THE CRITICS LOVE
WOMEN ON THE CASE

"EXCELLENT . . . THE STORIES RANGE FROM
GRITTY AND REALISTIC TO BIZARRE AND LAUGH-
OUT-LOUD FUNNY . . . EACH STORY IN THIS FINE
COLLECTION IS WELL WORTH READING."
—*Booklist*

"THE STORIES ARE STARTLINGLY DIFFERENT AND
WILL APPEAL TO DIFFERENT TASTES."
—*Chicago Sun-Times*

"MOST NOTABLE AS A BAROMETER OF THE
IMPRESSIVE VERVE AND VARIETY OF
CONTEMPORARY WOMEN'S MYSTERY WRITING."
—*Kirkus Reviews*

"AN EXCELLENT COLLECTION!"—*Chattanooga Times*

"GOOD STORYTELLING."—*Publishers Weekly*

"BRAVO, PARETSKY AND SISTERS! A GREAT BOOK."
—*Today's Chicago Woman*

"[AN] OUTSTANDING . . . DIVERSE COLLECTION."
—*The Oklahoman*

WOMEN ON THE CASE

EDITED BY

Sara Paretsky

A DELL BOOK

Published by
Dell Publishing
a division of
Bantam Doubleday Dell Publishing Group, Inc.
1540 Broadway
New York, New York 10036

ISBN: 0-440-22325-3

Reprinted by arrangement with Delacorte Press

Printed in the United States of America

Published simultaneously in Canada

June 1997

10 9 8 7 6 5 4 3 2 1

RAD

Contents

Introduction

Sara Paretsky

Women on the Case is the second in an occasional series of original short stories by women crime writers. The first, *A Woman's Eye*, was published in 1991. Since then, women—and men—have continued to think about what it means to speak in a woman's voice.

There is room for improvement. There is definitely room for hope. For while rape and domestic violence remain appalling problems throughout the world, more women are helping others survive these abuses. Women are helping women start businesses in Bangladesh as well as on the south side of Chicago. And despite the problem of illiteracy, record numbers of women are readers. And writers.

Women have been poets—speakers and writers of the word—since the dawn of recorded speech in ancient Sumer. The line from the Sumerian poet Enheduanna to the American Rita Dove is a narrow one, with many breaks, but it is a persisting line of women struggling to find and maintain a voice.

A few years ago I helped in a literacy program at a Chicago institute that trains poor women for jobs in the skilled trades. Because they needed to be able to read and write to start their job training programs, the eight women in my group—ranging in age from twenty-three to forty-seven—were eagerly but painfully overcoming a lifetime of illiteracy. When I talked to them about the history of women in letters —both their writing and their exclusion from the world of letters—one woman asked why, in so many times and in so many places, we have withheld the written word from women. Another student answered, without missing a beat, without prompting from me, "Because when you can't read they can control you."

Women today fight an uphill battle. After two decades of movement toward full partnership in many areas of human endeavor, we are under assault for wanting that partnership. Orthodoxy in Rome, Mecca, and Washington condemns women outside the domestic sphere as destroyers of the family, indeed the destroyers of all peace in society (although, paradoxically, the head of the U.S. Marine Corps during Reagan's presidency accused working women of softening the spirit of America's fighting men). But you don't need to call yourself a feminist to know that the fundamental battle for human freedom begins with the written word.

In the nineteenth century, as European and American women finally found it possible to write publicly under their own names and earn a living doing so, they turned to one another for support. The Americans Elizabeth Stuart Phelps and Harriet Beecher Stowe corresponded with George Eliot and Elizabeth Barrett Browning. Barrett Browning, in turn, brought the intensity of a passionate nature to her relations with Italian women poets—as she did to all matters Italian. We would call it networking, but these women knew they needed to support one another's work if they were going to make it in a world that put many obstacles in their paths.

As Barrett Browning tried to define herself as a poet and a woman, she said she looked for "grandmothers" in the art who could serve as her guide. She could find at best one or two and determined that she herself would have to become the grandmother of future women poets. In the introduction to her fourth collection of poems, in 1844, she regretted that her earlier work had failed "to represent the age" for women and said in the future she would speak out about women's sufferings and their social position. She added that if women writers did not acknowledge this duty, "they had better use pen no more," but "subside into slavery and concubinage."

Barrett Browning's *Aurora Leigh*—about a young poet who

turns her back on the Victorian insistence that women be domesticated angels—inspired Louisa May Alcott and Elizabeth Stuart Phelps, among many other writers. Alcott and Phelps both frequently wrote about the female artist who is stifled by domestic demands. For them, Aurora's passionate defense of her art was something they longed for but could not achieve.

> For me,
> Perhaps I am not worthy, as you say,
> Of work like this: perhaps a woman's soul
> Aspires, and not creates: yet we aspire,
> And yet I'll try out your perhapses, sir,
> And if I fail . . . why, burn me up my straw
> Like other false works—I'll not ask for grace;
>   . . . I
> Who love my art, would never wish it lower
> To suit my stature. I may love my art,
> You'll grant that even a woman may love art,
> Seeing that to waste true love on anything
> Is womanly, past question.

Barrett Browning's face sometimes looks at me out of the mirror, as grandmothers are wont to do, and demands to know what if anything I am doing to acknowledge my duty to other women writers, and to the sufferings of women in my own age. It was her chiding that made me set aside my own work to put together this anthology.

Because—at least in theory—women no longer have to defend themselves as artists, no longer have to fight against a sea of domestic demands to do their work, we no longer feel the Victorians' passionate response to *Aurora Leigh*. We've benefited so much from the work of these heroic pioneers that we now have the chance to explore more fully what it means to write in a woman's voice. So part of what we're offering you in *Women on the Case* is the chance to hear a wide range of those voices all in one volume.

At the same time, it is still exceptional for women's work

to stay in print as long as men's, to be included in the sacred canon of worthwhile fiction, to be awarded major prizes (two women have won the Nobel Prize for literature in the last thirty years). It is still true that the most popular role for women in fiction and in film is as prostitutes and/or victims of horrific mutilations. Just look at the best seller lists and the top-grossing films for any recent year. So a second part of what we're offering you here is an alternative vision to the anorectic, sex-crazed victim of much contemporary popular culture.

While Alcott, Browning, and Stowe all fought actively against U.S. slavery, they were less active in supporting contemporary African-American writers such as Harriet Jacobs or Angelina Weld Grimké. Similarly, *A Woman's Eye* included many of the most important American and English crime writers, but it didn't have much to say about women of color, women south of the Thirtieth Parallel, or those outside the English-speaking world (with the notable exception of the Catalan Maria Antonia Oliver). So *Women on the Case* tries to widen the lens with which we look at women's experience.

We're pleased to have added some important voices missing from the first collection. Ruth Rendell, perhaps the leading noir writer of our times, is present here. Elizabeth George and Linda Barnes both have contributed stories that demonstrate their keen insight into human passion. We're delighted to have the return of such skilled storytellers as Dorothy Salisbury Davis, Liza Cody, and Antonia Fraser. We also mourn the passing of Dorothy Hughes, who died not long after *A Woman's Eye* appeared.

Women on the Case includes a story by Eleanor Taylor Bland that shows her depth and sensitivity. Nevada Barr, whose Anna Pigeon stories have brought an important new voice to the crime scene, gives us an expanded idea of her range as a storyteller.

While *A Woman's Eye* focused on writers who'd already succeeded, *Women on the Case* showcases some new writers whose talents we'd like to put in front of the public. We are publishing two women for the first time: Andrea Smith and Dicey Scroggins Jackson. With Chicago police officer Ariel Lawrence, Andrea Smith has given us an engaging character we should see more often in the years to come, while Scroggins Jackson widens the range of our knowledge of homeless women.

Four other writers are appearing here in English for the first time. Several years ago, Helga Anderle of Vienna edited a German-language collection of European and Middle Eastern women's crime fiction called *Da Werde die Weibe zu Hyanen* (*The Women Will Become Hyenas*, from a quotation by Schiller). Her own story and those of Myriam Laurini and the Algerian Amel Benaboura are from that anthology. Benaboura's emotionally charged picture of a girl under assault by her brother will leave you with a deeper understanding of what lies behind some of the back-page paragraphs in the daily paper. Laurini, an Argentinean in exile, gives us a disturbing look at life on the Tex-Mex border. We're also proud to present the Russian author Irina Muravyova, whose tale "Women on the Edge" shows what powers women may call on in order to survive.

The Berlin writer Pieke Biermann presents us with an apocalyptic vision that will disturb the reader already nervous about the impending millennium. Biermann, a longtime political activist, lives on the front line of the social disruptions caused by the collapse of the G.D.R. and the triumph of capitalism. Her story is less dystopic fantasy than the Realpolitik of "free market meets STASI agents."

We've gone pretty far below the Thirtieth Parallel to find not just Myriam Laurini but also the Australian Susan Geason, whose tale of politics and the environment is especially timely here. Along with this provocative group, Nancy Pickard appears with all her usual dramatic insight; Barbara Wilson once more treads gleefully on sacred corns; Lia Matera takes us on an empathic romp through the avenues of political correctness. P. M. Carlson has written a polished, important piece set among the lynch mobs of nineteenth-century Memphis that turned Ida B. Wells into a crusader for justice. Marcia Muller, one of today's most skilled artisans, has created a fraught relationship between a writer and a homeless woman that demonstrates just how much effect we can unwittingly have on other people's lives—and deaths. Susan Dunlap has as wicked a sense of humor about pretension in death as she does in life, while Amanda Cross once more shows that crime and ubrane literateness can go hand in hand. Linda Grant looks at a popular contemporary subject and turns it on its head in an unusual tale, as does the British writer Frances Fyfield, who takes the English village beloved by Agatha Christie and peels back its skin to show us the heart.

This collection is an attempt to continue the work that Barrett Browning began, to make it possible for women to broaden the range of their voices, to represent their age for women, to describe women's social position, their suffering —and their triumphs.

At the end of the last century, male writers and critics undertook a major effort to discredit the words of women. Barrett Browning's poetry was out of print for several decades, while writers like Elizabeth Stuart Phelps, Anna Dickenson, and Rebecca Harding Davis disappeared altogether. These women wrote about topics that offended the social decorum of the day: They weren't afraid to discuss interracial marriage, or incest, or the legitimate longings of the female artist. Their books had very large readerships, which made them all the more threatening. Henry James and his peers used the pages of prominent journals to persuade readers and publishers to ignore women's words. Women's books were described as "vapid," "unwomanly," "sensationalist," or "political, not literary," and women were urged to keep silent, to leave these topics to experts.

Women continued to write, but their books were considered trivial, consigned to the margins. They were not taught in university courses, which keep books alive, and makes them part of the common language of educated people. They were often not reviewed, they were out of print within a year or two of publication. Women did not become silent, but few people heard them speak. The same fate befell the best-selling women crime writers of the last century. Anna Katherine Greene's books sold in the millions of copies on both sides of the Atlantic, but she's out of print, while Wilkie Collins is reissued time and again.

As I write this introduction, in September 1995, the Women's Conference in Beijing is concluding, with its mixed messages of hope and fear for the world's women. In Washington there are lobbies demanding that candidates fall in line with repressive social agendas for American women. Some women, in the state of anxiety that attacks on women's voices provoke, are writing books that blame all the problems facing contemporary women on today's equivalents of Rebecca Harding Davis and Elizabeth Barrett Browning. If only we would stop alienating men, all our problems would be solved. We've been too loud, too angry. We've been crying "rape" where there is no rape, demanding child care when the market is the best place to sort out that problem, crying—shrilly—for reproductive freedom when government is the best judge of whether we need it.

As we hurtle toward the millennium we are experiencing social discomfort in many arenas: in the relationship of young and old, rich and poor, fundamentalists and humanists, not just in our vision of women's roles. At this time of great discomfort we are showing women two widely divergent pictures of what they may be. In one, they have the two-thousand-year-old choice between virgin and whore. They can be the wholly sexual creatures in *Showgirls,* a movie that breaks barriers for showing female sexuality outside a porn theater, or pure wives and mothers, but they must not be thinking feeling beings.

In the other picture, women continue to speak in a wide range of voices, to explore what it means to be female and human. Issues of maternity play a major part in all women's lives—but for most women maternity is not the whole of life. And almost none at all fill the role of sex-crazed prostitutes that much of popular culture assigns them. Instead, they have to struggle to discover what life's work means for women. They may not be correct, but they have the right to make mistakes and learn from them, as do all adult humans.

The stories in this collection explore that multiplicity of voices, that multiplicity of choices, trials, errors, and recoveries. They come from women "who love their art" as Barrett Browning did, and who yearn for a world that will listen to them.

I am proud to present to you so many valiant writers. Those that you already know you can greet as old friends. For those that you've never met before, a pleasure awaits you. With this many women on the case, surely we will never again know another season of silence.

AUTHOR'S NOTE: This story is fiction and the historical events and characters in it are treated fictionally; however, readers may be interested to know that most details about the lynching and about Ida B. Wells (later Ida Wells-Barnett) are drawn from contemporary newspaper sources and from Wells-Barnett's autobiography and her journal, including Mr. Carmack's fitting end, Wells-Barnett's early interest in elocution and theatrical performances, her friendship with Thomas Moss, her acquisition of a pistol at a time that Memphis forbade the sale of arms to people of color, and her superb skill in communicating with people of all races.

P. M. CARLSON taught psychology and statistics at Cornell University before deciding that mystery writing would be more fun. Carlson's novels have been nominated for the Edgar award, the Macavity award, two Anthony awards, and selection to the *Drood Review of Mystery's* Ten Best list. She was also the 1992–93 president of Sisters in Crime. Her most recent novel, ***Bloodstream,*** is the second with her deputy sheriff creation, Martine Hopkins.

Parties Unknown by the Jury; or, The Valour of My Tongue

P. M. Carlson

Please, I beg you! Don't ask me to recount the story of that cruel night in 1892! As Shakespeare says, "On horror's head horrors accumulate." I have nightmares to this day! Besides, I was not the tragedy's heroine. I'm bound to admit that I was merely the comic relief. Or worse.

But if you insist—

To begin with, my handsome gray bengaline gown with bouffant Parisian-style sleeves was not suited to the night wind that blew chilly as a graveyard into the open door of the railroad car. But the conductor remained adamant. "Madam, you must get off here."

I fluttered my eyelashes at him, doing my best to appear a proper lady, though I feared he had long since realized that I was of the theatrical profession. "But, sir, my family in St.

Louis can pay amply when we arrive. Surely you can allow a young lady a few more miles in the middle of the night!"

"Madam, St. Louis is more than a few miles on. The Chesapeake and Ohio is not in the business of giving free rides to St. Louis." So saying, the conductor thrust my small steamer trunk and my Gladstone bag onto the station platform. I leapt from the train and lifted my trunk, attempting to heave it back aboard, but with deafening blasts of steam and screeches of metal on metal, the train began to move. My trunk and I thumped down onto the platform. I shook my fist at the conductor and shouted into the departing clamor of iron and steam, "The worm of conscience still be-gnaw thy soul!"

There was no response. The train disappeared into the blackness. I shivered again and opened my trunk to get out my worn blue traveling cape, my blond wig—far warmer than any hat—and a cigar. I pulled the wig over my red hair, wrapped the cape about me, and sat down on my trunk for a smoke and a good think.

Was ever a lady so beset by misfortune? Ticketless, penniless, jobless, hungry, and lonely, I was in sympathy with the perturbed spirits that seemed to ride the frosty March wind. I missed my brother, who had long since died for the Union cause, and my dear Aunt Mollie. I sorrowed that my beloved elocution tutor, the illustrious English actress Mrs. Fanny Kemble, was failing and might soon join them in their heavenly abode. So, too, my famous colleague Edwin Booth was in decline, seldom leaving his grand home on Gramercy Park. I tapped the ash from my cigar and grieved for the passing of a glorious era.

The great Sarah Bernhardt was still alive and well, of course, but that was of limited consolation to me just now, for she too was touring the American provinces and had cut deeply into my troupe's profits whenever our paths crossed. I was hard put to leave enough with my friends in St. Louis to provide for my dear little niece's spring toilette. My troupe had continued to New Orleans, and not having to contend with Bernhardt, our first night there had been rea-

sonably profitable. I had dared to hope again. But disaster
had struck. Our handsome leading man, succumbing to the
charms of the French Quarter, had drunk himself into such
a stupor that the patrons began to stamp and to throw unpleasant objects at us amid shouts demanding their money
back. Leaving the drunken Richard in a blinking heap center
stage, we scurried for the stage door, only to find the manager's men there before us. We did not escape until they had
emptied our pockets completely so that they could reim-
burse the angry audience. Thus I was forced to board the
train in New Orleans in great stealth, and without benefit of
ticket.

And now, the Chesapeake and Ohio had struck the
crowning blow, removing me from the train and abandoning
me heartlessly in the middle of the night! Do you wonder
that I felt forlorn? I found myself longing for my dear departed friend Jesse James, who was handy at wreaking revenge on selfish banks and railroads.

I looked about. The few passengers who had alighted by
choice had long since left the station, and the ticket master,
snug in his office, would most likely chase me from the
waiting room. The rails, reflecting the dull gleam of the station lamps, disappeared north and south into the inky Tennessee night. To the west, the great dark Mississippi rolled.
A few shacks and piers could be made out along the near
shore, but they appeared to be deserted at this hour. To the
east, the city of Memphis slept. I remembered spending
three days here with dear Mr. Booth's tour five years before,
in 1887. Being short of funds, I'd inquired of a kindly Negro
letter carrier if there was a way for an honest lady to earn a
few pennies to get her dress repaired, and he had introduced
me to an ambitious young teacher at the colored school who
desired elocution lessons. Aside from these industrious people, who were doubtless fast asleep somewhere in the
colored section, I knew no one in Memphis, and remembered it as one of the sleepier river towns.

The ghostly wind rattled through the weeds and fluttered
a corner of my cloak. With a last puff on my cigar, I lifted

my Gladstone bag and my heavy trunk and hid them under a stack of grain sacks that were awaiting shipment. I headed for town on the slim chance that I might encounter a kind-hearted and helpful gentleman still awake.

I picked my way along the pitch-dark street that led away from the river. But when I reached Front Street, the first crossing, I saw lights and several small clusters of gentlemen standing and talking in the street. The Front Street tavern was doing a brisk trade even at this late hour. I paused to pull my rouge from a handy pocket in my bouffant sleeve, applied just a touch to my lips, and went in.

I know, I know, a proper lady would never enter such a low establishment, certainly not at night in a river town. But what do you expect a poor penniless lady to do? It would be many long hours before the pawnshops opened, and I could hardly book a suite at the Ritz.

Fortune smiled upon me immediately. I caught the eye of a blond fellow with a fine mustache waxed into stylish points and a watch fob ornamented with a golden fleur-de-lis. He wore a gunbelt with a small blue-black pistol. He was sitting at a round table with a plate of catfish, a glass of ale, a newspaper, and a notebook before him. As I entered he inspected my blond hair and elegant gray gown with Parisian sleeves, then jumped to his feet most politely. "Good evening, madam," he said.

"Oh, sir, what a joy to encounter a kind face like yours in this hour of my need!"

Several other gentlemen had turned to look at me, a couple of the more inebriated favoring me with loud suggestions that I shall not dignify by repeating. My fair-haired hero scowled at them, then bowed me into a chair at his table. I couldn't help eyeing his dinner plate.

"I would indeed be delighted to assist you, madam," said my new acquaintance, waggling his blond eyebrows at me. "Tell me—but no, I see that you have not yet dined. They prepare a tolerable catfish here."

"Oh, sir, that would be most delightful!" He signaled the

innkeeper and I continued, "Allow me to introduce myself. I am Miss Bridget Mooney, of the St. Louis Mooneys."

"Delighted, madam. My name is Reginald Peterson, and I write for the Memphis *Commercial Appeal*." He indicated the newspaper before him. It featured an editorial vehement on the subject of protecting southern womanhood.

Well, I wished someone would protect southern womanhood from the greedy Chesapeake and Ohio, but I didn't think that was what the editorial meant, so I kept mum about it. Instead I said, "I am pleased to make your acquaintance, sir, for I greatly admire your profession."

"Thank you, my dear Miss Mooney. A journalist's calling is to serve society by observing truly. Sometimes even the law fails, and then we must say so and fight for justice." Mr. Peterson smiled at me quite warmly, perhaps impressed by my conversation, perhaps by my rosy lips. I feared it was my lips. Since I did not want our acquaintance to progress so rapidly that I would miss my dinner, I looked about for a conversational topic that might distract him.

"I see that Memphis has its share of ambitious Negroes," I commented, indicating his notebook, which had jottings about a grocery store owned by three of that race.

My diversion succeeded. Mr. Peterson snorted, "More than ambitious! Saturday night a few fine white men were entering the grocery premises and the damn darkies shot at them!"

"How dreadful!" I exclaimed. "No doubt the men wanted only to purchase groceries!"

"Well, in fact—" My well-dressed and well-waxed companion cleared his throat. "But tell me, Miss Mooney, what misfortune brings you to this place?"

Just then the innkeeper arrived with a handsome plate of catfish, which was indeed as delicious as Mr. Peterson had predicted. I applied knife and fork most daintily while recounting a tale of a dreadful pickpocket who had stolen my money and train ticket.

But just as I was delicately approaching the subject of how eternally grateful I would be if he loaned me enough money for train fare, a stout man entered the room. He was wearing two diamond rings and an expensive dark woolen muffler that hid the lower part of his face. This man stopped briefly at several tables, including ours, and said with barely suppressed enthusiasm, "Let's go, Peterson."

"Yes, sir, Mr. Carmack." My new friend leapt to his feet and bowed to me politely. "Please excuse me for a moment, Miss Mooney. My employer calls." He strode swiftly out the door.

Well, did you ever hear of such dreadful manners on the part of a southern gentleman? Fearing that the innkeeper would make unreasonable demands that I pay for my dinner, I snatched up my blue cape and skedaddled out the door after my new acquaintance.

But Mr. Peterson's fine mustache was nowhere to be seen. Instead, many gentlemen were milling about in the middle of Front Street. They had all tied dark cloths about their faces, like Mr. Carmack, who had summoned my new admirer. Not wishing to anger gentlemen with covered faces, I shrank back into the shadows against the tavern wall, thinking that Mr. Peterson was a clever reporter indeed, masking himself in order to observe the activities better.

The men began to move along the street, quite silently. Not knowing what to do, but hoping to find Mr. Peterson when they had finished whatever mysterious business they were about, I stole along behind them, keeping to the shadows.

They did not go far. Soon I heard the ringing of a bell, and an answering voice, "Who's there?"

"I have a prisoner."

"All right. This is the place, and I am always ready to receive them."

I was hiding next to a large shadowy building and was just able to make out the sign: SHELBY COUNTY JAIL. The voice, no doubt the watchman's, had come from inside. In a moment I heard a click of keys and saw the gate swing open. Instantly, three of the masked men pushed inside. I heard the watchman cry out, "What does this mean?" Then the voices were drowned out by the tramping feet of the rest of the mob rushing into the jailyard.

Hang it, this was not the place for a proper lady! I decided to wait no longer for the attractive and just-minded Mr. Peterson. My Aunt Mollie had taught me that too much knowledge about gentlemen's affairs could be dangerous to a lady. Wrapping my cape about me, I slipped away from the jail and peeped into the Front Street tavern to confirm that every gentleman awake was behind a mask at the jail, excepting only the innkeeper, whom I wished to avoid. I turned back toward the river. Now that I had dined properly, a night among the grain sacks might be more easily borne.

Imagine my distress when I reached the railway and saw the very mob of men I had left behind, pouring out of Auction Street onto the rails! I scurried under a porch to hide, because I did not want these gentlemen upset with me. They turned north, marching briskly and silently along the tracks, and driving before them three Negroes, gagged and securely bound. The three must have done something unspeakable to a white lady, I told myself, to so outrage the law-abiding citizenry of Memphis. Otherwise, surely, these kind gentlemen would let the prisoners' cases be tried legally, in court.

In the lantern light, I could see no unspeakable evil in the prisoners' dark eyes. Only fear.

I waited until the secretive army had passed by. At least their activities would be reported, for one of the masked men, I saw, had a watch fob ornamented with a golden fleur-de-lis. Another wore two handsome diamond rings.

Their footsteps rang out loud and dreadful, and slowly receded into the night.

There hadn't been a lynching in Memphis since the war.

After a time, I heard the crackle of a far-off fusillade. My catfish dinner turned a slow somersault within me.

I waited under the porch, but no one returned along the tracks.

Shivering even in my cape, I tiptoed out into the darkness and back to the grain sacks on the station platform. I curled up among them, but could not sleep. I thought no one had seen me watching the mob, and yet I was nervous, and more than nervous. I had supp'd full with horrors.

I know, I know, a proper lady wouldn't fret about the sound of gunshots in the night. A proper lady wouldn't presume to think that gentlemen might be wrong, and that the virtue of white southern womanhood might be as well protected by judges and courtrooms as by midnight abductions of prisoners. A proper lady would be grateful to her protectors. But I'm just a poor foolish girl from Missouri, and never got the hang of thinking like a proper lady, and I couldn't sleep, not with the nightmare memories of dark fearful eyes and the crackle of far-off gunfire.

Shortly before dawn, a freight train pulled into the station. Although I knew I should wait for the pawnshops to open, I couldn't bear to spend another minute in Memphis, and decided to gamble. Taking advantage of the dark, I hauled my trunk and Gladstone bag to a boxcar door, and when the trainmen were occupied with unloading some bales of cotton, I shoved my trunk inside and scrambled up behind it. I found myself amid crates of turnips, beets, and onions. At last, I could doze.

Yes, my Aunt Mollie would agree with you. It was foolish to stow away in an ill-smelling boxcar when the morning would bring the opening of pawnshops, and perhaps even another meeting with kind Mr. Peterson, who might well be as upset as I at what his profession had forced him to observe. But hang it, those nightmares had me plumb scared and worn out, and I wanted to get shut of Memphis.

Alas, this proved to be very difficult. We had traveled a mere fifteen miles north when an overly alert attendant discovered me huddled half asleep among the vegetable crates. He was as heartless as the conductor of the passenger train. Before I could wake up to protest, he had tossed my trunk down the embankment, and I had to leap after it, Gladstone bag in hand, fortunate only in that the train had slowed considerably to round a curve. My bag and I skidded down the stony embankment and fetched up on a narrow road that paralleled the tracks. I stumbled back half a mile to where my trunk lay, hauled my baggage into a willow copse, and gave myself over to sleep, and nightmares.

I woke at noon, ravenously hungry and eager to continue my journey to St. Louis. But my o'er hasty departure from Memphis had left me worse off than before. It was now clear that the Chesapeake and Ohio was not in the mood to provide journeys on credit. I would have to obtain money somehow. Unfortunately, the nearest source of money was back in Memphis, with its pawnshops and Mr. Peterson. Much as I disliked the idea, the prudent thing to do would be to turn back.

But with no money, and with baggage to carry, it required two days to cover those few miles. I was delayed by an episode involving some fresh-baked loaves of bread that someone had carelessly left on the windowsill of a ramshackle house, and also involving two mangy yellow hounds that lurked under a porch nearby. They chased me into the woods, where the heel of my shoe broke off. I didn't want to shoot them as the sound might bring unwanted visitors, so I shinnied up a maple tree where I remained for a miserable night finishing the loaf and pelting the hounds with branches until they lost interest. I was further delayed because although a few farm wagons were going my direction, even the ones driven by colored men, who are usually compassionate and helpful, did not pause and even increased their speed. I consoled myself by muttering, "A ragged multitude of hinds and peasants, rude and merciless," and trudged on.

At last a rickety mule-drawn wagon filled with baskets of yams and driven by a rotund old Negro woman stopped.

"I reckon I'm gonna be sorry for this," she said in the warm rural accents of the South, "but you're lookin' like you need some help, ma'am."

"Oh, please, could you help? My money and ticket were stolen on the train, and if I could only get back to Memphis—"

"Memphis!" The woman snorted. "I wasn't plannin' to go

by that route, ma'am! There's trouble there, heaps of trouble."

I realized then that the colored men who had passed me by feared for their lives if they were caught in the company of a white lady. I clasped my hands in supplication. "Oh, please, if you could take me even part of the way—"

She considered and asked abruptly, "Can you read?"

"Of course!"

"No 'of course' about it, ma'am, if you're born a slave and nobody sends you to school. But my cousin's husband, he says this newspaper has a story 'bout the lynchin', and if you read it to me I s'pose I can swing down as far as the Memphis streetcar line."

I didn't want to read about a lynching, for the mere thought of what I'd seen made me quake, but I had little choice. I heaved my baggage onto the wagon bed and climbed up onto the seat beside her. Bessie, for such proved to be her name, handed me a copy of the Memphis newspaper, and as the mule picked his slow way along many bumpy, bone-rattling miles, I began to read the dreadful story, wondering if Mr. Peterson had written it.

The reporter explained that twenty-seven colored men had been arrested because they had ambushed and shot four deputy sheriffs while the officers were "looking for a Negro for whose arrest they had a warrant." Bessie snorted at that, and I decided that Mr. Peterson, out of delicacy, had not mentioned the true reason. Lynchings, I'd always been told, occurred when fine gentlemen became so incensed at the violation of their virtuous women that they lost their heads and dealt out justice themselves instead of waiting for the courts. This fact was so well known that my friend Phoebe in St. Louis, who'd consorted willingly and frequently with a handsome mulatto stevedore, was easily able to save her reputation when her aunt discovered her emerging from his cabin. Phoebe simply accused him of assault. A lynching party was formed but the young man had very prudently left town. Still, no violated virtue was mentioned here in Memphis.

I read on. The newspaper said that the mob had selected William Stuart, Calvin McDowell, and Theodore Moss as their three victims. This last name jolted me, for the kind letter carrier who'd helped me years before had been Tommie Moss. I prayed that Theodore was not a relative of his. The story said that the three prisoners had been marched to the edge of town. Every detail agreed with what I had seen. Then, "in an open field, near the Wolf River, the Negroes met their doom. For the first time they were allowed to speak. As the gags were removed Moss said: 'If you are going to kill us, turn our faces to the west.' Scarce had he uttered the words when the crack of a revolver was heard, and a ball crashed through his cheek. This was the signal for the work. A volley was poured upon the shivering Negroes and they fell dead."

"Oh, Lord, Lord!" exclaimed my companion. Tears were rolling down her cheeks.

Well, I didn't want to read any more of this terrible story either. Getting away from it was the reason I'd left Memphis in the first place. Pushing the image of the prisoners' frightened dark eyes from my mind, I skipped to the last paragraphs, cleared my throat, and continued. " 'The mob turned about after it had completed its terrible work and came toward the town. At the first crossing they scattered, and all disappeared as silently as they had arrived on the scene. Not a trace of any of them can be found this morning.' "

Bessie lashed at the mule with such vigor that I paused to glance at her, but she said only, "Please, go on, ma'am."

I read on about the angry though unarmed assembly of Negroes, and about the equipping of 150 white men with Winchesters to preserve order, and about the verdict of the jury at the inquest: " 'We find that the deceased were taken from the Shelby County Jail by a masked mob of men, the men overpowered and taken to an old field and shot to death by parties unknown by the jury.' "

Bessie snorted, "Parties unknown by the jury!"

I said with relief, "That's the end of the story."

"No ma'am, there's more coming, and I'm not goin' into Memphis."

Well, how could I argue with her? I myself was doubly eager to find a pawnshop, or my admirer, and leave the dreadful town where people shot each other with such abandon.

Late in the day our wagon came to a crossroads, and Bessie pulled the mule to a halt. "Here we are, ma'am. I thank you for the reading. I go east here, where I know folks. You go straight ahead, and 'fore long you'll be at the curve of the streetcar line."

My benefactress had been right to be worried. As I hobbled toward the streetcar tracks I saw bands of colored men around a shop that had been nearly destroyed, its windows broken, its door smashed, the sign PEOPLE'S GROCERY gashed and hanging askew. There were also bands of white men carrying Winchesters, as promised in the newspaper. They were led by men with sheriff's badges.

The setting sun threw slanting rays across the tense faces, and I paused by someone's henhouse to survey the situation. It appeared to be a wary truce, the colored men muttering and occasionally cursing but making no hostile moves, the white ones swaggering about with their rifles, all of them with that dangerous kind of anger men pretend when they are bone-scared. Under ordinary circumstances I might have tripped daintily across to the streetcar tracks, secure in the knowledge that as a proper white lady I would be defended by every rifle there. But nights without sleep, a broken heel, and bucketsful of road dust had somewhat diminished my ability to appear a proper lady. Thus, when a gunshot blasted through the late rosy light, I leapt into the henhouse, pulling the door closed behind me amid a great flapping and squawking on the part of the usual residents. Ignoring them, I applied my eye to a knothole.

Outside, no one appeared to be hurt, but most of the colored men had taken shelter behind wagons or houses. The men with sheriff's badges were laughing. One shouted something about a coon dance.

The hens quieted in the darkness, and I became aware of another sort of breathing the instant before a taut voice said, "Who's there?"

"A lady! Fear not!" I cried, diving to the floor as I pulled my well-oiled Colt from the hidden pocket in my bouffant sleeve.

"Yes, it is evident that you are a lady." The voice was a lady's too, educated far beyond the usual southern female's. I could not tell where she was.

I asked, "Pray tell, madam, why are you in this place?"

"Fear of that armed mob," explained the unseen lady. "And you, madam?"

"The same," I replied. "By a series of misfortunes I find myself here in Memphis today."

"I live in Memphis, I regret to say," replied the lady with considerable bitterness. I decided she had no plans to harm me and tucked my Colt back into its pocket as she continued, "I had thought my town had progressed beyond these barbarisms. Such dreadful stories I could tell! 'Hie thee hither / That I may pour my spirits in thine ear . . .' "

I was curious to know why a well-educated lady would be found in a henhouse in a colored section of town, but as the same question might be asked of me, I did not pursue it, and instead completed her quotation: " 'And chastise with the valour of my tongue / All that impedes thee from the golden round.' "

The lady gasped. "Can it be? Are you—pray, madam, are you Miss Mooney, who came to Memphis four years ago with the famed Mr. Booth, and for three days kindly instructed me in elocution?"

"Ida?" I gasped in turn, realizing my mistake. "Are you Ida Wells?" Amidst the clucking of the hens, I fumbled my way across the straw-strewn floor and embraced her, though I knew my Aunt Mollie would have frowned at such egalitarianism with a colored lady, even one as proper as Ida. I was so delighted to find a friend, I couldn't help myself. "Ida, I am so glad to see you! Well, hear you," I amended, as it was still pitch-dark. "You have forgotten none of your lessons!

My teacher, the illustrious English actress Mrs. Fanny Kemble, would be delighted with your elocution!"

"Thank you," she said. "Shortly after you and Mr. Booth left, a score of us formed a dramatic organization. We were very much enthused about improving our vocal skills and our knowledge."

"I well remember your enthusiasm. I never have had a student so apt. Your tongue has valor indeed! You could have a great success on the stage!"

"Thank you, but I find that my calling is journalism," she said. "Did you know that I am now part owner and editor of our black newspaper here, the *Free Press*?"

"How splendid!"

"But we meet again in cruel, cruel circumstances. Oh, how I wish I were allowed to buy a pistol, so that I could defend myself!"

Well, remembering the tenseness in her voice a moment ago when she first challenged me in the dark, I was just as glad she hadn't had a pistol then. I said soothingly, "Things are quieter outside now."

"Is it yet dark?"

I returned to the knothole and peered out. "Dusk has fallen," I reported, "and there are fewer men and rifles about. I believe it is safe to emerge."

"Then I will go home," she said. "I must finish my editorial."

"Oh, Ida, may I come with you, just for a few moments? My travels have left me dusty, and I crave a drink of water."

"Of course! You are most welcome, Miss Mooney."

"Bridget," I said firmly, though I knew it wasn't proper.

We slipped out into the twilit town. She looked much as I remembered, a short woman with a lively round face and eyes that telegraphed her emotions, sparkling with enthusiasm or simmering with scorn or anger. Her dress was dark and neat, yet stylish and very proper once she'd brushed off the straws. She exclaimed when she saw my sorry state. Soon we arrived at Ida's neat rented quarters, and she postponed her editorial for a few moments in order to fill the washtubs on her back porch for me and to take my unfortunate shoe to a cobbler across the street. I washed my face and hands and changed into a plain clean frock, then went out to the porch again to launder my road-soiled garments. When Ida returned, I looked up from the washtub to say, "Ida, I am considering bringing an action against the dreadful Chesapeake and Ohio Railroad. If a colored woman succeeded in the courts against them, surely I can too. Please, tell me how you won your case."

"Win? I didn't win," she said crossly.

"What? How can that be? When we last spoke, you had proved in court that they had not honored your first-class ticket, and had sent you to sit in the smoking car instead! The court had awarded you five hundred dollars!"

"Oh, yes, the lower court. I still remember the headlines: 'A Darky Damsel Obtains a Verdict for Damages.' But the railroad appealed to the Tennessee Supreme Court, and they overturned the decision."

"But the railroad didn't honor the ticket it sold you! How could the judges say a jim crow car was first class?"

"How could they not? My dear Miss Mooney—"

"Bridget."

"My dear Bridget, they could not allow the precedent! My case was the first with a colored plaintiff since the repeal of Sumner's federal civil rights bill. The repeal means that we can no longer go to the federal courts, and must abide by state decisions. This state does not want justice for my race."

"Oh dear." I rinsed out my muslin underskirt. "It's true, I have never found the law favorable toward those of us who are not rich."

"Rich and white," she agreed. "Oh, Bridget, when I heard the verdict, I wanted to gather my people in my arms and fly far away with them! There is no justice in this land for us."

"But surely it is better than it was!" I protested. "My brother died fighting for the Union side!"

"The war has been over for twenty-seven years," Ida said with dignity, "and despite the sacrifices of people like your brother, there has been so much backsliding since the days of Reconstruction that I have no confidence in the majority of white people. Our hard-won freedom is hollow without justice. At this moment I am so heartsore about the lynching that it is difficult to feel that anything has improved."

"It was terrible indeed," I agreed. I didn't wish to discuss the terrible affair, but I was curious about one point. "Ida, I believe the newspaper left out part of the story. Doesn't lynching spring from gentlemen's unreasoning anger about unspeakable crimes against womanhood? No such crimes were reported."

"I can hardly blame you for thinking that lynching is the product of unthinking outrage, because that is the story they always give out, and in fact I too believed it until last week," Ida said. She stretched up to pin my washed underskirt onto a clothesline stretched between the porch posts. "But of course there was no such occurrence here, and they lynched Tommie Moss all the same."

"Tommie?" I froze, the soapy bloomers in my hand dripping into the washtub. "Tommie Moss, the kind letter carrier who introduced us? He was lynched?"

"Yes." She nodded, her face a picture of grief in the light that shone out through the kitchen window. "Tommie Moss, the kindest, best-loved man in Memphis, and my dear friend Betty's husband. I am godmother to his little daughter Maurine."

"Oh, Ida!" Once again I embraced her, heedless of the soapsuds and of what Aunt Mollie might think. "But the newspaper didn't mention his name!"

"The white newspapers got the names wrong too. Misspelled Stewart, and called Tommie 'Theodore' Moss."

"But—how did it happen? How did such a kind man come to shoot a white man?"

"He didn't!" Ida explained indignantly. "He did something far more outrageous."

I had met Tommie Moss only briefly, but still found it difficult to imagine him committing outrages. "What did he do?"

"He owned his home. He saved his money. He took Mc-

Dowell and Stewart as partners and went into the grocery business with the same ambition that a young white man would have had. Tommie was the president of the company. He continued delivering letters during the day while his partners ran the business, and then took care of the books at night."

"I don't understand. That sounds perfectly proper."

A bitter smile twitched at Ida's lips. "Then you do understand. Tommie was an exemplary young man, with a sweet family. He worked industriously. He was succeeding. But you see, the People's Grocery was located across the street from a grocery owned by a white man."

"I see," I said, and I did. Gentlemen everywhere are like that, don't you agree? They're full of manly ideals and heroic aspirations and kindness in their conversation, but their actions are more often inspired by money. "Still, lynching seems an extreme measure, even for a grocer who was losing business."

"They made other attempts first," Ida explained. "At one point the white grocer and another man swore out warrants against Tommie and some others for defending a little colored boy who'd been flogged by a grown white man. But the judge merely fined them and dismissed the case. Then we heard that the vanquished whites were coming Saturday night to clean out the People's Grocery Company."

"Oh dear."

"Tommie consulted a lawyer, who said that since the grocery was outside the city limits, they were beyond police protection, and therefore would be justified in protecting themselves if attacked. That's what the law says."

Well, I could see what was coming, because I've never found that what the law says has very much to do with what happens. As I pinned my bloomers to the line, I grieved for Ida, who had tried to use the law to stop injustice on the part of the wicked Chesapeake and Ohio, and most of all for kind Tommie Moss, who foolishly believed that if he had freedom to buy a grocery, the law also gave him freedom to protect it.

Ida continued, "Tommie's company armed some guards
and stationed them in the rear of the store, not to attack, but
to repel the threatened attack, as allowed by the law. And
that night, as he was doing the books and McDowell was
waiting on customers just before closing, they heard gunfire.
Their guards had shot at several white men who were sneaking in the back way. Three were wounded, none killed."

"But the newspaper said they were officers with a warrant!"

"No, they were not. The newspapers also said the People's
Grocery Company was 'a low dive in which drinking and
gambling were carried on: a resort of thieves and thugs.'"
Ida's eyes blazed. "That's what the leading white journals
called this legitimate business owned by decent black businessmen!"

Could the just-minded Mr. Peterson work for such a
newspaper? I said, "So you think the problem was, Tommie
was successful."

"That's right, Bridget. Success was Tommie's outrageous
crime. Immediately there was a massive police raid on the
entire neighborhood. Over a hundred colored men were put
in jail on suspicion. They took our weapons, of course, and
forbade any sale of arms to Negroes, so we are completely
defenseless. The white newspapers said the wounded white
men would die, and for two nights colored men guarded the
jail. Then the newspapers announced that the wounded
were out of danger, and our men thought the crisis was past
and left the jail unguarded."

Had my brother died for this? I was thinking that my
handsome blond admirer's friends were about as low and
cowardly as they came. How could they claim they broke
the law in an unreasoning fit of rage if they waited coolly for
three days until they could break it in perfect safety?

No, it was clear that they'd lynched Tommie Moss because
he would have won in a fair public trial.

I asked, "So none of the wounded men died?"

"None. But of course that was not the issue. The lynchers
did not look for the men who had fired the shots. Instead

they took the three partners of the People's Grocery Company. Three decent, kind, successful men." Tears sparkled on Ida's dark face, and I found my cheeks wet too.

"I am sorry, I didn't know! The white newspapers reported so many lies," I said, my faith in Mr. Peterson crumbling.

"There is more!" Ida declared, her eyes flashing. She stepped into her kitchen, returned with a copy of the *Commercial Appeal,* and read, " 'McDowell's jaw was entirely shot away and back of his right ear there was a hole large enough to admit a man's fist.' "

I clapped my hands over my ears. "Stop! Ida, please, I can't bear to hear it!"

"Bridget, don't you see, that is the problem!" Ida's eloquent eyes blazed. "How can we ever stop this injustice if white people refuse to notice it? Did Tommie Moss and your brother die in vain?"

Hang it, all I wanted to do was avoid trouble and get myself to St. Louis. But what can a poor girl do, confronted with someone as persuasive as Ida Wells? Her words, like daggers, entered in mine ears, and I could think of no reply. Reluctantly I muttered, "Go on."

Ida read, " 'His right hand, too, had been half blown away, as if, in defense, he had grabbed the muzzle of a shotgun. Stuart was shot in the mouth and twice in the back of the head. His body was riddled with buckshot. Moss had one ear shot off and several bullet holes in his forehead.' "

Sickened, I moaned, "Oh no!"

Genteel and unstoppable, she read on: " 'As the gags were removed, Moss said, "If you are going to kill us, turn our faces to the west." ' " Her blazing eyes flicked up to my face. "Don't you see, Bridget? The journalist was there! This is an eyewitness account. He knew!"

In the fading hope that my admirer had been a mere observer, I said, "But isn't it true that journalists are often at the scenes of terrible events that they cannot prevent?"

"Even if you cannot prevent the crime, you can work for justice! You can publish the whole truth!"

"Isn't that story true?"

"The facts of the lynching are true. But listen to this: 'Not a trace of any of them can be found this morning.' Bridget, the inquest found that Tommie Moss and McDowell and Stewart were killed by 'parties unknown by the jury.' That's ridiculous! Everyone knows! And yet—no one tells."

Proper ladies don't involve themselves in such matters; but I was overwhelmed by her outraged dignity and sorrow, and blurted out, "Ida, I saw that mob assemble. Mr. Peterson and Mr. Carmack were both there, masked like the others."

As soon as I'd said it, I wanted to call back the words. Wouldn't you? It was dangerous to know such things, more dangerous still to speak of them. But Ida did not seem shocked. "Yes, a friend said he thought he'd seen them. It's not surprising. Carmack writes hateful editorials. But they won't admit to being there, and they won't identify any of their friends in the newspapers and certainly not in the courts. There will be no justice for Tommie."

In my head Aunt Mollie was in full bray, pointing out that I must avoid the anger of armed, masked gentlemen, and that I'd best get me some money quick and light out for St. Louis, and other sensible businesslike things. But Ida's words batter'd me like roaring cannon-shot. I took a deep breath. "Suppose someone white testified against them?"

Ida looked at me with pity. "If you have any foolish notions about testifying, forget them. You're white, yes, that's a great advantage. But you're a woman, and an outsider, and an actress. They will make your reputation the jest and by-word of the street."

She was right, of course. This was not the first time I had faced the dreadful prejudices against those in my profession. I could not help Ida's cause in the courtroom.

I tried again. "Perhaps I could speak to a judge privately, and he could call for official inquiries."

"My dear Bridget, the criminal court judge too was a member of that mob."

"Oh."

"There will be no justice in this case."

I could almost hear Aunt Mollie breathing a sigh of relief as I realized the hopelessness of the situation. I turned sadly back to cleaning my gown and asked, "Ida, can you safely publish this story in your newspaper?"

"Safely? No. But publish it I will," she said firmly. "So much education is needed! Even I believed the lie that lynching occurs because of unreasoning outrage at the violation of an innocent woman. There is much work to do among both races to dispel that lie. But white people don't read my newspaper. I can tell my people the truth, and I will. But Bridget, how can I tell yours?"

That was a difficult problem indeed. Even I, kindhearted as I was, had done my best to avoid noticing these horrors. I said slowly, "Well, they have revealed their weakness with this lynching. As you say, what they fear is not damage to white womanhood, after all. It is not even being shot, for when a man of their own race shoots at them, they allow fair trials to take place. No, what they fear is colored success. Tommie's grocery won your race's patronage, and they killed him. That means they fear the loss of your business."

"So we are not powerless after all. We must use our power. But how?" Ida began to pace up and down the porch, ignoring the flapping garments on the line. "Ah, Oklahoma is opening up. Tommie said, turn our faces to the west. I'll urge my people to move west!" Ida paused in the light from the kitchen window, her small immaculately dressed person erect, her luminous eyes flashing. "There is only one thing left that we can do; save our money and leave behind a cruel town which will neither protect us nor give us a fair and legal trial, but instead murders us in cold blood!"

I applauded. "Ida, that will work! Money always works!"

"I only wish I could make them see the immorality of their actions."

"I fear they are not yet rich enough to be moral."

"Was your brother rich?"

"Well, no, but he was hired by the Northern army."

"The money's northern, even now," Ida pointed out. "Our streetcar line is owned by northern capitalists, although it's run by southern lynchers. Suppose we stop riding the streetcar? We walked before it was built, we can walk again!"

"Good! Withholding patronage from the streetcar may catch the attention of northerners too. And here's another idea!" I exclaimed. "Ida, go on stage! Tell your story, just as you've told it to me. Other white people will be as moved as I if they hear you tell of these outrages. But don't go west. Go north, and speak to the moneyed classes. Southerners look up to those with money!"

"I don't know," Ida said dubiously. "My acquaintance Mr. Fortune is the editor of a New York newspaper, and he tells me that it's difficult to get white people to read it there too. It's like a great stone wall without a door."

"Then talk to those who are richer and more powerful than New Yorkers! Tell your story to the English, Ida!"

"The English?"

"They are rich and powerful and highly moral. Well, most of them," I amended, thinking of my friend Lillie Langtry, but deciding not to mention her, as Ida was so proper that she might be offended. "And furthermore, the English have nothing to lose if your race gets justice in faraway America, so they can afford to be moral. And their opinion carries great weight among influential people in this country."

"But would they listen to a person of my race? To someone who was born a slave? To an American?"

I looked at her short, trimly attired person, her blazing eyes, her face, so vivid in its darkness, and smiled. "The English will find your story mesmerizing, Ida, because you'll tell it in the ringing accents of their own beloved Mrs. Fanny Kemble."

"So learning the rich folks' language can be a weapon too!" Ida bounced to the edge of the porch and raised both hands to the starry sky. "Do you hear, Tommie?" she cried. "We shall have justice yet!"

Well, I reckoned justice would take a while, but there was no need to say that to Ida Wells, who understood the world at least as well as I. She hurried off to write an editorial urging her people to move away from Memphis if they could, and to save their money and avoid the streetcar.

I hurried off, too, to pawn one of my genuine theatrical emerald necklaces before the pawnshops closed, and to purchase a ticket to St. Louis from the reprehensible Chesapeake and Ohio. Then I donned my blond wig and my striped dress trimmed with white guipure lace, screwed my courage to the sticking place, and made my way to Front Street.

I know, I know, it wasn't proper to return to such low haunts, and it was mighty risky besides, and in the usual run of things I never would have done it. But somehow Ida's words kept ringing in my head and nudging me on.

In the tavern, several of the gentlemen kindly offered their companionship, but I declined firmly and ordered a catfish dinner, which the innkeeper agreed to bring if I first paid for my interrupted dinner of Tuesday night. Presently, who should appear but my acquaintance of the waxed blond mustache.

"Why, Mr. Peterson!" I exclaimed with a shocked flutter of my eyelashes. "What am I to think of you?"

"My dear Miss Mooney! I beg your forgiveness!" He adjusted his gunbelt and dropped to one knee with an extravagant flourish of his hat. A couple of men in the room snickered, but lordie, his blue eyes and golden hair were handsome!

I gave him my prettiest pout. "Sir, it was not gentlemanly to leave a lady for so long."

"You are right, and you have my most fervent apologies. My business took considerably longer than I had anticipated, and I was desolate to think that you awaited me still. It was a matter of honor and of justice."

"It is true, sir, that the moment I first saw you, I took you for a gentleman of honor and justice."

"True, journalists too serve society. When the law is sure to fail, journalists too fight for justice!"

Hang it, how could a lady resist such a touching apology

and such a kindly regard for justice? " 'We will solicit heaven and move the gods / To send down justice for to wreak our wrongs!' " I quoted, and smiled at him. "And when the law is sure to fail, heaven sends down journalists! Please, sir, sit down."

He called for a whiskey and took the other chair at my table with a hopeful glint in his blue eyes. "Thank you, my dear Miss Mooney, for your understanding. It is delightful to meet again."

"It is a pleasure to renew my acquaintance with a man of intellect, who helps society by publishing the truth."

He beamed. Handsome blond gentlemen have little difficulty believing that they also possess intellect. "It is true," he said. "Mr. Carmack and I are devoted to the betterment of society." The golden fleur-de-lis on his watch fob winked at me as he added gallantly, "I must say, the company of a lovely blond lady who knows Shakespeare is pure delight!"

"My dear Mr. Peterson," I said, leaning near so that he could appreciate my Parisian perfume, "I would be very pleased to discuss justice and journalism at greater length, but I find it very close in here, and fear that I may faint. Do you suppose we could take the air for a few moments?"

"An enchanting idea! But it is rather cool, and there is mist on the river," he warned.

"So much the better!" I exclaimed, most sincerely. "Nothing could be more helpful for light-headedness. Let us take a stroll along the riverside."

With a triumphant wink at his fellows, Mr. Peterson downed the rest of his whiskey, peeled a bill from his roll for the innkeeper, and offered me his arm. We made a lovely pair, yes indeed, such a blond and handsome couple! Smiling into each other's eyes, we passed through the tavern door into the night.

Mr. Peterson's friends never saw him again.

The next morning, a redhead once more, I redeemed my emerald necklace from the pawnshop, then collected my baggage and bid farewell to Ida. "Bend every effort to addressing the public," I urged her. "Your splendid voice moves people to action."

"It is not my voice, it is the justice of my cause," she said earnestly. "And you too will tell the truth to those you meet?"

"I will do what I can," I said, and handed her a blue-black pistol. "I hope you never have to use it, Ida. But even the most proper of ladies must occasionally defend herself."

Her expressive eyes glowed with pleasure upon receiving the gun she was forbidden to purchase. "Thank you, Bridget! I too pray that I never have occasion to use it, but I promise you, if I must die by violence, I will take my persecutors with me!"

I know, I know, I shouldn't have given it to her, but she might well need courage, and I only had room in my pocket for one Colt. Besides, I had the feeling that Tommie Moss would be pleased to see one of the guns that killed him in the hands of his crusading friend.

And crusade she did. Within a few weeks, at Ida's urging in the *Free Press*, hundreds of colored people disposed of their property and left town, leaving Memphis businessmen reeling. Six weeks after the lynching, the superintendent of the streetcar company came to the *Free Press* offices and begged Ida to use her influence to get the colored people to ride the streetcars again, because the company's losses were enormous. She naturally refused. In late May, when she was out of town, Mr. Carmack took exception to her editorial that revealed the truth about false accusations like that of my friend Phoebe, and he incited a mob to destroy the office of the *Free Press*.

That didn't stop Ida Wells. She began writing for Mr. Fortune in New York and telling her story to women's clubs and church groups. Through them she met the famed English Quaker Mrs. Impey, editor of *Anti-Caste*. At Mrs. Impey's invitation, Ida was soon in England and Scotland rousing the churches and newspapers there to protest lynching. They raised such a clamor that this nation could no longer ignore the problem. Chastised by the valor of Ida's tongue, Americans of both races formed antilynching societies all over the United States. There were setbacks in Congress due to southern filibusters, but more and more prominent whites publicly opposed lynching, and slowly, mob rule receded.

Justice, I fear, will be slower to arrive.

Or perhaps it arrives in scraps and fragments. Mr. Carmack, who moved to Nashville, was eventually gunned down in the streets there—but that's another story.

As for my admirer with the blond waxed mustache, surely he could have no complaints, for he himself believed that sometimes the law is sure to fail, and for the betterment of society, other means of justice must be found. Who could argue with such estimable sentiments? His corpse washed up near Natchez a couple of weeks after I left. The verdict at the inquest was that he had died at the hands of parties unknown by the jury.

A Rock and a Hard Place

Nancy Pickard

I'm not a hard woman; I'm only a private investigator.

You see me, you think I'm an athlete, a tough girl, even at my age, which is fifty-one. You hear my voice, my language sometimes, you think, she's a rough one. But I'm college educated, with two degrees, one of them in English lit, believe it or not. Besides, lifting weights never built up muscles between a person's ears, if you see what I mean. I work out on computers more than I do at the gym, that's the nature of this job.

It's fairly respectable, my profession.

I'm fairly respectable, is what I'm saying, even if I do carry weapons and use them, even if I did serve in Vietnam for six months that are supposed to be top secret, even now, and even if I have witnessed sordid scenes and participated in violent acts. I still maintain I am basically a respectable and mostly law-abiding person, or I was, until recently. Now, I don't know what I am. Except that one thing I am for sure is dying. Yeah, right, aren't we all? No, I mean, specifically me, specifically now, from breast cancer. My doctors claim they excised it with one of those "partials," but I don't believe them. I hear it growing, infinitesimal and stealthy, escaping their means of detection, but not mine. The saving grace is: I'm good at guns. Things get bad, too painful, I always have my stockpile of large and little friends, the ones with the long noses and the short ones, the loud voices and the soft. Dying definitely does not scare me; I would not move one foot off the sidewalk to get out of its way.

Are we clear on all this, so far?

I was already all of those things I have just described— except the part about not knowing any longer what I am—at the moment when Grace Kairn (not her real name) applied her knuckles to a tentative knock on my office door. I looked up from my Macintosh Quadra, where I was trying to hack my way into a database I wasn't supposed to be able to get into, and saw her: late thirties, really short blond hair, Audrey Hepburn bones, one of those women who makes a woman like me feel big and bulky and clumsy, like we're all muscle and cuss words and she's all lace and fragrance.

"Hello?" she said, from my doorway. "Angela Fopeano?"

Immediately, I was awkward, not at my best, barking back at her like I was an MP and she was a private caught off base.

"Yeah!" I said.

Yeah. As if my mother hadn't raised me to say "yes," or to be polite, to be a nice girl. *Yeah. Duh. I'm Angie.*

"Who are you?" I asked her, point-blank, like that.

God, sometimes I make myself cringe.

"I'm Grace Kairn, may I talk to you, do you have time?"

No appointment. I hate that. Who do people think they are, expecting me to drop everything for them? I always do, though, because one of my failings is curiosity. God knows, I would hesitate to call it intellectual. Still, I want to *know,* even when I'm pissed at people—who they are, what they want. People in general were starting to bore me, though, with their repetitive stories about infidelity and fraud and deception and greed. Big deal. Did they think that made them different? It was all starting to feel banal and sordid. My own clients were beginning to bore me. Bad sign for a working gal. What did I think I was going to do if I didn't solve crimes? *Crimes,* hah. Misdemeanors of the ego, was more like it, that was what I investigated. Who was sleeping with whom. Who cooked the books. Who stole the paper clips. Who the hell cared. Not me anymore.

Man, I sound angry, don't I? Even I can hear it.

At least this woman asked if I had the time.

I waved her into a chair, and she looked across my desk at me with the gentlest smile I ever saw in anybody's blue eyes. In a humble kind of way, definitely not boasting, she said, "What I have to say is . . . maybe . . . unusual."

"Uh huh."

Yeah right, I thought, tell me a new one, or better yet give me a cure for cancer.

"I want to hire you," she said, concisely, gently, "to prevent three murders."

"You have my attention," I said, wryly. "I'm taping this."

"All right." Her voice was a sweet, melodic breeze across my desk, and I couldn't imagine she could have anything so very "unusual" to tell me. In fact, her first words were ordinary, to my jaded ears. "Five years ago, before Christmas of that year, I was held up at gunpoint in a parking lot of the Oberlin South Mall."

She was surprisingly direct, for someone so soft.

I sat back and listened.

"It was one man, with a gun, and he pushed me into the car and made me drive him out of town to a riverbank. And he raped me and shot me and left me there, thinking I was dead."

Jesus, I thought, and was surprised to feel tears in my eyes.

I cleared my throat. "I guess you weren't dead."

"No." She smiled, a wonderful, calming, gentle expression of serenity that I instantly coveted. "I *was* dead."

"Okay."

"To be specific, I was still alive when he left me, but I was bleeding to death and I was in shock and I was starting to be hypothermic, it was winter, after all, and I was lying in the snow."

Dear God, I thought. I hated this story already, and I didn't want to hear any more of it, but at least it had a happy ending. Didn't it? I mean, she was there, telling me her terrible tale, wasn't she?

Raped. Shot. Lying in snow.

I stared at the gentle, delicate woman seated across from me, and tried very hard *not* to allow a picture of the warlike scene to come into my mind.

Sweet Mother Mary.

And I'm not even Catholic.

"I was still alive when the paramedics arrived," Grace Kairn told me, while my stomach knotted as she spoke, "because a passing driver with a phone in his car found me pretty quickly. But I died in the ambulance on the way back into town. I was dead for ten minutes. No heartbeat. No brain activity. No respiration. They said I was absolutely, clinically dead."

"Yeah? One of those near-death experiences?"

I sat up, interested for obvious reasons. It's always good to meet a tourist who has already visited your next destination. They can clue you in as to the weather, what to wear. I'd heard plenty of those tales in 'Nam, but that was a long time ago, and these days I have a more personal interest in collecting any available data. As she told the familiar tale of the tunnel, the light, the love at the end of it, her face was—aren't they all—glowing with happiness. She almost, but not quite, made me want some of it.

But I was still waiting to hear anything "unusual."

"While I was dead," Grace Kairn said, predictably, "I felt loved in a way that I can never fully describe to anyone who hasn't felt it. And I learned some things from that love . . ."

I couldn't help it, I had to ask: "Like, what?"

She smiled, almost a grin, catching me in my curiosity. Before she could reply, I realized we'd better skip the fantasies and cut to the chase. "So who do you want me to keep from getting killed?" I asked her.

But she would tell it at her pace, not mine.

"The man who attacked me was captured and tried and convicted of armed robbery and put into prison."

"Just armed robbery? Was it a plea bargain?"

"Yes. He served four years of his sentence."

"Four . . . you mean he's out now?"

"Yes," she said, gently, "he is."

I felt a chill for her sake.

At that moment, I also experienced a strange, physical sense of a compression of time; it seemed to cast my office in shadow, as if the day were drawing too quickly to a close. All in all, I had a sudden and unaccountable feeling of urgency, which I tried to quell within me, because it was weirdly close to panic.

I couldn't remember the last time I'd felt panic.

"And you're afraid?" I asked her.

Or was I talking to myself?

She glanced out my window, smiling a little to herself, before she looked back at me. "I'll tell you the truth, the answer to that is yes and no. I'm not afraid of anything for myself, certainly not of dying, not anymore. But yes, I'm . . . afraid . . . for other people."

"Who?"

"My husband." The expression in her eyes made me envy any person who occasioned such affection. "Rick absolutely believes that I really died. In Rick's eyes, the man who . . . killed me . . . is a murderer. Not an attempted murderer. A *murderer* who should have been convicted of premeditated homicide."

"But you're alive," I pointed out.

"But I was dead," she countered, quite firmly. "He did kill me."

I let out a whistle. "Try telling that to the law."

"We did—to the police, to the prosecutors, to the judge, to the jury, to anybody who would listen, but they laughed at us. Not openly, they weren't that unkind, but they didn't take us seriously, because, as you yourself said . . ." Grace Kairn touched her blouse above her heart. "I'm alive." Then she added the kicker: "Rick says he'll kill the man who murdered me."

"Murdered you."

"I was dead."

"And you want me to keep Rick from doing that?"

"Oh, yes!"

"You want me to protect the man who assaulted you?"

I heard my own voice rise in disbelief and protest at the idea of it, and yet, I understood the logic of her plea: She didn't want her husband to commit a murder—a real one—and go to jail for it. And he would, because—trust me—the law is an ass, and so are many of the men and women who administer it. It wouldn't matter that he killed a very bad guy, or that he was acting out of perfectly understandable rage at the man and the system. He'd still get the very sentence the true bad guy didn't get. Grace Kairn was correct to fear for her husband. Not to mention the fact that he could, instead, get himself killed by the bad guy, and then what would become of *her*, left alone in the universe with a monster?

Her thoughts were way ahead of mine. "Yes," she affirmed, "I want you to protect that man and I also want you to protect Rick, so he doesn't get himself killed."

"Who's the third person?" I asked her.

She had said she wanted me to prevent three murders.

"Well, it's me." She smiled that gentle smile. "The man who killed me—his name is Jerry Heckler—has friends who have sent me threatening letters and phone calls, all of them saying that Heckler will 'get me' when he gets out." She blushed at the phrase, "get me," as if she were embarrassed to be uttering such a cliché, but that's about as disturbed as she seemed to be. The fact that this vicious bastard—this Jerry Heckler (also not his real name)—was once again free to hurt her seemed not to perturb her peace of mind. I, on the other hand, felt a quickening of horror on her behalf and a heavy dose of rage. I utterly sympathized with her husband's vendetta. Like I always say, where's the goddamned death penalty when you really need it?

"Okay," I said, "so you want me to protect Jerry Heckler so your husband won't do something stupid and get arrested for it. And you want me to protect Rick, so Heckler doesn't kill him for trying. And you want me to protect you, so Heckler can't kill you. Again."

"No," she said, gently correcting me. "I want you to protect all of us, because killing is . . . wrong. Under any circumstances, for any reason, it's a . . . mistake." That weird look of serenity—the one I coveted—came over her face again. "That's one of the things I learned."

"Just a mistake?"

"An error."

"Mistakes can be corrected," I pointed out. "But if I kill somebody, he's never coming back."

She smiled at me. "I'm back."

I agreed to take the case. Not for her reason. I didn't believe her reason. I accepted her advance money for *my* reason: That bastard Heckler was not going to hurt this nice woman again—or any other woman—if I could prevent it, and he was also not going to lure her husband into making a stupid, possibly fatal mistake.

"Will you agree to do what I tell you?" I asked her, and then when she said she would, I asked her to give me a few minutes to think about what that was going to be.

Because I felt such urgency for her sake, I sent Grace Kairn immediately out of town to stay with my mother, figuring Heckler would never know to look there. I didn't even let her go home to pack. I told her not even to call home until I okayed it; I'd inform and deal with her husband—that was part of what she was paying me for.

Maybe you think I was wrong to take a chance on endangering my own mother, but then you've never met Mom. Her only child grew up to be in the military, and then became a private investigator. Think about it: This is probably a mother who can take care of herself. Anyway, who do you think first taught me to shoot? Not Dad, he'd have been the one she shot if he'd ever come back to the rotten neighborhood he left us in. She'd have told the cops she thought he was a prowler, and I'd have backed up her story, even while I was privately thinking, is this any kind of woman for a man to marry? My mother cracks me up; I think she's great, but I can see how she looks from Dad's point of view.

Anyway, once I had Grace safe, the next three steps on my list were: visits, of varying degrees of cordiality, to Rick Kairn, Lt. Janet Randolph, and Mr. Jerry Heckler.

In descending order of cordiality, I started with the cop.

"On a scale of clear water to cesspool, Janet," I said to her in her office, "where does this Heckler fall?"

"Close your mouth *and* hold your nose."

"That bad?"

"You can't be too careful with this one, Angie." The lieutenant, no beauty queen to begin with, hiked an eyebrow, which gave her the appearance of a quizzical rottweiler: black hair, brown skin, pugnacious face, aggressive nature. "What *are* you going to do?"

"Take a look at him."

"That's all?"

I grinned at her. "Somebody's got to be able to identify the body."

Her answering smile was grim. "We were all hoping some other prisoner would kill him."

"It's not too late for that. The world is full of ex-prisoners."

"Don't I know it."

"Can I see a picture of him?"

"You don't need to. He's not real hard to spot. He's a carrottop."

I had to laugh. "You're kidding."

"No. If I had carrot hair, I would never be a criminal. Criminals are so stupid."

"He's out after only four years. So who's stupid? Him or us?"

She handed me the address of the halfway house where he was residing. I wanted to say, "Good dog." Janet had been in Vietnam, too, but in spite of the fact that we were coffee friends, she didn't know I had been there, and there was no way she could look it up, because those files don't exist. Hardly anybody now living does know. It's not too difficult, pretending innocence. People don't expect a woman veteran, not even other women. When Janet or some other 'Nam vet starts in on their war stories or trauma tales, I know how to widen my eyes and look awed and sympathetic.

She doesn't know about the cancer, either.

I'm good at disguise, so I went home and put one together.

I put on my black wig that is long enough to make a ponytail and that has bangs down to my eyelashes . . . and I put in my false bridgework that gives me an overbite . . . and my green contacts and plain glasses . . . and from out of my Goodwill clothing pile I selected a soiled white waitress uniform and dirty white waitress shoes. But my best trick is probably the only one I ever really need: I increased my bust size dramatically enough to draw a man's eyes away from my face. I added makeup, which I usually don't wear, or dangly earrings, either, and I offered a silent apology to all of the legitimate, hardworking waitresses in the world.

One good thing about a DD cup is that you can snug a pistol right down in there between the pads, and nobody suspects a thing unless they try to hug you. If you ever see a buxom waitress reaching in to adjust her bra strap—duck.

Thus camouflaged, I set off to find Jerry Heckler.

Do not assume I took that visit lightly.

There's a writer, Andrew Vachss, who wrote a short story I read one time that I'll never forget, because he was so right. In the story, which was called "The White Crocodile," Vachss compares certain kinds of people to crocodiles. He says baby crocodiles get abandoned by their mothers, so they have to fend for themselves, and if they live to be adults, they spend the rest of their lives getting even.

I figured Jerry Heckler was one of the world's crocodiles.

It didn't matter how much theoretical pity I might feel for whatever abuse he might have suffered as a child, the fact remained he was a man now and he would rend other people limb from limb and eat them if they got within striking distance of him, as proved by what he did to Grace Kairn.

I don't mess around with the Jerry Hecklers of the world; there's no talking to them, no reasoning with them, no sympathy to be got from them, they have no conscience, they are the most dangerous kind of human being that exists, the crocodiles of the human kingdom, and they have—quoting Vachss again—no natural enemies. If I have to deal with them at all, I do the only thing you can do, what I was taught first by my mother and then in 'Nam: strike first.

I made him within half an hour of waiting at a bus stop across from the halfway house. Suppertime. Carrottop came out of the halfway house and walked two doors down to a deli.

While he ate, I made use of the time by getting on the pay phone across the street and calling Grace Kairn's husband, Rick. There was no need for me to go see him personally, not when I had only one basic message to deliver, which was: Don't do it, you'll get caught. According to the schedule Grace had given me, her husband should be home from work now, and only just beginning to wonder where his wife could be.

"Rick? My name is Angela Fopeano, and I'm a private investigator that your wife hired today. She wants me to keep you from trying to kill Jerry Heckler."

I couldn't mince words; Heckler might eat fast.

Kairn was incoherent, indignant, frightened, on the other end of the line, but I could tell he really did love his wife, because he verbally took his frustrations out on me, not on her at what she'd done that day to knock his pins out from under him.

I interrupted Kairn to tell him, "Here's how I'm going to stop you from making a dead man or a prisoner out of yourself, Rick. I have been to see Lt. Janet Randolph today and I have informed her of your intention to kill Heckler."

Dead silence from Kairn.

So often the simple way is the best way.

There was nothing he could do now, without getting himself—and by extension, his wife—in a hell of a mess. And if he loved her—which she believed, and I did too—he just wouldn't do that. It was one thing for him to rant in private; another thing entirely for those rantings to become police knowledge. Whether Grace knew it or not, this is why she had come to me—she couldn't be the traitor who betrayed her husband to the police in order to protect him, but I could be.

"He deserves to die," Rick said, sounding furious, paralyzed, sad.

"You bet," I agreed. "But you don't, and Grace doesn't deserve to be left alone if Heckler gets you first, or you get arrested."

"I can't get arrested, can I, just for wanting to kill him?"

"No, Rick, there's no law against that, yet."

"But this leaves him free to hurt Grace again!"

"It's my job to see that he doesn't."

Rick Kairn didn't sound convinced that I could do that, but then why should he, he didn't know me. I felt for him. When he asked me where Grace was, I said I couldn't tell him until I was absolutely sure that Jerry Heckler would never bother her again, no matter where she was. Kairn didn't like the mystery, probably half suspected me of kidnapping Grace, but he could see the point. If he didn't know where his wife was, he couldn't accidentally—or as the result of force—give that information away to Heckler. I wasn't worried about Heckler's friends, the ones who'd terrorized Grace and Rick with their messages that Heckler would "get her" when he got out; if they were going to do the job on her, they would have done it by now. No, Heckler sounded to me like a man who wants to take his pleasures for himself.

I assured Rick that I'd relay messages between Grace and him.

And then I got off the phone fast when I saw Jerry Heck-

ler in the deli start to dig in his pants pockets for cash to pay
for his supper.

When Heckler came back outside, I called out to him.

"Oh, sir!"

He turned, a beefy, red-haired, suspicious-faced man in
his thirties, bumpy-skinned and heavy-lidded as a croc.

I advanced, holding a man's wallet out so he could see it.

"Did you leave this—"

"That ain't mine."

By then, I was close enough.

Strike first, but know your enemy.

"Grace," I said, low and clear. He looked startled, but
then a corner of his mouth ticked, as if in amusement. "If
anything happens to her or to her husband or to anybody
she has ever met in her life, I will find you and I will kill
you."

He laughed, at my appearance, at my threat.

"Yeah? What if something happens, and it's not my fault?"

He was having fun now, playing with his food.

"If I were you, I would work under the assumption that
everything is your fault, Heckler."

He told me what to do with myself, his eyes on my chest,
and then walked off, in no hurry to escape from me. But
now I knew him: he was arrogant, unobservant, and care-
less, the kind of guy who never, never learns that he will get
caught, which means he will not only do the time, he will
do the crime.

What I said to him wasn't a warning.

Guys like that, they don't take warnings, because they
have no restraint. The shrinks call it "low impulse control."
No, what I was doing was making a positive identification
and scouting behind the lines to protect my own rear.

I have high impulse control. I am very careful, at least I
always have been. Now, with this cancer thing, something's
coming loose.

*   *   *

I spent the subway ride home considering my choices and the consequences of them. When I was in the military, they took intelligent advantage of my best skill, which is exactly that—the ability to observe multiple opportunities and to foresee the consequences of all of them, quickly. It was a rare example of the armed services actually matching ability to assignment.

I spent only ten minutes at home setting up my plan.

First, I called Lt. Randolph.

"I talked to the husband, Janet. How about if I set up an appointment for him to go to your office?"

"Sure."

"When? You say."

"Tomorrow morning, ten-fifteen."

"I'll send him in."

Next, I called Grace's husband back, and told him.

"But I'll be at work—"

"Tell them something. You gotta be there, Rick. You have to convince her you won't harm a strand of Heckler's red hair."

He cursed me, but he agreed to do it.

I could have asked the lieutenant to call him to set up the appointment, but I had to hear his acquiescence, had to be sure he'd really make the appointment. Without mercy, I said to him, "Rick, I want to be able to tell your wife that Lt. Randolph actually saw you at ten-fifteen tomorrow morning."

That got him. "All right!" he said, shouting at me.

Last, I called Mom.

She said things were cool, and she said, "Grace is a nice woman."

"Absolutely. You taking her grocery shopping with you tomorrow morning, Mom?"

"Grocery—?" She stopped herself. "Am I?"

"Big sale on at ten-fifteen. I'd get there before that, and then hang around a while afterward, introduce her to folks, let her see what a friendly little town you have up there."

"She'll want to move here, by the time I finish."

"That's fine."

"You take care, Daughter."

"Yes, ma'am."

My mother didn't know what I was up to, she rarely did anymore, but she was quick to *understand,* and you don't need facts for that. She used to tell me a story, drilled it into me, really, her favorite story from mythology. Where other girls heard about Snow White, I heard the one about Daphne and Apollo. Apollo's a god, Daphne's a wood nymph, and he wants her, but she runs away. Just when he's about to catch her, and she's desperate, she prays to her father, a river-god, for help. Her daddy, thinking he's doing a good thing, saves her by turning her into a tree. Thanks a lot, Dad. You couldn't turn Apollo into a tree, instead, and let your daughter run free? My mother always said the moral of this story is: Don't trust the fathers. Never ask the fathers for help. They will freeze you where you stand, always, to protect their precious status quo.

The inference was: When I need help, ask Mom.

I wasn't crazy about my own plan.

It was all more complicated than I liked, but I had a lot of alibis to arrange, my own included. I also had to work fast, because I couldn't stall Grace out of town forever. What I was planning to do was take Heckler out. Just like that. No farting around. Strike first. Set him up and take him out, in a way that protected Grace, Rick, and me from any suspicion. I was crossing a line here, a line I hadn't crossed since Vietnam.

The rest of the setup was easy, even enjoyable, requiring a couple of hours of scouting near the halfway house for a good shooting gallery, and a few hours of rehearsal with my clothing changes and with my equipment, to develop certain ambidextrous skills.

I went to sleep thinking about Vietnam. Bad move, resulting in weird dreams. By now, most everybody knows we had assassination squads working in country, but hardly anyone knows—and no one would believe it even if you showed them photographs, which I could—there were women involved. Let me put it this way: Not every peacenik who traveled to Hanoi was a pacifist, not every girl with a cross on her uniform was a nurse, not every female with a pencil was a journalist. This all happened, you understand, before I realized—it was a man vet who bitterly told me this —that all soldiers, especially draftees, are prisoners of their government. You don't believe me? Name one other job you can get shot for leaving.

I didn't dream about 'Nam, though.

I dreamed about my mother. She was coming toward me, smiling with determination, a bottle of almond-and-straw-berry-scented shampoo in her hand. She was going to wash my hair. I really didn't want her to use that stuff on me, and I really didn't want her to get hold of my head.

I woke up screaming.

Then I lay there thinking—what a dramatic response to such a nothing little dream. My heart was thudding with fear and my upper body was slick with sweat. I put my hands on my chest right above where the X rays had shown the shadow, and I thought: Weird.

After that, I slept like a baby.

A cancerous baby.

When I awoke, I realized that being trained as an assassin is like knowing how to type: it's a skill you can always fall back on. Ever since I sensed what I was going to do about Jerry Heckler, I'd been thinking about him, but also about a certain child molester I read about who was released on a technicality, and about a terrorist who has somehow fina-gled his way into a minimum security prison.

I have debts from 'Nam.

And I'd been thinking, maybe I could pay them off—*pick* them off—one by one, starting with Heckler. Then I could write up my stories—like this one—and get them published anonymously to scare some of the bad guys. Let them start looking over their shoulders and wondering if they could be next. I was getting real excited about this plan. Like Mom always said: Angie, try to leave this world a better place than you found it.

Yes, ma'am.

I was almost laughing as I dressed, turning myself into a plain little wren of a woman. My equipment—sniper's rifle, telescopic scope, silencer, ammo, tripod, cellular telephone —disassembled quickly and fit perfectly into an ordinary straw bag that I had reinforced for strength. Over my first layer of camouflage, I slipped on thin plastic gloves, then put on coveralls, a well-padded jacket with a hood, a baseball cap with a long bill, and men's work shoes over my thin ladies' slippers. I'd already stashed a tool chest in my car after my practice sessions the night before.

As the old song advised: Walk like a man.

I would go up on the roof of a building across from the halfway house dressed as a workman with a tool chest. I would come down as a little wren with a straw bag, a woman so plain as to be nearly invisible.

It was a gorgeous day, chilly, sunny, no clouds.

And it was 9:45 a.m.

Up on the roof, at ten-fifteen, I called the halfway house on my cellular phone and told the man who answered that I was from the gas company and that we had a major gas leak on the block.

"Evacuate. Get everybody out now."

"Right!" he agreed. People can be so gullible.

Then I called the lieutenant and asked her if Rick Kairn was there yet.

"Sitting right here," she announced, sounding smug.

At that moment, Jerry Heckler walked out the front door of the halfway house. He was a big man, with a lovely large chest for aiming at, and I had ammo that would take down a grizzly, no mistake. I had to fire a cannonball, because silencers dissipate power.

"Tell me what you're telling him," I suggested to Janet.

As she did, I placed one finger of my left hand on the Mute button on my telephone and eased the trigger of the rifle with my right forefinger. Ambidextrous, for sure! And right then—at the worst possible moment in terms of the job—my memory kicked in.

It wasn't a Vietnam flashback.

What I remembered was that fear resides in an almond-shaped organ deep in the brain, the amygdala. Trigger that, and you trigger terror.

Terror. Heart pounding. Cold sweats.

Like my dream. Mom and the shampoo. The almond-and-strawberry-scented shampoo. I didn't know what the strawberry meant, but I knew the almond meant: fear.

Mom?

Shit! I didn't want to think about this now!

As she had warned me, I had never gone to "the fathers" for advice. Thousands of my male contemporaries had and they'd ended up in 'Nam. I had only gone to "the mothers." And here I was with a gun in my hand anyway.

I felt confused, paralyzed.

In that moment, with one finger on the Mute button . . . and Janet talking into my ear . . . and one eye on Jerry Heckler's chest . . . and another finger on a trigger, I felt empty as a jar.

Then I resighted, and fired the rifle.

When what noise there was subsided, I released the Mute button. And all the while, the lieutenant was telling me what she was telling Rick Kairn, who was seated right there in her office while his wife was being introduced to a dozen people fifty miles away. If the cops got suspicious enough of me to go to the trouble of tracking this cellular call, I was in deep shit. But, hey, I was already in deep shit according to several doctors, so what was a little more? Especially if I kept a crocodile from eating people?

Some days, everything works.

It all went perfectly.

Last week, I had lunch with Grace.

"We're safe, aren't we?" she asked me.

"Yes, at least from Heckler, I can't say about the rest of your life."

She smiled at me. "Thank you, however you did it."

"You're welcome. Now will you tell me what else you learned while you were dead?"

"I learned that we're already forgiven."

"Well, that is good news."

She laughed. "I learned that every evil act is actually a cry from the heart for healing, it is a plea to be reunited with God."

"Okay," I said, while she smiled at the skepticism on my face. "Then tell me this, who's God?"

She laughed again. "There's no 'who.' There's nothing— no thing—out there. It's all in here." Grace pointed to her chest, right about where my tumor is. "God is a name we give to love."

"Great bumper sticker," said I, tactless as ever.

But it seemed Grace wasn't defensive and I couldn't offend her. I decided not to mention that some scientists would say her near-death experience was merely a release of endorphins in the brain.

As usual, she was way ahead of me.

"You don't have to believe me, Angie."

"Okay, then if you don't mind, I won't."

We laughed, both of us, while I wondered why in the world I was resisting the idea that I could be forgiven for every bad thing I had ever done. And then I knew why: because that would mean the Jerry Hecklers of the world were forgiven too.

I had called him, the evening after the morning when my shot had missed him by an inch. I had meant to kill him, had gone up on the roof to blast him. But in that instant when I stood empty—with the voices of both the mothers and the fathers silenced in my head—I changed my mind. I think that may have been the first truly independent act of my life, and I wish I could say I felt good about it.

"I told you not to mess with Grace," I said to him.

"I didn't do anything!" he protested. I knew he'd been frightened; I'd seen it in his face after my shot nearly hit him, after I'd purposely aimed off target.

"I know that," I told him. "That shot was for thinking about hurting her. Now consider what's going to happen if you *do* hurt her."

Maybe crocodiles don't take warnings, but they're not complete imbeciles. Even crocs will swim away to another swamp if they hear the sound of gunfire.

I was still worried about those other swamps, though.

"Jerry?" I said. "I'll be keeping tabs on you. If I hear that you are under suspicion for injuring any woman, not just Grace, I will come after you again."

"Who *are* you?"

"A good shot," I said, and hung up.

Who was I? A good question. I was no daddy's girl, and never had been. And now perhaps I was no longer my mother's girl, either. Who was I? A woman, empty, but for something shadowy growing in my breast. For once in my life, I can't foresee the consequences. But I know this natural law: Shadows cannot be cast in total darkness; where there is a shadow, there must be light.

LIZA CODY was brought up in London, where she studied painting and later worked at Madame Tussaud's Wax Museum. She is the author of six Anna Lee mysteries, but recently she has become tangled up in the world of women's professional wrestling with *Bucket Nut* and *Monkey Wrench*. She now lives in Somerset.

Solar Zits

Liza Cody

I woke up this morning and decided on plastic surgery. You really can't begin too soon. After all, the force of gravity starts to work on your face from the moment you are born, and it seems to me that I can't let gravity have its own way one minute longer.

I will shorten my nose, remove the bony bridge. Suck out fat deposits from under my eyes. A little nipping, a little tucking. You won't know me.

I'll change the color of my contact lenses. I'll change the color of my hair. Everything will be new. I won't know me.

All it takes is money. I'll sell the house. I was going to move anyway.

I find a number in the last pages of *Vogue*. I ring and make an appointment. It is simple. It is not like trying to see a doctor when you need help. This clinic wants to help me. I am not a problem.

Today will be a good day. I have a project, a purpose. I know what I am doing. I know where I am going.

It is a blazing day. The world looks brown through UV glasses and I get into my car. I am going to a clinic in the city. It will take hours through the heat and the traffic, but it is an investment. I will be changed. No one will know me.

The radio is zapped out with static—sunspot interference —solar zits. The airwaves are polluted with sonic whimper. The air conditioner whines. I do not listen. I shoot a disc into the slot. It is an old disc. Not mine. I am not responsible for the lyrics.

A man with a boy's voice sings, "It was a slow day and the sun was beating . . ."

It is a speedy day, and the sun is beating. It is even speedy in the slow lane. On the hard shoulder there is a burned-out wreck with blackened steel ribs and no glass. I cannot edge into the second stream: twenty-four-wheelers race by on the outside, bumper to bumper, nose to tail, metal to metal.

This is a long haul, a journey toward transformation and forgetting. Another burned wreck by the side of the road recedes in the mirror. It gets small and then smaller. I will leave it all behind.

I could ask for ECT. Not with asymmetrical electrodes. Asymmetrical electrodes, they say, leave the memory intact. But, they say, if you whack the current through, temple to temple, you can burn out selected memory sites. Then you forget. And when you forget it is exactly as if an occurrence never occurred. Never happened at all.

A fresh face. An empty mind. A different address. A new number. You really won't know me, and no one can ring and remind me. There will be no long-distance calls accusing me. No one can write and blame me. No blame. Surgical intervention, electrical interference, and a good discreet estate agent. "Don't cry, baby, don't cry, don't cry."

My baby didn't cry much in his Perspex incubator. He was quiet and good. A good baby is a quiet baby. A quiet baby is a good baby. My boy in the bubble was no bother. Even when they let him out he was no trouble, and I went back to work before he was old enough to miss me. The child minder loved him. And so did I. I wired his crib for sound and watched videos downstairs. He never interrupted once. I could have heard his smallest whimper but he didn't whimper. He didn't cry. Later, it worried me because he didn't laugh either, but not much. Quiet is good where babies are concerned.

He doesn't need me, I thought. The thought comforted. I had to earn a living. I had to earn the child minder. I had to earn the child. I couldn't do that if the child needed me.

The boy didn't need me either. He went to school. They liked him at school too. They wrote, "He has ability." They wrote, "He is self-contained."

At night, when we were alone in the house, I worked. He worked too. He worked through his units and modules. We rarely spoke, and if I spoke he rarely heard. He wore headphones and strapped his music to his belt. His music went from ear to ear, sound waves transmitted symmetrically, lobe to lobe, through his brain without destroying a single memory site. I couldn't hear it.

I couldn't hear the first accusation either, although it traveled along the telephone wire. It came in the night, arriving as a piece of paper on my fax machine, a soft growl of high-speed words delivered softly into the plastic tray. It growled, in black and white, "What sort of mother do you call yourself?" It said, "Call yourself a mother?" It said, "Your boy is a monster." It was unsigned. No one claimed responsibility.

In the fifth of five gears, fast on the slow lane, with sun searing on the sunroof, I sing, "The boy in the bubble and the baby with the baboon heart . . ." I am not responsible. I am on the motorway, far away from information highways and optical pathways. Human voices cannot reach me. No one can say, "Your boy is a monster. You must be to blame." I will not listen, and what I do not hear will not be true.

I will be nipped and tucked, without laugh lines, cry lines, or life lines. They won't know me. I will be received as a stranger with a phone number nobody knows. If nobody knows me no one can blame me and I will be a miracle of surgical technique.

The only time the boy saw his father was when he watched the video of our wedding—top hat and tailcoat in the burning sun, confetti like dandruff on his shoulders. The boy did not comment, but later that night he asked me about virtual reality. He thought it might be a good way to learn billiards. That was peculiar: the boy did not play games unless there was sophisticated software attached.

I joked with him and said he had been brought up by Super Mario. But he didn't laugh. So I bought him a Home Multi-gym because he needed the exercise.

And it was good to see sweat glisten on that fine white flesh. He filled out, but he never went out. He is allergic to the sun. A lot of us are these days. There are magnetic blemishes on the face of the sun and they say we are undergoing fluctuations in the cycle of solar activity. I never leave home without a carapace of UVA and UVB screen. My sunroof is sun-blocked. The air is conditioned. This bubble sustains life and protects from transient pollution. It is safe, and fast on the slow lane.

Later I will shed my tired old skin. I'll be reborn newborn and my new tight skin will fit me without crease or wrinkle. I will be shrink-wrapped and plastic-coated and never again will I need another generation's hero to alter my mood. The man with the boy's voice and images of alienation depresses and excites me. He is not mine to control. I reject him and eject him. When I am newborn, wrinkle free, not me, I will pop a Prozac into my mouth, not a disc into the machine. But soon I will not need to alter my mood because soon everything will be new and unproved.

But I can't wait, and these millions of racing spinning wheels are making me nervous. I can't wait for my new skin. The burned-out wrecks on the highway might be me. I am so tiny next to the trucks and tracks and trekkers. Ocean liners, condominiums, apartment blocks on wheels, flash past my tinted window. There isn't enough space between them for me to sneak into the fast lane and leave them all behind. I want an empty road ahead and an empty road behind. But the rearview mirror is bursting with cars racing as fast as I am. Everyone is chasing each other with violence and velocity beyond their control. Everyone is chasing me. It is not only the boy who can't run fast enough. I can't either. He was caught, but they won't catch me.

There is not enough conditioned air to breathe and I need my inhaler. At the last moment I see a sign and scream up a slip road, too fast. Too fast to read the signs, too fast to hold the road.

The corner at the top of the incline races forward and rears up. The wheel spins out of my hands.

Flying forward on two wheels, I notice the flash of the spy camera as I rocket over the intersection. The antilocking device grabs, releases, grabs, and then in slo-mo I tip over a green rim and tumble.

The bag inflates with a hiss and a sigh. I recall that I woke up this morning having decided on plastic surgery. As my face hits the air bag I remember that I do not need to protect my head. Amnesia was, in any case, on the menu.

The accident has a cinematic quality: simultaneously as I fly, tumble, and roll, a prisoner of seat belt and air bag, I watch from the stalls. A car dives off a dock, over a cliff, into a ravine, and falls, slowly, an incredible distance until it hits water, beach, rock. The car always explodes into a ball of flame. I expect conflagration. Nothing of the sort occurs.

A good baby is a quiet baby. I have become the baby in the bubble and I do not cry as I lie cradled in straps and trampoline, helpless, hanging. I am not hysterical. Undying, unburned, upside-down, I can feel nothing. There is nothing to feel.

"Wake up," the boy shouts. He taps on my door. "Wake up."

A man with a thin, dark face and horse's hair taps on the window. "Are you awake?" he says. "Are you all right? I'm going to get you out."

He gets me out. He says, "We called Rescue when we saw you shooting over the bank. But nobody came. Can you walk?"

I can walk, shaking, with help. "Don't touch me," I say. I don't like being touched. I'm not used to it. I walk more, without help. All it takes is control.

The sound of sirens comes from the other side of the bank.

The man says, "A pileup. On the highway. That's where

the emergency services are. There's not enough to go round."

We are walking across a field. I don't like grass. Things hide in grass. The grass boils in the sun.

"Sit down a minute," the man says.

"No."

We walk slowly on. The man has horse hair to protect his head and neck from the sun. But I have no hat and my Ray Bans are missing.

The man lives in a bus, in a disused cutting under the highway. His woman makes tea. His children stand, dusty, in the shade, staring. They are ulcerous and brown. Clearly they are allowed to play in the sun. My boy never played in the sun.

The woman gives me tea in a plastic mug. I do not think she has sterilized the mug, but the water was boiled. So I drink the tea. This is a strange world, a world of accidents, incidents, and side dents. It is not my world. I drink the tea. I am prepared for anything.

"Better?" the woman says. "She's white as a ghost."

"Call Rescue again," the man says.

The woman picks up a cracked old portable.

"No," I say.

The man and the woman exchange looks. The children stare.

"Not yet," I say. When Rescue comes they will want my name and number. They will want my fingerprint and voiceprint, and, however far these people live from the highway, they will have heard about me or the boy. I do not want a woman with brown and ulcerous children asking me what sort of mother I am.

I search in empty pockets for something to give them.

"What are your names?" I say to compensate for the empty pockets. They suck on dirty fingers without answering.

"What will you do?" the man asks. "Do you want to call someone? We'd give you a ride, but we've got no fuel."

They are stuck, stationary, under the highway. But they

can live in their transport. I expect they would call themselves Travelers, but they aren't going anywhere. I am not a Traveler, far from it, but I have a long way to go.

"What will *you* do?" I ask, to compensate for the inability to answer his questions.

"Wait," he says, "until we've enough money to fill up and leave."

"We're all right here," the woman says. "We've everything we need."

"What do you do," I ask, "for money?"

"Betty cleans sometimes," the man says, "in the town."

Dirty Betty cleans. Miracle and wonder.

"Al tells fortunes," Betty says. "He has the gift."

A fortune is not something you tell; it is something you make. I am in a world of un-reason. I recall that I woke up this morning having decided on plastic surgery. I am on my way to alter my face, my future, my fortune. All it takes is money.

"He can read your hand," Betty says. "While you wait."

"No," I say. I do not want Al to touch my hand. Coarse black hair obscures his features, but I can see his eyes. I have lost my Ray Bans, so I can see that his eyes are deep-set and unreasonable. His hand, when he helped me out of my car, was burning hot. His children are brown and ulcerous and his tea is contaminated. My fortune is not safe from a man like that.

"It'd pass the time," says Betty. "It won't cost you much. Aren't you curious?"

I am not curious. I know where I'm going, what I am going to do. It is Al and Betty who are curious. They will want to know what sort of mother I am. Well, I am the mother of a boy with flawless white skin, and my tea is not contaminated. We are unblemished by fluctuations in the cycle of solar activity.

"It's the truth," Betty says. "Al can see the future, and he can see through the window in your heart. It helps, believe me."

The heart does not have windows; it has chambers. It is a

muscular system of pumps and chambers which deliver blood to parts which would otherwise die. A miracle of engineering: it can be replaced.

Al stretches. His sinews are long and impossible. He says, "Don't bother the lady, love." His sigh inflates the cutting. It billows around the bus. The grass ripples, the dust swirls.

"Call Rescue again," Al says to Betty. "We can't help this lady."

"No," I say. "Read my hand." The impossible, the unreasonable, will, for a while, rescue me from Rescue.

"Now you're talking," Betty says. "Give me some money and I'll take the children into town."

I pay her, and she takes the children out into the burning sun, out of my sight.

"Give me your hand," says Al.

I will not. I hold it up for him to see.

"An empty hand," says Al.

It is not. I am not empty-handed: I have savings and securities. Money is all it takes.

"A clean hand," Al says, as if I don't know my own hand.

He says, "Your love line is short but your life line is long. I'm sorry for you."

"I have no opinion about that," I say. "It is not a matter for regret."

"That is why I'm sorry for you," says Al. "Your fate line is fractured."

My fate is in my own hands. The fracture was not mine. If my fate is fractured by a fault line it's not my fault.

"It's not my fault," I say.

"But your fate is in your own hands," Al says. "Isn't that what you've just been thinking?"

I clench my fist. Al's eyes are unreasonable, but he knows something.

"Give me the portable," I say. "I'll call Rescue now."

Al laughs and a ripple runs through the grass. "It'll take more than Rescue to rescue you, lady," he says. He gives me the portable, but I can't call.

The boy is in a high-security holding cell but at least he is safe from solar zits. He has returned to his Perspex incubator. When he leaves it he will die. An eye for an eye, a heart for a heart. Solar zits is the only thing he is safe from.

I say to Al, "What have you heard?"

"Nothing," he says. "Hearing is not what I do. Reading is my forte."

I am certain he has seen my face on TV, the way everyone else did. I couldn't hide my face and the camera followed me, spying, and telling tales.

I look but see neither dish nor aerial.

"Where's your TV?" I ask.

"No TV," he says. "There's too much interference here."

I don't believe this is so. Everybody saw. Strangers looked and saw my face. From transmitter to aerial, from coast to coast, from satellite to dish to receiver to eye to brain to memory; my face was transported into offices, houses, pubs and clubs, a spectacle to boost ratings: entertainment for strangers.

"Give me your hand again," Al says.

I do not. I hold it up between my face and his burning eye.

"Yes," he says. "I can see that someone close to you has caused you pain."

The boy did not cause me pain. He was a quiet boy, a clean boy. Quiet boys are good boys.

"Can you see what will happen to the boy?" I ask.

"What boy?" Al says. "There's no boy in your hand."

"Then what will happen to me?"

Al says, "Pain is no bad thing. Pain can bring wisdom if you will only open yourself to new experiences."

As if I don't know my own life.

"I see death in your hand," says Al.

It is not my death. It was not my hand. My baby has a foreign heart. It is not my fault. I am not the mother of a monster in spite of what everybody says. The boy's heart is to blame. The boy's heart is an orphan.

I get up. I must go. I have an appointment. Time with Al

is not time well spent. His children are brown and ulcerous; they have been polluted by dust and dead sun.

"Good-bye," says Al. "Take care." He smiles and the dry earth cracks.

I cross the field to my wrecked car, but it is no longer isolated. An official vehicle has drawn up beside it. Two men in uniform are poking around inside and muttering messages into their mobiles.

One of them says, "Is this yours?"

"No," I say.

I point across the field to the cutting under the highway. If anyone is to blame it might as well be Al. And I woke up this morning having decided on plastic surgery. No one will know me so I might as well not be me, and the car might as well not be mine. It might as well be Al's.

"Don't I know you?" says the man in the uniform.

RUTH RENDELL has been writing for the past thirty-one years and has won the Crime Writers Association's Gold Dagger Award four times. Sixteen of her novels feature Chief Inspector Wexford, the subject of a television series. She is a Fellow of the Royal Society of Literature and holds honorary degrees from the University of Essex and East Anglia and Bowling Green State University in Ohio. Her latest books are **Blood Lines,** a collection of short stories, and writing as Barbara Vine, **No Night Is Too Long.**

The Astronomical Scarf

Ruth Rendell

It was a very large square, silk in the shade of blue called midnight that is darker than royal and lighter than navy, and the design on it was a map of the heavens. The Milky Way was there and Charles's Wain, Orion, Cassiopeia and the Seven Daughters of Atlas. A young woman who was James Mullen's secretary saw it in a shop window in Bond Street, draped across the seat of a (reproduction) Louis Quinze chair with a silver bracelet lying on it and a black picture hat with a dark blue ribbon hiding one of its corners.

Cressida Chilton had been working for James Mullen for just three months when he sent her out to buy a birthday present for his wife. Not jewelry, he had said. Use your own judgment, I can see you've got good taste, but not jewelry. She could see which way the wind was blowing there. "Not jewelry" were the fateful words. Elaine Mullen was his second wife and had held that position for five years. Office gossip had it that he was seeing one of the management trainees in Foreign Securities. I wish it was me, thought Cressida, and she went into the shop and bought the scarf—appropriately enough, for an astronomical price—and then, because no one gift-wrapped in those days, into a stationer's round the corner for a sheet of pink and silver paper and a twist of silver string.

Elaine knew the meaning of the astronomical scarf. She

knew who had wrapped it up too and it wasn't James. She had expected a gold bracelet and she could see the writing on the wall as clearly as if James had turned graffitist and chalked up something to the effect of all good things coming to an end. As for the scarf, didn't he know she never wore blue? Hadn't he noticed that her eyes were hazel and her hair light brown? That secretary, the one that was in love with him, had probably bought it out of spite. She gave it to her blue-eyed sister who happened to come round and see it lying on the dressing table on the very day Elaine was served with her divorce papers under the new law, Matrimonial Causes Act, 1973.

Elaine's sister wore the scarf to a lecture at the Royal Society of Lepidopterists, of which she was a Fellow. Cloak-room arrangements in the premises of learned societies are often somewhat slapdash and here, in a Georgian house in Bloomsbury Square, Fellows, members, and their guests were expected to hang up their coats themselves on a row of hooks in a dark corner of the hall. When all the hooks were in use coats had either to be placed over those already there or else hung up on the floor. Elaine's sister, arriving rather late, took off her coat, threaded the astronomical scarf through one sleeve—in at the shoulder and out at the cuff —and draped the coat over someone's very old ocelot.

As soon as the lecture, on the subject of Taxonomy of Genera and Species, was over, one of the guests made an immediate departure. She told the Fellow who had brought her that she had to be at the Savoy by seven-thirty and it was already twenty to eight. Everyone else gathered in the Fellows' Drawing Room for sherry and biscuits. The guest, whose name was Sadie Williamson, went to collect her coat.

Sadie Williamson was a thief. She stole something nearly every day. The coat she was wearing she had stolen from Harrods and the shoes on her feet from a friend's clothes cupboard after a party. She was proud to say (to herself) that she had never given anyone a present that she had had to pay for. Now, in the dim and deserted hall, on the walls of which a few eighteenth-century prints of British butter-

flies were just visible, Sadie searched among the garments
for some trifle worth picking up.

An unpleasant smell arose from the clothes. It was compounded of dirty cloth, old sweat, mothballs, cleaning fluid,
and something in the nature of wet sheep. Sadie curled up
her nose in distaste. She hoped there was a place nearby
where she could wash her hands. Not much worth bothering about here, she was thinking, when she saw the handrolled and hemstitched corner of a blue scarf protruding
from a coat sleeve. Sadie gave it a tug. Rather nice. She
tucked it into her coat pocket and because she could hear
footsteps coming from the lecture room, left in haste.

Next day she took it round to the cleaners. Most things
she stole she had dry-cleaned, even if they were fresh off a
hanger in a shop. You never knew who might have tried
them on.

"The zodiac," said the woman in the dry cleaners. "Which
sign are you?"

"I don't believe in it but I'm Cancer."

"Oh dear," said the woman, "I never think that sounds
very nice, do you?"

Sadie put the scarf into a box which had contained a pair
of tights she had stolen from Selfridges, wrapped it up in a
piece of paper that had originally wrapped a present given to
her, and sent it to her godchild for Christmas. The parcel
never got there. It was one of those lost in the robbery of a
mail train traveling between Norwich and London.

Of the two young men who snatched the mailbags, it was
the elder who helped himself to the scarf. He thought it was
new, it looked new. He gave it to his girlfriend. She took one
look and asked him who he thought she was, her own
mother? What was she supposed to do with it, tie it round
her head when she went to the races?

She meant to give it to her mother but lost it on the way.
She left it in the taxi in which she was traveling from Kil-
burn to Acton. It was found, along with a pack of two hundred cigarettes, two cans of diet Coke, and a copy of
Playboy, the lot in a rather worn Harrods carrier, by the taxi

driver's next fare. She happened to be Cressida Chilton, who was still James Mullen's secretary, but who failed to recognize the scarf because it was enclosed in the paper originally wrapped round it by Sadie Williamson. Besides, she was still in a state of shock from what she had read in the paper that morning, the announcement of James's imminent marriage, his third.

"This was on the floor," she said, handing the bag over with the taxi driver's tip.

"They go about in a dream," he said. "You wouldn't believe the stuff they leave behind. I had a full set of Masonic regalia left in my cab last week and the week before that it was a baby's pot, no kidding, and a pair of wellies. How am I supposed to know who this stuff belongs to? I mean, I ask you, they'd leave themselves behind only they don't, thank God. I mean, what is it? Packets of fags and a dirty mag."

"Yes, well, I hope you find the owner," said Cressida, and she rushed off through the swing doors and up in the lift to be sure of getting there before James did, to be ready with her congratulations, all smiles.

"Find the owner, my arse," said the driver to himself.

He drew up at the red light next to another taxi whose driver he knew, and having already seen this copy, passed him *Playboy* through their open windows. The cigarettes he smoked himself. He gave the Diet Coke and the scarf to his wife. She said it was the most beautiful scarf she had ever seen and she wore it every time she went anywhere that required dressing up.

Eleven years later her daughter Maureen borrowed it. Repeatedly, the taxi driver's wife asked for it back, and Maureen meant to give it back, but she always forgot. Until one day when she was going to her mother's and the scarf came into her head, a vision inspired by a picture of the night sky in September in the *Radio Times*. Her flat was always untidy, a welter of clothes and magazines and tape cassettes and full ashtrays. But once she had started she really wanted to find the scarf. She looked everywhere. She grubbed about in cupboards and drawers, threw stuff on to the floor and fumbled through half-unpacked suitcases. The result was that she was very late getting to her mother's. She had not found the astronomical scarf.

This was because it had been taken the previous week—"borrowed," he too would have said—by a boyfriend who was in love with her but whose love was unrequited. Or not as fully requited as he would have wished. The scarf was not merely intended as a sentimental keepsake but to be taken to a clairvoyant in Shepherds Bush who had promised him dramatic results if she could only hold in her hands "something of the beloved's." In the event, the spell or charm failed to work, possibly because the scarf belonged not to Maureen but to her mother. Or did it? It would have been hard to say who its owner was by this time.

The clairvoyant meant to return the scarf to Maureen's boyfriend at his next visit but that was not due for two weeks and in the meantime she wore it herself. She was only the second person into whose possession it had come to look on it with love and admiration. The lepidopterist had worn it because it was obviously of good quality and because it was *there;* Sadie Williamson had recognized it as expensive; Maureen had borrowed it because the night had turned cold. But only her mother and now the clairvoyant had truly appreciated it.

This woman's real name was not known until after she was dead. She called herself Thalia Essene. The scarf delighted her not because of the quality of the silk, nor its handrolled hem, nor its color, but because of the constellations scattered across its midnight blue. Such a map was to her what a chart of the Atlantic Ocean might have been to some early navigator, essential, enrapturing, mysterious, indispensable, life-saving. Its stars were the encyclopedia of her trade, the impenetrable spaces between them the source of her predictions. She sat for many hours in meditative contemplation of the scarf, which she spread on her lap, stroking it gently and sometimes murmuring incantations. When she went out she wore it, along with her layers of trailing garments, black cloak, and pomander of asafetida grass.

Roderick Thomas had never been among her clients. He had just moved into one of the rooms below her flat in the Uxbridge Road. It was years since he had had any work and longer than that since anyone had shown the slightest interest in him, wished for his company, paid attention to what he said, let alone cared about him. Thalia Essene was one of the few people who actually spoke to him and all she generally said when she saw him was "Hi" or "Rain again."

One day, though, she made the mistake as it turned out of saying a little more. The sun was shining out of a cloudless sky.

"The goddess loves us this morning."

Roderick Thomas looked at her with his mouth open. "You what?"

"I said, the goddess loves us today. She is shedding her glorious sunshine on to the face of Earth."

Thalia smiled at him and walked on. She was on her way to the shops in King Street. Roderick Thomas started shambling after her. For some years he had been on the lookout for the Antichrist, who he knew would come in female form. He followed Thalia into Marks and Spencer's and the cassette shop where she was in the habit of buying music as background for her fortune-telling sessions. She was well aware of his presence and, growing increasingly angry, then nervous, went home in a taxi.

Next day he hammered on her door. She told him to go away.

"Say that about the sunshine again," he said.

"It's not sunny today."

"You could pretend," he said. "Say about the goddess."

"You're mad," said Thalia.

A client who had been having his palm read overheard it all and gave Thalia a funny look. She told him his life line was the longest she had ever seen and he would probably make it to a hundred. When she went downstairs Roderick

Thomas was waiting for her in the hall. He looked at the scarf.

"Clothed in the sun," he said, "and upon her head a crown of twelve stars."

Thalia said something so alien to her philosophy of life, so contrary to all her principles, that she could hardly believe she'd uttered it. "If you don't leave me alone I'll get the police."

He followed her just the same. She walked up to Shepherd's Bush Green. Her threats gave her a dark aura and he saw the stars encircling her. She fascinated him, though he was beginning to see her as a source of danger. In Newcastle, where he had been living up until two years before, he had killed a woman he had mistakenly thought was the Antichrist because she told him to go to hell when he spoke to her. For a long time he expected to be sent to hell, even after the woman was dead, and although the fear had somewhat abated, it came back when he was confronted by beautiful evil women.

A man was standing on one of the benches on the green, preaching to the multitude. Well, to four or five people. Roderick Thomas had followed Thalia to the tube station but there had to abandon his pursuit for lack of money to buy a ticket. He wandered on to the green and the man on the bench stared straight at him and said,

"Thou shalt have no other gods but me!"

Roderick took that for a sign, you'd have to be daft not to get the message, but he asked his question just the same.

"What about the goddess?"

"For Solomon went after Ashtoreth," said the man on the bench, "and after Milcom the abomination of the Ammonites. Wherefore the Lord said unto Solomon, I will surely rend the kingdom from thee, and will give it to thy servant."

That was fair enough. Roderick went home and bided his time, listening to the voice of the preacher which had taken over from the usual voice he heard during his waking hours. It told him of a woman in purple sitting on a scarlet-colored beast, full of names of blasphemy, having seven heads and ten horns. He watched from his window until he saw Thalia Essene come in, carrying a large recycled paper bag of a dull purple with CELESTIAL SECONDS printed on its side.

Thalia was feeling happy because she hadn't seen Roderick for several hours and believed she had shaken him off. She was going out that evening to see a play at the Lyric, Hammersmith, in the company of her friend who was a famous water diviner. To this end she had bought herself a new dress, or rather, a "nearly new" dress, purple Indian cotton, with mirror work and black embroidery. The blue starry scarf, which she had taken to calling the *astrological* scarf, went well with it. She draped it round her neck, lamenting the coldness of the night. All this would have to be covered by her old black coat, as a shawl would be inadequate.

A quick glance at her engagement book showed her that Maureen's boyfriend was due for a consultation next morning. The scarf must be returned to him. She would wear it for just one last time. As it happened, Thalia was wearing all these clothes for the last time, doing everything she did for the last time, but clairvoyant though she was, of her imminent fate she had no prevision.

She walked along, looking for a taxi. None came. Thalia had plenty of time and decided to walk. Roderick Thomas was behind her but she had forgotten about him and she didn't look round. She was thinking about the water diviner, whom she hadn't seen for eighteen months but who was reputed to have split up from his girlfriend.

Roderick Thomas caught up with her in one of the darker spots of Hammersmith Grove. It was not dark to him but illuminated by the seven times seventy stars on the clothing of her neck and the sea of glass like unto crystal on the hem of her garment. He said not a word but took the two ends of the starry cloth in his hands and strangled her.

After they had found her body, her killer was not hard to find. There was little point in charging Roderick Thomas with anything or bringing him up in court, but they did. The astronomical scarf was Exhibit A at the trial. Roderick

Thomas was found guilty of the murder of Noreen Blake—
for such was Thalia Essene's real name—guilty but insane
and committed to a suitable institution "during the Queen's
pleasure."

The exhibits would normally have ended up in the Black
Museum, but a young police officer called Karen Duncan,
whose job it was to collect together such memorabilia,
thought it all so sad and distasteful, that poor devil who
never should have been allowed out into the community in
the first place, that she put Thalia's carrier bag and theater
ticket in the shredder and took the scarf home with her.
Although it had once been dry-cleaned, the scarf had never
been washed. Karen washed it in cold water gel for delicates
and ironed it with a cool iron. Nobody would have guessed
it had been used for such a macabre purpose, there wasn't a
mark on it.

However, an unforeseen problem arose. Karen couldn't
bring herself to wear it. It wasn't the scarf's history that
stopped her so much as her fear other people might recognize it. There had been some publicity for the Crown Court
proceedings and much had been made of a midnight-blue
scarf patterned with stars. Cressida Chilton had read about it
and wondered why the description of it reminded her of
James Mullen's second wife, the one before the one before
his present one. She didn't think she could face a fourth
divorce and a fifth marriage, she'd have to change her job.
Sadie Williamson read about the scarf and for some reason
there came into her head a picture of butterflies and a dark
house in Bloomsbury.

After some inner argument, reassurance countered by denial and self-rebuke, Karen Duncan took the scarf round to
the charity shop where they let her exchange it for a black
velvet hat. Three weeks later it was bought by a woman who
didn't recognize it, though the man who ran the charity
shop did and had been in a dilemma about it ever since
Karen brought it in. Its new owner wore it for a couple of
years. At the end of that time she got married to an astronomer. The scarf shocked and enraged him and he explained

to her what an inaccurate representation of the heavens it was, how it was quite impossible for these constellations to be adjacent to each other or even visible at the same time, and if he didn't forbid her to wear it that was because he wasn't that kind of man.

The astronomer's wife gave it to the woman who did the cleaning three times a week. This woman never wore the scarf, she didn't like scarves, could never keep them on, but it wouldn't have occurred to her just the same to say no to something that was offered her. When she died, three years later, her daughter came upon it among her effects.

The daughter was a silversmith and member of a celebrated craft society. One of her fellow members made quilts and was always on the lookout for likely fabrics to use in patchwork. The quiltmaker, Fenella Carbury, needed samples of blue, cream, and ivory silks for a quilt which had been commissioned by a millionaire businessman, well known for his patronage of arts and crafts and for his charitable donations. No charity was involved here, for Fenella worked hard and for long hours and the quilt would be worth every penny of the two thousand pounds she would be asking for it.

For the second time in its life the scarf was washed. The silk was as good as new, its dark blue unfaded, its stars as bright as they had been twenty years before. From it Fenella was able to cut forty hexagons which, interspersed with forty ivory damask diamond shapes from someone's wedding dress and forty sky-blue silk diamond shapes from a fabric shop off-cut, formed the central motif of the quilt. When it was finished it was large enough to cover a king-size bed.

James Mullen allowed it to hang on exhibition in Chelsea in the Chenil Gallery for precisely two weeks. Then he collected it and gave it to his new bride for a wedding present along with a diamond bracelet, a cottage in Derbyshire, and a Queen Anne four-poster to put the quilt on.

Cressida Chilton had waited for him through four marriages and twenty-one years. Men, as Oscar Wilde said, marry because they are tired. Men, as Cressida Chilton said, always marry their secretaries in the end. It's dogged as does it and she had been dogged, she had persevered, and she had her reward.

Before getting into bed on her wedding night, she contemplated the two thousand pound quilt and said to James that it was the loveliest thing she'd ever seen.

"The middle bit reminds me of when you first came to work for me," said James. "I should have had the sense to marry you then. I can't think why it reminds me, can you?"

Cressida smiled. "I suppose I had stars in my eyes."

IRINA MURAVYOVA was born in Moscow in 1952. She was raised by her grandmother, to whom most of her writing is dedicated. She came to Boston in 1985, where she held a variety of positions teaching and translating, and also made a documentary film. She has spent three years in the Department of Slavic Languages at Brown University. Now she is Editor in Chief of a weekly published newspaper, *The Boston Time*.

On the Edge

Irina Muravyova

Translated from the Russian by Marian Schwartz

Originally published as "Na Kraiu," in *Grani*, no. 167 (1993): 12–23.

It was a green, gushing, gritty world. Dirty, dark-faced people walked down its dusty roads. They stopped at a clump of large trees, built fires, and cooked supper. In the morning, their ragtag, colorfully dressed women hustled to the bazaars, badgered passersby, holding out their nut-brown palms.

She was sixteen the first time she went to jail. She wasn't any worse at stealing than the others, but she was unlucky for some strange reason. People said she had the evil eye and could sense misfortune. There was that crumbly, blue-eyed, fragrant-lipped woman who laughed with those gold crowns in her mouth and held out her plump hand: "Tell me my fortune, sweetie!" She knew instantly . . . What? Well, that the woman only had an hour left. That blue-eyed laughing woman with the fragrant lips and gold crowns only had one hour left. She could see it all: the embankment, the body thrown onto it from the hurtling train, the blue-eyed, dead-eyed thrown-back head with the half-open lips. . . . She did not tell her that. She wove the kind of tale the woman was expecting—about love and a journey, about the king of wands in the house of government who was tired of waiting, but by morning the whole district knew that a woman of about forty-five had been thrown from the evening commuter train at full speed—Alferova, Nadezhda Vasilievna Alferova, mother of two, unwed. . . .

Her first sentence was short. Just three years. She never went back to the Gypsy camp. She lived in Arkhangelsk and took a job every once in a while. She was married twice, though not officially. She didn't steal very often, only when she liked something a lot and didn't have any money. She had a special weakness for furs—coats and hats. More than anything else in the world she loved romance novels and movies from India, which she watched over and over again until she cried. She herself sang and danced and played the guitar. Her name was Liubov Rakhmetova.

". . . and also, dear Liuba, I want to tell you that you are the most beautiful woman destiny ever brought my way. If you and I'd met in a town like Simferopol or Yalta, instead of here, I'd have shut my eyes, given up everything, and followed you like a dog. My little black-eyed seagull. Liubochka! See, sometimes I think about you and me stuck in this shitty little hole where we don't even know what else might happen to us. What a rotten deal! We can't go for a walk. We can't enjoy each other. We can't even look at each other like we should. . . . But write me, Liubov, I'm waiting impatiently for your reply. . . . Your Vasily."

The letter was written in pencil on the yellowed, smoke-impregnated liner of a tobacco pack.

"Vasya, none of it's my fault. My mother and father abandoned me, and evil people forced me to steal and wrecked my whole life. See, people say I'm a Gypsy, but who knows? They took me into the Gypsy camp right off the street where I was standing, completely abandoned and unwanted. . . . Just because I have black hair. Well, Vasya, Gypsies aren't the only ones with black hair. But I like you a lot. You might say I fell in love with you because I could really see what a good man you are and because you have a face they could put in the movies, a very beautiful movie. I'm sending you a present. Smoke it in good health and don't forget me. Your loving Liubov Rakhmetova."

Combing her shaggy gray head, the old woman with the brown bumps on her fingers told her:

"You're a fool, Liuba. A fool as sure as I'm looking! Living in the same cell with you is pure punishment! You toss and turn, you moan, you grate your teeth! And now you've up and fallen in love! What's that brain of yours for anyway?"

Turning her back to the gray, shaggy old woman with the brown bumps on her fingers, Liuba chuckled sadly, and her black eyes shone, greedy and underslept.

". . . but I beg you, Liuba. Don't try to find out what I'm in for because I'm not getting out" (from Vasily Lebedev's letter).

"Dear Vasya! I give you my word I won't keep any secrets from you, so I don't really understand why you're keeping a secret in your heart from me, as if I were a stranger. If you're telling me the truth, that you love me, then why should we hide anything from each other? What kind of crime could you have committed that you can't even talk about it? After all, I'd forgive you for anything in the world anyway" (from Liubov Rakhmetova's letter).

The old woman with the bumps on her fingers, the old witch with the wrinkled eyelids, was seeping into her soul through the sour, moist cough that was tearing up her throat:

"He's not going to tell you that as long as he lives. Ha! You listen to me. I wish you well, you little scamp! I know I shouldn't trust your breed, but still . . . I like you, lady, and I pity you. . . . People are talking. Very, very soon, they're saying, your Vasya . . . He did his wife in, or that's the way it looks. . . . Except it was really ghastly. Pretty unusual. Hey, what're you going all white for? That's not going to make it any easier. In our life, a man's worse than a noose. It all comes down to the same fancy. I'll never believe in this love of yours as long as I live. There's no such thing! You're lying to yourselves, fools!"

Night is such a lonesome time. What did we ever do to deserve it—this muffled, stifling black, a narrow cot, eyes open, doors slamming in the distance, someone coughing, someone moaning, someone dying.

That night she suddenly realized whom she should turn to.

"Lord! My sweet, good Lord!" Her lips were dry, her words halting. She had never spoken those words before, but she had caught snatches of them in the earth's tumult of sounds. The feeling surfaced from out of somewhere and started hammering away inside her until it found expression. "Oh Lord, my sweet, good Lord!," she repeated, headlong. Her dry lips felt like they'd been ripped off and couldn't keep pace with her thoughts. "Lord! Help me! Don't let them kill him, Lord!"

The main thing, of course, was what had he done? She didn't know. The night kept repeating itself, muffled, black, the life in her. She felt like she was melting away.

"No, Rakhmetova! No one's bringing him out. You're wasting your time gawking! How's he supposed to take his walk now when they barely brought him back to life yesterday! He cut himself, the viper! You've got about as much chance seeing him now as you do your own ears. Hold on to your stupid money! How am I supposed to bring him? What, should I carry him out on my back? He's swimming in blood over there. He's not coming to anytime soon!"

Was he asleep? Dreaming?

"Vasya! Vasya! Come here! Get off the floor! It's me! I got them to let me in for a minute, Vasya! Stick your head in the feed bag! Can you see me? How could you do a thing like that, Vasya? Did you think you could leave me behind?"

He pressed his face to the food slot in the door, and her frightened fingers touched his forehead, eyes, and cheeks.

"Why didn't they wash you, sweetheart? Why are you covered in blood? Oh, my love, my sweet love! You decided to cut yourself and leave me behind!"

Her fingers reached for him, clutched at him, stroked him.

"How am I supposed to kiss you, Vasya?"

"Get going, Rakhmetova. Move it! Have a heart! You had your little chat, that's enough! Get going! Come on, move it, or they're going to slap me in strict because of you!"

The old woman with the bumps on her fingers, the old witch with the wrinkled eyelids, was seeping into her soul through the sour, moist cough that was tearing up her throat.

"Well, girl, you're really off your rocker now! They're going to stand him up against the wall any day now and you're in here bawling into your pillow. Didn't you ever get that on the outside? It's the truth they're telling: prison makes females all fuzzy in the brain! Give 'em love, like in the movies, that's all they want! He can be crippled, he can be armless, he can be anything at all, just so she can tear her heart out! You're fools, little fools! So what are you going to do tomorrow? Who's going to take you to him the next time?"

"Tomorrow" clouded her head. Her eyes were open and sleepless; her lips whispered something like a gray spider web. She got up, groped for the piece of razor she'd stashed in the crack in the wall, screwed up her face, and slashed her left wrist with all her might. A guard came running at her scream. She was sitting on the floor, soaked in blood. Something weird danced in her black irises.

"Vasya, Vasenka! Are you alive in there? It's me! I'm walking by again! They're taking me to the infirmary! I cut myself, Vasya! I wanted to shout a word to you!"

"That is one bizarre female. Watch her with both eyes. . . . She slashed her wrist to get a look at her fancy man! They should get her, too, you know what for? Mutilation. . . . The main thing is, keep your eye on that peephole. No breaks. You never know what other tricks she might be up to."

The older woman took a drag on her Dymok and shook her head meaningfully. The younger frowned.

"Naturally. I don't trust those broads, not one of them. They're all bitches. On the outside, wherever you go, at least they've got some proper fear. They've got their husband and kids. But in here these thieves are absolute animals. Laying hands on themselves doesn't mean diddly to them. I figured that out a long time ago. I've been working here for two years, and I finally got the message. They're a hell of a bunch of liars, though! They can spin you a tale about mom and pop that'll turn your stomach! Everyone of 'em a regular Sarah Bernhardt!"

She had a dream about bread. A big, moist loaf of black bread that she tore apart with both hands and crammed greedily into her mouth. The bread was underbaked and salty, and its black insides smelled of blood. It didn't fill her up; it just made her hungrier. The old witch beside her was snoring in her sleep, tossing her loose gray mane over the flat headrest. This crust she'd dreamed was spiky to the touch, like his unshaven face under her hands. She stroked the bristly, bloody-smelling bread skin and held it with trembling hands. The bread didn't fill her up; it just made her hungrier.

"I'm not writing a letter to you, Liuba, it's like I'm talking to you. Because death is standing over my shoulder. I didn't think I could ever confide in you, and that's why I cut myself, so I wouldn't have to tell you the truth. I got scared you wouldn't love an animal like that. But now I've decided that there's no one in the world closer to me than you. Actually, to be honest, I don't have anyone in the world at all. I'm going to open up to you completely, and maybe that'll make it easier for me. If you decide you hate me, all the better. No matter what, I'm on my way to the other world soon, but maybe you can still build your life without me. It's not easy for me to write this, Liuba, because I would have married you and made you happy. You've got to believe that. I've never said or promised that to anyone before, but I'll tell you like a priest at confession: I'd have married you and made you happy. That's the truth. But now you have to listen to what happened that night. It was muddy and raining hard. The whole road was churned up, and my car could barely get through. I was coming home at the wrong time because my relief got discharged from the hospital unexpectedly and he asked to take my shift. That's why it all happened. Tasya and I had just started living together then. Before, I used to come back from the village, get drunk, and drop out of sight. But suddenly I got back together with my little brother. He was born a deaf-mute, and he's totally disabled with one thing or another. Our parents passed away a long time ago. Well, naturally, he got sent to the children's home then, and I visited him there and kept an eye on him. But it made me so miserable, Liuba. I couldn't breathe it made me so miserable. I thought he must be just dying out there. You could see right through him. Who cared about him? He just mumbled and they fed him. You can't imagine how they goaded him. It got so pathetic I couldn't take it anymore. I wanted to take him home with me. But how could I? My house was like a wolf's den. One folding cot, two chairs, and a bottle of vodka. No, I found out you can't get along without women. I needed a woman. Right about then Tasya turned up. I don't want to lie, Liuba. She was pretty and red like a fox. But we didn't really love each other. We just lived together. The first time she stayed over I didn't recognize the house when I got back after a twenty-four-hour shift. It was all nice and clean. She put a little rug on the floor and a cloth on the table and flowers in a tin can. It was completely different. That's when I decided she might as well stay. She was a woman after all. She'd make me my food and put me to bed, as the saying goes. But mainly I was thinking about my little brother. Now I had somewhere to take him—and I did, immediately. We started living like people. I even drank less and started earning good money. Going home I'd get all warm-feeling inside. Tasya's there, I'd think. My own brother and a hot meal. Everything just like people. So one night I drove up to the house. Are you listening to me, Liuba?"

Night is such a lonesome time. Someone is moaning nearby, someone snoring, someone dying. So lonesome! Lying on this damned iron cot, eyes open and sleepless, and nothing to breathe, nothing to live for. Nothing at all. The old woman tossed her shaggy head over the flat headrest.

Death was standing over his shoulder. That night they got very close. Her face was like that neighbor of hers—gray, with saggy skin, angry, yellow-eyed. She made him tell her everything and not hide anything from her. But he overdid it. He tried to embellish. He tried to make himself out completely innocent. He felt sorry for himself. So sorry he could cry. After all, death was standing over his shoulders. What could be worse?

". . . I saw this guy in my bed. A stranger, not from our village. Kind of rickety all over, puny, clipped mustache. Well, there was wine on the table and cookies, everything just like it should be. At first I don't even look at Tasya. I look and my brother's not sleeping. He's looking at me like a rabbit at a viper. He was whiter than the tablecloth. And hiccuping like crazy. Scared shitless probably. That guy jumped right up in his birthday suit, grabbed the empty bottle, and started waving it at me. I remember now, I was trembling all over. I must have raised my hand in my fright. I grabbed him by the throat and pummeled him a few times, but I didn't kill him. You've got to believe me, Liuba. I didn't. I guess I broke his arm because it was dangling there like it wasn't alive and I pushed him out onto the stairs just the way he was, without anything. I shut the door behind him and tried to think, but my head was all fuzzy. I tore the sheet off her. The snake, she was draped in that red hair of hers and she lunged for my face with her nails, like she wanted to scratch my eyes out. The way I remember it now,

Liuba, I started hearing a hammering in my head like a train coming, and I was hollering worse than a wild animal. Howling like a dog. I'm going to tear her to pieces, I thought. I'm not going to leave a single shred alive. That's how it seems to me now, anyway, now that I've had a chance to think, but I don't guess I understood much of anything then. I threw her down on the bed, and then she spat in my face with all her strength. I grabbed the bottle then . . . Well . . . I broke the bottle over her head, Liuba. And I could feel someone grabbing me from below, from the floor, by my leg. It was my little brother. He'd crawled up and clasped me with those pathetic arms of his, and he's looking at me, but he can't talk. He's just totally white. I lean over and lift him up off the floor, and Tasya just slips from my arms, dead. She did die instantly, after all. Just thinking about it makes me so bitter. Maybe she was a filthy bitch, and maybe she was okay. That's not the point. There was no point killing her. What was I, her master or something? But I didn't understand that until now. At the time, I was totally seething. I shook off my little brother, and he meowed like a kitten. My whole head was in some kind of dark fog, all smoky. Nothing made any sense. I couldn't feel my hands or my legs. It was like they were all separate from me. And then from downstairs, from the first floor, I heard this god-awful commotion! Howling, wailing, moaning, crashing, someone sobbing—you couldn't even tell whether it was a guy or a woman. . . . Well, I'll tell you this, Liuba. It didn't have anything to do with me, even if they did finger me for it, I'm still not copping to it. The landlord decided to rough up Tasya's little friend, who burst into his place with his face all smashed in, naked, his arm dangling, and his brains a little scrambled too. Well, our landlord first fucked him up the ass and then beat him to a bloody pulp. Threw the body down the stairs, and then fingered me for it. . . . First I crippled him, he said, and then . . . So that's the story, dear Liuba. You can see for yourself, it's nothing to brag about. I didn't try to defend myself because who was going to believe me? The landlord would have made sure I never talked anyway. No matter where I was, in prison or on the outside, he's got buddies everywhere, and they'd see to it for sure! Anyway, somehow I didn't feel like I needed to live very much anymore. It's an awful nasty thing, Liuba. But now I regret it. I don't want to give you up so much I feel like screaming. I don't guess I'm such a bad guy, maybe a little crazy, but you know I didn't have things so great. The world went nuts the minute I set foot in it. What was I supposed to do? But now I love you. You've got to believe that. You and I could have shacked up and had a couple of kids, right? My little black-eyed seagull . . ."

She learned, heard none of this. Her bound arms lay on top of the scratchy blanket, which was pulled up to her chin. Her dry lips twisted. He was shot at dawn, while she was still asleep, and to the snoring of the old woman on the next cot she dreamed of a black field, damp and sticky, with horned cows roaming over it. They were coming directly at her, and she was scared, like when she was a child, that they would gore her with their horns.

"Well, Liuba, you and I are moving to the zone! They're transferring us this week, and that's a fact. And with that Gypsy kisser of yours, lady, you'll always be okay. Believe an old woman. . . ."

She wasn't listening to the shaggy gray witch or even looking at her. She was writing hastily on a page torn from a pad:

"Dear Vasya! We're getting transferred soon. Look for me.
Liubov Rakhmetova."

Nightfire

Eleanor Taylor Bland

Every August for three years, Tori had come to Minneapolis and listened to Old Lat lie. Now, as Tori sat down, separated from Lat by a thick window of glass, she wondered how she would get the old woman to agree to make bail. Watching her—hands folded, eyes calm, shoulders stiffened by the resolve of the righteous, Tori knew Lat had told the truth. Tori did not doubt that the old woman had convinced police, public defender, and state prosecutor that she had indeed and with malice aforethought killed a man. Lat would do nothing in half measures. It was murder in the first degree or nothing. Lat's only concession was to be jailed in the infirmary, but only because it was less drafty.

"How are you, old woman?" Tori asked, speaking Vietnamese, a language native to Lat, a language Tori learned not because her mother had been an African-American soldier stationed in Vietnam, but because her father was Vietnamese.

"It is too cold in here for old bones," Lat said. "I must have a sweater."

"Let me take you home where you can sit on your own front porch in the warmth of the sun."

"It is not right that I am free and another is dead."

Lat was not brave. Lat feared prison, feared police, feared soldiers who marched in holiday parades. Lat would not sleep in the dark.

"You lie, old woman. You do not stay here because of a dead man. Tell me who or what it is that you fear."

Lat shook her head. "I am too old to be afraid."

Another lie. Were lies and truth intermingled in the story Lat told the police?

"I cannot talk with you in this place, Lat." It was as if the glass kept their emotions from flowing between them, and they communicated as much through feelings as through words.

Lat shrugged and seemed content to keep her secrets intact.

"They will let me take you home if you will agree to go with me."

"No."

The man had been stabbed as he went down the back steps.

"He was bad? He brought harm? You killed in self-defense? Then perhaps he is better off dead and his karma will not cause harm again."

The old woman just sat there.

"The man lived in the downstairs apartment all summer. Why did you wait until three days before I was to come? Whatever it was, I would have helped you."

Lat's chin quivered, then became resolute. What had happened from May until the man's death? Would Lat tell her if she was out of here, when there was no glass shield between them? Tori did not doubt that Lat had killed him. But why? There was just Lat in that apartment. For as long as Tori had known her, nobody else had time for a seventy-year-old woman from Saigon who had napalm scars on her face and hands and spoke English as seldom as possible.

"You will at least tell them to give me your keys. The birds will soon need food and water."

Lat nodded.

Tori checked with a guard on her way out. Lat had no money. The jail only accepted money orders. When that was taken care of, Tori drove the rental car to a small town west of Minneapolis. She turned off the air-conditioning and rolled down the windows, grateful for the wind that blew on her face, grateful for the warmth of the sun and worried because Lat could feel neither.

The motel she had checked into last night was close to Interstate 5 and right next to a restaurant. That was as much convenience and comfort as she required. Except for a bathtub. Tori was not a shower person. The plastic bathtub in the motel room was not intended for bathing. It was neither the right length nor was it deep enough nor was it in any way comfortable. Looking at it, and knowing the key to Lat's place was in her pocket, was almost enough to make Tori check out. Almost. Someone had died violently in the house where Lat lived. Tori preferred to confront that tomorrow, after time spent in meditation, after a good night's sleep, and before either, a bath in that plastic tub.

Lat lived on a quiet street where flowers grew in little plots in front of small houses that were built close together. When Tori let herself into the attic apartment, the stale, musty odor was unfamiliar. She raised the shades and opened the windows. Lat's birds lived in pairs in bamboo cages; a blue parakeet and one that was green and two canaries. It was still early and they began chirping and singing in the sunlight.

Tori looked at the back door that led to the steps where the man had been killed, then ignored it. Two cups and a teapot were arranged on the low table in the kitchen, in anticipation of her visit. There were two rolled-up mats instead of one. She cleaned the refrigerator, throwing out the contents—wilted bok choy, a shriveled orange, and a bowl of noodles.

The sleeping mat in the front room had been rolled up. Tori put her sleeping bag beside it. Lat's turquoise slippers, embroidered with gold and black thread, were aligned side by side near the closet door. Her meager supply of books, tattered but in Vietnamese, were stacked neatly on the floor beside a small radio, one of Lat's few concessions to the world beyond her door. The marigolds and dahlias in the vases placed on either side of a jade Buddha were wilted. The candles were new. Two *zafu* were placed before the altar: the green cushion for Lat, the yellow for Tori. As Tori tossed the flowers into the wastebasket, she made a note to replace them before Lat came home. Lat would come home. Soon.

A bare, low-watt bulb lit the rear hallway. Large dark pools of blood had congealed and dried on the five bottom stairs. Tori sat on the step just above them. Daily, they each recited the Mettasutta—the Sutta of Loving Kindness. Feelings of enmity were not Buddha's way. What had caused the old woman to kill? She glanced at her watch. It was almost eight-thirty and her meeting with Lat's public defender was at nine. She grabbed Lat's long black wool sweater on her way out.

Lat's attorney stared at Tori for a moment when she entered his office. That didn't surprise her. Like her mother, Tori was tall and slender with skin the color of copper. But, she looked like her father—broad face, high cheekbones, dark eyes, and straight black hair. The Asian-African combination occasioned second looks.

"Miss Roberts?"

"Yes. Tori Roberts."

He leaned across the legal-size manila folders stacked on his desk and extended his hand. "Just call me Bill." His grip was firm, his smile friendly.

"I'm Lat's friend."

"Crusty old bird, isn't she?" he said.

Tori had to smile. "Stubborn," she agreed.

"She admits that she did it but gets vague on the details. Her prints are on the weapon. If she pleads to a lesser charge I think I can get her off with a few years' probation. You know about the recognizance bond?"

"She refuses to leave."

Bill ran his fingers through thinning brown hair. "Talk to her. We won't have any problem with the plea if she agrees. I've tried to explain to her. When she doesn't want to listen she answers in Vietnamese, but I'm sure she understands me. I don't know if it's something in her culture, her religion. Talk to her, please. It's Wednesday already. We go to court next Monday."

"Do you know why she did it? What happened?"

He gestured toward the folders. "I'll do what I can. She's old—and those scars—a sympathetic defendant. They'll give us a lot of leeway—and leniency—if we plead."

Tori asked to read Lat's file. "I'm a college instructor—African and Asian studies—I'm not a lawyer, but . . ."

"Sure."

He sorted through the folders, some bulging with papers. The one he handed her was thin. The police and autopsy reports told her little. Jed Morgan was forty-one. He had two hundred dollars, a woman's ring, and a pack of gum in his pockets. He was stabbed once from behind. Lat would have known where to aim. The man, Jed Morgan, was five ten and weighed a hundred and eighty pounds. His size would not have made a difference. Although Lat was petite and didn't practice Tae Kwon Do any longer, she still did Tai Chi every day and had the strength and agility to stab him.

Tori didn't know much about criminal law, but she thought the attorney was right. A lesser charge was a generous concession, sympathetic defendant or not. When she went to see Lat that afternoon, the old woman still refused to accept bail. What did Lat fear?

Back at Lat's apartment, Tori checked the cupboards before going shopping, surprised to find them bare except for two boxes of birdseed. Lat's Social Security check required that she be frugal, but there was always something to eat. Even Lat's small supply of herbs and medicinals was depleted—no ginseng or red clover tea, no shark cartilage.

Tori checked the cabinet drawer where Lat kept what money she had in an envelope taped to the underside. Nothing. It was only the tenth of August. Disturbed, Tori got a bucket and knife to clean and scrape the blood from the stairs, and squeezed the last of the dish detergent into the water. There was a soggy rolled-up newspaper in the sink that had been lit at one end. She threw it away.

A man came to the second floor door while she was scrubbing. He was wiry and thin with a mustache that dangled down the sides of his mouth, and wore dirty torn jeans and a T-shirt. "Who are you?"

"Mrs. Nhu's friend from Connecticut." Tori remembered the elderly woman who'd rented the apartment last year. "Where's Mrs. Nordstrum?"

"Died. June."

Something about him troubled her. Perhaps it was just having another man living in the house with Lat instead of the senior citizens who used to.

"Did you know Mr. Morgan?"

"Didn't want to."

This tenant wasn't mentioned in the reports. Tori wanted to ask if he knew anything about what had happened, but decided to be less direct.

"Too bad," she said, gesturing toward the dried blood.

"Couldn't say," the man said, and closed his door.

When the stairs were clean, Tori went downstairs, the place where Morgan had lived. The door was padlocked.

Upstairs, she went to the closet to get the small mat that Lat kept her papers wrapped in. It wasn't there. Sitting cross-legged on the floor by the window, Tori let the sun warm her face and inhaled deeply. Three years ago, Tori wrote to a company that helped find missing persons. She received a list of everyone in Minneapolis with the surnames Nhu, her father's name, and Roberts, her mother's. None of the Robertses were related to or knew a Jayda Roberts. Lat was the only Nhu, and she'd kept Tori coming here for three summers, a taciturn but courteous Scheherazade weaving vignettes about Vietnam, about the war, about her family, into a meager tapestry intriguing enough to keep Tori wondering if perhaps, after seven years of searching, she had found someone who might have known or been related to her father.

No. She knew that Lat did not know anything about her father. That was not what brought her here. Lat knew the ways of her father's people with an intimacy that Tori could never acquire. Lat could create a heritage for her, a past, that she would not have without Lat. Child of separation and foster care that she was, Tori did not expect vague memories of living in Minneapolis and Seattle and Santa Fe to lead her back to her family.

Tori heard someone sweeping. Mrs. Lindquist tending to the sidewalk. She hurried downstairs.

"Tori, you have come! How is my friend Mrs. Nhu?"

"They would let her out, but she doesn't want to come home."

"She was always so . . . serene. I can't imagine what happened. Mr. Morgan was so friendly. Can I help you with anything, he would say. Or, I'm going to the store, do you need something? He was always such a nice man."

A nice dead man. Tori went to the library on Nicollet Mall. Both newspaper articles were brief. Neither made the first page. Morgan was a Vietnam vet. Was that important? The only person who could tell her wasn't talking. She walked to a restaurant that served Vietnamese food and ordered bun cha gio, egg rolls stuffed with a ground mixture of beans, beef, pork, and carrots served over rice noodles. A bowl of nuoc mam, fish sauce, was served on the side. If Lat weren't in jail, they would have prepared a meal like this together. Was Lat eating in jail? There was not much about American food that she cared for, except doughnuts. Lat loved gooey, glazed doughnuts. Tori thought of the empty money envelope. She always sent something the last week of the month, when she knew Lat's money was short. A small amount, which was all that Lat would accept. Lat was so frugal. There should have been something in the envelope now.

It was getting dark when Tori returned to Lat's apartment. She lowered the windows halfway and pulled down the shades. Sheer white panels hung at each window, but only because the landlord insisted. In the dim light of small lamps, Tori began a methodical search. Feeling along the walls of the closet, she found a seam in the wallpaper that was loose. Behind it, plaster had been scraped away to the wood frame and Lat's small mat with her papers was tucked in the hole.

Tori sorted through passport, rent receipts, and folded scraps of paper. Opening them, she deciphered the Vietnamese script, pleased when she found her name. There were two notes written in French, not uncommon for Vietnamese who lived in the cities, but Lat only spoke of the countryside. Tori translated "he who comes from hell," "nightfire," and "bad sleep." The dead man had brought back memories of the war. Lat was afraid of her dreams.

Tori called Lat's attorney in the morning and he arranged another visit.

"You were having nightmares again, old woman. That is not a good enough reason to stay here. Whatever Morgan did, his karma is gone. There is no harm from the dead. You need to come home now, while I am here and you don't have to dream alone."

To Tori's surprise, Lat agreed. On the way home they stopped for flowers and food and fresh-baked glazed doughnuts. Lat was embarrassed because there was nothing to eat and immediately busied herself talking to the birds and arranging the flowers, while Tori put produce and fish in the refrigerator and stocked the cabinet shelves. Together they prepared a meal and Lat ate as if she hadn't eaten in days.

That evening, they sat side by side on the *zafu*. With her hands resting on her midriff, left hand on right palm, thumbs joined, Tori concentrated on breathing. As thoughts came, she let go of them until there was only her breath.

Lat's dreams came toward morning. The old woman tossed on her mat and moaned, mumbling in what sounded like Vietnamese and French but wasn't distinct enough for Tori to interpret. Tori gathered Lat in her arms. She brushed sweat-soaked strands of hair from Lat's forehead, then touched the napalm scars on her neck and one side of her face.

"How much they have hurt you," she said in Vietnamese. "How much you have endured and forgiven."

Lat leaned against her, eyes squeezed shut, thick lashes wet with tears, and said nothing.

"Three years you have taught me like a mother teaches a child. Your own children died in the war. What did the war man do to you, little mother?"

Lat cried in harsh sobs, clutching Tori in a tight embrace.

"Tell me what happened," Tori said when the crying subsided.

Lat still did not speak.

"Why was the packet of papers hidden in the wall? Why is the money envelope empty? Did you give to him freely or did he take what was yours?"

There would be little difference to Lat between giving and stealing. She would not kill to keep or avenge the taking of something material.

Lat slumped against her, exhausted. There was no glass window between them now, but Tori still could not reach her.

"What was the war like for you, little mother? My mother was a soldier there."

"She was there before they brought the fire-death," Lat said. "She brought life. You are born of a Vietnamese man. When you come to me, it is almost as if my own daughter returns, even though you look much like your mother. You remind me of the time before the fire, when the fields were green, and the land a place of peace."

"And you soothe me in my searching," Tori said.

Lat sat back on her heels, rubbing her eyes with her fists.

"The war, it is a time of terrible pain. Whole villages are destroyed. I can lie to you no longer. The place where your mother worked, it is gone. If your father was there also, then I fear he is no more either. There are many called Nhu. I cannot name him."

"I know you don't know him," Tori said. "But when I come here, I learn who he was, and perhaps something more of who my mother was. That's enough. That's much more than I expected."

Lat went to the back door, stood with her ear pressed

against the wood, then opened it and turned off the light. She seemed to brace herself and held on to the banister. Tori followed as she made her way down the stairs. Lat stopped seven steps from the bottom and sat in the dark. Reaching down, she touched the scrubbed places. "Whore," she whispered softly. "Whore," she said again, using first the Vietnamese word and then the French. "Whore."

"He raped you," Tori whispered.

Lat sat very still, then she began rocking. A soft keening sound began deep in her throat. Slowly she raised her hands. Her moans became louder. Arms outstretched, she clenched her hands into fists. "No more," she said. "No more."

Tori sat on the steps and put her arms about Lat. "September seventeenth, 1980," she said. "I was eleven years old. A teenager in my foster home raped me."

Tears streamed down Lat's face. "June nineteenth, 1971." She began trembling. "I watch the Viet Cong rape and kill my daughters. Then again and again they rape me. I run, only to be caught by the fire. No more," she said. "Never again."

When Lat stopped shaking and slumped against her, Tori said, "What happened the night Morgan died?"

It seemed like a long time before Lat answered. "There is much that I cannot remember. He leaves. He is laughing. Then he is here on the stairs."

The next morning the man who lived in the apartment below came to the door. He shifted from one foot to the other, then looked at Lat. "Ma'am, Morgan was never in 'Nam. I'm a vet. I'm sorry for what happened to you." Anger flashed in his eyes and for a moment Tori felt afraid. Before she could speak, the man turned and went down the stairs.

Lat's nightmares continued. She refused to tell anyone else that she had been raped. She refused to speak of it at all, walking shamefaced from the room when Tori mentioned it. The day before Lat was to appear in court, Tori didn't know what to do. She wanted to respect Lat's right to keep silent, but the authorities should know what Morgan had done. Neither hugs, nor questions, nor Tori's fragmented memories of how she felt after it happened to her could bridge Lat's silence.

After supper they stepped through the front window and sat on the small porch overlooking the street. The sky was clear with stars scattered across the darkness. A breeze brought relief from the heat. While she was here last summer they had joined Mrs. Nordstrum on the porch below. Lat, seldom talkative and not given to laughter, had done both as Mrs. Nordstrum told them about her family and growing up on a farm.

"I'm sorry about your friend, Mrs. Nordstrum. How old was she?"

"Seventy-three."

"What happened?"

"They found her in her bed."

Lat's chin trembled.

"You miss her," Tori said. Lat always seemed so self-contained and had so little to do with her neighbors.

"The lady next door says Morgan was a nice man—friendly, helpful."

Lat stared at her hands. "Why is it that we think bad karma cannot also be all of those things?"

"Was he kind?"

"To others perhaps. I don't know."

"Did you let him help you?" As soon as she said it, Tori wished she had not. Lat's lips were compressed. She had lost their fragile thread of communication again.

"I paid him." Lat spoke in a whisper.

"For what?"

"To leave me alone."

"Why didn't you tell me?"

"You are far away. I am alone. I think I would have told you when you came."

"Did he take money from the others?"

"I do not know."

"Did he threaten you if you did not give him the money?"

Lat pressed her lips tight together. One hand gripped the other so tightly that the creases in the scar tissue stood out. She closed her eyes and breathed deeply until she relaxed.

"When the soldiers came, some were very kind. They shared their food. They did not kill civilians. Others, they are like him—filled with anger. They beat us and shoot us, even strangle. His hatred for me was very strong. Perhaps he liked the others."

Lat pulled the sweater tighter and turned her back to the wind.

"You are tired, old woman, but afraid of your dreams. Perhaps if you tell what happened the dreams will go away."

"Tell me again of your mother," Lat said.

"There isn't much that I recall. She hugged us a lot, and I remember eating cake for supper and wishing for mashed potatoes. Sometimes she spoke Vietnamese. It was like the sun coming out. She became happy and sang and danced. They told me she was crazy. Whenever she went into the hospital, there were foster homes. One day that's all there was, and I was alone and my mother and brothers and sisters were gone."

"You are like a daughter to me," Lat said, and moved closer. "Daughters. Mrs. Nordstrum had a daughter also. She wanted to have Mrs. Nordstrum's ring."

"The one that belonged to her great-grandmother?"

"Yes. But, when she comes, the ring is gone."

"Gone? She said she never took it off."

Tori remembered the contents of Morgan's pockets. "Morgan had a woman's ring when he died."

Lat took a deep, shuddering breath. "I think he killed her."

"Morgan?"

Without looking at her, Lat nodded.

"Then you must tell."

"No. I am an old woman. I am not from this country. To whom, besides you, does it matter?"

Tori thought not of Lat and Morgan, but of the boy who

raped her, of the times she was able to avoid his hands, and the times she was not.

"This was not the first time he raped you, was it?"

Lat moved away.

"He raped you before Mrs. Nordstrum died, didn't he? You think that if you told someone then . . . you blame yourself for her death, not his."

Lat looked straight ahead, blinking rapidly.

"Little mother, if you do not tell them this, your dreams will not leave you. And when they know, we will leave here."

"The newspaper," Lat whispered. "He lit the newspaper and held it to my face."

Lat came to Tori almost like a child, and curled up with her head in Tori's lap. Tori touched Lat's napalm burns again. It was almost daybreak when they went inside. When Lat slept, she did not dream.

NEVADA BARR earned her master's in acting at the University of California and worked in commercial theater for eight years in Minneapolis/St. Paul. At thirty-six, she changed careers and became a park ranger, currently working on the Natchez Trace in Mississippi. Barr has written five novels, with the second, *Track of the Cat,* winning both the Agatha and Anthony awards. Her latest book, *Firestorm,* featuring her park ranger sleuth Anna Pigeon, was published in the spring of 1996.

Beneath the Lilacs

Nevada Barr

Lilac trees, two in white, two in plum, and two in the palest lavender, had grown up as Gwen had grown. Now she was in her forties and the lilacs were higher than the eaves of the house. One of the plum-colored trees had died. Slash, piled shoulder-high, lay on the concrete between the garden and the alley. It had taken Gwen all morning to cut it down and haul the withered limbs out to where the garbage men might deign to take them.

Digging out the last of the grasping roots, Gwen uncovered the bone. A museum curator, she knew a finger bone when she saw one. Letting her rump fall back on the freshly dug earth, she contemplated her find.

The day was still and warm, a hint of the hard winter past making the fragile spring almost unbearably precious. Growing up in Minnesota, there'd been many days like this one. Payoff days, her mother called them. Days when you were paid in full for chilblains, dead batteries, frozen nose hairs.

Here in the arbor behind her mother's house in Minneapolis, two blocks from Lake Nokomis, Gwen had spent those days curled down in the fertile earth arranging tiny plastic soldiers on the rooted mounds beneath the lilacs and fighting glorious bloodless battles till the last Horatio fell heroically defending the last bridge.

When had a real corpse come to join those of her phantom armies?

An Indian, perhaps, buried before whites settled the area. A homesteader, laid to rest in a family plot long since forgotten, sold and resold till at length a city had crept over sod and sodbuster alike.

Gwen looked up from the earth between her feet. Beyond the shade-dappling the sun shone with an unwavering intensity that by July would seem harsh. So close in winter's shadow it was a promise of renewal and, so, eternal life. Every leaf, each blade of grass, was wreathed in light. Spring's coronation.

The glare was not so kind to man-made structures. Mullions in the many-paned bay window were peeling, white paint curling off in strips like sunburned flesh; a crack ran up the foundation where the water faucet poked through the cement; the little statue of the Virgin Mary listed drunkenly, attesting to a neglect Gwen's mother would once have been incapable of.

At some point during the twenty-six years Gwen had been gone, Madolyn Clear had gotten old. A pang of guilt and one sharper for opportunities lost, cut through Gwen's chest. She pulled up her knees and hugged them close.

She had always thought of her mother as a rock, remaining unchanged as the oceans of life broke against her. For a little girl that brought with it a strong sense of security and not a little loneliness.

A memory from childhood, a snapshot without cause or effect, rose in Gwen's mind. She was very young, not more than two or three. It must have been around the time her father died, though there were no cerebral Polaroids of that. She was dressed in a T-shirt and underpants, her short hair molded into sleepy spikes. Mud mottled the carpet under her bare feet. One plump hand, fingers spread like a starfish, was pressed against her mother's bedroom door at the top of the stairs. Inside she knew her mother was crying.

Idly, Gwen wondered if she'd pushed open that door or stayed lonely and lost in the hallway. Probably the latter.

There were no memories of seeing her mother cry. Not ever. Everybody cried. Madolyn must have felt safe only in private.

Privacy, her mother's one indulgence, was all but lost to her now. Since the stroke the sitting room had become her bedroom. The stairs effectively banning her from the rest of her house, she spent her days in the bay window, propped up in the hideous comfort of a hospital bed looking out on her garden.

Light glittered off the windowpanes. Gwen couldn't see inside, but she waved anyway.

Her mother was no longer a poor woman. Money could buy cooks and nurses and therapists. Gwen had been asked to tend the garden. So much needed to be done with love and not just with a spade. Turned firmly out-of-doors, she nurtured the flowers with the tenderness she was forbidden to lavish on her mother.

And a skeleton lay beneath the lilacs.

Gwen wondered if she should tell her. "No shocks," Dr. Korver had warned, but Gwen doubted a corpse would distress Madolyn. Pragmatism had soaked so deep into her mother's bones it was sometimes hard to reconcile the woman as she was with the photos of her as a young bride, dripping with white after the wedding mass, decked in the ruffles and lace of her going-away suit.

And, too, there was nothing awful about a skeleton so long and so quietly dead. Her mother might even be intrigued, delighted. Who wouldn't be delighted to find a skeleton in the arbor? A story to dine out on for years to come. Still Gwen felt an odd reluctance to tell her. Perhaps it was simply a reluctance to move. The heady scent of the lilacs wrapped around her in a gauzy cloak. Like Dorothy in her poppy field, Gwen was paralyzed with the perfume.

Wriggling her feet deeper in the warm soil, she watched the dirt cascade over the rolled cuffs of her trousers. The house had its ghosts, its lonely hallways, as all houses did, but not the arbor. Bootsies and Tippies and Pinky-Winkies lay interred in various corners and there were remembrances of skinned knees and broken arms and once she'd dislocated Ricky Harper's little finger, but none of that marred the garden's perfect peace. Despite Minnesota's snows Gwen remembered it always sunny, always in bloom. As one remembers childhood.

A second snapshot materialized. This one was captioned, a single line of dialogue in a familiar yet unnameable voice. Gwen was at the piano pretending to play. Her feet didn't reach the floor; a dress in rustling pink frothed around her little bottom. On the high back of the old upright sat a yellow cat. His tail, fat as a striped sausage, switched down near the pages of music. The window to the garden was open and there was a faint pleasant sound of distant laughter.

The voice wasn't her mother's—a neighbor lady probably. "At least now you can keep the house full of flowers," she'd said. "Small blessings."

Gwen's house in Pasadena, California, was always filled with flowers. Her first husband had been allergic to them and to her cats. After the divorce her mother said it wasn't wise to completely trust a man who was allergic to cats. It meant they were part rat.

". . . now you can keep the house full of flowers. Small blessings." Who had been allergic? Not Gwen, not her mother. Not you, Gwen thought, looking at the spectral finger beckoning amid the roots. At least not for a long time.

Gwen seldom thought of the past. She and her mother didn't discuss it by mutual if unspoken agreement. Yet here under the lilacs the past seemed to rise up from the earth as insistent and cloying as the scent of the blooms overhead.

Coming home, Gwen thought, and her mother's stroke proving a mortality neither wished to admit. Gwen's age. She'd found herself getting in touch with old college friends, thinking fondly of reunions. The mad scrabble to grow up, to do and be and speak, was over and there was a desire to recapture the things undervalued in the rush to adulthood.

Surely it had been more than a decade since she'd thought of Ricky Harper, though they'd dated in high school and he'd gotten even with her for dislocating his little finger by breaking her heart. Disasters of about equal magnitude.

"Lit out," Ricky had said. Gwen remembered the words clearly. He'd said it of her father, hence the damaged pinky.

She turned her thoughts back to the bony pinky protruding from the rich black dirt.

The strange and dreaming lethargy lifted and she rubbed her face like a woman coming out of a long sleep. A curator's instincts reasserted themselves and she pulled off her mother's gardening gloves—heavy white cotton decorated with apple-green sprigs. The kind old ladies wear. The hands that were exposed were starting to wrinkle, age spots beginning to form from so many years working out-of-doors and Gwen smiled at her snobbery.

Kneeling over the bone, she carefully swept away the earth. Without access to a lab, she couldn't tell how old the find was, but the knuckle was still intact. Bit by bit she removed the soil until wrist, thumb, and index finger were exposed. Probably it was nothing, still she felt excitement building. Anthropologists, even those who've long since left fieldwork, dream of finding a Lucy the way gamblers dream of the big jackpot.

Several more minutes work raised Gwen's hopes even further. On the third finger of the right hand—for it was a right hand—something glowed dull and coppery. Gwen allowed herself a snort of derision as images of Aztec gold and Ojibwa copper danced incongruously through her head.

With great care, not as if the finger could still feel, but as if prying eyes might see and suddenly cry "Thief!" Gwen worked the ring free and polished the face of it clean with the tail of her shirt.

1946. University of Minnesota.

Modern dead; not history but murder.

Panic clouded Gwen's mind. Nausea threatened to rob her of her senses, and though she was sitting, she felt as if she would fall and clung to the sturdy trunk of a lilac.

Numbers, clear and neat as arithmetic problems, clicked through her thoughts. In 1945 her parents were married and bought the house. One year later her father graduated from the University of Minnesota and went to work for the city.

Without looking at it again, Gwen slipped the ring in her pocket and gently pushed dirt back over the bones.

Cancer, her mother had said.

"Lit out."

Never once had Gwen visited her father's grave. Buried in Sioux Falls, her mother told her, in his hometown. Gwen had never been there. Madolyn was estranged from her husband's family. Religious differences was how she explained it and, assuming they were Protestant, Gwen hadn't asked again.

Cards addressed to Gwen came at Christmas and on birthdays till she was out of school. Grandparents she'd never seen and did not mourn died while she worked on her doctorate at Stanford.

Gwen eased up from the ground and started to brush the dirt from her trousers, but the effort proved too great. The forty feet to the back door stretched an impossible distance and she found herself shuffling along the walk, the noise of her dragging steps clogging her ears.

As she passed through the front hall her mother called to her, but she pretended not to hear. Mud from the newly opened grave tracked the sage-green carpet of the upstairs hall and the snapshot came again: the little bare feet, the starfish hand, the mud, the weeping behind the closed door. Someone had tracked freshly dug earth upstairs that day as well.

Gwen's head swam and she stumbled the last few steps to collapse on Madolyn's bed; hers now.

She closed her eyes and would have closed her mind had she been able. Images chased each other around inside her skull like maddened ferrets. She imagined she could feel the weight of the ring in her pocket pressing on her thigh. Soon she would take it out, examine it again, but there was no hurry. An old photograph of her father had served as the springboard for the ten thousand daydreams of a lonely child. The ring was his. She'd memorized it along with the grain, the light, and the shadows of the photo.

Anger plucked her from the bed like a giant hand and in anger, she snatched up the phone. There was no statute of limitations on murder.

Before the second ring she laid the receiver back in its cradle and sat down on the edge of the bed. Her knees were shaking too badly to support her.

Lots of men must have graduated from the University of Minnesota in 1946. They would all wear the same ring. The corpse could have been a classmate of her father's, a family friend.

Buried in the backyard.

A lover then; her mother took a lover, her father killed him then "lit out." Or died of cancer as her mother said, taking his secret with him. Madolyn may not even have known of the murder. It could have taken place when she was out of town for some reason.

Gwen felt herself calming down, her breathing leaving off the ragged pattern of tears. Hysteria was being replaced by a lifetime's habit of rational thought. Explanations could be found. Truth was seldom more awful than one's febrile imaginings. She smiled, if weakly, at the lurid picture she'd conjured of her mother wild-eyed and blood-spattered wielding Norman Bates's knife.

For several minutes Gwen sat, her feet flat on the floor, her back bowed, staring at the carpet and thinking nothing at all. Too many electrical impulses at once had short-circuited her brain. From below the sweet strains of Doris Day's "Sentimental Journey" filtered up through the heater vents.

Of course Gwen would have to pursue it. Letting sleeping skeletons lie was out of the question. Her mother was too fragile to confront, the police too abrasive. Not that the Minneapolis police weren't as polite as midwestern myth would paint them, but there would be digging literally and figuratively. Strangers couldn't be expected to take the time and energy that delicacy required.

Again she picked up the phone. Grandmother and Grand-dad were dead, but Gwen assumed Sioux Falls still existed. Seven phone calls to the seven cemeteries and mausoleums didn't turn up any Gerald Clear interred in 1950.

Nausea returned. Gwen put her head between her knees. Her hands fell to the carpet like leaves and she found herself staring at the dirt-encrusted nails with morbid fascination as if they were the hands that buried the corpse, not the ones to unearth it after so many years.

Pushing herself to her feet, she made her way toward the bathroom to wash. On the wall above the light switch was a small wooden cross adorned with a long-suffering silver Jesus. Clawing it down, she hurled it against the far wall. From downstairs her mother called: "Honey, are you okay?"

"I'm okay, Ma," Gwen shouted.

"Come downstairs when you're done."

Gwen turned on both taps to drown out her mother's voice and watched the dirt from her hands sully the white porcelain of the old-fashioned sink.

There was an uncle in Des Moines, she remembered. Once or twice as a child she'd seen him, but relations between him and her mother were strained. Gwen didn't even know if he was still living. If so, he would be close to eighty.

Her old bedroom had been converted to a study some years after she left home. Oblivious to the mess she made, or on some level relishing the release of destruction, Gwen turned it upside down searching for his address. She was almost disappointed when she found it fairly quickly under C in her mother's well-ordered Rolodex.

Lest thought rob her of courage, Gwen punched in his number not knowing what she would say if he should answer. When an old voice creaked "Hello," she was momentarily stunned. At the third repetition, she found her tongue. "Uncle Daniel?"

"This is Daniel Clear," the man said with unconcealed annoyance.

Gwen introduced herself in greater detail and the annoyance evaporated. She told him her mother had had a stroke.

Daniel took that as the reason for the call and Gwen didn't disabuse him of the notion. Had it not been for the skeleton, she wondered if she would have thought to inform him. Probably not.

"Tell me about Dad," she said when the preliminaries were behind them.

Uncle Daniel didn't find it an odd question and Gwen realized she'd been wanting to ask it for a long time. The romantic fog of perfect love her mother had generated around her father's memory had ceased to be enough after Gwen's own marriage failed in mutual acrimony.

The picture Daniel painted of his little brother had grit, sand, and spice, and Gwen knew when this was over she would seek the old man out.

Daniel remembered an altar boy, quick with his fists, hot-tempered, a favorite with the girls and the apple of his mother's eye.

His memories dwindled and he began wandering to second cousins and others Gwen neither knew nor cared about. She asked him why he—all of her father's family—had become estranged from her mother.

"It may seem like a little thing to a modern young lady like yourself," he said. "But to us it wasn't. It nearly killed your grandma. Your mother just went and buried him up in the cities. Never invited any of us to the funeral. Didn't even tell us till it was all over."

Gwen sat in the wreck of the study and grasped at straws of justification. Hot-tempered, quick with his fists, a favorite with the girls. People didn't kill without reason. Had her father cheated, been killed in a moment of passion? Had he beaten her mother? Was he killed to protect Gwen? Gwen had no memories of abuse, but people sometimes didn't.

The thought physically sickened her. A glimpse of herself, face half in shadow, hankie clutched to her eyes, on *Oprah*, leavened the horror with absurdity. Vaguely she remembered repressed memories, like chicken pox, were more or less age-specific. Mid-thirties rang a bell. She comforted herself with that.

And the lies of True Love and her sainted father? Fairy tales to delight a little girl? Or to rewrite history for a shattered and disappointed woman? The crosses, the statues, mass and communion and confession: the ultimate hypocrisy or lifelong penance?

The phone was still cradled on Gwen's knees. With one hand she flipped through the Rolodex, then punched in the number for Dr. Korver's office. In his seventies, he still ran a practice. Gwen pleaded emergency and because Annie, the receptionist, had known her since she was three years old, she was given an appointment.

Compelled by some outdated formality that overtook her when she returned to childhood haunts, Gwen divested herself of jeans and slipped on a fitted rayon dress and flats. The short, graying hair got a few licks with a brush but, as always, it did what it did. Without saying good-bye to her mother, she lifted the car keys from the hook under the kitchen cupboard and slunk out the back door.

Dr. Korver looked much as he had as long as Gwen could remember: bow tie, suspenders, a clean-shaven and age-defying baby face. His hair was white but was still so thick and lush, one could almost believe he had it bleached to reassure his older patients.

Perched fully dressed on the examination table, Gwen knew neither of them was completely at ease.

"Annie said an emergency," Dr. Korver said for starters.

"I need to talk to you." Dr. Korver didn't do anything so crass as to glance at his watch, but he fidgeted and Gwen could read the impatience just as clearly. From the look on his face, talk wouldn't take precedence over so much has an ingrown toenail. "I need to know how my father died," Gwen said abruptly.

"Cancer. Surely your mother told you?"

Gwen nodded. "Did you see him?" she pressed.

"If I remember rightly, he died in Sioux City or somewhere, visiting I think. You should be asking your mother these questions, Gwen."

"You never saw him dead?"

He shrugged his shoulders. This time he did look at his watch.

"So you don't know that he died?" Gwen sounded accusing and he reacted in kind, his avuncular manner disappearing behind a mask of injured pride.

"He had an inoperable brain tumor. Unless he got hit by a truck first, he died of it," he said bluntly, and stood to indicate the interview was over.

Gwen caught hold of his arm. "Please," she said. "Could I see my medical records and Mom's?"

Dr. Korver looked at her for a moment. His visage softened. He'd come to recognize pain in all its guises. "What's wrong, Gwen?"

She said nothing and the kindness was pushed aside by irritation. "You can see your medical records, though I don't know what good it'll do you. I can't let you see your mother's without her permission." He left and Gwen felt as cold and exposed as if she wore only a backless paper gown.

After pulling her file, Annie left Gwen alone in the records room. Quickly, she flipped through the pages. Though she was healthy, so many years of care made it thick. Before 1952 there were seven entries: three general check-ups, an ear infection, fever, a scald on her left forearm, and a hairline fracture of her left foot.

Taking advantage of Annie's trusting nature, Gwen moved to the filing cabinet and walked her fingers through the C's. Her father's file was gone, taken to storage years before no doubt, but her mother's was there. Still standing Gwen scanned the entries from 1945 to 1952: influenza, broken rib, tonsillitis, sprained wrist. The box marked INSURANCE/ HEALTH/LIFE had the word "None" scribbled in it twice. No wonder there was such a paucity of doctor's visits during those years.

Footsteps sounded on the linoleum outside the door and Gwen hastily fumbled the file back into place. Her heart pounded as if peeking at her mother's medical history were a capital crime. No one entered the records room and Gwen took a moment to pull herself together before she ventured out and said her good-byes to Annie.

She couldn't bring herself to go back to her mother's, not yet. She chewed mechanically through a late lunch at Kapoochi's on Nicollet and Eighth. The food was more an excuse for the glass of Chardonnay than an end in itself.

When the dishes had been cleared and only another solitary glass or dessert could excuse lingering, Gwen returned to the festive crush on Nicollet.

Because the sun shone, Minnesotans made it a holiday. Flower vendors lined the street. People walked and waited for buses and shopped and chattered in groups. Gwen joined the loiterers gathering sun on the wide brick sills of the Conservatory.

Fortified with wine, she could again think of the skeleton, her mother, and murder. Broken rib, sprained wrist, scalded arm, fractured foot; a history of abuse or just the vagaries of living? Gwen had nothing to compare it to, no government statistics on how often the average mother and daughter damaged themselves in the pursuit of daily life.

Why kill a dying man? Surely it was easier and safer to let nature take its course. Self-defense? Possibly. A favorite with the girls: killed in a moment of jealous rage or because he was going to leave? Also possible.

Madolyn Clear never remarried and Gwen had believed it was because she never stopped loving her dead husband. Could it be that memories of a bad marriage made her shy of the institution? And the lilacs? "Now you can keep the house full of flowers. Small blessings." Revenge? Planting a man allergic to lilacs under six trees of blooms? Each thought was more wretched than the last, sick-making, and Gwen shook herself free of them as a dog rids its fur of raindrops.

Too many years had passed since the death of a father she had never known for the lash of his murder to cut too deep. Betrayal of truth was the injury; loss of the idea that love existed, that she was born from it and to it. Death of the possibility, of the dream.

Gwen relinquished her place in the sun to a polite young woman with tricolor hair and two nose rings. There was one more stop to be made and then she must go home.

St. Bartholomew's was in South Minneapolis in what was considered a bad section of town, though to Gwen's perception—altered by years in other cities—the homes still retained their dignity and the people on the streets didn't appear to have lost their hope. The church was staid and conservative, an edifice of brick and mortar that blended well with the apartment houses that had sprung up around it in the 1940s. The front lawn was badly in need of attention and the steps had deteriorated, not from the constant tread of feet but from disuse and neglect.

The front doors were locked. Gwen picked her way through the struggling rhododendrons to the rectory behind the church. Decay had taken the small brick dwelling as well. Windows were draped as if against terrible cold, and leaves from the previous autumn lay in dusty piles in the corners of the porch.

After two tries with the doorbell and a rapping that left her knuckles burning, Gwen was turning to go. Soft shuffling from within stopped her. Unconsciously donning a pious look, she waited in feigned patience.

A man so old he looked elemental—cracked stone and sere earth—opened the door and blinked up at her from eyes made milky with cataracts. Beyond the changed flesh Gwen could barely recognize Father Davis, the priest to whom she'd poured out childish confessions. Cataracts and time had clearly robbed him of all recollection of her.

"I'm Gwendolyn Clear," she told him. "My mother, Madolyn Clear, and I used to attend mass at St. Bartholomew's."

For long moments he stared at her. Minute workings of the muscles around his mouth attested to some kind of mental process. "Gwennie," he said at last, and she was impressed. "Do come in. You're just in time for something I'm sure. Tea? Sherry? Coffee? It's always a good time for company."

Inside, the rectory was dark and stifling. Father Davis wore wool trousers and a pullover sweatshirt and tapped at the thermostat as he passed, his old bones needing heat from without.

Ensconced in a worn chair by a blessedly dead fire, Gwen accepted a glass of orange juice as the quickest way to absolve both of them of the niceties and waited while Father Davis settled himself. Scooping a tiger cat from the seat of the chair opposite her, he lowered himself carefully into its depths then arranged the cat across his knees like a rug.

"I no longer say mass," he said. "But I still occasionally hear confessions of the very wicked." He smiled to let her know he was teasing.

Because he was a priest and because he was Father Davis, Gwen told him everything. She finished and the silence between them was long and comfortable. The old man stroked the tiger cat, the muscles around his mouth twitching as he thought.

"As a priest I'm not allowed to speak of much the good Lord has seen fit to let me remember," he said at last. "But you mustn't let these shadows from the past blot out your faith in the things that are good: love and forgiveness, sacrifice, redemption. I have known you all of your life and known your mother most of hers. All I can tell you that might be of help is that to my knowledge your mother loved your father dearly. Indeed, loved him more than she feared God."

Blinking again in the clear sunlight, Gwen fished sunglasses from her bag as she skirted the shrubbery in favor of paving stones on the way back to where she'd parked the car.

Time had poured its obscuring dust over events but still she held some facts—or educated guesses that she would use in lieu of facts. Gerald Clear had a temper. Gerald Clear was beloved of the ladies. Gerald Clear had inoperable brain cancer. Her mother had killed him or knew the person who had, and hid the crime by burying him in the backyard. Madolyn loved him "more than she feared God." Medical records catalogued four possible abuse injuries in seven years.

Gwen drove back to Lake Nokomis so slowly that cars honked at her more than once, but she scarcely acknowledged them. At a stop sign less than a block from the house her car came to rest. Traffic was light and no other vehicle appeared to remind her of the business of driving. As the car idled in neutral, the doctor's reports filtered back through her mind.

No insurance. Not life. Not health.

In 1952 the Clears were poor—poor as church mice, her mother was fond of saying. There would be no money for the medical bills from an extended illness. Dad was going to kick the bucket anyway so what the hey?

Gwen shook her head as if disagreeing with some unseen adversary. Madolyn had loved her husband more than she feared God. And the pieces fell in place. Sudden tears choked Gwen and she sat at the intersection and cried till the pressure of a Volvo in the rearview mirror forced her to move.

Madolyn Clear was propped up in her hospital bed, sun from the bay window making a patchwork of light and shadow across her legs. While Gwen had been out she'd been given a shampoo and short snow-white hair fell in natural curls. A pair of reading glasses hung around her neck on a cord of psychedelic colors. One hand, slightly gnarled with arthritis, rested on the book she'd been reading.

When Gwen came in she smiled. The teeth were yellowed and crooked but they were all her own and Gwen thought her smile beautiful. It faded to a look of concern as Gwen crossed the hardwood floor close enough that her mother could read the strange lines her face had fallen into after the storm of tears.

Gwen sat in the window seat, the light at her back, and took the ring from the pocket of her dress. Laying it on the coverlet between her mother's hands, she said: "I know all about Daddy."

Madolyn stroked the dull gold with one finger as if it were a tiny living creature. "And do you hate me?" she asked without looking up. Beneath white lashes tears sparkled in the sun. Gwen pretended not to notice. Her mother had seen fit to hide them for over forty years. It would be ungracious to discover them now.

"No, Momma." Gwen wanted to take her hand but lacked the courage. Instead she laid hers on the coverlet touching her mother's as if by accident. "I admire you. I've always admired you."

They sat for a time without speaking. A house finch came and hopped along the windowsill beyond the glass and Madolyn's old Siamese cat crept close to fantasize.

"Why lilacs?" Gwen asked. "Dad was allergic, wasn't he?"

Madolyn looked startled then laughed. "That's right, he was. It's been a very long time. Gerry said they were his favorite flower because they gave me so much joy. He knew he couldn't be buried in consecrated ground so he asked to have lilacs planted over his grave. So I'd visit often, he said."

"Was he afraid of the pain? Of losing his faculties?" Gwen asked.

"Your father wasn't afraid of anything," Madolyn said. Then: "Of course he was. Who wouldn't be? But he would have faced it as he faced everything. He knew he was dying and that the medical costs would eat up our savings, our car, even our home. You and I would be left alone with nothing. He loved us very much." Tears trickled from beneath the papery lids and found channels in the wrinkled cheeks. This time Gwen did take her mother's hand and Madolyn held tight, her grip warm and dry.

"But he didn't kill himself," Gwen said.

"It would have meant his soul," Madolyn said. "And there never was a finer."

FRANCES FYFIELD is the best-selling author of seven crime novels. *A Question of Guilt, Trial by Fire, Deep Sleep, Shadow Play,* and *A Clear Conscience* feature Crown Prosecutor Helen West and the detective Geoffrey Bailey. As Frances Hegarty, she has also written two psychological thrillers, and a new novel, *Let's Dance,* was published in the UK by Viking in October 1995. Frances Fyfield is a practicing solicitor in London, currently working with the Crown Prosecution Service in a specialized capacity.

Nothing to Lose

Frances Fyfield

"Y ou like my country?"

"Oh yes. I like. I like very much."

She liked the way he regarded her with a smile so full of sweetness it was better than a pineapple, fresh plucked and sold for cents, sliced for her as if she were royalty at a banquet. She liked the way no one on this West African beach looked askance at her figure, but smiled into her eyes. She liked: she liked so very much that she had almost lost her command of English. Much, very. Words of more than two syllables had slipped to the edge.

Wherever Audrey looked, she was blinded by what she saw. The sand was canary yellow, the sky was blue; the colors of cotton iridescent. All skin was as brown and various as the polished wood of her own antique furniture. Walnut, mahogany, oak, stained pine, nothing quite black. There was no such thing as really black wood. Black was not a color, it was an illusion.

"It's good? Is it good?"

"What?" For a moment, she was confused. What was good?

"The pineapple?"

"Oh, very."

"See you later."

"Not much later?"

"Of course." She watched his progress away from her and

knew she would wait. For him to come back and look at her with the great kind eyes of a man who could not harm a fly.

Abdoulie had been squatting beside her heavy wooden sunbed, his pose laconic and restive, full of the spring of a tiger. He could look at ease with his elbows on his knees, his buttocks almost touching the sand, his long arms hanging loose until he spoke, and then his arms and fingers became the whirling tools of gestures. His was hesitant English, better by far than her own command of any foreign language, but still the level of fluency which would scarcely gain him admission to many an old-fashioned English secondary school. Mrs. Audrey Barett was aware of that. At home, she commuted from her village to teach difficult children in a school where half the problem was language. Punjabi versus English, own goal. In rapid reverse of her own childish belief that anyone who spoke a foreign language must be sublimely clever in order to get their tongues round all those sounds, she had advanced beyond the stage of imagining that either soul or intelligence could be gauged by what words came out of the mouth. Goodness had nothing to do with linguistics. She was also beyond imagining that her own admirable culture (and she did admire it, without apology) was better equipped than any other to rule the world. Audrey was an intelligent, middle-aged lady who read the quality newspapers and the better kind of novel which made one think. She was liberal and conservative in the same breath, her life without blame, and yet she still felt a sense of failure. No one had ever shouted admiration at Audrey Barett.

She chewed her nails, something she had always done. These days, she exerted control over her shyness.

"How many childrens, many, many, I think, Mrs. B., I think?" the hotel manager had asked, questioning her respectability and looking for a common denominator. People would always talk about their children, and in his family, any woman over fifty was obliged to be a grandmother by now.

"Thousands," she had said, grandly, startling him a little

until she explained. She failed to add, two, of my own. Anxious girls, long gone, phoning every week from London, which is very different from the North of England, you know. Long gone, along with their father. Such is history. She could not quite imagine how she had come by them, except for the fact that hormones do not dictate the best choice of partner. Her own husband had been a little vicious; something she liked to forget and translated into a fondness for men who would never consider violence, but splendid results sometimes arrive as the result of bad mistakes, her best friend Molly was fond of saying, and the mistakes can last for years, as hers had done.

"Abdoulie is a good boy," the manager said meaningfully. "He will look after you." Then he bent toward her, speaking confidentially. "He has had a sad life, that boy."

The description of "boy" was inaccurate, Audrey thought when she saw him. Abdoulie was not a boy; he was a man of almost forty and he needed looking after. There were fabulous young men on this Gambian beach; Audrey watched them, early on the first morning, with the same disinterested fascination she might have given to a series of moving pictures. They worked their lithe bodies with exercise, hoping for a big break into the football team; fitness could catapult a boy into employment, even stardom. Abdoulie was not one of these. He was immensely tall, with dark coffee skin, a broad torso, and a slight squint in one eye. His wife and child had long since died in a fire, he said, and he was not eligible enough or prosperous enough to begin again. He did what he could, he said. He might have been, in his own estimation, too old for hope and he was not a glamorous young lion. Audrey would not have looked at him twice if he had been a youth. As he was, in the high street of the prosperous village where Audrey lived, under her gray skies and mirrored in the green eyes of the inhabitants, he would surely look like a god.

In all her careful and independent life, Audrey had avoided the trauma of rash deeds just as she normally avoided sunshine. Nor had she ever gone out looking for a man. Europe had been the setting for travels where she made friends with other woman travelers. Africa was a brutal assault on the senses similar to a series of blows from a spiked mallet. The poverty moved her to despair; the corruption angered her beyond belief, the smells made her delirious, the colors invaded her eyes, and the sun made her beautiful.

That was June: this was November. Abdoulie lay on her spare bed in the tiny spare bedroom of her small cottage and he had shrunk to fit. He had never been more prosperous, and he looked like a dying man. The squint in his eye and the crookedness of his teeth were more noticeable than they ever had been against the golden sand or the green vegetation which had crept down to the shore. He was as pale as he could be against her own white pillow. She perspired inside her blouse; the sweat on his skin shone like water.

She loved him to death and she wanted, more than anything else in the world, to kill him.

They had been married ten weeks.

They did not seem to notice a woman's age, these Africans with the endless smiles for the tourists. Abdoulie had trembled when she touched him; he seemed drawn to her by invisible strings. He did not look at girls; he looked at her as if she were beauty incarnate. They had managed a whole repertoire of jokes with the aid of a small store of words and the universal language of gesture. The understanding between them seemed infinite. Undeniably genuine, provided it had seen its limitation, which was the scenery in which it grew. Neither of them saw this flowering love as being bounded by the beach. It was too fine a plant to depend on habitat. The hotel manager smiled benignly and touched his nose.

"Love is in the air, I think, Mrs. Barett. Or is it spring?"

* * *

After all, she reasoned then, while wondering gleefully about how Molly would react, what did she have to lose? It did not seem to her any great act of courage to fall in love and propose marriage; in fact it would have taken far more courage to walk away and know that she would spend the rest of her life wondering how it might have been. Sitting in her cottage with the roses round the door after the next round of educational cuts she had come away to escape, prematurely retired, financially okay and emotionally barren. No pupils, no one to look after, no sense of purpose. The opposite beckoned when Abdoulie told her he loved her and that love always found a way. Audrey Barett would educate this funny, sorrowful man who did not know the meaning of malice; she lulled herself to sleep with visions of benign influence while the air-conditioned hotel room chilled her overheated body to ice; she dreamed of her own triumph.

Now she was not only contemplating murder most foul; she was set on it. The light from the lamp outside cast strange shadows on the ceiling as the branches of the tree waved at her in breezy mockery. Fool, fool, fool; sighing and scolding at her, telling there is no fool like a liberated one. Audrey had aged a decade in as many weeks. They had never quite known one another in the biblical sense, as her daughter primly defined it. That had been one of those stored-up treats, which remained stored until after the use-by date until forgotten and no longer relevant. The knowledge gave her an inkling of what it had been like to be proud. There was something about herself she had not relinquished, even if the failure to do so had been because he had not wanted it; both of them had been paralyzed. There was still a little piece of England, perfectly preserved.

"I'm going to get married, Molly."

"You never!"

"Well, he's a widower and I met him on holiday and we get along just fine, why not?" There had not been a single tremor of doubt as long as she had been acting alone, organizing things, booking his flight as soon as she got home, paying for it without a murmur, looking into the whole vexed business of entry, being appalled and outraged, all that. Easier by far than telling Molly or her daughters, which certainly took the air out of her lungs.

"He's black, of course," she added as a throwaway line, not courageous enough to add that black was an illusion of a color and it was finding him asleep outside her bedroom door which had been the final decision time. Abdoulie slept like an angel, but the whole cut of his body adjusted to a concrete floor. A man accustomed to such, without the option of a bed, was a man who deserved better. You could not do damage to a man who had nothing. You could only transform him.

Silence on the end of a phone line was unnerving.

"Congratulate me, darling?"

More silence.

"Say something then."

"I can't. You must be mad."

There was nothing like resistance to get her going and make her prove she was right. Audrey had always moved sideways in the face of conflict, found another way. She did not fight, she merged into shadows until the fuss was over and then came out triumphantly and went on as before. Besides, it was not so much her daughters and Molly she wanted to impress; it was neighbors who had seen her as dull, sensible, sexless Mrs. Barett, manless and dutiful this twenty years in an area where to be without a mate was to be without sin or life. Boring and sad, in other words. Audrey did not want that kind of respect, and there she would be, in the eyes of the newsagents, the butcher and the baker, in the eyes of her contemporaries at school, taking life in both hands and embarking on adventure. With a man so much taller, so much kinder, than any of theirs.

How was she going to kill him? It was three in the morning and the cold was complete. Poor little Abbie had pneumonia. All she had to do was open the window and strip the bed. He was used to sleeping on mud floors, let him try this.

Audrey tucked the duvet round his chin and sat back. There was never a violent burglar high on drugs and homicidally inclined when you wanted one. She would have paid such a beast to make a decent job of it, although she would have preferred to donate her life savings to an undertaker who would make it look as if her brand-new husband had died a natural and dignified death.

It was a long vigil, midnight to dawn, leaving far too much room for thought. There were many options, apart from the brutal remedy of ice. She could give him extra antibiotics, not known to kill a man, but never mind. Extra sleeping tablets. A parcel of antidepressants saved from a long and distant time, in the fridge. She could give him a cocktail of pills, she could poison him with the alcohol he loathed and say he had done it to himself. He was weak: he was sick to death. The doctor had given her an armory.

Abdoulie opened his eyes. He had the nerve to smile.

"Banjie," he murmured. "Banjie."

The name of a girl, the name of a town. Never her name.

Audrey was a neat-figured, neat-faced person with a good crop of outstanding gray-black hair, better-looking than many, but not so vain as to contemplate a wedding with white gown and all the jazz. Besides, they would need the money for other things. Someone would give him a job, surely, on the basis of his gentle temperament alone. Audrey had worked it all out on a piece of graph paper. It would take him a year, she reckoned; a year or less to learn the system. In the meantime, there was enough to buy him the clothes he patently adored, or there might have been if the man had the faintest idea of the value of money. He did not. He could not understand that if she was willing to buy him a suit worth eighty pounds, she would balk at the one priced at three hundred which he preferred. He did not understand why she lived in a cottage with low ceilings when there were other houses on the market. He did not (and she laughed herself sick at this one) understand the difference between rich and poor. If you had any money at all, you could buy the world. All this from a man who could sleep on concrete. Whose shoe size defeated condescending persons in shops and whose feet ached from the cold.

Abdoulie looked like a puzzled giant at their nuptials. These took place two weeks after his arrival. She had asked him if he was sure.

"Of course. Of course. I am very sure." He had fingered the cloth of his imperfect suit, doubtfully, smiled his crooked smile. Moved from the embrace of her arms, where her head nestled against his chest.

"Then," he said, "we make love."

Oh yes, he had caused a stir. But the modesty of the wedding, the Anglo-Saxon reserve of it, was simply another of her mistakes. He wanted her to look like something from television, the way she had never looked. He spoke his lines with the aplomb of Sir Laurence Olivier and he looked like Othello, but he might as well have killed her then, the way she would kill him now.

This kind of wedding meant nothing to him. He had no particular belief, he had said. Only the beliefs which were buried in his bones, made him mutter alien prayers and meant that this was no wedding at all. The same beliefs which made him a kind of thief.

Audrey was the sum of all her parts. She had wanted a man, this man, so gentle, malleable and different from the last, to complete the circle of her existence and surround that hole in the middle, making the vacuum a captive space which no longer bothered her. There's always that space, her friend Molly had said: we are none of us born to know contentment at all times. Look at what you have achieved, Audrey, dear; take pride in that. A lovely home with roses round the door, the liking and respect of your peers, freedom, the ability to live with grace.

"Grace is a virtue; virtue is a grace,
Grace is a naughty girl who will not wash her face. . . ."
Audrey chanted the words under her breath and wiped

Abdoulie's face, roughly. She could put the pillow over his head, press down and wait: she doubted he would even fight because he had never had any fight in him.

It would be a lovely funeral, better than a wedding.

She sat and considered how his premature death would give back to her what she had lost. She could see herself following the coffin to the crematorium, dignified in grief, wearing her black suit, holding her head high, admired by those who would give her the accolades of their pity, talking about her admiringly behind her back. Oh, she's so brave. Brave to marry again in the first place, and them so happy, and him dying so soon. Extraordinarily sad. Tragic. She would be restored to her place in the pecking order, with the added cachet of widowhood and eccentricity. After all, no one had heard them quarrel. She and Abdoulie had never quarreled. They had merely been silent, with him frozen into ghostly quietness by his own despair. He could not admit mistakes; nor tell her in words the devastating homesickness which began to eat him like a cancer as soon as he finally got it into his mind that this was where, and how, he was supposed to live.

The despair had followed fast on the heels of novelty.

"What's so wrong with it, Abbie? Why do you negate me by hating everything about this place? Why have you fouled up everything important to me?"

She spoke softly, the venom in her mind turning to plaintive speculation. He hated the cold, he hated the low beams of her cottage, he shied like a frightened animal in the supermarket, he did not like the food, and he treated her cat like something with the evil eye. The doctor said he could be allergic to the cat; the pneumonia was compounded by fits of wheezing. What a joke that would be if it was the cat killed him. She could bring it into the room, wake him up and watch him expire out of terror. Pathetic, a big man like that. And what was more to the point, it was his frigid, frightened, monumental, animal loathing which made her follow and detest all the same things which so affected him.

She looked at her possessions and her status and wondered what they meant, mistrusting everything she had done and all she owned. All turned to dust as she gazed at it. He was like someone who had seized an exquisite piece of crochet and systematically reduced it to threads. He, who was without violence, had smashed everything to pieces.

On the nights on which murders take place, or so she had read, the wind howled outside; thunder and lightning heralded the worst crime known to man, but at the time, murder seemed the most natural thing in the world and the night had grown calm and clear. She looked out of the window at the village street, a tidy piece of England, far from the sea.

"Banjie," he muttered, turning so that his face pointed to the white ceiling. "Banjie." Then he opened his eyes, looked straight into her own as she moved closer to him. In his dream he screamed. Once, loudly. A single expulsion of desperate sound, before his eyes closed again.

Poor man, who would not hurt a fly.

You are not really a tolerant person, Molly had said. None of us, apart from those peculiarly gifted to the point of being a little mad, are so tolerant that we can be comprehensive about what we are able to accept about another. You liked his country; you didn't love it or understand it, which isn't your fault. Why should he suddenly love yours?

Because he loved me.

That, said Molly, is nowhere near enough. You can't put cactus in a pond and expect it to grow. You can't expect a husky dog to love the desert, even if it is a champion breed. Molly was expert on gardening and dogs.

He is so gentle, Audrey said; I cannot bear it.

There was sobbing from the bed. Audrey sat on the edge. She touched his face. His hand held her palm against his hot skin. She cradled his head and gave him water. She knew she had the power of life and death. He knew it, too and did not seem to mind.

"You had nothing," she whispered to him. "Nothing." That was where he had lied. He had had plenty. The only thing not included had been money.

The dawn was beginning when she went downstairs to let the cat back indoors. Autumn had been fine. The sky was streaked with red, delicately pretty. No comparison to the awesome splendor of the West African sunset, where Audrey had fallen in love. Where a man could bury his heart in the sand and let the clouds take his head. Murder belonged with the dark. Audrey became efficient with the daylight. She waited, impatiently, for the hour when other people would be in their offices, ready to receive calls and respond to her authoritative voice. In the meantime, she busied herself, frowned over her bank balance, shrugged and planned the week. She pushed down the bitterness inside her with the same determination she used to knead bread. She suppressed all the feelings of insult and outrage and put them to one side together with all those comfortingly violent sensations which had been her companions for the night. She was not, after all, that kind of woman.

Yes, she was. She was no better than she ought to be and worse than he was, suffering in silence, turning his face to the wall while she planned necessary termination. He had not pleaded; he had not even considered violence. He was what she first discovered, a good man, in his way. He had never wished her harm, would never do as she had done, contemplate hurting her. Audrey was not ashamed about any of her decisions.

It was ten o'clock when she went upstairs. His eyes were closed, his sleep profound and peaceful, as if he had known what she was doing. She flung back the curtains and let in the sun. Pale, watery, English sun.

"You're going home," she said firmly. "In a day or two. When you feel a bit better, eh?"

It was the look of intense relief that he could not begin to hide as his eyes flew open and his face came alive, which made her want to weep. Such an innocent, totally unaware of what she had been thinking. Of course he would rather have nothing.

After he had gone, both of them laughing and crying at the airport and making meaningless promises, she came home and cleaned the house. Stripped his bed and wondered if she would ever use it again. Prepared a barrage of explanations to save what dignity she could. Vowed she would never say a bad word about him. Audrey felt bereft and utterly relieved about her soldierly behavior. He had never seen into her soul, never guessed she could be so foul.

Turning the mattress in order to resettle it upside down against the divan base, she found the knife at the level of the pillow. It was an unfamiliar, lethal-looking thing, sharper than the ones the tourists bought for fun.

Ready for her.

On balance, Molly said, she should be grateful. The discovery redressed the delicate balance of one, last night.

The Surprise of His Life

Elizabeth George

When Douglas Armstrong had his first consultation with Thistle McCloud, he had no intention of murdering his wife. His mind, in fact, didn't turn to murder until two weeks after consultation number four.

Douglas watched closely as Thistle prepared herself for a revelation from another dimension. She held his wedding band in the palm of her left hand. She closed her fingers around it. She hovered her right hand over the fist that she'd made. She hummed five notes that sounded suspiciously like the beginning of "I Love You Truly." Gradually, her eyes rolled back, up, and out of view beneath her yellow-shaded lids, leaving him with the disconcerting sight of a thirtysomething female in a straw boater, striped vest, white shirt, and polka-dotted tie, looking as if she were one quarter of a barbershop quartet in desperate hope of finding her partners.

When he'd first seen Thistle, Douglas had appraised her attire—which in subsequent visits had not altered in any appreciable fashion—as the insidious getup of a charlatan who wished to focus her clients' attention on her personal appearance rather than on whatever machinations she would be going through to delve into their pasts, their presents, their futures, and—most importantly—their wallets. But he'd come to realize that Thistle's odd getup had nothing to do with distracting anyone. The first time she held his old Rolex watch and began speaking in a low, intense voice about the prodigal son, about his endless departures and equally endless returns, about his aging parents who welcomed him always with open arms and open hearts, and about his brother who watched all this with a false fixed smile and a silent shout of *What about me? Do I mean nothing?*, he had a feeling that Thistle was exactly what she purported to be: a psychic.

He'd first come to her storefront operation because he'd had forty minutes to kill prior to his yearly prostate exam. He dreaded the exam and the teeth-grating embarrassment of having to answer his doctor's jovial, rib-poking "Everything up and about as it should be?" with the truth, which was that Newton's law of gravity had begun asserting itself lately to his dearest appendage. And since he was six weeks short of his fifty-fifth birthday, and since every disaster in his life had occurred in a year that was a multiple of five, if there was a chance of knowing what the gods had in store for him and his prostate, he wanted to be able to do something to head off the chaos.

These things had all been on his mind as he spun along Pacific Coast Highway in the dim gold light of a late December afternoon. On a drearily commercialized section of the road—given largely to pizza parlors and boogie board shops—he had seen the small blue building that he'd passed a thousand times before and read PSYCHIC CONSULTATIONS on its hand-painted sign. He'd glanced at his gas gauge for an excuse to stop and while he pumped super unleaded into the tank of his Mercedes across the street from that small blue building, he made his decision. What the hell, he'd thought. There were worse ways to kill forty minutes.

So he'd had his first session with Thistle McCloud, who was anything but what he'd expected of a psychic since she used no crystal ball, no tarot cards, nothing at all but a piece of his jewelry. In his first three visits, it had always been the Rolex watch from which she'd received her psychic emanations. But today she'd placed the watch to one side, declared it diluted of power, and set her fog-colored eyes on his wedding ring. She'd touched her finger to it, and said, "I'll use that, I think. If you want something further from your history and closer to your heart."

He'd given her the ring precisely because of those last two phrases: *further from your history and closer to your heart.* They told him how very well she knew that the prodigal son business rose from his past while his deepest concerns were attached to his future.

With the ring now in her closed fist and with her eyes rolled upward, Thistle stopped the four-note humming, breathed deeply six times, and opened her eyes. She observed him with a melancholia that made his stomach feel hollow.

"What?" Douglas asked.

"You need to prepare for a shock," she said. "It's something unexpected. It comes out of nowhere and because of it, the essence of your life will be changed forever. And soon. I feel it coming very soon."

Jesus, he thought. It was just what he needed to hear three weeks after having an indifferent index finger shoved up his ass to see what was the cause of his limp-dick syndrome. The doctor had said it wasn't cancer, but he hadn't ruled out half a dozen other possibilities. Douglas wondered which one of them Thistle had just now tuned her psychic antennae onto.

Thistle opened her hand and they both looked at his wedding ring where it lay on her palm, faintly sheened by her sweat. "It's an external shock," she clarified. "The source of upheaval in your life isn't from within. The shock comes from outside and rattles you to your core."

"Are you sure about that?" Douglas asked her.

"As sure as I can be, considering the armor you wear." Thistle returned the ring to him, her cool fingers grazing his wrist. She said, "Your name isn't David, is it? It was never David. It never will be David. But the *D*, I feel, is correct. Am I right?"

He reached into his back pocket and brought out his

wallet. Careful to shield his driver's license from her, he clipped a fifty-dollar bill between his thumb and index finger. He folded it once and handed it over.

"Donald," she said. "No. That isn't it, either. Darrell, perhaps. Dennis. I sense two syllables."

"Names aren't important in your line of work, are they?" Douglas said.

"No. But the truth is always important. Someday, Not-David, you're going to have to learn to trust people with the truth. Trust is the key. Trust is essential."

"Trust," he told her, "is what gets people screwed."

Outside, he walked across the Coast Highway to the cramped side street that paralleled the ocean. Here he always parked his car when he visited Thistle. With its vanity license plate DRIL4IT virtually announcing who owned the Mercedes, Douglas had decided early on that it wouldn't encourage new investors if anyone put the word out that the president of South Coast Oil had begun seeing a psychic regularly. Risky investments were one thing. Placing money with a man who could be accused of using parapsychology rather than geology to find oil deposits was another. He wasn't doing that, of course. Business never came up in his sessions with Thistle. But try telling that to the board of directors. Try telling that to anyone.

He unarmed the car and slid inside. He headed south, in the direction of his office. As far as anyone at South Coast Oil knew, he'd spent his lunch hour with his wife, having a romantic winter's picnic on the bluffs in Corona del Mar. The cellular phone will be turned off for an hour, he'd informed his secretary. Don't try to phone and don't bother us, please. This is time for Donna and me. She deserves it. I need it. Are we clear on the subject?

Any mention of Donna always did the trick when it came to keeping South Coast Oil off his back for a few hours. She was warmly liked by everyone in the company. She was warmly liked by everyone period. Sometimes, he reflected suddenly, she was too warmly liked. Especially by men.

You need to prepare for a shock.

Did he? Douglas considered the question in relation to his wife.

When he pointed out men's affinity for her, Donna always acted surprised. She told him that men merely recognized in her a woman who'd grown up in a household of brothers. But what he saw in men's eyes when they looked at his wife had nothing to do with fraternal affection. It had to do with getting her naked, getting down and dirty, and getting laid.

It's an external shock.

Was it? What sort? Douglas thought of the worst.

Getting laid was behind every man–woman interaction on earth. He knew this well. So while his recent failures to get it up and get it on with Donna frustrated him, he had to admit that he was feeling concerned that her patience with him was trickling away. Once it was gone, she'd start looking around. That was only natural. And once she started looking, she was going to find or be found.

The shock comes from outside and rattles you to your core.

Shit, Douglas thought. If chaos was about to steamroller into his life as he approached his fifty-fifth birthday—that rotten bad luck integer—Douglas knew that Donna would probably be at the wheel. She was thirty-five, four years in place as wife number three, and while she acted content, he'd been around women long enough to know that still waters did more than simply run deep. They hid rocks that could sink a boat in seconds if a sailor didn't keep his wits about him. And love made people lose their wits. Love made people go a little bit nuts.

Of course, *he* wasn't nuts. He had his wits about him. But being in love with a woman twenty years his junior, a woman whose scent caught the nose of every male within sixty yards of her, a woman whose physical appetites he himself was failing to satisfy on a nightly basis . . . and had been failing to satisfy for weeks . . . a woman like that . . .

"Get a grip," Douglas told himself brusquely. "This psychic stuff is baloney, right? Right." But still he thought of the coming shock, the upset to his life, and its source: external. Not his prostate, not his dick, not an organ in his body. But another human being. "Shit," he said.

He guided the car up the incline that led to Jamboree Road, six lanes of concrete that rolled between stunted liquidambar trees through some of the most expensive real estate in Orange County. It took him to the bronzed glass tower that housed his pride: South Coast Oil.

Once inside the building, he navigated his way through an unexpected encounter with two of SCO's engineers, through a brief conversation with a geologist who simultaneously waved an ordnance survey map and a report from the EPA, and through a hallway conference with the head of the accounting department. His secretary handed him a fistful of messages when he finally managed to reach his office. She said, "Nice picnic? The weather's unbelievable, isn't it?" followed by "Everything all right, Mr. Armstrong?" when he didn't reply.

He said, "Yes. What? Fine," and looked through the messages. He found that the names meant nothing to him, absolutely nothing.

He walked to the window behind his desk and looked at the view through its enormous pane of tinted glass. Below him, Orange County's airport sent jet after jet hurtling into the sky at an angle so acute that it defied both reason and aerodynamics, although it did protect the delicate auditory sensibilities of the millionaires who lived in the flight path below. Douglas watched these planes without really seeing them. He knew he had to answer his telephone messages, but all he could think about was Thistle's words: *An external shock.*

What could be more external than Donna?

She wore Obsession. She put it behind her ears and beneath her breasts. Whenever she passed through a room, she left the scent of herself behind.

Her dark hair gleamed when the sunlight hit it. She wore it short and simply cut, parted on the left and smoothly falling just to her ears.

Her legs were long. When she walked, her stride was full

and sure. And when she walked with him—at his side, with her hand through his arm and her head held back—he knew that she caught the attention of everyone. He knew that together they were the envy of all their friends and of strangers as well.

He could see this reflected in the faces of people they passed when he and Donna were together. At the ballet, at the theater, at concerts, in restaurants, glances gravitated to Douglas Armstrong and his wife. In women's expressions he could read the wish to be young like Donna, to be smooth-skinned again, to be vibrant once more, to be fecund and ready. In men's expressions he could read desire.

It had always been a pleasure to see how others reacted to the sight of his wife. But now he saw how dangerous her allure really was and how it threatened to destroy his peace.

A shock, Thistle had said to him. *Prepare for a shock. Prepare for a shock that will change your world.*

That evening, Douglas heard the water running as soon as he entered the house: fifty-two-hundred square feet of limestone floors, vaulted ceilings, and picture windows on a hillside that offered an ocean view to the west and the lights of Orange County to the east. The house had cost him a fortune, but that had been all right with him. Money meant nothing. He'd bought the place for Donna. But if he'd had doubts about his wife before—born of his own performance anxiety, growing to adulthood through his consultation with Thistle—when Douglas heard that water running, he began to see the truth. Because Donna was in the shower.

He watched her silhouette behind the blocks of translucent glass that defined the shower's wall. She was washing her hair. She hadn't noticed him yet, and he watched her for a moment, his gaze traveling over her uplifted breasts, her hips, her long legs. She usually bathed—languorous bubble baths in the raised oval tub that looked out on the lights of the city of Irvine. Taking a shower suggested a more earnest and energetic effort to cleanse herself. And washing her hair suggested . . . Well, it was perfectly clear what that suggested. Scents got caught up in the hair: cigarette smoke, sautéing garlic, fish from a fishing boat, or semen and sex. Those last two were the betraying scents. Obviously, she would have to wash her hair.

Her discarded clothes lay on the floor. With a hasty glance at the shower, Douglas fingered through them and found her lacy underwear. He knew women. He knew his wife. If she'd actually been with a man that afternoon, her body's leaking juices would have made the panties' crotch stiff when they dried, and he would be able to smell the afterscent of intercourse on them. They would give him proof. He lifted them to his face.

"Doug! What on earth are you doing?"

Douglas dropped the panties, cheeks hot and neck sweating. Donna was peering at him from the shower's opening, her hair lathered with soap that streaked down her left cheek. She brushed it away.

"What are *you* doing?" he asked her. Three marriages and two divorces had taught him that a fast offensive maneuver threw the opponent off balance. It worked.

She popped back into the water—clever of her, so he couldn't see her face—and said, "It's pretty obvious. I'm taking a shower. God, what a day."

He moved to watch her through the shower's opening. There was no door, just a partition in the glass-block wall. He could study her body and look for the telltale signs of the kind of rough lovemaking he knew that she liked. And she wouldn't know he was even looking, since her head was beneath the shower as she rinsed off her hair.

"Steve phoned in sick today," she said, "so I had to do everything at the kennels myself."

She raised chocolate Labradors. He had met her that way, seeking a dog for his youngest son. Through a reference from a veterinarian, he had discovered her kennels in Midway City—less than one square mile of feedstores, other kennels, and dilapidated postwar stucco and shake roofs posing as suburban housing. It was an odd place for a girl from the pricey side of Corona del Mar to end up professionally, but that was what he liked about Donna. She wasn't true to type, she wasn't a beach bunny, she wasn't a typical southern California girl. Or at least that's what he had thought.

"The worst was cleaning the dog runs," she said. "I didn't mind the grooming—I never mind that—but I hate doing the runs. I completely reeked of dog poop when I got home." She shut off the shower and reached for her towels, wrapping her head in one and her body in the other. She stepped out of the stall with a smile and said, "Isn't it weird how some smells cling to your body and your hair while others don't?"

She kissed him hello and scooped up her clothes. She tossed them down the laundry chute. No doubt she was thinking, Out of sight, out of mind. She was clever that way.

"That's the third time Steve's phoned in sick in two weeks." She headed for the bedroom, drying off as she went. She dropped the towel with her usual absence of self-consciousness and began dressing, pulling on wispy underwear, black leggings, a silver tunic. "If he keeps this up, I'm going to let him go. I need someone consistent, someone reliable. If he's not going to be able to hold up his end . . ." She frowned at Douglas, her face perplexed. "What's wrong, Doug? You're looking at me so funny. Is something wrong?"

"Wrong? No." But he thought, That looks like a love bite on her neck. And he crossed to her for a better look. He cupped her face for a kiss and tilted her head. The shadow of the towel that was wrapped around her hair dissipated, leaving her skin unmarred. Well, what of it? he thought. She wouldn't be so stupid as to let some heavy breather suck bruises into her flesh, no matter how turned on he had her. She wasn't that dumb. Not his Donna.

But she also wasn't as smart as her husband.

At five forty-five the next day, he went to the personnel department. It was a better choice than the Yellow Pages because at least he knew that whoever had been doing the background checks on incoming employees at South Coast

Oil was simultaneously competent and discreet. No one had ever complained about some two-bit gumshoe nosing into his background.

The department was deserted, as Douglas had hoped. The computer screens at every desk were set to the shifting images that preserved them: a field of swimming fish, bouncing balls, and popping bubbles. The director's office at the far side of the department was unlit and locked, but a master key in the hand of the company president solved that problem. Douglas went inside and flipped on the lights.

He found the name he was looking for among the dog-eared cards of the director's Rolodex, a curious anachronism in an otherwise computer-age office. *Cowley and Son, Inquiries,* he read in faded typescript. This was accompanied by a telephone number and by an address on Balboa Peninsula.

Douglas studied both for the space of two minutes. Was it better to know or to live in ignorant bliss? he wondered at this eleventh hour. But he wasn't living in bliss, was he? And he hadn't been living in bliss from the moment he'd failed to perform as a man was meant to. So it was better to know. He had to know. Knowledge was power. Power was control. He needed both.

He picked up the phone.

Douglas always went out for lunch—unless a conference was scheduled with his geologists or the engineers—so no one raised a hair of an eyebrow when he left South Coast Oil before noon the following day. He used Jamboree once again to get to the Coast Highway, but this time instead of heading north toward Newport where Thistle made her prognostications, he drove directly across the highway and down the incline where a modestly arched bridge spanned an oily section of Newport Harbor that divided the mainland from an amoeba-shaped portion of land that was Balboa Island.

In summer the island was infested with tourists. They bottled up the streets with their cars and rode their bicycles in races on the sidewalk around the island's perimeter. No local in his right mind ventured onto Balboa Island during the summer without good reason or unless he lived there. But in winter, the place was virtually deserted. It took less than five minutes to snake through the narrow streets to the island's north end where the ferry waited to take cars and pedestrians on the eye-blink voyage across to the peninsula.

There a stripe-topped carousel and a Ferris wheel spun like two opposing gears of an enormous clock, defining an area called the Fun Zone, which had long been the summertime bane of the local police. Today, however, no bands of juveniles roved with cans of spray paint at the ready. The only inhabitants of the Fun Zone were a paraplegic in a wheelchair and his bike-riding companion.

Douglas passed them as he drove off the ferry. They were intent upon their conversation. The Ferris wheel and carousel did not exist for them. Nor did Douglas and his blue Mercedes, which was just as well. He didn't particularly want to be seen.

He parked just off the beach, in a lot where fifteen minutes cost a quarter. He pumped in four. He armed the car and headed west toward Main Street, a tree-shaded lane some sixty yards long that began at a faux New England restaurant overlooking Newport Harbor and ended at Balboa Pier, which stretched out into the Pacific Ocean, gray-green today and unsettled by roiling waves from a winter Alaskan storm.

Number 107-B Main was what he was looking for, and he found it easily. Just east of an alley, 107 was a two-story structure whose bottom floor was taken up by a time-warped hair salon called JJ's—heavily devoted to macramé, potted plants, and posters of Janis Joplin—and whose upper floor was divided into offices that were reached by means of a structurally questionable stairway at the north end of the building. Number 107-B was the first door upstairs—JJ's Natural Haircutting appeared to be 107-A—but when Douglas turned the discolored brass knob below the equally discolored brass nameplate announcing the business as COWLEY AND SON, INQUIRIES, he found the door locked.

He frowned and looked at his Rolex. His appointment

was for twelve-fifteen. It was currently twelve-ten. So where was Cowley? Where was his son?

He returned to the stairway, ready to head to his car and his cellular phone, ready to track down Cowley and give him hell for setting up an appointment and failing to be there to keep it. But he was three steps down when he saw a khaki-clad man coming his way, sucking up an Orange Julius with the enthusiasm of a twelve-year-old. His thinning gray hair and sun-lined face marked him at least five decades older than twelve, however. And his limping gait—in combination with his clothes—suggested old war wounds.

"You Cowley?" Douglas called from the stairs.

The man waved his Orange Julius in reply. "You Armstrong?" he asked.

"Right," Douglas said. "Listen, I don't have a lot of time."

"None of us do, son," Cowley said, and he hoisted himself up the stairway. He nodded in a friendly fashion, pulled hard on the Orange Julius straw, and passed Douglas in a gust of aftershave that he hadn't smelled for a good twenty years. Canoe. Jesus. Did they still sell that?

Cowley swung the door open and cocked his head to indicate that Douglas was to enter. The office comprised two rooms: one was a sparsely furnished waiting area through which they passed; the other was obviously Cowley's demesne. Its centerpiece was an olive-green steel desk. Filing cabinets and bookshelves of the same issue matched it.

The investigator went to an old oaken office chair behind the desk, but he didn't sit. Instead, he opened one of the side drawers, and just when Douglas was expecting him to pull out a fifth of bourbon, he dug out a bottle of yellow capsules instead. He shook two of them into his palm and knocked them back with a long swig of Orange Julius. He sank into his chair and gripped its arms.

"Arthritis," he said. "I'm killing the bastard with evening primrose oil. Give me a minute, okay? You want a couple?"

"No." Douglas glanced at his watch to make certain Cowley knew that his time was precious. Then he strolled to the steel bookshelves.

He was expecting to see munitions manuals, penal codes, and surveillance texts, something to assure the prospective clients that they'd come to the right place with their troubles. But what he found was poetry, volume after volume neatly arranged in alphabetical order by author, from Matthew Arnold to William Butler Yeats. He wasn't sure what to think.

The occasional space left at the end of a bookshelf was taken up by photographs. They were clumsily framed, snapshots mostly. They depicted grinning small children, a gray-haired grandma type, several young adults. Among them, encased in Plexiglas, was a military Purple Heart. Douglas picked this up. He'd never seen one, but he was pleased to know that his guess about the source of Cowley's limp had been correct.

"You saw action," he said.

"My butt saw action," Cowley replied. Douglas looked his way, so the PI continued. "I took it in the butt. Shit happens, right?" He moved his hands from their grip on the arms of his chair. He folded them over his stomach. Like Douglas's own, it could have been flatter. Indeed, the two men shared a similar build: stocky, quickly given to weight if they didn't exercise, too tall to be called short and too short to be called tall. "What can I do for you, Mr. Armstrong?"

"My wife," Douglas said.

"Your wife?"

"She may be . . ." Now that it was time to articulate the problem and what it arose from, Douglas wasn't sure that he could. So he said, "Who's the son?"

"What?"

"It says Cowley and Son, but there's only one desk. Who's the son?"

Cowley reached for his Orange Julius and took a pull on its straw. "He died," he said. "Drunk driver got him on Ortega Highway."

"Sorry."

"Like I said. Shit happens. What shit's happened to you?"

Douglas returned the Purple Heart to its place. He caught sight of the graying grandma in one of the pictures and said, "This your wife?"

"Forty years my wife. Name's Maureen."

"I'm on my third. How'd you manage forty years with one woman?"

"She has a sense of humor." Cowley slid open the middle drawer of his desk and took out a legal pad and the stub of a pencil. He wrote ARMSTRONG at the top in block letters and underlined it. He said, "About your wife . . ."

"I think she's having an affair. I want to know if I'm right. I want to know who it is."

Cowley carefully set his pencil down. He observed Douglas for a moment. Outside, a gull gave a raucous cry from one of the rooftops. "What makes you think she's seeing someone?"

"Am I supposed to give you proof before you'll take the case? I thought that's why I was hiring you. To give *me* proof."

"You wouldn't be here if you didn't have suspicions. What are they?"

Douglas raked through his memory. He wasn't about to tell Cowley about trying to smell up Donna's underwear, so he took a moment to examine her behavior over the last few weeks. And when he did so, the additional evidence was there. Jesus. How the hell had he missed it? She'd changed her hair; she'd bought new underwear—that black lacy Victoria's Secret stuff; she'd been on the phone twice when he'd come home and as soon as he walked into the room, she'd hung up hastily; there were at least two long absences with insufficient excuse for them; there were six or seven engagements that she said were with friends.

Cowley nodded thoughtfully when Douglas listed his suspicions. Then he said, "Have you given her a reason to cheat on you?"

"A reason? What is this? I'm the guilty party?"

"Women don't usually stray without there being a man behind them, giving them a reason." Cowley examined him from beneath unclipped eyebrows. One of his eyes, Douglas saw, was beginning to form a cataract. Jeez, the guy was ancient, a real antique.

"No reason," Douglas said. "I don't cheat on her. I don't even want to."

"She's young, though. And a man your age . . ." Cowley shrugged. "Shit happens to us old guys. Young things don't always have the patience to understand."

Douglas wanted to point out that Cowley was at least ten years his senior, if not more. He also wanted to take himself from membership in the club of *us old guys*. But the PI was watching him compassionately, so instead of arguing, Douglas told the truth.

Cowley reached for his Orange Julius and drained the cup. He tossed it into the trash. "Women have needs," he said, and he moved his hand from his crotch to his chest, adding, "A wise man doesn't confuse what goes on here"— the crotch—"with what goes on here"—the chest.

"So maybe I'm not wise. Are you going to help me out or not?"

"You sure you want help?"

"I want to know the truth. I can live with that. What I can't live with is not knowing. I just need to know what I'm dealing with here."

Cowley looked as if he were taking a reading of Douglas's level of veracity. He finally appeared to make a decision, but one he didn't like because he shook his head, picked up his pencil, and said, "Give me some background, then. If she's got someone on the side, who are our possibilities?"

Douglas had thought about this. There was Mike, the poolman who visited once a week. There was Steve, who worked with Donna at her kennels in Midway City. There was Jeff, her personal trainer. There were also the postman, the FedEx man, the UPS driver, and Donna's too youthful gynecologist.

"I take it you're accepting the case?" Douglas said to Cowley. He pulled out his wallet from which he extracted a wad of bills. "You'll want a retainer."

"I don't need cash, Mr. Armstrong."

"All the same . . ." All the same, Douglas had no intention of leaving a paper trail via a check. "How much time do you need?" he asked.

"Give it a few days. If she's seeing someone, he'll surface eventually. They always do." Cowley sounded despondent.

"Your wife cheat on you?" Douglas asked shrewdly.

"If she did, I probably deserved it."

That was Cowley's attitude, but it was one that Douglas didn't share. He didn't deserve to be cheated on. Nobody did. And when he found out who was doing the job on his wife . . . Well, they would see a kind of justice that Attila the Hun was incapable of extracting.

His resolve was strengthened in the bedroom that evening when his hello kiss to his wife was interrupted by the telephone. Donna pulled away from him quickly and went to answer it. She gave Douglas a smile—as if recognizing what her haste revealed to him—and shook back her hair as sexily as possible, running slim fingers through it as she picked up the receiver.

Douglas listened to her side of the conversation while he changed his clothes. He heard her voice brighten as she said, "Yes, yes. Hello . . . No . . . Doug just got home and we were talking about the day. . . ."

So now her caller knew he was in the room. Douglas could imagine what the bastard was saying, whoever he was: *"So you can't talk?"*

To which Donna, on cue, answered, "Nope. Not at all."

"Shall I call later?"

"Gosh, that would be nice."

"Today was what was nice. I love to fuck you."

"Really? Outrageous. I'll have to check it out."

"I want to check you out, baby. Are you wet for me?"

"I sure am. Listen, we'll connect later on, okay? I need to get dinner started."

"Just so long as you remember today. It was the best. You're the best."

"Right. Bye." She hung up and came to him. She put her arms round his waist. She said, "Got rid of her. Nancy Talbert. God. Nothing's more important in her life than a shoe sale at Neiman-Marcus. Spare me. Please." She snuggled up to him. He couldn't see her face, just the back of her head where it reflected in the mirror.

"Nancy Talbert," he said. "I don't think I know her."

"Sure you do, honey." She pressed her hips against him. He felt the hopeful but useless heat in his groin. "She's in Soroptimists with me. You met her last month after the ballet. Hmm. You feel nice. Gosh, I like it when you hold me. Should I start dinner or d'you want to mess around?"

Another clever move on her part: he wouldn't think she was cheating if she still wanted it from him. No matter that he couldn't give it to her. She was hanging in there with him and this moment proved it. Or so she thought.

"Love to," he said, and smacked her on the butt. "But let's eat first. And after, right there on the dining room table . . ." He managed what he hoped was a lewd enough wink. "Just you wait, kiddo."

She laughed and released him and went off to the kitchen. He walked to the bed where he sat, disconsolately. The charade was torture. He had to know the truth.

He didn't hear from Cowley and Son, Inquiries, for two agonizing weeks during which he suffered through three more coy telephone conversations between Donna and her lover, four more phony excuses to cover unscheduled absences from home, and two more midday showers sloughed off to Steve's absence from the kennels again. By the time he finally made contact with Cowley, Douglas's nerves were shot.

Cowley had news to report. He said he'd hand it over as soon as they could meet. "How's lunch?" Cowley asked. "We could do Tail of the Whale over here."

No lunch, Douglas told him. He wouldn't be able to eat anyway. He would meet Cowley at his office at twelve forty-five.

"Make it the pier, then," Cowley said. "I'll catch a burger at Ruby's and we can talk after. You know Ruby's? The end of the pier?"

He knew Ruby's. A fifties coffee shop, it sat at the end of Balboa Pier, and he found Cowley there as promised at twelve forty-five, polishing off a cheeseburger and fries with a manila envelope sitting next to his strawberry milkshake.

Cowley wore the same khakis he'd had on the day they'd met. He'd added a panama hat to his ensemble. He touched his index finger to the hat's brim as Douglas approached him. His cheeks were bulging with the burger and fries.

Douglas slid into the booth opposite Cowley and reached for the envelope. Cowley's hand slapped down onto it. "Not yet," he said.

"I've got to know."

Cowley slid the envelope off the table and onto the vinyl seat next to himself. He twirled the straw in his milkshake and observed Douglas through opaque eyes that seemed to reflect the sunlight outside. "Pictures," he said. "That's all I've got for you. Pictures aren't the truth. You got that?"

"Okay. Pictures."

"I don't know what I'm shooting. I just tail the woman and I shoot what I see. What I see may not mean shit. You understand?"

"Just show me the pictures."

"Outside."

Cowley tossed a five and three ones onto the table, called, "Catch you later, Susie," to the waitress and led the way. He walked to the railing, where he looked out over the water. A whale-watching boat was bobbing about a quarter mile offshore. It was too early in the year to catch sight of a pod migrating to Alaska, but the tourists on board probably wouldn't know that. Their binoculars winked in the light.

Douglas joined the PI. Cowley said, "You got to know that she doesn't act like a woman guilty of anything. She just seems to be doing her thing. She met a few men—I won't mislead you—but I couldn't catch her doing anything cheesy."

"Give me the pictures."

Cowley gave him a sharp look instead. Douglas knew his voice was betraying him. "I say we tail her for another two weeks," Cowley said. "What I've got here isn't much to go on." He opened the envelope. He stood so that Douglas only saw the back of the pictures. He chose to hand them over in sets.

The first set was taken in Midway City not far from the kennels, at the feed and grain store where Donna bought food for the dogs. In these, she was loading fifty-pound sacks into the back of her Toyota pickup. She was being assisted by a Calvin Klein type in tight jeans and a T-shirt. They were laughing together, and in one of the pictures Donna had perched her sunglasses on the top of her head the better to look directly at her companion.

She appeared to be flirting, but she was a young, pretty woman and flirting was normal. This set seemed okay. She could have looked less happy to be chatting with the stud, but she was a businesswoman and she was conducting business. Douglas could deal with that.

The second set was of Donna in the Newport gym where she worked with a personal trainer twice a week. Her trainer was one of those sculpted bodies with a head of hair on which every strand looked as if it had been seen to professionally on a daily basis. In the pictures, Donna was dressed to work out—nothing Douglas had not seen before—but for the first time he noted how carefully she assembled her workout clothes. From the leggings to the leotard to the headband she wore, everything enhanced her. The trainer appeared to recognize this because he squatted before her as she did her vertical butterflies. Her legs were spread and there was no doubt what he was concentrating on. This looked more serious.

He was about to ask Cowley to start tailing the trainer when the PI said, "No body contact between them other than what you'd expect," and handed him the third set of pictures, saying, "These are the only ones that look a little shaky to me, but they may mean nothing. You know this guy?"

Douglas stared with *know this guy, know this guy* ringing in his skull. Unlike the other pictures in which Donna and her companion-of-the-moment were in one location, these showed Donna at a view table in an oceanfront restaurant, Donna on the Balboa ferry, Donna walking along a dock in Newport. In each of the pictures she was with a man, the same man. In each of the pictures there was body contact. It was nothing extreme because they were out in public. But it was the kind of body contact that betrayed: an arm around her shoulders, a kiss on her cheek, a full body hug that said, Feel me up, baby, 'cause I ain't limp like him.

Douglas felt that his world was spinning, but he managed a wry grin. He said, "Oh hell. Now I feel like a class-A jerk."

"Why's that?" Cowley asked.

"This guy?" Douglas indicated the athletic-looking man in the picture with Donna. "This is her brother."

"You're kidding."

"Nope. He's a walk-on coach at Newport Harbor High. His name is Michael. He's a free-spirit type." Douglas gripped the railing with one hand and shook his head with what he hoped looked like chagrin. "Is this all you've got?"

"That's it. I can tail her for a while longer and see—"

"Nah. Forget it. Jesus, I sure feel dumb." Douglas ripped the photographs into confetti. He tossed this into the water where it formed a mantle that was quickly shredded by the waves that arced against the pier's pilings. "What do I owe you, Mr. Cowley?" he asked. "What's this dumb ass got to pay for not trusting the finest woman on earth?"

He took Cowley to Dillman's on the corner of Main and Balboa Boulevard, and they sat at the snakelike bar with the locals, where they knocked back a couple of brews apiece. Douglas worked on his affability act, playing the abashed husband who suddenly realizes what a dickhead he's been. He took all Donna's actions over the past weeks and reinterpreted them for Cowley. The unexplained absences became the foundation of a treat she was planning for him: the purchase of a new car, perhaps; a trip to Europe; the refurbishing of his boat. The secretive telephone calls became messages from his children who were in the know. The new underwear metamorphosed into a display of her wish to make herself desirable for him, to work him out of his temporary impotence by giving him a renewed interest in her body. He felt like a total idiot, he told Cowley. Could they burn the damn negatives together?

They made a ceremony of it, torching the negatives of the pictures in the alley behind JJ's Natural Haircutting. Afterward, Douglas drove in a haze to Newport Harbor High School. He sat numbly across the street from it. He waited two hours. Finally, he saw his youngest brother arrive for the afternoon's coaching session, a basketball tucked under his arm and an athletic bag in his hand.

Michael, he thought. Returned from Greece this time, but always the prodigal son. Before Greece, it was a year with Greenpeace on the *Rainbow Warrior*. Before that, it was an expedition up the Amazon. And before that, it was marching against apartheid in South Africa. He had a resumé that would be the envy of any prepubescent kid out for a good time. He was Mr. Adventure, Mr. Irresponsibility, and Mr. Charm. He was Mr. Good Intentions without any follow-through. When a promise was due to be kept, he was out of sight, out of mind, and out of the country. But everyone loved the son of a bitch. He was forty years old, the baby of the Armstrong brothers, and he always got precisely what he wanted.

He wanted Donna now, the miserable bastard. No matter that she was his brother's wife. That made having her just so much more fun.

Douglas felt ill. His guts rolled around like marbles in a bucket. Sweat broke out in patches on his body. He couldn't go back to work like this. He reached for the phone and called his office.

He was sick, he told his secretary. Must have been something he ate for lunch. He was heading home. She could catch him there if anything came up.

In the house, he wandered from room to room. Donna wasn't at home—wouldn't be home for hours—so he had plenty of time to consider what to do. His mind reproduced for him the pictures that Cowley had taken of Michael and Donna. His intellect deduced where they had been and what they'd been doing prior to those pictures being taken.

He went to his study. There, in a glass curio cabinet, his collection of ivory erotica mocked him. Miniature Asians posed in a variety of sexual postures, having themselves a roaring good time. He could see Michael and Donna's features superimposed on the creamy faces of the figurines. They took their pleasure at his expense. They justified their pleasure by using his failure. No limp dick here, Michael's voice taunted. What's the matter, big brother? Can't hang on to your wife?

Douglas felt shattered. He told himself that he could have handled her doing anything else, he could have handled her seeing anyone else. But not Michael, who had trailed him through life, making his mark in every area where Douglas had previously failed. In high school it had been in athletics and student government. In college it had been in the world of fraternities. As an adult it had been in embracing adventure rather than in tackling the grind of business. And now, it was in proving to Donna what real manhood was all about.

Douglas could see them together as easily as he could see his pieces of erotica intertwined. Their bodies joined, their heads thrown back, their hands clasped, their hips grinding against each other. God, he thought. The pictures in his mind would drive him mad. He felt like killing.

The telephone company gave him the proof he required. He asked for a printout of the calls that had been made from his home. And when he received it, there was Michael's number. Not once or twice, but repeatedly. All of the calls had been made when he—Douglas—wasn't at home.

It was clever of Donna to use the nights when she knew Douglas would be doing his volunteer stint at the Newport suicide hotline. She knew he never missed his Wednesday evening shift, so important was it to him to have the hotline among his community commitments. She knew he was building a political profile to get himself elected to the city council, and the hotline was part of the picture of himself he wished to portray: Douglas Armstrong, husband, father, oilman, and compassionate listener to the emotionally distressed. He needed something to put into the balance against his environmental lapses. The hotline allowed him to say that while he may have spilled oil on a few lousy pelicans—not to mention some miserable otters—he would never let a human life hang there in jeopardy.

Donna had known he'd never skip even part of his evening shift, so she'd waited till then to make her calls to Michael. There they were on the printout, every one of them made between six and nine on a Wednesday night.

Okay, she liked Wednesday night so well. Wednesday night would be the night that he killed her.

He could hardly bear to be around her once he had the proof of her betrayal. She knew something was wrong between them because he didn't want to touch her any longer. Their thrice-weekly attempted couplings—as disastrous as they'd been—fast became a thing of the past. Still, she carried on as if nothing and no one had come between them, sashaying through the bedroom in her Victoria's Secret selection-of-the-night, trying to entice him into making a fool of himself so she could share the laughter with his brother Michael.

No way, baby, Douglas thought. You'll be sorry you made a fool out of me.

When she finally cuddled next to him in bed and murmured, "Doug, is something wrong? You want to talk? You okay?" it was all he could do not to shove her from him. He wasn't okay. He would never be okay again. But at least he'd be able to salvage a measure of his self-respect by giving the little bitch her due.

It was easy enough to plan once he decided on the very next Wednesday.

A trip to Radio Shack was all that was necessary. He chose the busiest one he could find, deep in the barrio in Santa Ana, and he deliberately took his time browsing until the youngest clerk with the most acne and the least amount of brainpower was available to wait on him. Then he made his purchase with cash: a call diverter, just the thing for those on-the-go SoCal folks who didn't want to miss an incoming phone call. No answering machine for those types. This would divert a phone call from one number to another by means of a simple computer chip. Once Douglas programmed the diverter with the number he wanted incoming calls diverted to, he would have an alibi for the night of his wife's murder. It was all so easy.

Donna had been a real numbskull to try to cheat on him. She had been a bigger numbskull to do her cheating on Wednesday nights because the fact of her doing it on Wednesday nights was what gave him the idea of how to snuff her. The volunteers on the hotline worked it in shifts. Generally there were two people present, each manning one of the telephone lines. But Newport Beach types actually didn't feel suicidal very frequently, and if they did, they were more likely to go to Neiman-Marcus and buy their way out of their depression. Midweek especially was a slow time for the pill poppers and wrist slashers, so the hotline was manned on Wednesdays by only one person per shift.

Douglas used the days prior to Wednesday to get his timing down to a military precision. He chose eight-thirty as Donna's death hour, which would give him time to sneak out of the hotline office, drive home, put out her lights, and get back to the hotline before the next shift arrived at nine. He was carving it out fairly thin and allowing only a five-minute margin of error, but he needed to do that in order to have a believable alibi once her body was found.

There could be neither noise nor blood, obviously. Noise

would arouse the neighbors. Blood would damn him if he got so much as a drop on his clothes, DNA typing being what it was these days. So he chose his weapon carefully, aware of the irony of his choice. He would use the satin belt of one of her Victoria's Secret slay-him-where-he-stands dressing gowns. She had half a dozen, so he would remove one of them in advance of the murder, separate it from its belt, dispose of it in a Dumpster behind the nearest Vons in advance of the killing—he liked that touch, getting rid of evidence *before* the crime, what killer ever thought of that? —and then use the belt to strangle his cheating wife on Wednesday night.

The call diverter would establish his alibi. He would take it to the suicide hotline, plug the phone into it, program the diverter with his cellular phone number, and thus appear to be in one location while his wife was being murdered in another. He made sure Donna was going to be at home by doing what he always did on Wednesdays: by phoning her from work before he left for the hotline.

"I feel like dogshit," he told her at five-forty.

"Oh, Doug, no!" she replied. "Are you ill or just feeling depressed about—"

"I'm feeling punk," he interrupted her. The last thing he wanted was to listen to her phony sympathy. "It may have been lunch."

"What did you have?"

Nothing. He hadn't eaten in two days. But he came up with "Shrimp" because he'd gotten food poisoning from shrimp a few years back and he thought she might remember that, if she remembered anything at all about him at this point. He went on, "I'm going to try to get home early from the hotline. I may not be able to if I can't pull in a substitute to take my shift. I'm heading over there now. If I can get a sub, I'll be home pretty early."

He could hear her attempt to hide dismay when she replied. "But Doug . . . I mean, what time do you think you'll make it?"

"I don't know. By eight at the latest, I hope. What difference does it make?"

"Oh. None at all, really. But I thought you might like dinner . . ."

What she really thought was how she was going to have to cancel her hot romp with his baby brother. Douglas smiled at the realization of how nicely he'd just unhooked her little caboose.

"Hell, I'm not hungry, Donna. I just want to go to bed if I can. You be there to rub my back? You going anywhere?"

"Of course not. Where would I be going? Doug, you sound strange. Is something wrong?"

Nothing was wrong, he told her. What he didn't tell her was how right everything was, felt, and was going to be. He had her where he wanted her now: she'd be home, and she'd be alone. She might phone Michael and tell him that his brother was coming home early so their tryst was off, but even if she did that, Michael's statement after her death would conflict with Douglas's uninterrupted presence at the suicide hotline that night.

Douglas just had to make sure that he was back at the hotline with time to disassemble the call diverter. He'd get rid of it on the way home—nothing could be easier than flipping it into the trash behind the huge movie theater complex that was on his route from the hotline to Harbour Heights where he lived—and then he'd arrive at his usual time of nine-twenty to "discover" the murder of his beloved.

It was all so easy. And so much cleaner than divorcing the little whore.

He felt remarkably at peace, considering everything. He'd seen Thistle again and she'd held his Rolex, his wedding band, and his cuff links to take her reading. She'd greeted him by telling him that his aura was strong and that she could feel the power pulsing from him. And when she closed her eyes over his possessions, she'd said, "I feel a major change coming into your life, not-David. A change of location, perhaps, a change of climate. Are you taking a trip?"

He might be, he told her. He hadn't had one in months. Did she have any suggested destinations?

"I see lights," she responded, going her own way. "I see cameras. I see many faces. You're surrounded by those you love."

They'd be at Donna's funeral, of course. And the press would cover it. He was somebody after all. They wouldn't ignore the murder of Douglas Armstrong's wife. As for Thistle, she'd find out who he really was if she read the paper or watched the local news. But that made no difference since he'd never mentioned Donna and since he'd have an alibi for the time of her death.

He arrived at the suicide hotline at five fifty-six. He was relieving a UCI psych student named Debbie who was eager enough to be gone. She said, "Only two calls, Mr. Armstrong. If your shift is like mine, I hope you brought something to read."

He waved his copy of *Money* magazine and took her place at the desk. He waited ten minutes after she'd left before he went back out to his car to get the call diverter.

The hotline was located in the dock area of Newport, a maze of narrow one-way streets that traversed the top of Balboa Peninsula. By day, the streets' antique stores, marine chandleries, and secondhand clothing boutiques attracted both locals and tourists. By night, the place was a ghost town, uninhabited except for the new-wave beatniks who visited a dive called the Alta Cafe three streets away, where anorexic girls dressed in black read poetry and strummed guitars. So no one was on the street to see Douglas fetch the call diverter from his Mercedes. And no one was on the street to see him leave the suicide hotline's small cubbyhole behind the real estate office at eight-fifteen. And should any desperate individual call the hotline during his drive home, that call would be diverted onto his cellular phone and he could deal with it. God, the plan was perfect.

As he drove up the curving road that led to his house,

Douglas thanked his stars that he'd chosen to live in an environment in which privacy was everything to the homeowners. Every estate sat, like Douglas's, behind walls and gates, shielded by trees. On one day in ten, he might actually see another resident. Most of the time—like tonight—there was no one around.

Even if someone had seen his Mercedes sliding up the hill, however, it was January dark and his was just another luxury car in a community of Rolls-Royces, Bentleys, BMWs, Lexuses, Range Rovers, and other Mercedes. Besides, he'd already decided that if he saw someone or something suspicious, he would just turn around, go back to the hotline, and wait for another Wednesday.

But he didn't see anything out of the ordinary. He didn't see anyone. Perhaps a few more cars were parked on the street, but even these were empty. He had the night to himself.

At the top of his drive, he shut off the engine and coasted to the house. It was dark inside, which told him that Donna was in the back, in their bedroom.

He needed her outside. The house was equipped with a security system that would do a bank vault proud, so he needed the killing to take place outside where a peeping Tom gone bazooka or a burglar or a serial killer might have lured her. He thought of Ted Bundy and how he'd snagged his victims by appealing to their maternal need to come to his aid. He'd go the Bundy route, he decided. Donna was nothing if not eager to help.

He got out of the car silently and paced over to the door. He rang the bell with the back of his hand, the better to leave no trace on the button. In less than ten seconds, Donna's voice came over the intercom. "Yes?"

"Hi, babe," he said. "My hands are full. Can you let me in?"

"Be a sec," she told him.

He took the satin belt from his pocket as he waited. He pictured her route from the back of the house. He twisted the satin around his hands and snapped it tight. Once she opened the door, he'd have to move like lightning. He'd have only one chance to fling the cord around her neck. The advantage he already possessed was surprise.

He heard her footsteps on the limestone. He gripped the satin and prepared. He thought of Michael. He thought of her together with Michael. He thought of his Asian erotica. He thought of betrayal, failure, and trust. She deserved this. They both deserved it. He was only sorry he couldn't kill Michael right now too.

When the door swung open, he heard her say, "Doug! I thought you said—"

And then he was on her. He leapt. He yanked the belt around her neck. He dragged her swiftly out of the house. He tightened it and tightened it and tightened it and tightened it. She was too startled to fight back. In the five seconds it took her to get her hands to the belt in a reflex attempt to pull it away from her throat, he had it digging into her skin so deeply that her scrabbling fingers could find no slip of material to grab on to.

He felt her go limp. He said, "Jesus. Yes. *Yes*."

And then it happened.

The lights went on in the house. A mariachi band started playing. People shouted, "Surprise! Surprise! Sur—"

Douglas looked up, panting, from the body of his wife, into popping flashes and a video camcorder. The joyous shouting from within his house was cut off by a female shriek. He dropped Donna to the ground and stared without comprehension into the entry and beyond that the living room. There, at least two dozen people were gathered beneath a banner that said SURPRISE, DOUGIE! HAPPY FIVE-FIVE!

He saw the horrified faces of his brothers and their wives and children, of his own children, of his parents, of one of his former wives. Among them, his colleagues and his secretary. The chief of police. The mayor.

He thought, What is this, Donna? Some kind of joke?

And then he saw Michael coming from the direction of the kitchen, Michael with a birthday cake in his hands, Michael saying, "Did we surprise him, Donna? Poor Doug. I hope his heart—" And then saying nothing at all when he saw his brother and his brother's wife.

Shit, Douglas thought. What have I done?

That, indeed, was the question he'd be answering for the rest of his life.

AMEL BENABOURA was born in 1966 in Algeria, and started to write at a very young age. She has written three crime novels, all of which have been published in France to critical acclaim. Several of her stories have also been published in Czechoslovakian and German. This is her first story to be published in the United States. She lives in Algeria with her husband and two children.

Only a Woman

Amel Benaboura

Translated from the French by Jeremy L. Paretsky

"Ikrame, go see who's knocking at the door," her mother calls from the kitchen.

The little girl carefully stores her little picture book under a pillow and runs to the door. Suddenly she freezes. Suppose it's Nabil? No, Nabil has a key. Furthermore, he never knocks before entering. Ikrame gets up on tiptoes in her slippered feet, works the bolt, and opens the door. A lady is standing on the landing, tall, beautiful, wrapped in a velvet coat. Her manner of dress disturbs the child, who glances fearfully toward the staircase. Suppose her brother Nabil saw that! she thinks, shuddering.

"Are you Yamina's little sister?" the lady asks.

"Yes."

"Is she home?"

Ikrame raises her fingers to her mouth in an agony of indecision. She hesitates at the foolhardy getup of this unknown woman. "Nabil doesn't like women who wear European clothes," she thinks it necessary to point out.

"Oh? And why?"

"He says that women who do not wear the *hajib* aren't real Muslims and deserve to be punished."

The lady pats her on the cheek. "He's entitled to think whatever he wants, but that doesn't mean he's right. Go tell your sister that Mrs. Raïs is here."

Ikrame acknowledges this with a nod and runs to her sister's room.

Yamina is feeling the bruises on her face. Her hand is shaking as she picks up the mirror. The olive-dark circles ringing her eyes are still there. The swollen lip deforms her mouth. The scar on her cheek is hideous.

She drops the mirror, weary, infuriated, her face haggard.

"Tell her I've gone out."

Ikrame raises her eyebrows in amazement. "I can't lie to her. That's a sin. Nabil hates liars. He beats them horribly."

Against her will Yamina gets up painfully and follows her little sister. The lady heaves a sigh of relief. "Thank God, you're on your feet. I thought you'd been laid up by some illness. I . . . Good God! What's happened to you, my dear?"

Yamina invites the visitor in, conducts her to the living room, and offers her a rickety chair. Mrs. Raïs sits down, mouth agape, incredulous. She lets out a squeak: "My poor girl!"

"Please," Yamina begs, "let it be."

They remain silent for a long while, Mrs. Raïs unable to find her voice and Yamina leaning against the wall. "Was it an accident?" the visitor mumbles at last.

Yamina asks her younger sister to go fetch a cup of coffee for the lady. Then she lets herself drop down onto a pillow, not raising her head. "Why have you come, Mrs. Raïs?"

"Come now, it's the least I could do. You're not in the habit of being gone two weeks in a row without letting us know. We're beginning to worry about you at the office."

"That's all over and done with."

"What is?"

"The office!" Yamina groans, as though something is caught in her throat.

Mrs. Raïs does not quite seem to catch on. "What exactly does that mean?"

"I'm not going to work anymore. I'm finished with it."

"That I understood. But why? Is it because of Redouane? You know very well that he loves to tease the girls. I'll admit he's something of a creep, but he doesn't have any ulterior motives."

Yamina pushes her hair to one side and continues to stare at the floor. Slowly her shoulders hunch and start to shake. Her sobs suddenly pour forth into the silence of the room.

Mrs. Raïs gets up from her chair and goes over to put her arm compassionately around her. "Oh, my dear, my poor little darling, why, what's the matter? Won't you tell me anything? I'm your friend. Confide in me. Every problem has a solution."

"You're wasting your time," Yamina's mother says as she comes in with a tray.

Mrs. Raïs gets up, kisses the mother respectfully on the forehead, and introduces herself. "I am a colleague of your daughter. Since we've had no sign of life from her for two weeks, the director told me to come and see what the matter was. What has happened to your daughter?"

"The same thing that happens to girls in this country every day," the mother sighs sadly.

Yamina looks up and pleads with her mother to be quiet. The old woman shrugs, puts the tray down on a pedestal table, and sets about pouring the coffee into three cups. "I ruined my own life for her education," she begins in the singsong voice of a storyteller. "I suffered night and day, did all sorts of degrading jobs so that she could earn the degrees she needed. But instead, when she became an executive in some firm, she abandoned—"

"Mother—"

"Be quiet! I sacrificed my best years for your education. You don't have any right to give up. Go back to work. It's the only friend you'll ever have. One day I'm going to die. Nabil will marry, have children, and start to want the house all for himself. He'll throw you out, you and Ikrame. Only, then you'll be sorry for what you do today."

Mrs. Raïs guesses that something serious has happened. The mother explains.

"It's her stupid brother, Nabil, who's plaguing her. He's one of those 'enlightened.' He can speak only in terms of prohibitions. To listen to him you'd think the whole world was a garbage dump, where everything is noxious and disgusting. He's riding like hell all over her. He throws everything she does back in her face, but privately he admits to me that it's only because he's jealous of seeing her succeed, where he always seems to fail. So he beats her. Each time her scars close, he manages to make them bleed again, just to keep her locked away. He has forbidden her to take work anywhere men are around. As far as he is concerned, any place where women and men get together is suspect, unhealthy, accursed. He says he is ashamed to see his sister make herself up indecently, so that every morning she can go join the 'incubuses' and other degenerates that lurk behind the walls of the firm."

Mrs. Raïs is not unduly astonished. At the same time she cannot approve of her colleague's decision. "It's not that bad, Yamina. You're an executive, remember that. You're not going to turn your back on all the years you put in at the university, just because some ignoramus of a brother—"

"He swore he would kill me!" Yamina explodes.

"They all say they'll do that. We're not cattle."

"He's a lout. He's capable of anything."

"He makes you believe it, dear. Come now, the age of the all-powerful male is over and done with."

"He's a brute, a brute!"

The lady is deeply moved; she stretches out her hand to tilt up Yamina's face lined with scars, and looks her in the eyes. "I, too, am a woman. What you resent, I, too, have suffered. I have been forbidden to do things, and I have received affronts and warnings for my actions. But I answered back. I took responsibility for myself. I fought like a maniac. Today I enjoy the well-earned rest of a successful warrior. I marked out my road with my own hands. I go where I want, with my head held high. And know that I married the man I love. We can no longer speak of acquiescence. We must resist, always resist, even if it's just on principle. If we oppose *them,* we can escape their control once and for all."

"My brother is a ravenous beast. Nothing anyone says or does makes any impression on him."

"So? Our ribs are not some stepladder at the disposal of others. This coming Friday, the Women's Association is organizing a march to protest against men's unpunished acts of violence, and for the liberation of women. You should come with us and cry out your bitterness and defiance for our whole society to hear."

"You're crazy!"

"If you come— Look at me. I am a woman who burst her bonds, who threw off the straitjacket of prejudices and taboos. I said enough! I am *free*. No one will ever put *me* back on a leash again."

Yamina's head sinks down; she hunches her shoulders and cries. Her mother leaves the living room, muttering her annoyance. Through the window the sun is casting its late afternoon light on the two women who stand facing each other.

"Go away," Yamina begs.

"I'm not going, my dear."

"Oh yes, you must, and right away. You don't know what you're talking about. You've had some good luck, but not me. It's not that I've given up. I never had the nerve to begin with. This discussion is pointless! You ask me to look at you, but you forget to take a look at me, *me*. You don't see my flayed face, my bent back, my haunted eyes."

Mrs. Raïs suppresses an involuntary whimper of rage. Her hands shake, doing their utmost to shape the air, to give form to her anger. "I can see you perfectly, Yamina. They are trying to make you believe that you don't count, that you are *nothing*, nothing but a bruise that can't be comforted. But that's not true. Sharpen your nails, make them into claws to defend yourself with, to tear out *their* eyes with, to bite and to scream. If their arms are stronger and their blows nastier, fight back with your heart. Remind yourself how many times a day you bend your back. Think of your luscious cheeks under *their* blows, of your ears under *their* reprimands. Then your tongue will become a wild, unleashed tentacle, whipping out of control; it will be your instrument for expressing your silences, your refusals, your thirst for a life of dignity. You are the warrior's hope and his mother as well, or have you forgotten this?"

Nabil is beside himself with fury. With a predatory glare his eyes dart arrows at his younger sister, who is forbidden to be in the hall. His breathing fills the house with an apocalyptic rumbling.

His mother is at her prayers. Veiled from head to foot, she is silently reciting verses from the Koran. She leans forward, straightens up, kneels and prostrates herself, facing east.

Nabil shakes with all his being. His mother finishes praying and puts the mat away in a recess. "All right, where is she?" thunders her son.

His mother turns away, unable to bear the burning gaze of her offspring. He grabs her by the shoulders and forces her to turn. His saliva splatters the old woman when he growls, "Where did she go?"

His mother quivers with rage and tears away the talons clutching her shoulders. "Cursed be the day that saw you born! How dare you raise your hand against your mother!"

Nabil works his jaws as he snarls, "I'll bet she's gone and taken part in that women's protest march."

His mother's gaze wavers. Nabil immediately sees that he has hit the mark. He utters a wild yell and rushes down the stairs. The few children who are playing on the sidewalk clear off, frightened away by this human tornado.

Nabil looks all around him, trying to spot a friend with a car. He hails a young neighbor on a motorcycle, climbs on behind him, and orders him to drive to Martyrs' Square.

About a hundred women, banners held aloft, are clustered together in a small group on the esplanade, under the mocking gaze of the idlers. Nabil dashes into the crowd, punching with his elbows as he pushes his way roughly through them, spitting and hitting out to clear a path. There is a buzzing in his head. It howls to him in a voice full of malice, "That demon, that bitch, she dared to disobey the law." He brushes women aside, looking, looking. Every glance, every back turned to him, every gesture inflames his hatred. For a moment he imagines himself armed with a flamethrower, setting these cows, these whores, these witches on fire. His eyes glitter with murderous sparks. The voice in his head buzzes, "Sluts! sluts!" He knocks a woman down and tramples on her as he flails all around him.

A touch of panic rattles the march. Shouts ring out. "He's crazy!" Nabil hears nothing. Coming upon a cluster of demonstrators he sees *her*! There she is, standing in front of him, wrapped in that skirt he can't stand. She sees him coming. She waits for him . . . without wavering . . . without drawing back. . . .

"She's sneering at you," the voice ululates. "She's taunting you, she's challenging you, the bitch!"

On her lightly made-up face there is a smile, a sardonic smile that has always rubbed him raw. He thrusts his hand into his jacket. His fist closes around a knife. Bitch! Whore! He strikes—just under the left breast, there! where the soul of perversity lurks. Then in the left kidney. Next a thrust to the stomach, at the height of the navel. Each stab is like the release of an electric charge. His sister's blood spurts out. Smoking-hot red spots splash onto his wrist. In his head the murmuring of the voice mounts until it reaches an unbearable intensity. He is now quite mad.

The day wanes, the twilight sun flickering like a dim lamp placed in a room where the dead are laid out. Night falls as if the sun were putting on mourning for love betrayed. Shortly the moon will insinuate its eye like a hole punctured in the faceless sky. The rain is weeping on the city.* Yamina doesn't notice it. She is floating in a universe shrouded in fog, a glacial, echoless place. She is already wandering in some parallel world. A voice calls out to her. Is it someone trying to attract her attention? Or is she only talking to herself. She does not know.

* "La pluie pleut sur la ville." Cf. Paul Verlaine, "Il pleut dans mon coeur / comme il pleut sur la ville . . ." (Trans.).

The place makes a turn and becomes a dark river. Yamina is a pebble, a bit of wreckage, a suicidal wave. She is a path wandering through a graveyard, a cobblestone humping up in the roadbed like a fossilized bruise, a bend in the road surprised and trapped by a dead end, and she is the crowd turned to stone as it watches her die.

Die? Is living all she ever did? Did she ever kiss the mouth of one she loved, did she ever shiver under a loving caress, or weep the orgasm of a body set free, of a body that shouts for joy?

In her death throes she returns to a yesterday rendered phantasmal like an illusion. A woman . . . to be a woman . . . to be nothing, nothing but a woman . . . To be of no account . . . deprived of hope . . . To be nothing but a bundle of sour wounds, blackened by the fates. Cursed be yesterday, a wretched sleepwalker lurching about in the infinite night.

Her mouth fills with blood, a blood that intoxicates her. She no longer recognizes her brother. She no longer even remembers him. Is it because he has disowned her?

She drops to her knees, the upper part of her body sways, she falls. Her face crashes against the roadway, her gaze fixed on something not there.

She is no longer anything, only a virgin who has just flickered out like a candle in a room where the dead are laid out.* She has flickered out like the day, at that hour when the sun crucifies itself on the shirttail of the horizon.

* Play on *cierge* and *vierge* (Trans.).

DOROTHY SALISBURY DAVIS received the Grandmaster Award of the Mystery Writers of America in 1985. Her early novels and short stories held close to her Midwestern roots, but after *A Gentle Murderer* was published in 1951, New York became the scene of her fiction. The author of twenty novels and twenty-four short stories, Mrs. Davis has been nominated for the Edgar award seven times and is a member of the Adams Round Table.

Miles to Go

Dorothy Salisbury Davis

Laura set her weekend bag, her purse, and the gifts of chocolate creams—one for her aunt Mattie and one for her father-in-law—by the hall door. She tucked a scarf into the pocket of her reversible where it hung on a hall tree and went to find her husband. You could smell the paint throughout the apartment, and God knows, the whole apartment needed painting. It was in anticipation of a financial gift from her aunt Mattie that they decided to go ahead with the paint job now. Tim wanted to see how much he could do himself while she was away.

The paint bucket gave a perilous shudder as he came down the ladder. Much better for her nerves, Laura thought, that she was getting out of the house. Tim stooped low and Laura stood on tiptoe to kiss him. He was a tall man and she had to stretch to make five feet two. They were both crowding middle age, married for almost twenty years. No children. Alas! both of them always added. Tim worked variously in the entertainment field, a magician who built his own illusions, a folk singer who improvised modern metaphors on old legends. He made most of his living in summer camps. He was what those with scorn for the race —or so much pride in it they could not abide mere affinity —called a professional Irishman. Laura was a lay teacher of English and music at a convent school just up the Hudson River from New York. The Mallorys owned the apartment on the Upper West Side, partnered to be sure with Chemical

Bank. Large and high-ceilinged, it was full of books, the tools of Tim's trades, and quite a number of things having nothing to do with modern employment, such as a spinning wheel, a loom, and a butter churn streaming now with ivy. Laura would be driving home from Vermont with the grandfather clock that had been in her family for more than a hundred years. It was a trip she cherished. She loved to drive. Tim was barely tolerant of her Honda, a 1993 Accord LX coupe, feeling it was built for Japanese midgets. He liked to say that if they had put the front seat in backward, and he lowered the back of the rear seat so that he could extend his legs into the trunk, it would just about fit him. Otherwise that convenience was great for a Christmas tree or, in the present circumstances, for the grandfather clock.

"You have the map and a flashlight," Tim started his usual rundown. "Take the cellular phone. I'll only get it all paint if you leave it here."

"I don't need it, Tim. Aunt Mattie would say it's an affectation."

"So is a grandfather clock."

"Tim . . ."

"Okay, okay. Just drive carefully. It's a car, not a palomino pony you're driving. If it starts to rain skip the hospital. You can call them when you get to your aunt's. And call me when you get there. Promise?"

"On my palomino," she said.

When they reached the door he said, "Give Dad my love. I'll write him soon. And mind you don't commit us with the hospital people, not yet."

"Wasn't it decent of them to let me come today?" Laura said.

"They can't wait to see you," Tim mocked. "I'll expect you back Sunday night."

Laura had taken that afternoon and Friday off. Friday was St. Patrick's Day and most of the school was going to the annual parade on Fifth Avenue. She tried not to show how eager she was to get away. "I wish you were coming with me."

"To watch the speedometer," Tim said.

He waited at the apartment door until the elevator arrived, an ancient carriage of brass and wood paneling. A prickle of anxiety caught at Laura as she touched the lobby button. It passed with the door's closing and she put it out of her mind.

Once in the car she was in her element, secure. She made a U-turn out of the parking space and headed for the West Side Highway, accelerating to beat the first traffic light. The car seemed to anticipate her, leaping ahead. "Go for it, baby," she said, and patted the puffed-up center of the steering wheel, fat thing. It carried its air bag like a pregnancy.

The river was pewter gray and choppy with only occasional tugboat and barge traffic. Most of the pleasure boats were still in drydock. She could remember snow on St. Patrick's Day. This part of the drive was familiar, her schoolday route. Yet she rarely drove it without seeking something new to weave into the pattern of her day's work. It was not easy to match imaginations with the young.

When she passed her usual turnoff, her mind went solely to the first stop on her journey. Tim didn't have to tell her not to commit them to the care and guardianship of his father. Guardianship? He hadn't used the word but it had occurred in their communication with the hospital. She and Tim had talked for years about the possibility of taking his father into their home when the authorities considered it feasible. When Aunt Mattie decided to give them their inheritance before her demise, they could no longer weigh their finances into the decision. The moment of truth was near. She was not afraid of the old man; nor was Tim. If Tim feared anything, it had to do with being his father's son. Joseph Mallory had killed a man and had been confined for the past fifteen years in a psychiatric hospital.

Word would get out that Joseph Mallory was living with them. It had been a well-known case at the time. She had sat in the courtroom among a passionate lot of Mallory partisans. They brought him oranges and cigarettes, and the bailiffs allowed the gifts to be passed along. The courtroom had to be cleared when Mallory was found not guilty by reason of insanity. They had wanted him exonerated.

By the time she turned off the Taconic Parkway the sky had grown lumpy with clouds too swift for the rain, too heavy for the sun to part. The hills were a tawny stubble, patched with the brown of early plowing, the green of winter wheat. Greening willow trees hung over the reservoirs. It was almost spring.

The hospital gates were closed. On regular visiting days they were open, a larger staff perhaps. The gatekeeper came out of his shelter and checked her identification. She signed his register and tried to fix in her mind his direction to the Administration Building, where she was expected. Groundsmen were raking leaves. Traffic was sparse, mostly delivery trucks. Signs pointed to Laundry, Rehabilitation, Workshop, Drug Center, a Children's Unit. It always surprised her that there was a children's facility in a place like this. Their building was like the rest, dusty yellow brick. Not a swing or a jungle gym in sight. She drove into the Administration lot and parked the Honda among cars more expensive than itself, most with MD license plates.

It was not until she was waiting alone in the reception office that she remembered the chocolates she had brought her father-in-law. She had left them in the car. The question of whether to go back for them was settled when the attendant said Dr. Burns's secretary would be right along. Dr. Burns was superintendent of the hospital. When the attendant turned his back she could see the outline of a gun and holster beneath his uniform jacket. She looked up quickly to the one picture on the wall, a huge golden eagle with the American flag clutched in its talons. This was a terrible place, she thought, to call a hospital.

Dr. Burns's secretary was male, all male to judge by his size and the shoulders that shaped him like a triangle. He did try to accommodate his step to hers as they clattered down the corridor. She could hear the broken rhythm of her own footfalls. "Do you know Mr. Mallory?" she inquired.

"Uncle Joe? Oh, sure. Everybody knows Uncle Joe. He's a card."

There didn't seem to be anything else to say. "I brought him some candy and then left it in the car."

"He's not much for sweets as I remember."

"What could I bring him that he'd like?"

"A songbook maybe. He's taken up music lately."

Dr. Burns, too, spoke of Joe Mallory's turn to music. "We got him a violin and he's taught himself to play it. He's very good—I'm something of an amateur musician myself." The hospital superintendent took her from his office to a small adjoining sitting room—plastic chairs, ceiling light, one window, and a small round table with a white chrysanthemum in its center. Burns was a rumpled-looking man with tired eyes and a mustache that needed trimming. Laura thought a violin would become him. "I've sent for Mr. Mallory. You'll be comfortable in here and you and I can talk afterwards. I wouldn't mention to him what you wrote me. Unless you already have?"

"No."

"Time enough."

Laura was looking out the window when two men came in view, one wearing a white hospital uniform, the other a heavy sweater that looked to weigh him down, Joe Mallory. He had to skip a step now and then to keep up with the orderly. She waved when they were near, and the old man saw her. He pulled himself up and saluted, military fashion.

He was even more jaunty when he came into the room and held out his arms to her. She said it to herself every time: If she had not been at the trial, she wouldn't believe this man could commit murder. They pulled up two chairs to the table. Mallory took the white chrysanthemum to the window. The sill was too narrow. He set it on the floor. "Flowers should come in colors," he said, and pulled his chair closer to hers. "I've never got over the Easter lily they gave me to carry on Holy Thursday. The smell of it made me sick and I threw up right in the middle of the procession. You came alone again, did you?"

"Tim sends you all his love."

"There must be more of it than I'm getting," the old man said, "or it wouldn't be worth sending." He blinked his very blue but rather cold eyes at her. "Is he ashamed of me? It's far too late for that. I get letters to this day from people saying they're proud to have known me. And me with no recollection of them at all." He glanced at the office door and leaned toward her. "I think they're intercepting any letters I get now. I'll tell you why in a minute. And listening in on everything. If we was to turn up this table, do you think we'd find one of them listening gadgets? Or in the blossom I took from the table? Oh, I'm serious. If you was to look on the other side of that door, you'd see Leroy sitting there, his chair tilted to the wall, and his ear bent to the crack. He's the one brought me over. His name isn't Leroy, but I call him that. You have to feel superior to somebody in this place that isn't in a worse state than yourself. Do you think Tim's afraid of me—my bucking boy who pretends he's an Irishman when it suits him? I don't like a man who denies his blood."

"But he doesn't deny it, Joe. He was born in this country, remember."

"Will I ever forget it, the death of his darling mother."

"That's not fair," Laura said softly. Tim was hard enough on himself for all the sadness in his life.

"Then I'm the blame!"

"Must there be blame?"

Mallory sat back in his chair. He puckered his lips thoughtfully. "You're a soft woman, Laura. He's lucky. I wish I'd seen you first myself."

Laura was straining to be natural. "Is it true, everybody calls you Uncle Joe?"

The old man chortled, more at her clumsiness, she thought, than at the benevolence of institution and residents. "Somebody must have started it and the rest picked it up and passed it around. You know I've been studying the law. Did they tell you that?"

"And the violin," she said.

"Oh, they'd tell you that all right, but not about me informing myself of the law in as rare a case as mine—as the law was fifteen years ago and is today. I learned the ins and outs of it pretty damn well. Then I wrote the governor a masterful petition for retrial. I pointed out that the insanity plea on which I was acquitted would not stand up today. Whereas if I'd been convicted of murder in the second degree I'd have been eligible for parole two years ago. I was a pawn of the politicians. I had a court-appointed lawyer with a brogue as thick as you'd hear in County Mayo. He thought himself a genius getting me put in here instead of the brig. And me a hero. Oh, yes! The blow I struck was for Ireland when I cleaved his skull in two. He was on the docks and supposed to be handing off the occasional crate of rifles marked for Arabia to them who'd see them transported to Ireland. . . ."

Laura had heard him tell the story before. He told it often, filling in more and more details that were utterly blank to him at the time. Certified by three psychiatrists. The transport worker he killed had betrayed the very men to whom he was handing off the munitions: he was that dread character in Irish lore, an informer.

"So what does the governor say?" Laura eased the question in.

"I've not heard a word, and my informant in the bureaucracy here tells me the bastards never sent him the petition at all. That's enough. I'll not spoil your visit. Time is no longer of the essence to me as it must be to you. It was grand of you to come. Is it the same little car you have?"

"It's my love," she said.

"I can understand that. Where is it again you're going?"

Laura explained.

The old man pushed away from the table. "I'm going to ask Leroy to run back for my fiddle. I'd play you a tune before you go." He pulled open the office door without knocking. The orderly was sitting, his chair tilted against the door frame, even as Mallory had foretold of him. "So you see, I'm not paranoid," the old man said, returning to the table. "We're supposed to stay close as Siamese, him and me, but there are privileges to be had if you know when to behave and when to act up. Do you follow the news, Laura?"

"Not as closely as I'd like to."

"Come on, girl. If you wanted to follow it closely, you would."

Laura nodded.

"Do you believe there's going to be peace in Ireland now?"

"I hope so."

"Would you rather peace or justice?"

"Why can't there be both?"

"Well, they've sent a fellow over here now who'd say you're right, and he's getting a hero's welcome—a new fashion in heroes." He looked about as though for a place to spit.

A few minutes later the orderly returned and handed in the violin case with the admonition "You don't have much time, Uncle Joe."

"As though I have anything else," the old man said, and took the violin from the case as tenderly as he might a baby from its cradle. He tuned the strings to a pitch pipe he put back in the case.

The orderly returned to his tilted chair and closed the office door three quarters this time.

Mallory tightened the bow and started to play. The tunes were out of a beginner's manual—"Humoresque," "The Old Refrain." Laura was moved that he had wanted to play for her and pondered again what it would be like if he came to live with Tim and her.

Mallory tuned one of the strings while Laura said how good he was. He winked at her then, tapped a martial beat with his foot, and sawed the strings in a wild lament that was more a wail than a melody. Bagpipes could not have screeched worse.

Both the orderly and Dr. Burns burst in from the office. The old man, a gleam in his eyes, kept playing until the orderly confronted him, hands half clutched. Mallory waited till the last minute and then handed over fiddle and bow.

"They'll be waiting for you, Uncle Joe," the orderly said. He put the instrument in its case.

Laura's father-in-law came to her, his hands outstretched. He pulled her to her feet and kissed her on the mouth. "I'd go to the gate with you, darling, if they weren't waiting for me in Babel." At the hall door he imperiously motioned Leroy out ahead of him. He turned and threw Laura a kiss.

She remembered the chocolates again. Again too late.

Dr. Burns joined Laura in the sitting room as soon as Mallory and the orderly had gone. He closed the hall door. "Would you rather talk here or in my office, Mrs. Mallory? People come and go in there. Better here perhaps. How did you find the old gentleman? He looks well, doesn't he?"

"Is he not, Doctor?"

"Not my meaning. He takes good care of himself. With our help, of course." While he spoke he retrieved the chrysanthemum from where Mallory had set it on the floor and put it on the table again. Laura wondered at the possibility of a listening device. Surely not. Once again she sat at the little table. The doctor straddled a chair. "You didn't mention to your father-in-law your inquiry about his possible release?"

"No."

"I wonder what his reaction would have been. He likes it here, you know."

"That's hard to believe," Laura said.

"Well, for one thing, he's top banana." Dr. Burns laughed a little. Not easy for him. "He taught me the expression—top banana. He talks about his son being in show business. Says he taught him all he knows. And he is clever. I'm not sure what to say to you, Mrs. Mallory. There are times—" He broke off when his secretary came in bringing two mugs of coffee. "Here we are. Sugar and something like milk can be provided. . . ."

"Just black," Laura said.

"Not exactly down home. You've met Tony? Yes, of course, when you arrived. Thank you, Tony. I'll be available in a few minutes, tell them if they're waiting for me."

The secretary retreated into the office and Laura said that she had to go soon, that most of her trip lay ahead of her.

"Miles to go before you sleep," the doctor quoted.

She nodded and sipped the coffee, bitter as alum.

"We do review your father-in-law's case periodically, you understand. I've said he likes it here. I'm not sure that's true. He's a great manipulator."

"He's an Irishman," Laura said.

The doctor smiled. It was spontaneous and she liked him better. "What about these Irish fraternal organizations he talks about? He gets letters from them now and then, harmless things, like 'Cheer up, the world's not getting better waiting for you. . . .' We used to censor mention of Irish politics, but with things looking better, and he is allowed newspapers . . . but what I want to ask you: Would any of these organizations help you support him?"

"I don't know. I don't even know the names of them—except when they march on St. Patrick's Day."

"That's coming up tomorrow, isn't it? Let me get Mallory's file. Do you want more coffee?"

Laura shook her head and said, "Thank you." Her cup was more than half full.

"Don't throw it in the plant," the doctor said. "It's had its quota for the week."

Laura leaned back and relaxed for the first time since arriving. They were human here after all. Which, strangely, made her want to reconsider the enormous undertaking of making a home for a man who had been institutionalized for fifteen years. She remembered the dog Tim and she had bought from a kennel. They got it cheap because it had been living in the kennel for two years. The first day in the house it bit Tim and wouldn't let him come near Laura.

Dr. Burns was gone for several minutes. She could hear him on the telephone and sounds within the building seemed to be picking up, muted bells and intercom messages. She supposed that, as in all hospitals, they had their evening meal early. Daylight was fading and it looked as though it might be raining. She did not know why but she

did not want to get up and go to look out the window, and
she thought of the moment of fear in the elevator, at home,
and then of a tale from her adolescence involving an elevator: "Room for One More." One thing about growing up,
you didn't enjoy getting spooked anymore.

The doctor returned, apologized, and forgot to bring the
file with him. He called out to his secretary. But just as Tony
came into the room, an alarm sounded on the intercom
system. Laura could feel the shock of it at the back of her
neck. It was an eerie repetitive hee-haw, like the bray of a
donkey. Both men stood still and counted. The signal was
repeated. Dr. Burns excused himself to Laura and instructed
the secretary to stay with her, but to monitor communications. He returned to his office, half closing the door this
time so that Laura could only see him go toward his desk
and soon come back from it. She wondered if he had
stopped there for a gun. "Check seventeen, will you?" he
said to Tony, and left by the hall door.

Laura knew from having written Joe Mallory that Block
Seventeen was part of his address. She followed Tony to the
door of the office. He watched her, waiting for his call to get
through. The braying signal let up. She could hear her own
heartbeat drumming in her ears. Tony spoke on the phone
and then listened for what seemed a long time. Laura leaned
on the frame of the door. The secretary signaled her to take
one of the office chairs. She remained standing at the door.
When he hung up the phone he said to Laura, "Mr. Mallory
is in his room."

"Thank God," Laura said, "and thank you for telling me."

"It could be a false alarm. That's happened before. I'm
sorry you had to get caught in it."

"I don't think I ought to wait for Dr. Burns. . . ."

The secretary was shaking his head. "The building's
sealed. Nobody leaves just now. Why don't you sit down
again? I'll bring you a magazine or two. Can't keep them in
here. They disappear."

Laura was not going to remember a single word she read.
What kept going through her mind was that they had

checked out *Joe Mallory*. That had to mean something, some appraisal of his behavior. But what? And it was strange how they had broken in on his playing a dirge. If she didn't get away soon, she would backtrack on the whole idea of taking him into Tim's and her home. A few minutes later one long bray came over the alarm system. Tony came to the door and said he'd been right. It was a false alarm.

She waited another twenty minutes. Dr. Burns had not returned. Alarms must upset the inmates. Not inmates, patients. It was ridiculous but her nerves were getting ragged. She looked into the office where the secretary, his back to her, was working on a computer. She put on her coat and simply walked out the hall door and down the corridor by which she had entered. The guard checked her pass and opened the heavy door to let her out into a drizzle of rain.

The Honda was sitting alone, the cars with MD registrations she had parked between were gone. When she got in, she patted the steering wheel. "Oh, baby, am I glad to see you."

There was even less traffic on the grounds than when she had arrived, but lights had come on in all the buildings, and she told herself she ought not let her imagination run wild. It was a shabby thing she had done, leaving without a word. A little more courage and she'd go back. No way, not tonight. At the gate she was required to sign out. A state trooper got into his cruiser and with a wave to the gateman, followed her off the grounds. As soon as they hit the highway, he turned on his flashers and passed her, picking up speed. "Follow that car!" she said aloud, and wished she could. Not on a winding, two-way road. She intended to go on to the Taconic Parkway, but to get away from traffic decided on Route 22 for part of the way. It was getting dark too soon. In the rearview mirror she saw that the sky was brighter behind her than ahead. She also saw a car turn in where she had turned. He gained speed until he was almost up to her. She slowed down to let him pass. He slowed down. She accelerated. So did he.

"We didn't need this," she said, again aloud. She did not

like driving scared. She settled for fifty-five miles per hour; so did the driver behind her, and the uneasiness let up a little. She had read somewhere that fear and guilt went together. *Mea culpa, mea culpa.* It wasn't as though she'd let Joe Mallory himself down. Not yet anyway. She braked suddenly when a rabbit dashed into the road. It zigzagged in front of her, and kept to the road. Finally, she doused her lights. A pale, damp twilight. When she turned them up again, the rabbit was gone. But the driver behind her had kept even pace. There was a car behind him now too. She hoped it would follow him until she could get to the village ahead. Then, as they approached it, she decided to take a chance that he would turn off there. He didn't but the car behind him did, and she was soon beyond the village. She was in farm country, hollows in the road and fog she drifted into and out of. The rear of the car gave a thump. She didn't think she had hit an animal. It came again. She slowed down and checked the dashboard. Normal. Then she looked in the rearview mirror.

In the light of an oncoming car, she saw Joe Mallory palely, a face without a body. She swerved wildly, the right wheels jolting off the pavement.

"It's Joe Mallory, for the love of God," the old man called out. Stowed away in the trunk, he had pushed down the backseat and was pulling himself through the opening. "Keep us out of the ditch, girl!" and when she braked, "Don't stop!"

The Honda thumped itself back onto the pavement. Laura's mouth was so dry she couldn't speak. Her hands quivered on the steering wheel. Behind her the old man was struggling out of a white jacket such as Leroy wore. The car behind overtook them and slowed down alongside.

"Wave him on or I'll kill him," the old man shouted.

Laura waved. She did not look, afraid to take her eyes off the road. The driver gave his horn several jolly beeps and sped into the night.

Mallory pulled the coat off. "Free at last! Free at last!" he sang out. "I'll crawl up with you in a minute. Have you no radio in the car?"

"No."

"Mother of God."

Laura coaxed saliva into her mouth. "I park on the street overnight. The one in my last car was stolen."

"Savages." Then: "What did that sign say?" They had come up on a road sign and passed it.

"I didn't notice."

"Damn it to hell, I'm here without my glasses. Where are we?"

"On Route 22, going north."

"I don't want to go north. Turn around the first chance you get."

"Let's go back," Laura said. "You shouldn't be here, Joe. They'll never let you out and Tim and I asked if they would soon."

"The hell you did, and him never writing to me. Don't lie to me, girl. They wouldn't even send my brief to the governor." A hand with fingers like talons grasped her shoulder. "I'm not going back so get it out of your head. I never heard of Route 22. Keep going ahead till I get my bearings. Isn't it a wonder I'm here at all?"

Laura didn't say anything.

A brief silence. Then she thought he was chuckling. "The key in the very place I taught him to hide it when he was a kid. They don't make bumpers like that anymore, but it was there."

Laura knew what he was talking about although she'd forgotten: After she had once locked herself out of the car, Tim had soldered a pocket on the underside of the bumper.

"Drive easy, I'm coming up front with you." He reached forward and put something on the passenger seat, a small, snub-nosed gun, terrible to see in the pale light of the dashboard. She wanted to grab it and throw it out the window but she was as afraid of the gun as she was of him. She opened the wrong window and closed it. He cursed the headrest as he twisted around and came over feet first.

Sneakers, thin pants, and a sweater. His knees on the seat, he put the gun in his pocket and pushed the back of the rear seat into place, closing the trunk.

"Bastards won't even give you a belt to hold your pants up with." He wriggled around, a slight, wiry figure on the seat beside her. But deadly. Or was he?

"Is the gun loaded?"

"Ha! Would I carry a dummy?" He giggled and then laughed. He rocked back and forth in the seat, the laughter bubbling out of him. It quieted down to a cough. Finally: "You want to know where I got it, don't you?"

"No. I want you to throw it away and let me take you back." Once she had spoken she knew she could speak, and it occurred to her then, she had a mighty weapon of her own, the car, the Honda, which Tim said would go through hoops for her. "Listen to me, Joe. Dr. Burns asked me if some of the Gaelic organizations—the ones who wrote to you—he wanted to know if they'd help support you if you came to live with Tim and me. Now do you believe me?"

"Tell it to me again. My ears are stopped up."

She repeated more or less what she had said.

"Bloody spy. He was looking for information. Did he say the word 'Gaelic'?"

"He did," she lied.

"And what did you tell him?"

"I never got to tell him anything. The alarm cut us off."

He was on the verge of laughing again. He choked it back. "And me lying in my bed innocent as a babe."

"Yes," she said.

"What do you know about it? Nothing. I was under the bed, and Leroy rolled up like a pig in the blankets."

Dead? she wondered. She wondered also at the strength and agility of the man beside her. The orderly must weigh nearly two hundred pounds.

"What are we going this way for? Read me the road signs we come to."

Laura missed the next ones purposely; chief among the directions was that to the Taconic Parkway. She said she was sorry, and began to contrive a desperate gambit. When the next sign came, it also pointed to the Taconic. She read it aloud, but took the road in the opposite direction.

"How long before we'll make the city?"

"Two hours."

"They'll be looking for me with dogs by then. Is there no way you can go by side roads?"

"I can try. Where do you want me to take you?"

"Aren't you taking me home? Isn't that what you said you came for? Won't Tim be waiting for us?"

"Okay, Joe. Let's go for it." She drew a deep breath and took firm hold of the steering wheel.

"I'm pulling your leg, girl. Isn't that the first place they'd look? You'll put me down near the heart of the city, and I'll get lost among my own. I'll have a night on the town." Once again he broke into high, hysterical laughter.

Laura, trying to watch both him and the road, came up too fast on a broken-down car, the driver outside it trying to steer and push it off the road. She swerved wildly and must have missed the man by a hairbreadth. She could hear him screaming after her. She could only hope he'd contact the police. Rolling with it, she straightened the Honda.

"You did that on purpose, didn't you?" the old man said. "You could've cracked my skull. You could dump me on the road and be off to Vermont or wherever the hell you're going."

"I'm taking you home," Laura said grimly.

"There's a tune to that. I wish I could've brought my fiddle. I don't wish that at all. It'll be alive and well when I'm writhing in hell. Ah, Laura, there's times I wish I could pray. . . ."

"We could pray together," she said.

"Not if you knew what I'd pray for."

"What?"

"That I'll find the motherless bastard who sold out Ireland for a penny's worth of peace."

"Oh, my God . . . Don't, Joe. Ireland's not worth it!"

The old man didn't hear her, intent now on his own resolution. "If I live through the night and the parade is tomorrow, I'll send him home in a coffin."

There was no way he could make it, surely. And yet, he had found a man seventeen years ago, after a four-year search for him.

The rain had almost stopped and the sky to what she supposed was the south was a musty yellow and pink. She turned toward it.

"What's that ahead making all the color?" he wanted to know.

"New York."

"It lit up the sky when I was on the run there. Can you go no faster?"

She sped up and, glimpsing the speedometer top seventy, passed two cars, and shot between a third and an oncoming truck, her wheels squealing.

"You're a Barney Oldfield!" the old man shouted.

He twisted his scrawny neck to look after a passing sign. "Where are we now?"

"Near Yonkers," she said. It was a familiar name, though they were miles and miles away from there.

"Cows?" said Mallory. "Did I see a cow?"

"An ad," she made up. "Borden's milk."

"And no more traffic than this? What time is it?"

"Look at the clock." It wasn't seven yet.

"I can't read it. Do you have a pair of glasses I can try?"

"Try my reading glasses. My purse is on the floor at your feet."

He plundered her purse while she sped on, praying to attract police attention, but there was no traffic at all. She thought they'd soon be in reservoir country and she'd have to slow down.

"I've money in my pocket I saved all these years," he said. "Will you go to the police as soon as you leave me?"

"I don't know."

"If you don't know, who does?" He was trying her glasses. "Can't see through the damn things at all." He put them back in her purse. "I've lived my life, Laura. Half dream, half horror. You wouldn't begrudge me a last hurrah?"

"What about Leroy?"

"Leroy. What about him?"

"Did he help you escape?" What she had wanted to ask was if he had killed him.

"Not by choice. He'll sleep till they wake him. I put every pill in my box down his throat." Mallory threw back his head and laughed. "Oh my God, he won't wake up for a week and they'll send him back to Sing Sing where he came from. . . . I'll miss the bastard." And after a minute, "No, he'll miss me."

"Go back while there's time," Laura pleaded. At the intersection, she made a right turn, again the tires squealed. So did the brakes of a car coming on behind her. She had run the stop sign and cut in front of him. He was not going to be able to stop. She all but lifted the Honda into the left lane, in the path, but at a distance she could handle, of an approaching car. The car behind zoomed past on the passenger's side, his horn blasting. He started to stop and then went on. Laura cruised back into the lane behind him.

"Tim's wrong," the old man said. "It's a darling car."

They were both silent for a time, the road winding and rutted. There was little oncoming traffic, but in the rearview mirror Laura could see a police car approaching. She was of two minds what to do, but before she could settle on one of them, it was too late. The vehicle passed them, its siren sudden and shrill. "Now where are they going?" the old man said.

Laura said nothing. Having slowed down to let them pass, she had read STATE POLICE CANINE CORPS.

Soon they could see the sky ahead lit up, the color of alarm, of search. The iron fence loomed in the headlights as though rising from the ground. "Now I know," the old man said, and for a few seconds rocked himself in the seat. "Put me down here," he ordered, "and get the hell away."

Laura stopped. The ceiling light came on when he opened

the door. He noticed the two boxes of candy on the backseat. "Is one of them for me?"

It was an hour later when Laura stopped near the Massachusetts border, intending to call both Tim and her aunt Mattie. When she went to get money out of her purse, she found the snub-nosed gun. It was of carved wood, polished to a sheen. She also found a small roll of dollar bills tightly bound with a rubber band.

ANDREA SMITH grew up in Chicago and plans for Ariel Lawrence, her Chicago police detective, to join the ranks of African American female protagonists in the mystery genre. Mrs. Smith has completed a novel, **Brother's Keeper,** featuring this spunky, saucy member of Chicago's Finest. She lives in Indianapolis and manages employee communications for a corporation.

A Lesson in Murder

Andrea Smith

Ariel Lawrence had vowed to do things differently this time. Vowed not to become consumed again. Yet here she was, dragging up the back stairs of headquarters past nine in the evening, bone-aching weary after working five straight twelve-hour days. And still had another two hours to put in if she was going to turn in a thorough report. With all the crap thrown at her, all the suspensions, why did she keep doing this? She was crazy, that's all. Yes, that was it —crazy.

Maybe she wouldn't do her usual detailed job tonight. Maybe she could get away with sketching out the key points like everybody else and—

"Let me go! They killed my baby and you don't want to do nothing about it. Let . . . me . . . go!"

The shrieks sliced through the evening quiet as Ariel hit the top of the stairs. She paused on the step. Just a few feet away the slight black woman who had cried out those words was trying to wrestle free of two uniforms. Her mouth opened into another scream, and one of the men, who was tall and husky and had a marine buzz cut, clamped his hand over it and twisted her arm, bending her forward. The heavy wool coat she wore to protect her from Chicago's bitter February popped open and fell off one shoulder. The husky one's baby-faced partner held the woman's other arm. Wegglin, who was pulling front desk duty, stood wooden-faced with his thin arms folded as if he were watching the scene on television instead of right in front of him.

The woman was a fighter; she wasn't going down easy. She kicked baby-face in the calf with a heavy-booted foot and yanked away from him. The husky cop twisted the arm he gripped even more and raised his knee to put it in her back. Ariel could take it no longer. Anger propelled her tired body over the top step toward the three.

"Hold it! Just hold it!"

The uniforms scowled at her, and the husky one snapped, "Mind your damn business, lady!"

Ariel flashed her identification. "This *is* my business"— she read his tag—"Rogers. And you, my friend, are going to regret swearing at a superior."

The uniforms bucked eyes at each other. If she hadn't been so mad at how they were treating the woman, Ariel might have been amused at their reaction. Even cops still expected detectives to be big, white, and male. Not a woman of five two with deep chocolate skin and natural hair that hung in heavy ringlets to her shoulders.

The woman was still struggling. "Help me, please! They killed my baby! Oh, Chloe!"

"I suggest you take your hands off of her," Ariel said.

Rogers's grip slackened. "Eh, Detective . . . we—"

"Let her go!" Ariel ordered.

He dropped the woman's arm. Ariel bent down to her. "You okay, ma'am?"

The woman held her shoulder and whimpered, "My baby . . . my baby."

Ariel straightened up. "How about saving me a trip to your sergeant."

The uniforms looked at each other and Ariel knew what they were thinking. Did they really have to explain anything to this runt of a woman, even if she did outrank them? Rogers reverted to that *manly* gesture of pulling up his pants at the waist, a gesture Ariel had long decided was carried in the X chromosome.

"Just following orders," he said.

"Whose and for what?"

He chewed on his lower lip a minute. Finally, he said, "She's been waiting to see Detective Donnelly since four-thirty, but he didn't come back in. I beeped him and he gave orders to remove her from the station," Rogers said.

"Four-thirty! She waited four hours and he says throw her out? What a cop."

Orville Donnelly was in her unit and a classic bigot. Hated blacks. Hated Hispanics. Hated Jews. Hated women.

Rogers shrugged his shoulders. "I don't ask questions. I just follow orders."

"So you said already. I'll take it up with your sergeant," Ariel said, dismissing them. "Ma'am, would you like to talk to me about this?"

The woman's nod was slight.

Feeling angry eyes on her back Ariel led her to an empty interview room. "May I get you something to drink? Coffee? A Coke?"

"Wa—water will be just fine," the woman rasped.

Ariel went for the water. When she returned, the woman had her arms folded on the table and her head down.

"Here you are," Ariel said, sorry she had to interrupt the woman's brief moment of rest.

The woman lifted her head and blinked teary eyes. "Oh, thank you." She took the glass, put it to her lips, and sipped. "Thank you," she said again.

Ariel sat across the table from her. She could tell she'd been a pretty woman in her younger days. Years of too much hard work and struggle had turned her beauty into functional. Salt-and-pepper hair—mostly salt—styled in a plain pageboy. No makeup.

"I'm Detective Ariel Lawrence. Are you up to telling me what happened to Chloe?"

She didn't answer at first. Then her lips began to quiver and tears filled her eyes again. "My baby was going to be somebody too," she said, then began sobbing in loud shaking gasps.

Ariel waited until they subsided. "What's your name, ma'am?"

"Sondra Love," she sniffed. "Chloe was my oldest daughter. She was a good girl. A really good girl."

Ariel hated to ask the next question. "How was she killed?"

That got more sobs.

Again Ariel waited.

"On Forty-seventh Street about three weeks ago," Mrs. Love finally said. "In some vacant building. I told them my Chloe would never go to that neighborhood."

Her head went up proudly. "My baby was a senior at City University. She was going to be a lawyer and then a judge. She was a good girl. They said she was in the wrong place at the wrong time. Got shot because she was doing something she had no business doing. Not my baby. She went to school and she studied. I'm a widow but I work two jobs so Chloe wouldn't have to sell hamburgers to help pay for school. So she could concentrate on getting good grades. Only job I let her work is . . . was . . . as a teacher's assistant because she was a senior and she said she needed the experience. It was more like studying. Being black *and* a woman we have to know twenty times more to get ahead."

Ariel smiled slightly, thinking about her own battles with Sergeant Mancuzek about her detective work.

Mrs. Love folded her arms across her stomach and rocked back and forth in the chair. "Every night she was working on something. Schoolwork or some story for the paper. You would have thought she was that Carole Simpson newswoman the way she worked for that paper. And they not even looking for the lowlife who killed my baby."

"Have you spoken with Detective Donnelly at all?"

Mrs. Love threw her head back. "Humph. I spoke to him all right. I'm ashamed to repeat what he said. He laughed and said what a pretty thing. Said he'd wished he'd gotten a piece of that before she died. Said it right in front of me when I went to see my Chloe's body!

"She was nobody to them," Mrs. Love went on, looking

toward the wall. "Just a little ol' black girl whose life wasn't worth their time."

She turned back to face Ariel. "Can you help me? Find out who killed my baby?"

Ariel winced inwardly. She felt Mrs. Love's pain; Ariel was only fifteen when she'd lost her father to violence. But Mancuzek had dumped a case load on her that would sink a ship. And she had just come back from suspension a week ago, the third one he'd given her for working cases she hadn't been assigned. It didn't matter that she'd gotten arrests on all of them. Mancuzek was more interested in his people following regulations than solving murders.

"Mrs. Love," Ariel said, "there are detectives already assigned to this case. I can't just decide that I'm going to work it."

"They don't care about what happened to my baby. I've been calling and calling and you saw for yourself how they treated me for coming down here. They won't do anything." Mrs. Love's voice was pleading.

"I'm sorry," Ariel said. She was pleading too—for understanding. "But there are procedures we have to follow."

Mrs. Love looked at Ariel with somber eyes. She stood up on her sturdy boots and buttoned up against the cold. "Well. Thank you very much, Ms. Lawrence," she said, her voice heavy with disappointment. Then, head up, she walked slowly to the door.

Mrs. Love's teary face replaced Ariel's sleep that night. She knew there'd be no rest for her until she at least read the case file. So the next morning after roll call she pulled it.

Now she knew what a knockout Mrs. Love had been. The file portrait could have been her at twenty. A beautiful young woman with clear skin the color of nutmeg, sparkling almond-shaped eyes, and a saucy smile.

In sad contrast, the crime scene photo showed a body riddled by ten bullets from a semiautomatic. Ariel's chest tightened and she fought back the tears that wanted to fill in

her eyes. Seven years of police work, and she'd never understand how anyone could kill another person.

Two brothers, ages eight and nine, on their way to school
that morning had taken a detour to play in the building and
had found Chloe's body. Their mother, Debra Green, called
911. There was no lab report on the crime scene. No autopsy or ballistics report. No interviews with Chloe's family
or classmates.

What irony, Ariel thought. Mrs. Green had done her duty
only to have Donnelly slough off his.

Ariel took the crime scene photo and went down to the
evidence room in the lower level. "How's it going,
Kornfein?" she asked the uniform at the counter.

"If it was any better, I couldn't stand it," he said dryly.

Ariel chuckled. "Those new babies keeping you up
nights?"

Kornfein's round face beamed. He and his wife were getting used to month-old twin boys. Kornfein whipped out his
wallet and opened it to a photo. "Aren't they the cutest fellas
you ever saw?"

Two fat faces and two pairs of sky-blue eyes stared at her.
"Just like their daddy," Ariel teased.

Kornfein beamed some more and put his wallet back.
"What brings you to my castle this morning?"

"I need to see the evidence on the Chloe Love case, number 231264."

"Forty-seventh Street?"

"You got it," Ariel said.

"Be right back."

Kornfein disappeared among the shelves and Donnelly
chose that moment to show up.

"Don't tell me you workin' today, Lawrence, that's a new
one," he quipped, waddling his three hundred slovenly
pounds up to the counter.

"It's a new one for you too, Donnelly, and you haven't
been on suspension."

"Hah. Same ol' smart mouth. Gonna git you more than
suspended one of these days."

Kornfein came back with the package. "Here you go, Lawrence."

Ariel tried to take it before Donnelly figured out what it was, but he caught the tag. Grabbed at it.

"Hey, wait a minute. This looks familiar." He read the tag. "This from my case! Whatchoo doin' nosin' in my case?"

Damn, Ariel thought. Fine time for him to become eagle-eyed. She looked at Kornfein, who was rubbing his temple nervously. Probably thinking about those twins he had to feed. She decided to try to reason with Donnelly cop to cop.

"Look, Donnelly—"

"Naw, you look, girlie. You putchoo nose in my case and I'm goin' straight to the sergeant."

Ariel wanted to tell him that *somebody* needed to put their nose in it because he sure wasn't. How could one human being be so despicable?

She scooted the evidence back to Kornfein.

Since Donnelly had spoiled her look at the evidence, Ariel went to see the medical examiner. "Best I can tell, time of death was somewhere between six-thirty p.m. and ten-thirty p.m.," Robert Holifield said. Ariel was in his office at the morgue.

"That's an awfully big spread," she said. "You can't be more specific?"

"I didn't get to examine the body until the next morning," Holifield said, in a tone that made his feelings clear about it. A short man with thick white hair and heavy bifocals on a large nose, Holifield had been the city's chief medical examiner for twenty years. And ever since Ariel had been in the detective division she'd heard the same complaint from him.

"They don't call me when they should and then they expect me to perform miracles," Holifield said. "I had to base the time of death on the amount of rigor mortis that had set in. So that spread, as you call it, is as accurate as I can get."

He looked at the photo. "Beautiful girl. Such a shame."

"Anything else you can tell me that might be of help? This case is getting icicles on it and I don't have a single lead."

He shook his head. " 'Fraid that's about it."

"No other signs of abuse?"

Holifield shook his white head again. "No. Not raped or beaten." He handed her a manila folder. "Stick this in the case file. It's the autopsy report; Donnelly never picked it up."

Forty-seventh Street was like a hundred other streets in Chicago. Back in the sixties it had pulsated with black-owned businesses and theaters. Ariel's aunt Lela often told how she and Ariel's mother would go to the Regal Theater on 47th and South Park Way, which was now King Drive, and watch the best of Motown—the Miracles, the Temptations—over and over. Could stay at the Regal all day for the price of one ticket. Now 47th Street was just another example of the urban blight that uncaring politicians had allowed to take away the life of the city. From State Street to Cottage Grove, every other building on 47th Street was a hole in the landscape the politicians had created.

The abandoned building where Chloe's body had been found had been a department store. It claimed the whole corner. Ariel stepped through what was once a display window on the 47th Street side. She flicked on her flashlight so she could see in the shadows that winter cast during the day.

A gust of wind whipped through. Ariel steadied her booted feet and turned her face away from its sting. She let the wind die down, then took out her photo of the crime scene to try and pinpoint where the police markers—if there'd been any—might have been. Gingerly she stepped over the bricks, wood, and bottles to as near the spot where Chloe had been found as she could.

"This is ridiculous," she was muttering to herself twenty minutes later as she searched around the area. "Why didn't evidence take photos of the blood droplets? This is worse than looking for a needle in a haystack."

She left, clueless and disgusted.

*   *   *

Ariel walked both sides of the street, three blocks from the building that had been Chloe Love's deathbed. She interviewed every store owner. There was a shack of a fast-food place called Sam's, and a tiny overpriced grocery store. There was a liquor store where the line to buy lottery tickets snaked to the back. She interviewed the folks who hung on the corners. If Ariel was to believe any of the people she talked to, the night somebody pumped ten bullets into Chloe Love, 47th Street had been as quiet as a Sunday in church.

The trees on City University's grounds were breathtaking in their winter clothes of snow and ice. From its cocoon of wealth, surrounded by some of the city's most poverty-stricken neighborhoods, the school had produced Nobel scientists and celebrated authors. And had her young life not been stolen, most likely would have produced a bright lawyer named Chloe Love.

Ariel got a list of Chloe's professors and activities from the dean's office. Chloe had carried a 3.8 grade point average out of 4.0. Had written for the campus newspaper, tutored a student, and still found time to work as a professor's assistant.

The professor was Michael Trenton, and he taught criminal justice. Ariel found him in a small cluttered office, his desktop littered with papers. He was younger than Ariel had expected, early forties, and stockily built with blond hair that fell into his eyes. Dressed in khaki pants, blue jean shirt with a print cotton tie, he looked more like a news reporter, yet he exuded a scholarly calmness.

"This is one reason I miss her," he said, holding up a stack of papers. "Chloe kept my paperwork up-to-date."

He began cramming the papers into a tan leather briefcase. "You mind walking with me to the parking lot while we talk? I have an appointment to get to."

"Sure," Ariel said.

Trenton opened the door for her, followed her out, and turned to lock it. Started down a narrow corridor.

"Chloe was one of the brightest, most hardworking students I've taught in a long time," he said. "She was like a sponge; trying to soak up as much knowledge as she could. Believed that the law would always win. That's rare to find in anyone these days. A lot of us don't hold on to that childlike optimism."

In the parking lot Trenton stopped in front of a red sports car.

"How long had she worked for you?"

"She took the assistant job in September. Usually came in for about three hours on Monday, Wednesday, and Friday afternoons. She reviewed exams, kept my records. Just kept everything in good order. We're all just devastated by what happened." He opened the car door and climbed in. "She had such a good life ahead of her. If anybody didn't deserve to die, it was Chloe."

By the time Ariel had talked to the rest of Chloe's professors it was after three. Deadline time at the *City Weekly,* where the budding journalist had worked. The staff was scurrying around the newsroom like rats trying to get out of a maze. She went up to a young woman with russet hair past her waist who was intently banging on her computer keyboard. "I'm with the Chicago Police Department. Is your editor around?"

The young woman paused and absorbed Ariel for a minute.

"Is he?" Ariel asked again.

"*Her* office is in that corner." The young woman jerked her head toward the back and returned to her banging.

The editor, a tall black woman with close-cropped natural hair, was huddled with a short guy with blotchy skin.

"This photo looks like something my little sister would take, Arthur. Too grainy. Take Pete and see if you can get Professor Wickham to give us ten minutes for another shot."

Arthur screwed up his face. "Walking on hot coals would be a lot easier than getting that prima donna to give me more time."

"Yeah, well, Cartwright will have our butts if we print this."

Arthur sighed dramatically, took the photos, and stormed past Ariel.

The editor rolled her eyes at the ceiling. "Photographers," she said. "You here about the reporter's job?"

Ariel smiled. She hadn't had a compliment like that in a while. "Actually I came about a reporter."

The woman looked puzzled. Ariel showed her identification.

"I'm looking into the death of Chloe Love. . . ."

"Kind of late aren't you—*sister*?" the woman snapped.

The change in attitude took Ariel aback. "What do you mean?"

"It's been three weeks since Chloe was killed. That's three years in your line of work."

"You know a lot about my work?"

The tall woman shrugged. "Criminal justice courses. Chloe and I took a couple together."

"Nobody came to talk with you about Chloe?" Of course, she knew the answer, she just wanted to hear it firsthand.

"Not a soul. Chloe was good people. She was going to make one hell of a reporter or judge, whatever she ended up doing. But who cares. She was just another—"

"Don't say it. That's why I'm here. Her mother asked me to find Chloe's killer, and that's what I intend to do. Maybe you can help."

They looked at each other squarely. Ariel extended her hand. "Detective Ariel Lawrence."

The woman let her hang out there alone for a few awkward seconds before she accepted it. "Eva Phillips."

"Can you tell me who Chloe hung out with? Could she have been involved in some bad business?"

Eva shook her head vigorously. "Not Chloe. She was straight as an arrow. A crusader."

"What about her personal life. Boyfriend or anything?"

Eva hunched her shoulders. "I really don't think she was seeing anybody. She came in here three times a week to work on her stories. We didn't party together or anything like that; we were both too busy trying to make the grades and graduate, so we didn't see each other much outside of this place."

Ariel thought a moment.

"How about her stories? Anything there that could have caused any problems?"

Eva laughed. Her laughter was loud and deep. "You kidding? This is not the *Washington Post.* We don't run anything that, in my adviser's words, is not a positive representation of this prestigious institution."

Sean O'Hallihan was a freckled-face sophomore with thick carrot hair. In three quarters, Chloe had helped him pump up his English grade from a D to a B.

"She was cool," he said. "Real cool."

"You two ever talk about anything other than English? Did you ever see or meet any of her friends?"

Sean looked down at his gray Nikes. "Not really. I know she was dating some guy. I saw her with him once." His tone was wistful. He bent his head and studied the red swooshes on his shoes. Had Sean O'Hallihan had a crush on Chloe?

"He was real tall and sort of skinny."

"A student here?"

Sean finally looked up. "I'd seen him around." He wrinkled his nose as if he smelled something bad. "Wouldn't know his name, though."

"The last time you saw Chloe was she her normal self?"

Sean shrugged. "Guess so. We didn't get to talk much really."

"Too busy going for that A, huh?"

"She said she had to get out early." He looked at his Nikes again. "I figured she had a date or something."

Mrs. Love, her tired eyes drawn into slits, led Ariel to what had been her daughter's bedroom. "I haven't been able to bring myself to put her things away." She said it almost as if that made her a bad mom.

"That's understandable, Mrs. Love," Ariel assured, elated that Mrs. Love hadn't touched anything. That boosted her chances of finding something that would tell her why Chloe had to die. Mrs. Love left Ariel to her rubber-gloved search of the room. Chloe had the typical college wardrobe. Jeans, jeans, and more jeans. Wore an imitation of Fred Hayman's 273 perfume and listened to En Vogue and Salt-N-Pepa.

And she was organized. Her books and notes arranged by class in a steel bookcase that had three shelves. Ariel went through each one carefully, checking between pages for notes that might have gotten stuck. Then she searched her dresser drawers. Maybe Chloe kept a diary on her personal life. But there was nothing, and after three hours Ariel gave up.

Her only hope was the evidence. Ariel went back to the station about seven-thirty; Donnelly wouldn't be around that late. Wilson was on duty, and he was extremely cooperative. Ariel took the evidence package to an interview room.

Chloe had been wearing blue jeans, white sweatshirt, and pale blue starter jacket. The jacket and shirt were ripped by the bullets and hardened with Chloe's blood. Ariel went through Chloe's cloth briefcase. There was the lesson book she had used for tutoring Sean that evening. Her political science textbook.

Ariel went through Chloe's black sack purse next. Makeup. Comb and brush. Wallet with ten dollars and some change. And . . .

A calendar and address book.

The girl would have made a first-rate detective; she had filled in every day of her life like clockwork. Right down to the Wednesday that she'd cut her tutoring session short. In fancy, curly script she had written: *Meet Anthony. 6:30 p.m. 7723 West 22nd Street. Berwyn.*

Anthony? Berwyn?

Chloe wouldn't go near Forty-seventh Street, Mrs. Love had said. So what was this young black woman doing meeting some guy all the way out in a suburb that Donnelly would call home if the department didn't require him to live in the city?

Ariel tucked the black book in a plastic bag and put it in her purse. Then she went back to Wilson and gave him the rest.

The next morning Ariel cross-checked the address for a phone number and when she called, she got "Riley's Gun Shop."

"Gun shop? This is a gun shop?" She felt stupid repeating what he'd said.

"Yeah, can I help you?"

"No. Think I misdialed." She hung up.

Confused? Ariel was baffled now.

Behind the counter was a scrawny white man wearing a plaid shirt and blue jeans so faded the color was just about gone. A good ol' boy. Probably had animal skins and deer heads on the walls in his den.

Cold gray eyes pierced Ariel.

"How're you doing?" Ariel asked, smiling big enough to show off the dimple in her left cheek.

Didn't impress good ol' boy. He just looked at her. Didn't say a word.

"Chicago Police Department," Ariel said, displaying her identification. "What's your name, sir?"

He didn't deserve the courtesy, but maybe it would get her what she needed.

"Riley," he said. Not quite a snarl, but almost.

"You own this establishment?"

"It's my place."

Ariel took the eight-by-ten portrait she had of Chloe out of the large manila envelope and laid it on the glass counter. Beneath the glass, small handguns were displayed. The kind you could strap around your calf.

"Mr. Riley, have you ever seen this young woman?"

Riley was still hard-faced.

"Have you?"

His eyes flicked down.

"I don't do business with that kind," he said, his gray eyes glinting.

"Excuse me?"

He took in enough air to make his scrawny chest expand and give him the courage to say, "Niggers know not to come in my place."

Once upon a time a comment like that would have brought Ariel's blood to a boil instantly. But she'd learned to deflect and ignore the worst in her years with the department. So Ariel gave Riley her smile again. "Oh, that's a good one. Real intelligent response."

Riley balled his fists on the counter.

Ariel picked up the photo of Chloe and put it back in the envelope. "Well, I've got some time before I head back to the city so I think I'll drop in on some friends of mine in the county sheriff's office and tip them off about all the violations I've discovered in this place."

Riley's gray eyes flashed with anger.

Ariel showed her dimple again.

"See you soon," she said.

Jack Meyers was in a wonderful mood. "You ain't the only one in a hurry, Lawrence," he blustered into the phone. I got—"

"Come on, Meyers. You can get this information with a snap of your fingers." He'd been in the gang crime unit for ten years, and knew all the ins and outs.

"Don't try to use flattery. That won't get you nowhere." She could hear him chomping on one of his nasty cigars.

"For God's sake, Meyers, it's a homicide. I don't have time to argue with you."

His sigh was loud and drawn out. "I'm just a pushover. You know that? Just what is it that you need?"

Ariel told him. "Any reports of gunfire in the area on that night? And I need you to tell me whose turf that is—"

"Disciples territory," Meyers interrupted.

"Yes, well, I think Chloe had a boyfriend that she didn't want her mother to know about. Think he was in a gang and that she may have been with him that night. His rivals opened fire on him and she got it."

"Happens all the time," Meyers said. "Young girls get mixed up with the wrong type and it costs 'em big time. I'll call ya back."

Ten minutes later, he did just that. "Like I said, Forty-seventh Street was Disciple territory. But six months ago, the Black Vice decided to take it. Easier thought than done. Disciples been battling; knocked off five Black Vice this month. None of 'em were drive-bys though. They've been hits on their headquarters and some of their houses.

"What we haven't been able to trace is where they got the guns. Before these hits, they were using handguns. Now they got a lot of sophisticated weapons. Like the one that did your victim."

Mrs. Love's anger sizzled through the line. "My daughter wasn't dating no gang-banger. I raised her better than that."

"It's not your fault if she was, Mrs. Love. Sometimes girls just fall for the wrong guy. Maybe that's what Chloe did."

"You have to prove it to me. I'll never believe that about my baby." Ariel could see the woman shaking her salt-and-pepper head. "No. Not my Chloe."

A mother's love and faith, or did Mrs. Love know what she was talking about? Or was Chloe everything her mother said she wasn't?

Eva Phillips was preparing to leave when Ariel got to the newspaper office. "Good news?"

"I wish. Want to ask you about Chloe's articles again. What had she covered this year, and what was she working on just before she was killed?"

Eva went over to a file cabinet and pulled out a binder. "I keep my copies of back issues in this."

She opened it and flipped back to January. "Chloe's beat

was criminal justice and black studies. Criminal justice was pretty dry. She always had to dig to find something there."

Eva flipped Ariel through the back issues, pointing out stories on new members of the criminal justice faculty. A story on a new curriculum that the department was going to implement in the fall. What the black studies department planned for Black History Month. Nothing worth anybody getting killed over. Eva's assignment log didn't turn up anything controversial either.

"You know, Eva. I went through Chloe's things at her home. The girl was so organized she could have been a consultant on the subject. I found information on everything. But there were no notes from her work here at the paper. Where would she have kept that stuff?"

Eva nodded. "Yeah, that was Chloe. Me I'm scattered as paper on a windy day. But Chloe could go right to anything you asked her for."

Ariel was silent.

"What about her computer files? That's where I keep a lot of my notes."

Eva nodded again. "Let's check."

She led Ariel over to a desk in the corner of the room and turned on Chloe's computer. The system beeped as it booted up. She entered a few key strokes, watched the cursor blink and then stopped.

"Heck, I forgot about her password. I don't know it."

Ariel sighed. "Anybody around who would?"

Eva looked at her watch. "There's a slight chance somebody in Info Service might be working late."

Eva grabbed the phone and punched out a number.

"Phillips at the *Weekly*. I need the password of one of our former reporters. Chloe Love. Yeah, the woman who was killed."

Eva listened. "Yeah it was a tragedy. Look, I'm on deadline and . . . yeah." She listened again. "Mama? Okay. Thanks a lot."

"That's appropriate," Ariel said when Eva hung up.

Eva typed in the four letters, and she and Ariel watched

the message *Password accepted* flow across the screen, watched the system scan for viruses and then a blank screen appear.

"Okay. List files."

Ariel said, "Let's start with the ones close to the date of her death."

They did that. All they got were the dry stories that had already been printed.

"Go back to the month before," Ariel said.

Eva brought up the files again and scrolled the cursor down each one.

"What's this?" Ariel said. Pointed her finger at a document called "Guns."

"Got me. We never did a story on guns," Eva said, and opened the file. Chloe's notes were short:

> *I'm going to make Tony give me all the details on the guns. When this story breaks, I'll be able to get a job on one of the dailies right after graduation.*

Eva laid a puzzled look on Ariel and said, "Tony?"

The guy who got the call to open the records office and help Ariel identify Tony didn't appreciate it.

"Anthony is a common name," he snarled.

"Check only Chloe's classes first," Ariel instructed, ignoring his attitude. "There can't have been that many Anthonys in them."

There were five. One had transferred to a school on the West Coast. Another was from Boston; chances of his being in the Disciples were slim. Anthony No. 3 was a white student who lived on the North Side. No. 4 was a Hispanic whose name was actually Antonio, but records had made a mistake. But No. 5 was Anthony Stevens. He was in Chloe's criminal justice class and attendance records showed him AWOL in the three weeks since her murder. He lived at 6129 S. Cottage Grove. Disciples territory.

* * *

"I know my boy didn't do nothing," Anthony Stevens's father stated from the small living room of his third-floor apartment. He was dressed in a laborer's uniform of green overalls, and reminded Ariel of her own dad, who had worked day and night to support his family.

"He go to school every day and he's doing real good. Gonna be the first in our family to finish college," he announced proudly. "My wife and me gonna see to that."

"I need to ask him a few questions," Ariel said.

"He ain't here. He takes classes in the evening too. Sometimes he studies so late, he just stays at a friend's house and go to school from there."

Poor man really believes that, Ariel thought. Probably doesn't know about Anthony's sidelines. She was about to ask if she could wait, but at that moment the front door opened and a tall, gangly guy about twenty years old walked through it.

"Hey, Pops," he called. He threw a puzzled glance at Ariel, who couldn't believe her luck. Couldn't believe that he'd just walked right into her hands.

"Tony, this lady's from the police. She say—"

The elder Stevens didn't have a chance to finish. Anthony's eyes popped in surprise, he backed out the door and took off.

Ariel was right behind him, taking the stairs in chunks.

"I just want to talk to you, Anthony," she called.

Anthony kept running. Out the door and onto the sidewalk that was slick with hardened snow. "Knew slacks were a wise wardrobe choice today," Ariel muttered.

Anthony's legs were long, but Tai Chi training made Ariel fast and agile. She was about six steps behind him when she left her feet and flew into his thighs. He slid face first into the dirty snow the way Pete Rose used to slide into the bases.

The fact that she caught him must have shocked Anthony because he didn't immediately try to get up, which gave Ariel the few seconds she needed to whip out her handcuffs and lock his hands behind his back.

"You get off me, lady. I ain't done nothing."

"Ain't? What are they teaching you at that snotty university?" She stood him up. "I just want to talk to you. I need to ask you some questions about Chloe Love."

Anthony's stare was defiant, but Ariel thought she also saw something else in his black eyes. Sadness maybe?

"Don't know no Chloe Love."

"Well, why don't we talk about it at police headquarters."

Fifteen minutes later he was cuffed to the wall in an interview room and still denying he knew Chloe Love.

"Come on, Anthony. This is tiresome. Chloe Love was in your criminal justice class so don't tell me you didn't know her. I know for a fact that you were supposed to meet her the night she was killed. What was that about?"

Anthony didn't say anything. Just stared at the dark window in the room.

"Were you two dating? You fit the description of the guy people say she was seeing."

That got a loud groan. "How many times do I have to tell you, lady? I didn't know the girl."

This time Ariel groaned. "You know, Anthony. You better get your father's hard-earned money back because you're not learning a darn thing at that university."

With nothing to hold Anthony Stevens on, Ariel let him go and went home to leftover pizza and her thoughts.

Plopped on the sofa with a pad and pencil, Ariel went back to the beginning. She had a crime scene that had no evidence of a crime having been committed. She had two rival gangs fighting over turf with illegally purchased guns. That same type of gun had killed her victim. She had the victim's classmate who happened to belong to one of those gangs run like a jackrabbit when he got a visit from the police and lie about knowing her.

Pretty pat.

She chewed on her pencil.

Too pat.

Chloe's notes hadn't pointed to Anthony Stevens as the

buyer. He was going to give her the details, she had written. The details. Chloe had been good about details.

Ariel picked up the notebooks she'd borrowed from Mrs. Love. Went over them again and again. English literature, political science, advanced reporting . . . all these notes from her classes, yet something seemed to be missing. She pored over them again. One more time before it hit her.

Of course. Why hadn't she seen it before?

She dialed Meyers at home and after letting him complain for five minutes, explained what she wanted him to do.

"Hate stakeouts," Meyers grumbled. He ran an impatient hand through what was left of his sandy hair.

"Just think about the big bust you're getting ready to make," Ariel told him.

They had been sitting in their regulation Chevy across the street from Berwyn's friendly neighborhood gunshop for two hours, since seven-thirty that morning, and Meyers had been moaning the whole time.

"You know—"

"Shush!"

A beat-up Ford pulled into the parking lot, and Anthony Stevens and a guy who looked like he could snap a neck with one hand got out.

"Well, your undercover buyer got them here," Ariel said.

"Of course," Meyers said matter-of-factly.

They let them go in and waited for their other guest. Not five minutes later, a red Corvette drove up and Michael Trenton got out.

"Police. Everybody freeze," Ariel announced.

They did, but not before Anthony's friend grabbed Riley by the collar and put a semiautomatic to his temple. Anthony pointed his at Trenton.

"Guess these gentlemen don't know about your business rule, huh, Riley," Ariel said.

Riley had panic in his eyes. "A-a-rrest these punks. They —they trying to rob my place," he stammered to Meyers.

Ariel looked at Trenton. "Good to see you again, Professor. Though I wouldn't have expected it to be under these circumstances."

Trenton smiled crookedly. "Man, are we glad you folks showed up. I came out here just to browse. I'm starting to get into hunting. And here I walk into a robbery."

"Is that right?" Ariel said. "And here I thought you were here because you got a call saying the Disciples wanted to do some more business."

Trenton's face flushed just a bit. "What? What business are you talking about?"

"Illegal sale of firearms. You and Riley have quite an operation going. And Chloe, poor idealist that she was, had her sights set on getting a story in the school press. Now you and I know that the university would never have allowed itself to be tainted like that. But you figured you couldn't risk it."

"That's absurd," Trenton said.

"Is it, Professor?" Ariel stepped closer to him, holding her gun straight out. "You said it yourself. Chloe was like a sponge, soaking up all she could about the law. She watched your every move so she could learn. And she was very detailed, took copious notes on everything she did. Except for your class and the work she did for you. Now doesn't that seem strange to you? It did to me."

Trenton's chin went up. "I have no idea what you're talking about."

"Studying you she found out about your little sideline. You bought the guns from good ol' Riley here and sold them illegally in the city to street gangs. Having a Disciple in your class made it work smooth as silk. Made you quite a bundle. Lot more than you earn as an associate professor. You have the priciest set of wheels in the teachers' lot."

"That's—"

"Absurd? I don't think so. But what I do think is you found Chloe's notes. You lured that poor, innocent girl to a meeting—easy enough since she didn't suspect you knew that Anthony had told her about the scheme—killed her and dumped her body in that building on Forty-seventh Street so the gangs would be blamed.

"Now if my colleague here checks you, I bet he'll find the piece you used to kill Chloe and that you were going to use on Anthony."

A smiling Meyers stepped up to Trenton and patted him. Took a semiautomatic from his pants at the middle of his back.

Trenton curled his lips.

"He would have gotten you earlier, Anthony, but you've been hiding out because you thought the Vice killed Chloe and were after you too."

Anthony's eyes got dangerously big. "You killed Chloe?"

He stared at Trenton. A vein throbbed in his skinny neck. "She was my lady, man," he said in a voice that was too calm. He lifted his gun.

"Anthony, don't," Ariel pleaded.

"I loved Chloe. I was leaving the Disciples for her."

Anthony moved the gun closer to Trenton's face. "You killed my lady."

"She wouldn't want you to go out that way," Ariel said.

"Don't matter what way I go out." His voice was shaking. "He killed Chloe!"

"And we've got him now. He's going to pay for it."

Anthony put the gun almost at Trenton's cheek. The professor's expression was smug, as if he dared Anthony to fire.

After what seemed like a year, Anthony lowered the gun. Ariel saw his eyes were shiny with tears.

"Told you fooling with niggers be nothing but trouble," Riley piped.

Anthony's friend whacked Riley on the head with his big bare fist. The county sheriff's police walked in as he hit the floor.

Mrs. Love was waiting at the front desk. This time she had a smile on her face, and it was saucy.

"I just wanted to thank you again for finding my baby's murderer."

"There's no need," Ariel said. "I was only doing what they pay me to do." She didn't add that it was worth the dressing-down she'd received from Sergeant Mancuzek for working Donnelly's case. Donnelly had been royally pissed and, of course, had run whining to Mancuzek claiming she had stolen his collar.

"Well, you sure showed him. Showed him he couldn't get away with killing people. Let him think about *that* in jail."

Ariel grinned. "Yes, let that be the last lesson he teaches."

In 1981, **LINDA BARNES** wrote her first mystery novel featuring Michael Spraggue. After three more Spraggue mysteries, Barnes introduced Carlotta Carlyle in 1985 in the award-winning story "Lucky Penny." Since then, Carlyle has appeared in six novels, the latest being *Hardware,* published in 1995. Barnes has won the Anthony and American Mystery awards, and has been nominated for the Edgar and Shamus awards. Born in Detroit, she currently lives near Boston with her husband and six-year-old son.

Miss Gibson

Linda Barnes

I hate to travel except by car or cab. Even then I like to call the shots, do the driving. If you see me on board an airplane, someone else is surely footing the bill. If you find me flying first class—United #707 to Denver, connecting first class to United #919 to Portland, Oregon—you can be absolutely certain that the lady paying the freight is Dee Willis.

You remember Dee, the pop/blues singer who snatched seven Grammys after twenty years of hard-luck bar gigs. The hot new songbird with—can it be? is it possible?—a shred of dignity, a smidgen of integrity. Stubborn as they come, Dee couldn't be bothered following trends. She just kept on doing what she always did. Never dumbed down her act for an audience. The fans had to catch up to her.

Hell, even I have to admit it: Dee's got more than a few remnants of tattered integrity. She supports good causes, sings her heart out at benefits for sick musicians and AIDS-infected kids. I tend to choke on her acts of kindness because I've been jealous of Dee as long as I can remember: first and always for her sweet soaring soprano; second, because some time ago she ran off with a Cajun bass player, my then husband, Cal Therieux.

No surprise that her hastily scrawled plea hadn't been enough to make me abandon my Cambridge, Mass., digs. Neither was her promise of primo plane and concert tickets.

Only a carefully negotiated fee had me peering nervously from the Boeing 737's pitiful excuse for a window.

Dee owns one item I'd rather have than anything you can name, and I certainly do not speak of my ex-husband, who's no longer a member of Dee's band and was never her "possession" to give or to take. Twenty-five years ago, Dee studied at the feet of the Reverend Gary Davis, the blind bluesman who wrote holy spirituals and, when the spirit moved him, played such hymns to human weakness as "Baby, Let Me Follow You Down." The Reverend was so taken with Dee that he willed her Miss Gibson, his favorite guitar. Dee hardly plays Miss Gibson anymore, what with her stock of custom-made electrics and glittering Stratocasters. I'd treat Miss Gibson right, give her a better home.

The vision of the Reverend Davis's Gibson keeping company with my old National Steel guitar had me up above the clouds, grasping the armrests, trying to fly the plane via mind control.

Ridiculous. I took six deep breaths, accepted the futility of telekinesis, and lapsed into fitful sleep.

I switched planes at Denver's International Airport, wandering into a nearby ladies' room, where I splashed my face with cold water, shook out my red hair, glared at the mirror, and hoped the lighting was bad. A mother of twins maintained serene calm while one offspring vomited and the other wailed.

While we were waiting to take off for Portland, a guy across the aisle asked the flight attendant for a Bailey's-on-the-rocks. I hadn't indulged during the Boston-to-Denver leg in spite of the free flow of liquor, but Bailey's sounded like such a good idea I decided to join the party.

Bailey's was my dad's home tipple of choice. At bars, it was a shot and a beer, like the other Irish cops. Even after my folks split, Mom kept a bottle for him. She drank schnapps. Peppermint. Disgusting.

Many Bailey's later, the jolt of the plane's wheels smacking the Portland landing strip made me grind my teeth. I didn't relax my jaw till the damn thing slowed. Out of control, that's how airplanes make me feel.

Dee Willis always had style, now she's got the cash to go with it: a guy in full livery waited at the gate with CARLYLE printed neatly on a signboard. Broad-shouldered and burly, he resisted conversational gambits and stood at attention until the luggage carousel disgorged my bag. Hefting it, he gawked at its pathetic lightness, staring me down with narrowed eyes, as if he wanted to ask why I couldn't have carried my stuff on board and saved us the twenty-minute wait.

I saw no reason to explain that I needed to check my luggage because it contained a Smith & Wesson 4053, two magazines, and sufficient ammunition to turn an aircraft fuselage into Swiss cheese. I'm no U.S. marshal, just a private investigator; I can't carry on planes. To carry at all, I'd have to check in with the Portland cops, explain my mission, and get a temporary license.

I'd told Dee to hire somebody local. Seems like I've been giving Dee good advice all my life and she never takes one word to heart.

"Stalker," she'd said in her increasingly urgent phone calls. At every concert in every city, always seated in the same section, wearing colorful western gear, almost like he wanted her to notice him, wanted to stand out in the crowd. Always too damn close.

Ron, Dee's longtime lead guitar, and some of the other guys in the band had brace͏   ͏e man one night. He hadn't seemed fazed, hadn't backeu ͏ʋf an inch. Showed up at the next performance bold as brass—and now he, or somebody, was sending wilted flowers, sending nasty letters. She'd FedExed a sample, of a semilyrical nature:

> Our lives are linked with chains of steel,
> Chains of steel, my Lady Blue.
> Saw a chainsaw in a hardware store.
> Thought of you, babe. Thought of you.

Block print in a Neanderthal hand. Cheap ballpoint ink. Unsigned. Hardly Dee's favorite fan mail. And no proof that the "stalker" had sent it.

Dee was set for three shows in Portland due to a venue screw-up. She'd been scheduled to play one date in a major arena; her manager had discovered the booking error after the tickets went SRO. Not wanting to disappoint the legions who'd finally made her a star, she'd rented a smaller hall. Intimate. Close to the audience. Close to the stalker. She was scared.

Bodyguard, I'd advised.

You, she'd insisted. We'd discussed terms, including Miss Gibson. Then the tickets came. For the planes and all three shows.

Great seats.

"I thought it didn't snow in Portland," I muttered as the chauffeur and I struggled through gusts of icy wind layered with flakes as soft and wet as soapsuds.

"First blizzard since '89," he grumbled. "Just for you."

"You drive in snow much?" I asked.

"Nope," he said, brushing ineffectually at the windshield with a gloved hand.

In the terminal I'd noticed folks standing around, eyes glued to picture windows, staring with wide-eyed wonder at a paltry six inches Bostonians would have shrugged off with a laugh. I felt a jolt of pity for these two-season folk—rainy and dry—wished I had a shovel to offer the driver instead of a handgun.

I blinked bleary eyes, figured that since the flight had landed after one in the morning, it was now past 4:00 a.m. Boston time. The little sleep I'd enjoyed on the Denver leg had been more than countered by the Bailey's binge. I could barely stand upright in the slashing wind.

I was grateful when the chauffeur opened the passenger-side back door, understanding when he didn't wait politely to close the door behind me. I heard the lid of the trunk open, felt a brief stab of regret. Separated from my luggage again.

I drive a cab part-time when I can't make enough PI money to crack my monthly nut. My eye went automatically to the front visor. No photo, no license. Not to worry, I told myself. It's not a cab; it's a limo. No regulations, most cities.

I halted, one foot poised on the shag carpet. The front door locks were shaped like tiny letter *T*'s. The rear locks were straight, smooth, and short, like the filed-off jobs in the backseats of patrol cars.

I engineered a quick reverse, backing into a pile of slush that soaked through my thin boots. "Have a scraper in the trunk?" I asked as casually as I could manage, trying to come up beside the chauffeur.

He gave way. "Jeez, I dunno. You wanna look?"

The leather soles of my boots slipped on the slick stuff coating the pavement. I had to concentrate on my footing. No excuse, just the truth. When the "chauffeur" tackled me high, midback, he had no trouble flipping me head over heels. I barely had the presence of mind to tuck my head to my chin. If I hadn't, I might have snapped my neck as the huge trunk lid came slamming down.

Thank God and the Ford Motor Company for the depth of Lincoln Town Car trunks. Ditto for the plush carpeting. My head thunked against my soft-sided duffel.

Dammit. Yes, I was jetlagged, half drunk, in a strange city at a beastly hour, but Dee had described her "stalker": heavyset, big as a small refrigerator, built on the same square lines as my "chauffeur." I cursed and cursed again. Uniforms'll get you every time; you *trust* a guy in livery, a guy parading your name on a signboard.

The engine revved far too quickly for my assailant to have cleared the windows properly. As we fishtailed into motion I tested the limits of my confinement, reaching out with my right arm, then my left, pushing the trunk lid with both arms, then both feet, in case the latch had failed to catch. No such luck.

Seven plus two, I thought. Seven plus two.

I drive an old Toyota, but as a car freak in good standing, I pore over *Consumer Reports* New Car Yearbooks at newsstands or libraries, anyplace I don't have to fork over cash. Seven plus two is the way *CR* indicates a huge trunk, one with room for seven pullman cases and two weekenders. I spent a while pondering the word "pullman," which reeked of ancient railroad lore, and rubbing my head. Cubic feet, as in amount of available air, would have been a better measurement considering my predicament. Dual exhausts on a new Town Car. I hoped they were working well, discharging their fumes behind the car, not underneath it.

Lying on my back, I approximated the position of a helpless turtle. My duffel bag, probably less than "weekender" size, was next to my head. My knees grazed the top of the trunk. The darkness was total, absolute. We careened around a corner and I found myself unwillingly shifted to an even less comfortable angle.

Did the Lincoln Town Car possess a trunk pass-through to the backseat? I didn't think so. Most of those are found in cars with less trunk capacity. I tried a crab-crawl deeper into the trunk, felt around for some doodad that might lead to the passenger compartment. Lots of effort; no result. Except sweat.

It was going to have to be the duffel bag, maneuvering it, opening it, locating the 40 in its silica-lined case, finding a magazine, loading it. Not shooting off a round by mistake. I imagined one ricocheting through the trunk till it found a soft, cozy home in my body. Imagined igniting the gas tank. Even if the slug miraculously missed me and any flammable fluids, I'd wind up stone-deaf from the enclosed explosion.

We turned a corner too fast. I tried to anchor myself, but I slid to the right, away from my bag.

The "stalker" had an ally in Dee's camp. Deeply embedded there. Dee's no loudmouth, no idle gossiper. She doesn't share her plans with roadies or groupies. Would she have told anyone I was arriving? Left a note by the telephone? Had someone overheard her call a travel agent? Had she relegated the duty to some gofer who'd been suborned by the stalker?

Who'd want to stop Dee? Scare Dee off the circuit?

She'd never harbored a female backup vocalist, didn't tour with a regular opening act. Nobody in her entourage would cherish delusions of replacing Dee Willis.

Her recording company might hire a goon to get her off-stage and into the studio. Dee doesn't cut many albums; she likes the rush of live performance. Says she's the leader of a road band and proud of it. Her last two CDs went platinum practically overnight. More studio recordings might make a mint for some MCA/America exec.

Would an entertainment giant hire a thug to frighten one of their stars? Not much I'd put past those L.A. suits.

I wriggled closer to my suitcase.

First step: simple. Unlock the duffel. Keys in my back pocket; I'm not a handbag toter. For the first time since high school I found myself wishing I were less than six feet one. I rolled onto my side, slid an arm behind me, and inched the key out. Might sound easy. Try it in the dark, in a trunk, in a lurching, skidding vehicle.

My fingers found the lock, unbuckled and unzipped the bag from memory and touch, located the gun case. I placed it between my shaky knees. Then it was a race against time, my fingers steadily more numb, more unwieldy as they grew icy. It was not a job for gloved hands.

I couldn't find a magazine. Something sharp jabbed my hand. What? A nail scissor protruding from my plastic makeup sack? Blood welled from the cut and I made sure to smear some on the carpet. Evidence. Just in case. A snake-like garment grabbed my wrist. Panty hose. There. My hand closed on a rectangle of metal. The box of shells was at the bottom of the case.

Which way to face when he opened the trunk? Should I try for a full rotation, a rollover to get my elbows on the floor? The car stopped. Red light? Traffic jam? I heard a door open, slam. What if he was stopping for backup? What if he abandoned the car? "Woman frozen in freak Portland blizzard." Maybe he'd come back in a week, dump my body in a river.

I clicked the magazine home.

I forced myself to breathe. In and out. Slowly, regularly. I couldn't hear footsteps.

The trunk opened so fast I only caught a glimpse of a hand holding an upraised crowbar before the flashlight blinded me. The beam gave me a target to sight on. My neck ached from holding my head upright. I kept my teeth from chattering as I yelled, "Hold it there. Drop the iron."

Never pull your piece unless you intend to shoot. Never shoot unless you mean to kill. That's what they taught me at the police academy. I'd have shot the chauffeur without a qualm, just for being a lousy goddamn driver, but I wanted answers.

If he'd flicked off the light and made a sudden move, he might have gotten me. My finger tightened against the trigger. If the light died I'd fire.

It didn't. It wavered and I heard a soft thud, like a tire iron landing in snow.

"Hey," he said, his voice a good two notes higher than before. "Relax. Take it easy. I look mean, but I'm not."

"I don't look mean, but I am," I said menacingly, wondering how the hell I was going to get out of the trunk without at least wounding the jerk, giving him something to hold his attention while I clambered over the rear bumper.

"You got the safety catch on?" he asked nervously.

"Guess," I said. "Take five steps back and lie down in the snow."

"Lie down?"

"Faceup. Make me a snow angel, and I mean a good one."

"A snow angel?" he echoed.

"It's like doing jumping jacks lying down," I said. "What's your name?"

"Why?"

"Because I've got a gun and you don't, moron."

"Name's Clay," he muttered.

"Well, Clay. I want to hear you flap those arms and legs. I want to hear your hands clap over your head, okay? Real loud and regular. If I even suspect you're going for the tire iron, not to mention anything else, you're going to be missing a kneecap."

I didn't move till I heard a snort, followed by the scuffing of snow, and rhythmic clapping. Then I stretched my legs over the edge of the trunk, and lifted myself to a semi-sitting position using a combo of abdominals and my left arm.

"Okay, angel," I said once I'd struggled to my feet. My legs felt tingly and achy. My left arm burned. I wanted to sit in the snow and cry. Lie down. Make my own angel.

"What?" he said.

"Are we going to chat or shoot?"

"Can I get up?"

"Why? You want to die like a man?"

"It's colder than a witch's tit down here. If we're gonna talk this thing out, let's get in the car and turn on the heater."

"I have a better idea," I said, reaching behind me and lifting my bag out of the trunk.

"What?"

"Keep flapping those arms. I am now going to take ten steps away from the car. Don't worry. That won't put me out of firing range. Then you will stand *when I tell you to,* and you will march over to the car, and get in the trunk."

"In the trunk?"

"We're trading places."

"Then what?"

His voice hailed from somewhere south. No wonder he didn't know how to make a snow angel. His accent reminded me of someone else's; its cadence was familiar, but not the same. His voice was higher pitched.

"I didn't get a chance to ask 'then what?' when you shoved me in," I said reasonably. "Now, did I?"

He glared. No reply.

"I'm taking my ten steps," I said. "You can get up now."

He followed orders.

"Who hired you to freak Dee Willis?" I asked.

No response.

"Come on," I urged. "You think I couldn't shoot you dead

and walk, buddy? Think it over. I'm a legit private eye on a
legit case. My gun's legal. There's evidence—my blood and
sweat and hair—in the damn trunk. Your fingerprints on the
tire iron. There's self-defense written all over this baby."

Nothing.

"So who hired you?"

I was freezing my ass for nothing. I don't know, in the
movies, somebody's got a gun, they ask questions, and people tell them what they want to know. In real life, I get perps
too stupid to plan beyond their next meal.

I blew out a steamy breath, said, "Okay. Let's do it the
hard way. Empty your pockets. Drop everything straight
down in the snow. I want to see the car keys drop. I want to
see your wallet drop. I expect you have a knife, and I would
like to see that hit the ground, too."

"Shit." His drawl split the word into two syllables. "I ain't
got a knife."

I sighted to the left of his foot, pressed the trigger gently,
hit closer than I'd intended. The ground jumped four inches
from his toe.

"Knife," I said.

"Jesus, lady," he said. "It's in my boot."

"Well, sit your fat butt on the ground and take your boots
off. Easy, now. Rest your weight on your right hand. Like
that. Take your boots off with your left. One at a time. Slow
and easy. Lay the blade on the ground. Take your socks off,
too, while you're at it."

"I could get frostbit."

"You could get dead," I said pleasantly. "Okay. Now stand
up and walk to the car. Hands over your head, please. Take
one step toward me, make a move for the knife or the tire
iron, and you're meat, understand? My hands are getting too
cold to go for anything but gut shots. And, trust me, I will
empty the magazine. I've got seven left. And they're not
twenty-twos."

I felt better as soon as I'd slammed the trunk. I grabbed
the keys from the snow and locked the damn thing just to
make sure.

I slung my bag into the backseat, then gathered up the "chauffeur's" belongings, boots, smelly socks, and all.

In the driver's seat, I turned on the engine and let blessed heat flow over my shaking hands and chilled feet. I set the safety on the 40 and stuck it in the glove compartment.

I searched for a map. Nothing in the dash. Nothing in any of the fancy seat pockets. As dawn brightened the sky, I settled down for a thorough exam of the man's wallet.

Cash: one hundred and eighty-seven bucks. A crumpled note giving my name—spelled wrong—airline—spelled right—and arrival time. I stuck it in my pocket, went on to examine a mine of contradictory ID. He had a California driver's license in the name of Claude Fillmer. A Discover card for one Clyde Fulton. Several business cards for Clyde, one introducing him as a claims rep for State Farm Insurance, another asserting his connection to California Security, Incorporated. He'd made himself vice-president. I wondered why he hadn't gone for the top job.

A motel key. Room 138.

A video-rental card for Claude.

A Burger King receipt. I was getting nowhere; I should have made him strip.

Mooney, my former boss at the Boston PD, once told me that ex-cons tend to keep more than knives in their boots. I could practically hear his voice. I hoped I wasn't starting to hallucinate.

Inside the left boot, I felt the raised outline of a cardboard rectangle. I upended the sucker, shook it hard, but the card was stuck to the insole. It felt too thick and stiff for a manufacturer's label. I used Clay's (or Claude's or Clyde's) knife to pry it out, taking grim satisfaction in the gouges I hacked in the leather.

I found the kind of ID card that comes with cheap wallets. Clayton Fuller had filled out parts of it in a barely legible scrawl. If anything happened to Clayton, anything necessitating the removal and examination of his boots, he thought Mrs. Caroline Fuller of Hazlehurst, Mississippi, was most likely to care.

Hazlehurst, Mississippi. The name swam before my eyes.
Memphis means Elvis.
Detroit is Aretha.
Liverpool equals Lennon and McCartney.
Hazlehurst, Mississippi, is the birthplace of the legendary
Robert Johnson, a man who recorded forty-one tunes in a
tragically short twenty-nine-year life span and left his im-
print on country blues forever. King of the Delta Blues, they
called him. Any blues musician worth his salt would boast
of sharing a hometown with Robert Johnson, even a player
born years after Johnson's mysterious death in 1938.
One had.
I needed to rock the car to get us moving. I may have
done it more vigorously than necessary out of consideration
for my passenger in the trunk.
I had no idea where we were. I drove, searching for a
convenience store, a phone booth, a police station. The Lincoln had half a tank of gas.
I pulled into the parking lot of a little mom-and-pop store
near a crossroads, taking care to remove the keys and lock
all the doors. Wouldn't do to have my possibly stolen car
possibly stolen again. Mom-and-pop sported a Pacific Bell
logo on their door. The clerk shook his head sadly as he
informed me that I was in the town of Gresham, Oregon.
Women drivers, his glance said, hardly ever knew where the
hell they were. I was glad I'd left my gun in the glove compartment.
I requested a phone book and ten dollars' worth of
change. I learned that all of Mississippi shares one area code:
601.
Clayton's mama was home, practically housebound, she
said, what with the "artheritis" actin' up like it done, and
just full of chitchat about her son and his best boyhood pals.
What a memory.
I was exhausted by the time I talked her off the line. I
used some of Clay's cash to buy a local *Oregonian*, a map, a
cup of steaming coffee, and a huge Nestlé's Crunch bar.
Breakfast.

I knocked on the trunk in passing.

"I'm gonna faint in here," Clay yelled.

"Good," I hollered back.

God knows what the nosy clerk, peering through the blinds, thought. I gulped the coffee without tasting it, ate half the candy bar standing in the chill morning air. It felt fine to be outdoors in sunlight.

The air was different, canned and smoky, at Dee's first Portland gig. After managing a few hours' sleep, I entered the hall as soon as the doors opened, the first fan inside the tiny auditorium. The stalker was not in the house. The police had been glad to take him off my hands. We'd had a little private eye–to-felon chat before I turned him in. I'd mentioned the inadvisability of naming Dee Willis, unless he wanted his fifteen minutes of fame fast, followed by a lifetime of hate mail and hard prison time.

Dee's popular with inmates. She does jailhouse concerts.

I kept my lies simple. I'd landed late at the airport. No cabs. Guy had pretended to be a legit limo driver, offered me a ride into town for twenty bucks, tried to attack me. I showed my license, my Massachusetts permit to carry. Perp had picked on the wrong victim. The cops were sympathetic. I presented them with Clayton's various IDs, suggested they check outstanding warrants and parole violations in all his assumed names as well as his own.

I didn't think they'd come up empty.

I watched the crowd filter in, young and old, dressed up, dressed down. Joking, laughing, getting ready for a great time.

No opening act. The curtain rose on the band, playing "For Tonight," the early rocker Dee had made her anthem. Her voice came from everywhere, amplified. The audience gawked, expecting her to enter from stage right, stage left, down one aisle, then another. She chose her moment brilliantly, theatrical as always, appearing suddenly behind an onstage scrim, rainbow lights glistening her white satin tux.

I settled into my crushed velveteen seat and fell for the

magic. For glistening bodies shiny with sweat. For the beat and the lyrics and the glorious close harmonies. For the old songs, by John Lee Hooker and Robert Johnson and Son House and Mama Thornton, that Dee had taken, transformed, and made her own. I saw her through a looking-glass of memory at first, but she shattered the barrier with song after song, dragging me into the moment, her moment.

That's her gift. She makes you forget everything but the song. Makes you care about lyrics written seventy years ago by a Mississippi sharecropper, makes them more important than a crummy day at the office or a fight with the kids. Dee gets so deep into the music, it's a wonder she ever climbs out.

I didn't leave my seat at intermission. I didn't move until the last encore ended. Didn't stand till everyone else had gone. Then I parted a red velvet drape and mounted the steps leading backstage.

The dressing rooms were upstairs, eight of them, two per floor, four floors. The "chauffeur" had outlined the setup. I knew which room was Dee's. First floor back. I kept climbing, up to the second floor front. I knocked once, stepped inside. I kept my voice low; I didn't want Dee to hear.

The room was Spartan, linoleum floor, peeling paint on bare walls. Air freshener and body odor warred, neither victorious.

Dee and I have long shared a taste in men: tall, bone-thin, and musically inclined. Ron, in his early forties now, and Cal, my ex, shared enough superficial similarities to pass as a pair of matching bookends.

Ron was buttoning a purple silk shirt over his skinny torso, tucking the shirttail into tight jeans. The jeans disappeared into high snakeskin boots. His guitar lay across a countertop. I brushed a string to get his attention.

He glanced at my reflection in the mirror, sank into a hardbacked chair.

"Carlotta," he said, both grin and voice forced.

"Don't bother smiling for me, Ron."

"No bother," he lied. "Long time."

"I've had a talk with your boy, Clay."

He fumbled for an answer, an excuse. "Clay doesn't know shit," he said, after a long pause. "Clay's not my 'boy.' "

"He knows who hired him, Ron. He's real sure about that."

"You don't fuckin' understand," the lead guitar player said, slamming his fist down against the countertop.

"I understand that you love Dee, Ron. I understand that's hard."

He nodded, so slightly it was barely perceptible.

"I mean about Clay," he said. "There's no understanding Dee. I've given up on that. But with Clay, it got out of hand, Carlotta. I never meant it to get ugly."

"Ugly, Ron? You're talking about scaring somebody half to death. You're talking about a stalker. You're talking about a guy who tried to kill me last night."

"Shit." He split the word into two syllables, just like Clayton Fuller.

"Did you tell him I was coming?"

"Only reason I did was to scare him the hell off, Carlotta. Told him Dee'd hired a pro, somebody who'd nab his sorry ass. I figured he'd split. He's changed, you know? People fuckin' change on you. . . . He's somebody from the old days. Guy I played football with in high school. That's all."

"Hazlehurst," I said.

"Hazlehurst High, yeah. He was a tough guy then. Still is."

"You send for him?"

"He came to a concert. Out of the blue. We went out for a drink. He wanted me to introduce him to Dee. That's what every guy in the fuckin' country wants, an intro to Dee."

"So?"

"So I told him that Dee and I were . . . together, but we were having our troubles. You know, like we always had."

"Trouble staying faithful, you mean?"

"You know her."

I folded my arms under my breasts, gave him a look. "Whereas you were always a saint, Ron. I remember that."

"I only care for Dee. If she'd—"

"Did you ever ask her to marry you?"

"I always ask. Says she doesn't want kids, so what's the point?"

"And she likes men," I observed.

"Probably sucking some guy's dick right now," he said without skipping a beat. "Celebrating 'cause Clay didn't show." Ron's voice sounded dead as an urn full of ashes. "Wanna go check? It's not like I never walked in on her before."

"Let's not change the tune here, Ron. It's not illegal to sleep around. It is illegal to threaten somebody's life."

"Honest to God, I tried to stop him, Carlotta. Everybody in the band'll tell you that. He was like a hound on the scent, out to do me a favor whether I wanted one or not."

"You should have called the cops."

Ron swallowed. "I thought about it. I told him it'd gone too far. He kinda laughed, then he said he'd cut my hand, cut the tendons, so I'd never play again. He swore if I turned him in he'd tell everybody it was my idea from the get-go."

"Wasn't it?"

"Carlotta, I *love* her. I might have said something to Clay, probably did after I'd downed a few shots. Like, you know, I wish to hell she'd stop screwing around. Clay took it real personal. Said he'd been through two divorces and every time it was his wife cheatin' on him, bangin' this guy or that guy while he's out earnin' bread for the table."

"And you believed him?"

Ron stared at his boots. I noticed a deep scratch across one toe. "I reckon if his wives ran off, they had good reason. I knew a girl he dated back in high school. She'd look at another guy, he'd smack her 'cross the mouth. She moved away, didn't tell anybody where she was headed. What I understand, one of his wives, at least, has got a restraining order out on Clay, maybe an arrest warrant. He told me he can't see his kids, called his wife a castrating bitch. Really got off on it, how wicked she was. Couldn't tell me enough about that evil woman."

Good, I thought, hoping for the arrest warrant. I wanted the bastard locked up, but not at the expense of involving Dee. She didn't need the tabloid coverage. She didn't need every jerk who could read the *Star* or the *Enquirer* getting the idea that stalking Dee Willis might be a fine way to pass the hours.

"Did she sound evil to you?" I asked Ron. "The wife?"

He shook his head. "Sounded like she didn't like gettin' the shit kicked out of her. Sounded like she'd had enough and wanted out."

I repeated, "You should have called the cops."

He faced me directly, stared at me with ice-blue eyes. His voice sounded low and raspy, exhausted. He shook his head, kept shaking it slowly, side to side, as he spoke. "I thought he'd stick around a few nights, maybe make her realize a true thing, Carlotta. Like it's not how it used to be out there. You know it isn't."

"How'd it used to be, Ron? I forget."

"You could get crabs, Carlotta. Maybe the clap. Shot of penicillin. Big fuckin' deal."

"You afraid she'll bring home AIDS? Stop sleeping with her. Use a condom."

"You think I'm just worrying about myself here? Goddammit, I love her."

"So you hire some jerk to scare her to death. What's he supposed to do for a finale? Kidnap her? Rape her?"

"I'd never—I only thought he'd keep her home nights. I thought she'd turn to me, for help, for protection. Instead, she called you."

The way he looked at me, I could tell Dee's cry for help, for *my* help, had been bitter medicine. Yet another injury to his pride.

"And just what was Clay going to do to me, Ron?"

"I dunno," he said studying the linoleum like it was a

work of art. "Man's a fool. I guess he figured he could scare you."

I thought about my time in the trunk. Especially the few moments when I hadn't known whether Clay would open it or walk away. . . .

He'd done his job.

Ron was speaking. "I think Clay's way past thinkin' about me, Carlotta. I'm afraid he really wants Dee. I'm scared he'll hurt her." He swallowed audibly. "I guess I'm ready to go to the cops."

I said, "No reason to, Ron. I've taken care of the cops. You're going to do something harder. Tell Dee. Every nasty detail."

"No."

"Then pack your bags and update your resumé, because she'll fire your ass. You know she will, if I tell her."

He didn't say anything, just stared into the mirror like he was saying good-bye to the best part of himself.

"Do it, Ron. Apologize. Stay with her."

"She's never loved anything but the music, Carlotta," he said, his Adam's apple working. "She doesn't love me."

"She comes back to you, Ron."

"She comes back."

"Maybe that's her kind of love. Maybe that's all the love she's got."

"I don't know if I can live with that," he said.

I wasn't sure if he was talking to me or to the pale skinny man in the mirror.

"Two days, Ron," I said. "You have two days to tell her, or else I will."

I flagged a cab and went straight to the airport. No trouble changing the tickets. Fly first class, they give you leeway.

Dee called late the next night, woke me from a sound sleep. I suppose Ron will always be her lead guitar.

Miss Gibson arrived via messenger. I've stroked her, held her, but I can't bring myself to play her. I try, but something keeps me mute. When I touch the strings, finger a chord, I'm overwhelmed by a sense of awe.

Maybe fear. With that precious battered guitar in hand, I guess I'm scared that I've come as close to the magic as I'll ever get.

SUSAN GEASON lives in Sydney, Australia, where she is the literary editor of the *Sun-Herald* newspaper. Her first three novels featured private investigator Syd Fish, with journalist Lizzie Darcy, the heroine of "Green Murder," as best mate and invaluable source. Her latest suspense novel, **Wildfire,** featuring homicide detective and psychologist Rachel Addison, and set against the cataclysmic bushfires of January 1994, has just been published by Random House.

Green Murder

Susan Geason

Like all big cities, Sydney is also a small town, so I wasn't surprised to run into Margo Daniels at a fund raiser for a women's research library. Margo and I had attended a girls school that made no secret of its ambition to produce Australia's first female prime minister. As New South Wales's minister for the environment and one of only three women in Cabinet, Margo was the most obvious contender.

A plodder with good political instincts masquerading as character, Margo had ended up head girl. I, on the other hand, had narrowly escaped expulsion for attitudinal problems. Neither of us has changed much. I'd been quietly gleeful when Margo had dropped out of an arts degree to marry a good Catholic boy, but five children later she'd completed a law degree and entered politics. You can't keep a good woman down—or an egomaniac.

Over glasses of chardonnay, we circled each other warily.

"How's the environment?" I asked, knowing full well the portfolio was in chaos. Only a week back, thousands of outraged middle-class voters had marched on the airport to protest against noise from a new runway, and any minute now, loggers might blockade Parliament House with their trucks to protect their traditional right to destroy the state's old-growth forests.

"I'm dealing with it by calling it a baptism of fire," she

said, and I liked her a little more. "What's happened to you?"

"I'm on sabbatical," I said. Panicked by my thirty-seventh birthday, I'd negotiated a year's leave of absence from my newspaper to write a book about a controversial media magnate. I was bogged down in research and terminally bored, but Margo didn't need to know that.

"I miss your pieces in the *Herald*," she said.

"You're kidding me!"

She laughed. "I didn't always agree with you, but I never found you unfair. Besides, you were quite useful to me sometimes when I needed leverage against the troglodytes in Cabinet."

Margo's generosity gave me a twinge of guilt for the jokes I'd made about her in the past, but as remorse is useless unless it leads to a change of heart and I had no desire to reform, I ignored it.

"How do you do it all?" I asked.

"I had nannies when the kids were small, and now I've got a housekeeper, a mother and two sisters whom I shamelessly exploit, and a husband who's a workaholic too."

"What if he gets midlife crisis and bails out with his secretary?"

"In some ways it would be a relief," she said, in a rare moment of candor. "I wouldn't have to feel so guilty about neglecting him."

But I'd been hogging one of the movement's stars, and a gym-honed, besuited young woman interrupted to do some networking. "Good luck, Margo," I said.

"My old dad used to say you make your own luck," she replied. She'd live to eat those words.

I awoke a week later to the news that the body of Margo Daniels's press secretary, David Valentine, had been found in an inner-city park. No mention was made of the well-known fact that Green Park was a notorious homosexual beat, probably because of the victim's political connections.

I'd come across David Valentine through my work, and though I'd assumed he was gay, I never saw any proof. Consequently, I'd put him down as one of those homosexuals who are terrified of exposure, deep in the closet. His caution was understandable: Margo Daniels, his boss, was noted—notorious, in homosexual circles—for her advocacy of family values and her tough line on crime.

"Can't stay away from it, can you?" said Chrissie Wilmot, one of the *Herald*'s crime reporters, when I rang her for the juicy details. "It looks like the usual Saturday night gay bashing. Did you know Valentine was homosexual?"

"I suspected it, but I would never have thought he'd risk his career for a rent boy. What's Margo Daniels saying?"

"Maintaining radio silence so far. Doubtless we'll get a media release expressing her deep sadness at the untimely death of a trusted and valued employee and decrying the breakdown of standards in a society where a citizen can be struck down while going about his lawful business in a public place."

We laughed. As soon as I'd put the phone down, it rang again.

"Miss Darcy," said a breathy female voice, "the minister would like to speak to you."

"Which minister?"

The young woman was flummoxed for a moment. "The minister for the environment, of course. Mrs. Daniels."

"Okay," I said, nonchalantly, pulse racing, curiosity aflame.

"Lizzie?"

"Margo."

"I assume you've heard about David."

"Of course. It's terrible. You must be upset."

Margo's protestations of shock and disbelief were as unconvincing as mine: her sympathy lay entirely with herself. Her mind was on damage control.

"Lizzie, I don't want to sound cold-blooded, but David's death has left me in a hole. I can't function without a press secretary with these airport protests going on."

Assuming she was asking me to recommend someone, I racked my brains for competent journalists with sufficient political wit to navigate the minefield of state politics without getting their legs blown off. I mentioned a name, but it seemed she wanted me.

"Just for a couple of weeks until I can fill the position permanently," she promised.

The offer was like the scent of smoke to an old fire horse. I was constitutionally incapable of resisting the lure of a political murder, but knowing how politicians despise the needy, I played hard to get, finally allowing myself to be won over by an appeal to our shared history.

I slept badly that night. I have no illusions about politics. Years ago, I'd done a stint on the staff of a federal politician and had quickly mastered the arts of the positive spin and the strategic leak, and had begun playing politics as a game, a game I had to win at any cost. Then I'd heard myself, in a meeting, demolishing the argument of a lobby group I had once belonged to, realized what I'd become, and handed in my resignation.

But I'd lost faith in my book and had long ceased to believe the half-truths journalists tell to convince themselves they haven't wasted their lives breaking the news while other people make it. I wanted to get close to the levers of power again. As I tossed and turned, I told myself that age and wisdom would protect me from temptation, and that I could not refuse an old friend's cry for help. It was half true: Margo certainly needed a good operator on her team. Once the media started gunning for her, the hyenas in her own party would begin to circle.

Qualms quelled, buttoned into my best and only suit, I presented myself at Margo's office on the city's North Shore the next day. First stop was the office of Maureen Noonan, Margo's personal assistant, a large, attractive, fortyish woman with an air of quiet authority.

Maureen introduced me to my new colleagues, who responded coolly. Like all ministers' offices, Margo's was a shark nursery, stocked with would-be politicians and bureaucrats on the make. Margo's minders made it clear they had opposed my appointment and were suspending judgment until I proved myself. One way or another. If it was supposed to frighten me, it didn't work: the atmosphere reminded me of every newspaper office I'd ever worked in.

It took me ten minutes to work out that all this professional poise masked a state of barely suppressed panic. If David Valentine's murder scuttled Margo's career, they'd all go down with the ship.

Eventually Maureen turned me over to Abigail Huntley, Margo's assistant press secretary, who'd been keeping the propaganda machine ticking over in David Valentine's absence. Bottle blond, brittle, and far too thin, Abigail quickly inducted me and dumped a stack of pressing files on my desk.

"I'll field the phone inquiries till you've gotten across the files," she said, and fled.

I read files till my eyes crossed, then knocked out a bunch of media releases. Free to snoop, I set about mapping the power lines.

Margo's chief executive officer, Rowan Sherwood, was now top dog. I'd run into him around the traps and had found him pompous, devious, and utterly ruthless. A political mercenary, he'd been one of the few ministerial staffers to survive the last change of government. A man to watch. Today Sherwood seemed tense and jumpy. Shocked by David's death, or just worried about the political fallout?

When I went in to his office for a briefing, he looked up from a file and said: "Margo must have flipped her lid, letting a snoop like you in here."

"I'm delighted to see you, too, Rowan," I said, itching to slap his supercilious mug.

He pursed his lips. "Just watch your step. If there are any leaks from this office, we'll know who to blame."

It was pure provocation. We both knew any gossip about Margo's business would be professional suicide for me. Before I could return the insult, his phone rang, and he turned his back and began to talk. I got up to leave, but before I could make my escape, he put his hand over the receiver and said: "You'll find the Queen of Macquarie Street a hard act to follow."

No love lost there.

A little later, I saw him buttonhole Lindsay Groenewegen, the deputy director of the Environment Protection Authority, as he came out of Margo's office and engage him in a serious tête-à-tête. It must have been bad news, because Groenewegen left looking grim.

As the day wore on, I set about ingratiating myself with my new colleagues, laying on the sympathy with a trowel. I discovered that David Valentine had been too reserved to be popular; that Abigail Huntley was widely regarded as a bitch; that Rowan Sherwood was cordially detested but feared; and that the parliamentary assistant, Ted Simms, liked a drink.

They also told me that Margo ruled the place with an iron hand, forbidding backbiting, complaining, and long faces, and refusing to listen to excuses. Several people repeated her mantra: "Don't come to me with problems; come to me with solutions." Margo, it seemed, inspired respect rather than devotion.

To a person, however, Margo's minders agreed that Maureen Noonan was the power behind the throne. The way they described her, Maureen had the logistical skills of a general, the tact of a diplomat and the unflappability of an air traffic controller. She had an encyclopedic memory and never lost track of a piece of paper or an item of gossip. Discreet as a boulder, sharp as an ax blade, she never had to raise her voice to get what she wanted. Even the cynics invoked her name with awe.

I caught myself thinking that the day she lost Maureen's support would be a sorry day indeed for Margo.

In what little time I had between phone calls from reporters maddened by the whiff of a sex scandal, I tried to chart the informal networks in the office. Though I would have expected the policy staff to stick together, the two researchers—Evelina Villanelle and Sean Kelly—were colleagues rather than friends; Evelina and Abigail Huntley seemed close but gave Rowan Sherwood a wide berth; the departmental liaison officers, evidently feeling marooned in enemy territory, stuck together, and the support staff didn't socialize with the professionals because they couldn't talk about anything but politics.

The only odd note was the apparent alliance between Rowan Sherwood and Ross Harvey, the EPA liaison man. On the surface, they couldn't have been more different. Sherwood was a BMW-driving, well-tailored yuppie who occasionally appeared in the social columns with a federal politician's daughter; whereas Harvey was a typical sedentary public servant, about thirty-five, going to seed, who appeared to own only one suit, a shiny-seated number he'd probably worn to his confirmation. In pride of place on his desk was a photo of a chubby wife, two fair little girls, and a boy in a wheelchair. Perhaps the two men shared an interest in stamps, or racing pigeons.

Exhausted, I crawled home about seven o'clock, poured myself a drink, and slumped down in front of the television. On a current affairs program, a journalist hinted heavily at a sex angle in David Valentine's death. As the item finished, the phone rang: it was Margo.

"Did you see that?" she asked, no chitchat, no preamble. "What should I do?"

"If you're absolutely certain he wasn't gay, you could come out and quash the speculation; otherwise, you're stuck with sad but puzzled. Whatever you do, though, you're going to be accused of hypocrisy before this is over."

Her voice rose. "I hired David because he was the best in the business. How was I supposed to know he was gay? What am I supposed to do, run checks on people's sex lives? And anyway, just because I believe in families, it doesn't mean I have to discriminate against homosexuals."

"I'll come up with a form of words for you first thing tomorrow morning," I said.

Realizing she'd been told to pull herself together, Margo subsided. "Thanks for coming aboard, Lizzie. It means a lot to me."

I put down the phone thoughtfully, and tried to translate Margo's tirade. I couldn't decide if she'd known David was gay and decided to take the risk, or if she had been too naive to sense his sexual orientation.

Day two began with a crisis over a lost departmental file dealing with an application to extend a toxic chemicals plant. After we'd turned the place upside down to no avail, Maureen buzzed me and asked me to pop in.

"Could you do us a favor?" she said.

Us, I thought. So Maureen gives orders for Margo.

"The only place we haven't looked for the Sharrock file is David Valentine's apartment. I wondered if you'd mind going out there and having a look for it."

I'm not superstitious, but this felt a bit like grave robbing. I hesitated.

"Rowan's out, and I thought the others would find it too upsetting," said Maureen. It had been an order, not a request.

"He often took files home?" I asked.

"Oh, yes. And Margo asked him to have a look at the Sharrock file a few days ago because the local rag has started a campaign against the plant. They reckon it's too close to a new residential development."

"Where does he live?"

"Bondi Beach. Here, I've written down the address for you."

"How am I going to get in, Maureen?"

"I've spoken to the police, and they're sending a key over."

Game, set, match, Maureen Noonan.

While I waited for the key, I made myself a cup of coffee and went out into the courtyard to sneak a smoke, all government offices being smoke free these days. Abigail Huntley was there already, talking to one of the researchers, Sean Kelly, a thin, slightly stooped nerd with a scraggy scientist's beard and watchful brown eyes behind heavy glasses.

"Margo's so upset . . ." Abigail was saying. Seeing me, she stopped guiltily.

"Were David and Margo close?" I asked.

Abigail hesitated, then decided the question was innocuous. "In some ways. Nobody really got close to David, but if Margo wanted any dirty work done, she always got him to do it. He was very discreet."

"What sort of dirty work?"

They exchanged a look. "It was just a figure of speech," said Abigail.

"David was closer to Maureen, actually," said Sean Kelly.

"Really?"

"Yes, they used to shut themselves in Margo's office when she was out and gossip and laugh," said Abigail. "Thick as thieves, they were. Quite frankly, I don't know what she saw in him."

She turned on her heel and left. Watching her go, Sean Kelly smirked and said: "Abby was just jealous; she wanted his job. If I were you, I'd watch my back. That's a very ambitious lady."

Later, armed with a key delivered by a nervous and ridiculously young police officer, I drove out to Bondi. Feeling like a burglar, I unlocked the door to David Valentine's flat and went in. It was stale and stuffy, so I threw open the windows, letting in an expensive view of the beach and the roar of the surf and traffic. David had good taste: parquet floors, minimal furniture, a couple of arresting Aboriginal paintings, a wall of books, and a sophisticated sound system. But there was no sign of a file in the eerily tidy living room.

I had no excuse to go into David Valentine's bathroom, but that didn't stop me: the desire to peer into people's medicine cabinets is coded into the human DNA. Alongside the usual patent medicines were several packs of condoms, and on a glass shelf, five expensive bottles of aftershave stood, lined up like hussars. It looked as if David Valentine had a sex life, but with whom?

I got the answer from a photograph album I found in the top drawer of the bedside table. It was filled with shots of David with a slightly built, fair, attractive younger man, whose name, according to the inscriptions on the back of the pictures, was Heath.

Needing a surname, I dialed the automatic number marked Heath on David's phone. An answering machine told me Heath Robertson wasn't available to take my call and asked me to leave a message, but I declined to do so.

Later Margo called me in to Parliament House, in the city, for a briefing. The buzz of purposeful activity in Macquarie Street gave me a brief nostalgia hit, but I knew it was just a Pavlovian response. I'm too old and cynical now to take most politicians as seriously as their egos demand. Margo was still agitated about the media's reaction to David's death, wondering if we needed to change our strategy. Reminding her that reporters have a short attention span, I advised her to hold the line. With any luck, an earthquake, a cyclone, or an intemperate outburst by the Prime Minister would send them all rushing off in another direction, and they'd forget to come back.

That night I rang Chrissie Wilmot at the *Herald* and asked her if the police had made any headway on the murder.

"The postmortem showed he had a very thin skull, that he died from a blow which probably wouldn't have killed your everyday knucklehead," she told me.

"So it could have been one unlucky punch?"

"Yes. And the gang-bashing theory is starting to look a bit sick. I heard a whisper that a transvestite who works the street near there saw a man dragging something heavy from a car into Green Park that night. But before you get your hopes up, he's a speed freak. He could have imagined the whole thing."

"But if he didn't . . ."

"Someone killed Valentine elsewhere and dumped him in the park."

"To make it look like a sex murder," I said. "There's no other reason they'd take such a risk. Which means we should be looking for another motive."

"We?" asked Chrissie. "I thought you were on leave."

I ignored this dig. "If he wasn't hanging around Green Park trying to score, where was he that night?"

"Your guess is as good as mine."

If anyone knew, it would be Heath Robertson. He was in the phone book, and this time he was in when I rang. He was very guarded, though, wanting to know how I'd tracked him down. When I confessed, he said the police had been there before me, and had given him a hard time until he'd established his alibi. A policy adviser in the Health Department, he'd been at a conference on the Gold Coast, six hundred miles north, when his lover was killed.

When he discovered I had inside information on the case, he agreed to trade.

We met in an empty, miraculously quiet coffee shop in the espresso strip in Darlinghurst. A bored, black-clad waiter served us cappuccinos, then sloped off and picked up a dog-eared paperback copy of Middlemarch, leaving us alone.

I recognized Heath Robertson from his photos, but now there were purple stains under his gray eyes and fine lines bracketing his mouth. I told him about the new witness, and he put his head in his hands and almost wept with relief. He said he'd thought he was going mad, wondering if he'd completely misread the man he'd loved.

"It just didn't make sense. He was terrified to go near any gay joints in case someone recognized him and the word got around. And even if he had decided to cheat on me, he wouldn't have been confident enough to try to pick someone up in a public place. I had to throw myself at him when we met, and he was ten years younger then. . . ."

A sob escaped him, but he quickly regained his composure. "I hated the secrecy, all that creeping about feeling like a criminal, but he wouldn't come out. In the beginning he used his old man as an excuse: said it would kill him. But when his father died, he wheeled Mad Margo in; said she'd sack him if she found out." He paused. "All those wasted years, and now the whole world knows."

"If it wasn't a gay bashing, there has to be another motive," I said. "Was he acting differently before the murder?"

"Yes, he was. He was very tense, not sleeping properly, and he started smoking again. I told the police all this, but they said it made sense if he was playing around on me. But they're wrong: it was his job."

"How?"

"He was squabbling with Rowan Sherwood."

"What about?"

"I'm not certain, but it started after he went home to Dolphin Bay, to his father's funeral. He was fit to be tied when he got back. Apparently the Japanese were planning to build a mega-resort there, and his parents' friends had got into his ear about it."

"But surely he would have already known about that development?"

"I don't think he'd realized what the resort would do to the town. He was determined to stop it. Do you think . . ."

"I don't know what to think yet," I said. "Did he tell you what he was going to do?"

"No. He didn't discuss political business with me. . . . Sometimes he acted like an equerry to the queen. Queen Margo." His voice grew bitter. "He idolized that cow, and she exploited him because he didn't have a family to go home to."

"You didn't live with him?"

He lowered his eyes. "No. I've got my own place."

I felt real sympathy for Heath Robertson, who'd obviously been no match for his lover. Out of fear, David Valentine had treated him like a backstreet mistress, and that betrayal still hurt. He'd probably heard about his lover's death on the morning news, like any stranger. I wasn't at all sure I would have liked David Valentine. When we parted outside, I asked if he'd be all right.

"No, I won't. But there's nothing you or anybody else can do about that."

I suppose I'd asked for that.

Next morning, Abigail told me that Maureen Noonan had

located the toxic chemicals file under a pile of stuff on Margo's desk. It seemed like an uncharacteristic lapse, but these were difficult times. Sanity, or what passes for it in politics, returned.

Emerging from the kitchen with a coffee later that morning, I noticed Rowan Sherwood and Ross Harvey engaged in an intense conversation at the photocopier. Then Sherwood stalked outside. Curiosity piqued, I scuttled to a window and saw him pacing and gesticulating wildly with his cigarette, arguing with someone on his cellular phone. It might have been his girlfriend or his bookie, of course, but I wanted to know for sure.

Shortly after, he came inside, threw the phone into a desk drawer, and set off in the direction of the Men's. After a quick scan for spies, I whipped into his office, grabbed the phone, and pressed the redial button. A female voice answered: "This is the mayor's office. Can I help you."

"I'm not sure I've got the right number," I purred. "Is this the mayor of Casterbridge?"

"No," said the woman. "It's the mayor of Dolphin Bay."

Why was Margo's chief political adviser screaming at the mayor of a town slated for a major development? And what had Rowan Sherwood and the EPA liaison man been arguing about?

I needed more information about the Dolphin Bay development.

In a quiet moment, I started researching Dolphin Bay, which turned out to be a village on a river estuary on the state's north coast. All I could find in my first trawl was a briefing paper, one of those waffly ministerial replies insisting that plans were still in the developmental stage, and assuring the public that "the resort would not go ahead unless the appropriate environmental impact assessments indicated that it would not damage Dolphin Bay's fishing industry." It was a standard bureaucratic fob-off.

Jane Gunn, a contact at Coast Guard, an environmental pressure group, had all the dirt. A Japanese consortium had submitted a development application for a seven-hundred-room resort, complete with casino and marina, catering mostly to Japanese tourists. The town was split, with some residents appalled by the inevitable destruction of their way of life, and others seduced by the promise of jobs and the glitz of a casino. Arguing that development on this scale would almost certainly pollute the river estuary, destroy the mangrove beds, kill off most of the marine life in the area, and wreck the fishing industry, the north coast greens had joined the fray.

"Margo Daniels is backing it, as is the tourism minister," said Jane. "The proposal was fast-tracked through the Dolphin Bay council, and the environmental impact statement gave the development a clean bill of health."

"What's the story on the council?" I asked. Despite the best efforts of the government's anticorruption commission, corruption was still rife, though less blatant, in local government in New South Wales.

"Well, we have no proof that would stand up in court, but the mayor did buy a Jaguar convertible three months ago."

"What color?"

"Silver," she said, and we laughed.

"Who did the environmental assessment?" I asked.

"A shonky bunch called McCluskey and Farrell. McCluskey used to work in the EPA till he took a suspiciously early retirement, but he's still got lots of mates in the department. Including Lindsay Groenewegen, the deputy director."

"Wasn't the new Coastal Protection Act supposed to stop this sort of thing?" I asked.

Bowing to green pressure, the government had finally drafted legislation designed to stop the galloping development that was concreting the coastline, destroying sand dunes and beaches, and even changing tidal patterns in some places.

"It hasn't come into effect yet, Lizzie," said Jane sadly. "It's scheduled to go to Parliament in about two weeks."

I rang off, wondering why the city media hadn't picked up on the controversy, then realized that David Valentine had probably been responsible for keeping it tamped down.

At the beginning anyway; later, he'd woken up and decided to do something about it. Now I could understand why he'd been so disturbed: To save Dolphin Bay he would have had to confront Margo and risk losing his job. Had he been about to blow the whistle?

Ross Harvey did a double-take when I hove into view.

"I want a look at the environmental report on Dolphin Bay," I said.

He blinked. "What for?"

I gave him the gimlet eye, and he colored. "I don't have a copy," he said.

"So get me one from the department, Ross. Today."

As soon as he thought I was out of sight, he slid into Rowan Sherwood's office.

Thinking laterally, I looked for the file containing correspondence about the development. It seemed to have disappeared. Thwarted, I decided to pump Evelina Villanelle. It was a gamble; an environmental economist employed by a conservative minister was unlikely to be emerald green, but she might be honest.

On my way into Evelina's office, I bumped into Maureen Noonan, coming out. Flashing me an enigmatic smile, she sailed off. Wondering what that was about, I went in and closed the door behind me.

Frowning, Evelina was staring into middle distance behind a desk covered in teetering stacks of files and documents, two used mugs, a vase full of wilted roses, and a silver-framed picture of Evelina and a handsome black horse.

"What do you know about Dolphin Bay?" I asked.

Her eyes narrowed. "Why?"

"I think it's connected with David's death."

Evelina gasped, and one hand flew to her mouth. She looked up at me and our eyes locked, and she made up her mind.

"Politically, the minister of tourism just happens to be the local member, and he's hot for it to go ahead, as is the mayor, who is a slug.

"Economically, it would get the town out of a hole in the short term; you know, laboring jobs on building sites, that sort of thing. In the long term, it's a dud. The resort will get its supplies from the city, Japanese operators will transport the tourists to and from the resort and take them out fishing and sightseeing, and Japanese boutiques will sell the imported fashion and the souvenirs. There will be some low-level work in the resort for locals, but because they don't speak Japanese and don't understand the intricacies of bowing, they won't get the good jobs. Japanese workers will be brought in."

She paused for breath.

"Environmentally?" I prompted.

"The picture there isn't totally clear. . . ."

"Meaning?"

Cornered, she took refuge in bureaucratese. "There are those who would question the highly positive findings of the environmental impact statement carried out by carefully selected contractors under conditions stipulated in the Dolphin Bay local environment plan."

"What's the timetable?" I asked.

"The Dolphin Bay development proposal is scheduled to go to Cabinet next week, strongly supported by the minister for the environment."

Evelina dropped her eyes and said softly: "On the advice of certain members of her personal staff."

At 6:00 p.m. Maureen poked her head round my door and said: "We're having drinks in Margo's office. She's asked me to invite you."

I had a wash, looked at my face in the mirror and decided there wasn't much I could do, and went in to get a look at Margo's inner circle. Arrogant Rowan Sherwood, downtrodden Ross Harvey, and bitchy Sean Kelly were there, as were the ambitious Abigail Huntley, the dipsomaniac Ted Simms, and Margo's young, handsome driver, Ron.

The chatter, mostly political gossip and football, was eye glazing. At about seven, Ross Harvey got up to go, and

Rowan Sherwood decided he'd join him. As the others trickled out, Margo signaled me to stay.

"The media seem to have lost interest in David's death at last," she said, abandoning her mineral water for a double Scotch.

"It will hot up again if they find out who did it."

"Maybe they never will," she said.

I thought that unlikely, but held my tongue.

Then she surprised me. "I miss him . . . though it's a lot more peaceful around here lately."

"How do you mean?"

"They were careful around me, but David and Rowan were hardly speaking toward the end."

This felt like an opening. "Margo, what do you know about the Dolphin Bay development application?"

"Not much." She was alert now, concerned about where this was leading.

I waited, and unable to bear silence, like most politicians, she caved in. "The project looks like a good thing, though," she said, watching me closely. "That area needs a lift, and tourism seems the only way to go." She laughed: "Rowan calls it Doldrums Bay."

I'll bet he does, I thought. "What about its environmental impact?"

"I've only seen a summary report, but it looked pretty good, I thought. . . ." Then she cracked. "What's this all about, Lizzie?"

I plowed on. "What did David think about it?"

"He was dead against it. He grew up there, you know, and his old mother still lives there. I suppose he didn't want it to change. Rowan said he was just being a dog in the manger."

"So Rowan's pushing it?"

I could almost see her hackles rise. "He thinks it's a good thing for the state."

Margo was no fool: she'd been busily connecting the dots as I spoke. She got up and walked to the window, gazed out at a view few taxpayers could afford, and said: "You're not about to tell me there's a problem with the paperwork, are you, Lizzie? Not on top of David's murder . . ."

"I've got no proof, Margo, but if I were you, I wouldn't wait for it. Rowan Sherwood and Ross Harvey are in cahoots, and Rowan is yelling at the mayor of Dolphin Bay on his private phone. One of your research staff has serious doubts about the development, and Coast Guard thinks the company that did the environmental work is too close to Lindsay Groenewegen at the EPA."

I paused. "And, of course, David Valentine, who opposed the development and was at loggerheads with Rowan Sherwood, is dead."

Margo hugged her glass like a life jacket: "But David was killed by gay bashers." I didn't reply. Her voice rose: "Wasn't he?"

"It's more likely he was killed elsewhere and dumped in Green Park to make it look like a sex murder, Margo. That was to deflect attention from the real motive."

"Which was?"

"Money, of course. Wheelbarrows full of it."

Margo instigated her own investigation into the handling of the Dolphin Bay development application, and turned her findings over to the anticorruption commission. In the meantime, I went to the police with my suspicions.

When the heat was applied, Ross Harvey caved in and confessed, but said he'd simply acted as a go-between for Rowan Sherwood and Lindsay Groenewegen, who'd organized the bogus environmental assessments through George McCluskey. Harvey insisted he'd done it for his disabled son. The mayor of Dolphin Bay and Rowan Sherwood hung tough, but a disgruntled employee of McCluskey and Farrell defected and gave up his boss, who implicated Lindsay Groenewegen.

Forensic tests on fibers found on David Valentine's body matched those from the carpet in the trunk of Rowan Sherwood's BMW. Confronted with the evidence, he admitted knocking down David Valentine in a rage, after David told him he had enough evidence to sink the conspiracy. Sherwood was a gambler, it seemed, and had been under pressure from the loansharks to pay debts of close to a quarter of a million dollars. Groenewegen was just plain greedy.

I didn't stick around long after my heart-to-heart with Margo: there was too much suspicion in the air. As I was cleaning up my desk, Maureen Noonan dropped in.

"We'll miss you," she said. "You know what you're doing."

"Maureen, you make me look like an amateur," I said, shoving the last of my junk into my bag and rising to leave.

We both knew Maureen had masterminded the entire investigation. All she'd had to do was wind me up and point me in the right direction. She'd avenged David Valentine's death, saved Dolphin Bay—for the time being, anyway—punished Margo Daniels for her hypocrisy, and got clean away with the lot of it.

It doesn't look now as if Margo Daniels will be the first female prime minister of Australia, but if Maureen Noonan ever decides to run, I know where I'll put my money.

When **CAROLYN HEILBRUN** first started writing, she used the name Amanda Cross to protect her academic identity as an English professor at Columbia University. Since then she has done very well both in the academic field and the mystery field, with her latest book, *An Imperfect Spy,* released in 1995. Heilbrun has also been president of the Modern Language Association.

The Baroness

Amanda Cross

The invitation to dinner at the House of Lords was startling enough, and the more so in that the Baroness knew perfectly well I was in New York City and would have to make my way to Parliament and the Peers' entrance at considerable expense and effort. True, she had no reason to doubt that I could afford both the time and the money, but that hardly served to minimize my astonishment. Phyllida—though I liked, since her elevation, to call her "my lady," exhibiting an American's scorn for British titles—must have had something very serious on her mind, the more so since she had been in New York not many weeks before, and we had met then, although for a shorter visit than we usually allowed ourselves: Phyllida was on some sort of business visit and had almost to do a turn-about. She well understood—I had known her through five decades—that I would come at even a moment's notice if summoned by her. As it happened, being essentially old-fashioned in the best sense—that is, regarding electronics and not morals—she had written a short letter and sent it by ordinary post. (I can never convince Phyllida how unreliable New York mail is; I shudder to think the letter might never have arrived.)

She had written simply enough, in her pleasant, legible hand: "My dearest Anne: Please come to dinner at the House of Lords in a month, about a fortnight after you are likely to receive this letter. I must talk to you, and somehow the terrace at the House of Lords seems the place. (I shall also offer you dinner, though the food, I warn you, is quite uninspired. But I seem to remember that you always liked what you call 'plain English food.' You will get it.) Do not disappoint me. I shall await you at six-thirty [and she gave the date] at the Peers' entrance. If you cannot come, a message can be left for me at . . ."

Dear, dear Phyllida. Her extraordinary tact had only matured, like wine, with the years. She knew that a letter left me time to think and to refuse if I had to; she knew that a more direct message would, were refusal necessary, have required immediate personal explanations and apologies. Phyllida, my dearest friend.

Of course I went—was, if truth be told, glad to go. I lead an extraordinarily pleasant life, but a sudden summons is exactly what it needs from time to time for spice and the right amount of excitement. One does not want too much excitement in one's sixties; certainly I don't. On the other hand, the occasional adventure, if sufficiently benign, is not to be lightly shunned. The question of how benign this adventure would be was one I determined not to engage with.

I was early at the Peers' entrance, partly because, since England was having one of its regular railroad strikes, thus putting extra pressure on London taxis, I had left more than ample time; and partly because I rather anticipated, if early, a chance to look around. I found I could not imagine what the Peers' entrance or, for that matter, the House of Lords would be like; the House of Commons, through films and television news, was a far more familiar ambience.

I watched the Lords come and go, all smoking, all assertively male, all moving under the watchful eye of a man in white tie and stiff shirt front, with a large medallion hanging round his neck. Sitting there, I contemplated England, which I had left—permanently, however often I visited—at the age of twenty. Phyllida and I, friends since the age of ten, had married brothers; mine had immediately decamped with me for the United States. Both brothers had been obsessed by flying since boyhood, but hers, remaining in England, had managed fatally to crash himself and his plane some ten years after my departure, leaving her with children to support and no professional preparation for supporting them. My husband, although he too remained enamored of planes, had gone to work in a small airfield and ended up owning both the field and an airline or two. I was a wife and mother as they used to say before the women's movement, but both Phyllida and I had the usual Englishwoman's competence, then (and I suspect still) too often revealed only in the comfort and success of her husband.

Phyllida went to work for the government, eventually achieving one of those administrative positions that runs the whole show and does not change with elections or parties. She became immensely valuable, if underpaid, and when, after the women's movement, they wanted one or two women on various important boards and such, she was appointed. Phyllida, as I never ceased to remind her, was a natural conservative and did not, therefore, flutter the dovecotes—that is to say, frighten the men. She was firm but gracious, ladylike, and, more to the point, with a natural deference to the male and his need to dominate, or appear to dominate. We argued the point frequently, but Phyllida might have been said to have won when England showed its appreciation of her opinions and capabilities by making her a baroness.

I, eventually (but hardly soon enough), bored with my husband and no longer needed by my children, carved out my own life working for a law firm. What I became, in fact, was a kind of private detective, working on behalf of the lawyers in the firm who defended criminals, or those accused of crimes. Most of these clients were guilty, but that did not stop them or me from seeking out evidence that brought their guilt into question at the trial. I became very good at this.

Phyllida's and my children flew back and forth constantly to visit one another and became friends. Most of the flying was at my expense; I used also to help Phyllida out when circumstances grew tight. I will say for Phyllida that she did not make a fetish of taking money, recognizing perfectly well that had our situations been reversed, she would have expected me to be a courteous recipient. Besides, she agreed with me that a friendship such as ours deserved to be extended into the next generation.

Waiting just inside the House of Lords, and staring alternately at a television monitor reporting on the current debate or question before the house and, beyond the formal man in the white tie, at endless coat racks, I thought how nearly our situations had reversed themselves. Phyllida was now well off, and a prominent figure in many circles, a baroness by god. I, with an interesting job devoid of status, and alimony (which I took gladly, feeling I deserved it after so many years advancing my husband's career) to pad my meager salary, was clearly the less exalted of us two.

Phyllida greeted me with a modest hug that to anyone observing us would have seemed cool; we had never gone in for those dramatic embraces with which in the States even men greet each other these days. But the love I felt for her, and she for me, was—although Phyllida would never have dreamed of saying any such thing—stronger than family bonds. Not only sisters-in-law, Phyllida and I had long been the chief members of each other's family.

When we were seated on the terrace, when, on the way there, I had admired the continuous red carpet (green for Commons, Phyllida told me), when the server had taken our order, when we had expressed our shared admiration for the Thames and answered each other's perfunctory questions about our children—perfunctory not because we did not care, but because we recognized that the children were not, this evening, our subject—only then, when we had raised our glasses, did Phyllida come to the point. That she came to it so directly—for Phyllida was a mistress of the indirect approach—bespoke her sense of urgency.

"The most awful thing has happened," she said.

"So I have somehow gathered. Whatever it is, Phyllida, knowing will be better than this suspense."

"You know the small Constable drawing that was stolen with the Vermeer a short time ago in New York, from that elegant small museum?"

I nodded, mystified. The theft had indeed been widely publicized, mainly because the main haul had been a Vermeer—there are less than forty of them in the world— and no trace of it had been found. The robbers had taken, in addition, one other item, valuable but not altogether beyond price as the Vermeer was. I had remembered about the drawing because it was by Constable, a favorite of mine, and with all the strange delicacy that an initial drawing may have that the finished painting, however magnificent, always lacks.

"Well," Phyllida took a large sip of her drink and could be clearly seen to be gathering all her forces for the next announcement. "I have it," she said.

I admit that for one frightful moment I was simply worried about Phyllida, not because she had, it seemed, stolen a valuable drawing if not a Vermeer, but because she gone mad—quietly mad, but mad nonetheless.

"Oh don't look at me as though you thought I'd grown a brain tumor," Phyllida said, annoyed.

"So you stole the Constable because we had always admired him even as girls," I snapped, cross at having my mind read. We used to joke, in school, that Turner, who painted fog, had produced endless pictures, but Constable, who painted English sunshine, had, inevitably, painted fewer.

"Of course not. As you know, I was exceedingly busy when I was last there—no time for even a small museum."

"I'm well aware of how busy you were," I said with some asperity. "Phyllida, for God's sake, what happened in New York? Someone gave you the drawing as a gift and you thought it was a reproduction?"

"Well, at last you're thinking about the problem," she said. "That's not true, but at least not insulting."

I determined to wait for further information before uttering another syllable.

"What I *think* happened is that the rolled-up paper was slipped into my bag, the one I carried on the plane with me, and of course no one examines luggage these days, at least they never examine mine. Yours?"

"No," I said. "But that's probably because—"

"Exactly. Old ladies with gray hair are hardly likely smugglers of stolen goods, or contraband, or drugs, or whatever does get smuggled these dreary days." Neither Phyllida nor I thought of ourselves as old; but we had faced the fact that so we appeared to the unperceptive multitudes.

"But if the thieves know that, why don't the customs people know it."

"Because the thieves don't know. I think the whole horrible thing was a mistake—the wrong carry-on bag. Mine is rather ordinary and so, I can only suppose, resembled the one designed to receive the stolen drawing."

"How long have you had it?" I asked. I knew I had to get the facts, but my mind was mainly engaged with thinking of how the drawing might be returned with no one the wiser as to how or by whom. In this, as it soon transpired, I was, as is so often the case with us two, anticipating Phyllida. But she answered my question.

"Since I returned from New York, of course."

"Really, Phyllida."

"I know; spare me representations of my stupidity, I know them all. But the whole thing has been a shock. Later, I just about decided to call the authorities and simply tell them what happened, how it had been a mistake, how I didn't realize it was the actual drawing, how I was terribly sorry, had been frightfully busy, how I hoped that, since I am in the House of Lords, I would simply be believed when I turned it in. The, suddenly I realized with horror that because I *was* in the House of Lords, the whole scandalous matter would make a tasty headline in all the tabloids: 'Baroness clings to stolen Constable for weeks.' I got cold feet."

"Well, it was a good idea to turn it in," I said, "but I do see what you mean about the tabloids. There's something about women doing hanky-panky, especially baronesses and royalty, that seems to be irresistible to the gutter press. It's the same in the States."

Phyllida rose to her feet and waited until I had risen to mine. "Shall we go in to dinner? I'll tell you my plan." We were about to leave the terrace but stopped a moment for a last glimpse of the Thames in the setting sun. Suddenly, an extremely noisy motorboat shattered the air with its cacophony. "I don't steal art," Phyllida said between her teeth, "but I would very much like to throw a bomb at that boat; a quick explosion and the noise of the motor would cease; it might even frighten off others. Come on, then." I was suddenly back in our girlhood, when Phyllida would snap "Come on, then" after keeping *me* waiting. I said nothing, but myself composed another tabloid headline: BARONESS BOMBS BOAT FROM HOUSE OF LORDS TERRACE.

Feeling rather anxious, as though I had learned that Phyllida had been diagnosed with something fatal and hideous, I followed her along the red carpet, watching her nod amiably to a few acquaintances, until we entered a smallish dining room ("much better food than in the larger one," she muttered as we were led to a table) and the waitress greeted her with dignity and called her "my lady." The waitress smiled at me too, and I realized that I, who thought of myself as spectacularly out of place, probably resembled with alarming closeness most of the peers' wives who were taken from time to time to dine in this hallowed place; indeed, a few of them, I noticed glancing around the room, were even now there.

"Phyllida," I said when we had got to the Dover sole ("of course not filleted," Phyllida told the waitress, "it tastes altogether different off the bones"), and I was concentrating on lifting the meat neatly from the skeleton—one does not seem to eat Dover sole frequently in New York—"where exactly is the drawing now?"

"Here," she said.

"In this dining room?"

"The lady members' cloakroom."

"Are you completely mad?"

"It seemed the best place. I simply asked the attendant if I might leave a carrier bag there for a time, with things that I would need someday soon. Of course she said I might. It seemed the safest place, just in case the drawing had been 'planted' on me instead of getting into my bag by mistake. I do, of course, have to consider that possibility." Phyllida had uttered this Americanism without a shudder; she was concentrating on her sole. "No doubt anyone from the police to the Mafia could search my home, but it's a bit more difficult to penetrate the lady members' cloakroom."

I suddenly thought of something. "Phyllida, listen: In the States, the statute of limitations on theft runs out after five years. I suppose you can be prosecuted for possession of a stolen article, but not for theft. Do you think it's worth looking into? Simply leave it in the cloakroom for five years?"

Phyllida, with a touch of hauteur, ignored this.

"All right," I said, by now past amazement. "What do you want me to do? I can't penetrate the lady members' cloakroom, or so I assume. Naturally, there are special facilities for guests like myself."

"Naturally, I'll get the drawing and pass it on to you. You will then return it to the museum who owns it."

"And why, when I wander in and say, pleasantly, 'You'll never guess what I found in *my* luggage,' won't they regard me with the same suspicion they would direct at you? And if your answer is that I'm not a baroness, forget it, Phyllida, it won't do."

"Do stop babbling, Anne." Phyllida was six months older than me and had always considered that additional experience of the world endlessly significant. "Here's the drill, as my father used to say. I retrieve the drawing from the cloakroom, which will almost certainly be deserted this time of night, and hand it to you in a large brown envelope I've also got in my carrier bag. You accept it happily, right in front of the man at the entrance. . . ."

"The one with the white tie and medallion?"

"That one. I say something like 'Let me give you this now, in case I forget once we're in the taxi,' you take it, we leave the building, a nice policeman will find us a taxi, and I'll drop you at your hotel." (I always stay at a hotel in London, not being fond of joining other people's households, even Phyllida's.)

"Why are you going to pass it to me so publicly?" I asked. I know I'm supposed to be a detective and am actually rather good at it, but the thought of being handed stolen goods by Phyllida—never mind that she hadn't been the thief—was leaving me in a state typical of those who are only slowly emerging from shock.

"I'm confident you'll manage to return it to the museum, Anne; I have no doubt. I've seen you at your most inventive, as well as on the trail, and I know you'll pull this off"—Phyllida liked Americanisms delivered with her best upper-class English accent—"with your usual acuity. But, just in case you don't, just in case something goes, despite your most punctilious efforts, awry, we will have a witness to the fact that I handed the drawing to you and am, therefore, ultimately responsible."

I opened my mouth to protest—we were at the dessert stage—but Phyllida held up an admonishing hand. "I've got it all worked out," she said. "Just listen. You put the drawing in the bottom of your suitcase, and forget about it until you get home. Should you be, by the merest fluke, questioned by a customs person, you say you don't know what's in it, you were asked by me to deliver it to someone in New York. I've put the name of my American agent inside the envelope, just in case the worst occurs. But you will simply get home with the drawing."

She seemed to wait for me to "babble," as she unkindly put it, but I said nothing. "Coffee, my lady?" the waitress asked.

"In a few minutes, thank you," the Baroness responded, waiting until the waitress had retreated to continue outlining her preposterous plan. "After that you do this. You go to the

Metropolitan Museum, look around a bit, then drift into the gift shop and buy a number of small posters—that sort of thing. Pay for them in cash. Ask for a shopping bag, though they'll probably give you one without being asked. Take it to somewhere—the cloakroom, a telephone booth, a deserted gallery—and drop the rolled-up Constable drawing into the bag. Then go to one of the places where you check your coat and packages, and check it. Walk about the museum a bit more, and then leave. End of assignment. What will happen is that eventually the unclaimed bag will be examined, the drawing found and returned to its proper owner. No doubt there will be sufficient brouhaha and much speculation, but none of it need worry you. Except, and I do emphasize this, Anne, if anyone should recognize or greet you while you are in the Metropolitan, instantly abandon the plan."

"Suppose someone recognizes me while I'm checking the bag?"

"Then don't check it, of course; wave to your acquaintance, leave the museum, bag in hand, go home, and try again, perhaps at the Museum of Modern Art."

I had to smile. Phyllida had planned it all so nicely, and I was the one taking all the risks. Except that, were I to be caught, she would step nobly in and take the blame. It had been that way at school. The plans were hers, the execution mine. We only were caught once, Phyllida immediately took the blame, and I was allowed innocently to withdraw. I trusted Phyllida. All the same I wondered, not for the first time, why I had become a paralegal and a detective, while she had remained a so much more obviously conventional person.

It all worked out as Phyllida had planned it; I did my little number at the Metropolitan late one afternoon, when I thought it unlikely anyone I knew would be there. Nothing went wrong. I had brought the rolled-up Constable drawing fastened with masking tape to my blouse under my jacket. (I had suggested folding the drawing to make it small, but Phyllida had told me not to be a barbarian; Phyllida does tend to get above herself if not restrained.) After I made my purchases I dropped the drawing into the bag, wholly unobserved, in front of some antique male statues in the basement, lacking noses and penises, and indifferent to me. Then I checked the bag—excuse ready, but they asked for none—did a turn around the Temple of Dendur, and departed.

The news of the drawing's recovery broke several weeks later. Apparently it took the Metropolitan some time to figure out what they had on their hands, and even longer to establish that what they had found was, indeed, the real thing. Endless speculation about why, who, above all where was the Vermeer? By this time I had recovered my wits and figured out, as subsequently did the newspapers, that the Vermeer had been stolen on consignment, the drawing picked up as an afterthought, unauthorized and no doubt resented. It had been cleverly dumped, as it turned out, on Phyllida.

And that should have been the end of the story. The Constable drawing went back into its place at the small, elegant museum where each day it attracted a small group of viewers, and the Vermeer was, for the second time, broadly bemoaned by the media and the art world. But, as it happened, I became once again involved in this strange affair, this time closer to home and, thank God, in a more indirect way. A young art historian who had gone to work for the small, elegant museum that owned the Constable drawing and had owned the Vermeer called me up at the insistence of her lawyer husband who knew the lawyers I worked for and had heard of my detective skills. These had become, within a small legal circle, rather celebrated. The young woman, named Lucinda, informed me that there was an intriguing and disturbing problem at the museum; she thought I might be able to advise her. When people think that problems they come across are intriguing, they are usually wrong. But I could hardly refuse to meet with her at least once, and the chance to stand right in front of the Constable drawing and admire it—which I had felt diffident about doing before—tempted me to agree to lunch and a consultation. Phyllida would, I had no doubt, have suggested a courteous refusal, but I did not consult Phyllida. We had, in fact, never again mentioned the matter of the stolen drawing, not in letters, faxes, or the transatlantic telephone conversations in which, both of us now being more than comfortably off, we frequently indulged.

Lucinda launched into her account the moment our food was served; I do like people who can come to the point. "There used to be a criminal scam going on in the museum," she said. "They found a way to stop it, and no one was fired." I lifted an interrogative eyebrow. "Oh, it was simple enough; the members of the staff selling tickets simply pocketed some of the money, not ringing up that admission. The museum blocked this scheme rather cleverly; each morning they weighed all those little buttons that would be given out when admission was paid; at the end of the day, they weighed the remaining buttons, and could therefore figure out how many had been distributed. This number had to agree with the number of recorded admissions."

"Neat," I said. "One problem solved."

"Yes." Lucinda was one of those who eat their food so slowly that I have to fight the temptation to snatch it off their plate. (At school, Phyllida used to tell me that ladies do not demonstrate quite so much enthusiasm for food.) "What has happened now, is that one of the guards who has been in the place forever, and with whom I've become friendly since we both arrive in the morning before anyone else, told me how worried he was because he was being harried by the head of security. He wouldn't say how he was being harried, I couldn't get that out of him, but he did let on that the scheme to steal the admissions money had been his, that is, Guido's, the head of security, and that he had taken the greater part of the proceeds, offering protection as his excuse."

"Can't you get rid of him?"

"Not easily; he's been here a long time, and is friendly

with all the men on the board. They would believe him and fire the staff members. What I wanted to consult you about is that I think he was the inside man on the robbery."

"The Vermeer and all?"

"Exactly. I'd like to prove it. We could get rid of him and get the Vermeer back."

"You might get rid of him; I very much doubt you'd get the Vermeer back. I'd guess it's being held as collateral somewhere, probably in a drug deal. Your man was paid off but not, I'd guess, told who was in back of the whole thing."

"The point is, I think he took the Constable drawing when it hadn't been part of the original plan, expected to be praised, and was shocked to see it returned. If we could prove that, we'd at least get rid of him *and* get some lead on the robbery. He acted very peculiarly when it turned up here; he kept returning to stare at it, pretending curiosity but it seemed more like astonishment to me."

"Did he say anything in particular that made you suspicious?"

"Yes; he kept asking me if I was absolutely sure it was the same Constable drawing, almost as though he couldn't believe it was. Why ask that unless he had reason to suppose it couldn't be? I think those who hired him to help in the robbery simply dumped the drawing, which they didn't want, at the Metropolitan."

"An interesting theory," I said. "Ingenious. But how on earth can you prove it was him?"

"I was hoping you'd think of something."

"Could I have the other half of your sandwich," I asked, "if you're not going to eat it?" She handed it over and we both thought and thought; I always think better while munching.

"I'll have to go away and ponder," I finally said, "but let me ask you one vital question. Please be sure of your answer. Does he suspect at all, in the slightest, that you suspect him? Would the guard, however unconsciously, have tipped him off?"

"I'm sure not; 'no' to both your questions. Guido, who by

the way is no more Italian than I am, which is one eighth—
has retained his unmistakable look of satisfaction. It's because he's named Guido that we got on what he no doubt
thinks of as intimate terms in the first place. He introduced
himself when I first came and I mentioned that my great-
grandfather was named Guido. After that we were 'chums,'
even though he thinks that I, like all women, am not up to
this or any job."

"You clearly can't stand the man, but apparently he's
pretty widely liked. Are you sure this isn't something personal with you?"

"I hate art thieves, and people who cheat museums." And,
I thought, she particularly hated this thief.

When I got back to the office, one of the partners called
me in and told me how grateful the firm would be if I could
help Lucinda out; something to do with her husband. "Take
all the time you need, Anne."

So I began by taking the time to view the Constable drawing in place. It was still evoking comment, though it was
not, I thought, that easily distinguishable from the other
Constable drawings. They were all framed and under glass.
When I got home I called Lucinda at her home; we had
agreed not to discuss the matter on the museum phone.

"How do people go about stealing paintings and drawings?" I asked her. "Aren't they rather bulky to move?"

"With paintings, they take the canvas from the frame and
then roll it up.

"Cut it out, you mean?"

"Usually. They did this time. That's why paintings on
boards are rarely stolen. With drawings, they have to deal
with the glass. Drawings are always kept flat, in drawers, but
when they're exhibited they're mounted under glass. Whoever stole the Constable broke the glass and grabbed the
drawing; he was probably feeling confident at the time,
looking for a final thrill."

"You seem to have remarkable insight into art thieves."

"Naturally; we all think about it and how it was done.
That's how you prevent its being done again. There's some-

thing else I forgot to mention: The motion detectors have a record of where the thieves went in the museum; they didn't wander about. They went directly to the Vermeer and, later, to the Constable drawing. They took the tape from the surveillance cameras."

"Where were the guards at the time?"

"Tied up. They weren't involved, by the way. The whole thing's been cleared as an inside job, but of course no one ever suspected Guido. No one but me."

"Couldn't the guards give a description?"

"They did; it seems obvious the robbers were wearing wigs and false mustaches. They got the guards to open the door to them pretending to be police detectives. It's much simpler than those things are in the movies, more's the pity."

It certainly looked like a thief who knew what he was doing; of course, anyone could have cased the joint, but a visitor to the museum that attentive and that constant would have been noticed. He had led the other man right to the Constable. Had he taken a fancy to it and if so, why? Looking around the other exhibits in the museum, I decided that one of the Constable drawings was the obvious "extra." To determine why he had picked that particular one was beyond knowing, but probably he had taken the closest to hand.

Would he, given the chance, steal a Constable drawing again? Perhaps he knew their worth and had expected kudos for adding it to the Vermeer. Slapped on the wrist, he might yet, if the bait was juicy enough, steal another such drawing for his own purposes, and then we would have him. But what would be the bait? I detested the idea of entrapment, of leading someone to commit a theft he might not, on his own, have undertaken.

And then I recalled Phyllida when we were at school: she was very much the head girl—that was probably why she did so well on important boards—with me following admiringly behind. There had been a series of thefts at school, always of money that each girl kept in an obvious place. At first girls missed part of their stash (never much, gifts and allowances for food and the occasional school trip to the theater) but might have been mistaken. Then the thief got bolder and took more each time. As happens in small communities, everyone began regarding everyone else with suspicion, and as head girl, Phyllida knew she had to find the one guilty person to restore innocence to everyone else. (Now that I thought of it, that was probably the sort of thinking that had made her a baroness.) She also decided that the thief was stealing either out of need, in which case she could be helped, or out of malevolence, in which case she could be expelled. So Phyllida made it easy for someone to steal a fairly large sum of money: a girl in need could hardly resist; a malevolent girl could hardly resist the challenge. I tried to summon up the long-ago details: Everyone learned that a stash of money was in a certain place. Not entrapment, Phyllida assured me (though we did not, of course, use that word) because no one was being invited to steal or induced in any way. Phyllida did not take the school administrators into her confidence, and so was left (with my eager help) to deal with the results. It had a sad end, I did remember that. The girl was stealing the money for her brother, I forget why. We managed to help them out, again under Phyllida's direction.

Well, I consoled myself, what could we lose? Phyllida had asked that then, and I asked it now. Lucinda and I again met, this time not in a restaurant but in my apartment; I was not going to make finishing her food a habit. "I think we ought to offer Guido another Constable drawing," I said. Lucinda stared at me. "How does Guido regard you?" I asked. "Try to be exact, rather than modest or resentful."

"He thinks I'm in above my head, as any young woman would be. Curators should be men. He's offered to help me out, and thinks my reluctance is shame rather than distaste."

"Excellent. So if you confided in him, he would accept it as his due."

"I think so." She looked a bit wary.

"Here's what we're going to do, if you are willing. You are going to call Guido to your office in the late afternoon, one day soon to be decided upon. You are going to declare your-self in a panic. An old friend from school has pleaded with you to lend him a Constable drawing; not that you don't trust him, but it's so irregular; no artwork ever, ever leaves a museum except under the most controlled circumstances. Your friend's in a jam—don't worry, I don't think we have to explain the jam, but it's well to have a story ready. Say, your friend has to give a lecture on art theft, and wanted to make a real effect by producing a real Constable. Well, something like that," I added, as she looked more and more dubious. "Guido may well conclude your friend borrowed something and needs, temporarily, to replace it. Liars suspect everyone of lying, thieves of thieving. Your friend's coming around for the drawing—which you have already taken from the drawer and rolled up—that very day. Would Guido be will-ing to hand it to him when he comes by, about a half hour or so after the museum closes?"

"You think he'll fall for that?"

"If he doesn't, we've lost nothing."

"Unless he tells people in the museum I was 'lending' one of their Constable drawings."

"You deny it, and stick to your denial. He'll have no proof, and he'll look foolish. He can't very well produce the draw-ing if he hasn't handed it over when he should have. You can always burst into tears at the very idea—it's what women always do, isn't it?"

For the first time since we had met, she smiled. But she was soon frowning again. "You're suggesting I give him a real Constable drawing, hoping, well, expecting that he'll steal it? What do I do after he *has* stolen it?"

"Nothing. There will be an FBI contingent there, one of whom will pretend to be your desperate friend. If Guido hands over the drawing, fine, we were wrong, you've got the drawing back, no one the wiser. If he doesn't, well—Bob's your uncle, as we used to say at school."

"I think it's risky. Why should the FBI help?"

"Stealing artifacts from a museum is a federal offense. The FBI has been on this case from the beginning. Let me handle that end. No one will know your part in this but you, me, and Guido. I won't talk, and if he does, out of honest outrage, you'll deny everything. At least you'll have proved your suspicions wrong, and can turn your worries elsewhere."

Lucinda agreed in the end. I was, of course, a lot more nervous than I let on. But it all worked out exactly as I had planned. The FBI agent, posing as Lucinda's frantic friend, turned up to be told by Guido that no drawing had been left for him. The agent withdrew, and he and his colleagues watched as Guido, the Constable in hand, departed the building some hours later; theirs was a highly effective stakeout.

Guido turned state's evidence. I don't think he knew too much about who had hired him, and they haven't yet got back the Vermeer, but everybody at Lucinda's museum is resting easier. Hopes are high.

Lucinda and her husband and the lawyers in my firm were all very happy with the outcome, and Lucinda was appointed to ask if there was anything they might offer me as a reward. I said I would like a reproduction (different size, clearly marked) of the Constable drawing that had been stolen with the Vermeer. Lucinda had one made for me, and I flew with it back to England.

I met Phyllida once again on the terrace of the House of Lords, and as we watched the Thames and sipped our drinks, I presented her with my trophy. "You can leave it in the lady members' cloakroom if you like," I said, "but I was rather hoping you'd hang it on a conspicuous wall where it will remind you of me and my talents."

"I need no such reminder," Phyllida primly said, but I knew she liked my gift. What I didn't tell her was how close I'd come to lifting a real Constable drawing. Lucinda had shown me the drawers where they were kept, and I didn't really think one would have been missed. But resisting temptation is one of the lessons I had learned at school—with Phyllida's help, of course.

PIEKE BIERMANN is a free-lance writer from Berlin whose work includes essays, radio dramas, and television documentaries as well as a series of crime novels and short stories. Her novels include *Potsdamer Ableben* (1987), *Violetta* (1990), and *Herzrasen* (1993). She was awarded a second prize at the annual Klagenfurt literary contest for literature in German in 1992 and has received the best crime novel in German award in 1992 and 1994. She also is a translator of Italian and English works into German.

7.62

Pieke Biermann

**Translated from the German by Ines Rieder
and Pieke Biermann**

New school? What school? Am I supposed to have opened a new school? What's that cow want from me? At least the doors here aren't half as loud as they look. Never seen that kind: a metal door with a sound-absorber. At GSTI, the door can put your bowels in a panic if someone doesn't hold it back. Here—sounds like a walk-in freezer. *Vvvmmmpfff. Kllleggg.* The keys are terrible though. Now she's left with them. Thank God. That elephant. Squeaking with friendliness, that's what she is, definitely. Like her rubber-soles. Upwardly mobile, those shoes. Allow the foot its natural habitat. Claro: We've all taken to eating eggs from free-range hens only! Like we all step on other people's nerves with real health shoes only. Molded heelcups. Nose up like sports cars.

New school. Me—*ffhhh*! Me never. Not even with things I'm really good at. Better than them. All of them! *That's* why they were pissed in the first place. 'Cause next to me they all look older than they'll ever get. One day, someone's gonna blow them away. Sooner or later. Short good-bye. Happens fast. Big sleep. Sleeping bags, every one of them. Tombstone blues in their guts. Ivy already growing up their legs. *That's* why I'm here. Claro. That's as clear as the sweat on your palms on your first mission.

I'm here for their *old* school. Their disciple, finally. Otherwise they'd have put me someplace else. Not in front of a window that looks out on the inner-city highway, of all places. Six lanes. Right in the middle of the flight path to Berlin-TXL too! Claro. To make it finally clear to me who's the commander. Yessir! That's right, officer, sir! Click my heels with a real fine BANG! Nay nay nay nay nay—that crash came from up above. And it wasn't a bang either! Cool down: that was a thunderbolt. 'Cause up above the floodgates are opening. Thank God. And there's a bolt of lightning too now. Down southwest. But the picture, wasn't it down here? Claro: three cars, one crumble-zone. Clean job! Reporting-rear-end-crash-highway-north-two-lanes-blocked-heading-Tegel-airport-Jakob-Kaiser-Platz. Heavenly soundtrack for sure. Another bolt now. Southeast. Sweet little baby bolt. Waitasec. Hangon. What's that little cloud there, right under the—where did they *come* from, those four helicopters? How come I didn't *hear* them? Shit. I was fixed on the highway. Major mistake. Stay flexible and cover the *whole* area—I blew it. That's losing points for good. Now cool all down and start again: The first helicopter keeps going. The second is tumbling. The third—waitasec! Hangon! There wasn't any bolt anywhere! Why is it exploding? Ohmygodmagn'm! Its ass is being torn up! So that's what it looks like. But where's the—oh, there. Tumbling too, now. Turn back, man, turn! There—*that's* a bolt. That is— that means—bullshit, no. We haven't got *that* far yet—although: it couldn't be any harder to get a Strela than all the other toys, nowadays. Yeah, sure. Claro! All he needs to have is a safe place somewhere in Berlin-Mitte. Or Pankow. A Strela will knock everything out of the sky. If it's flying low enough. Like helicopters. Airplanes approaching the runway. Well well well. But one away. Wonder where the others came down. The second one in the community garden next door? Pieces of the third all over Westhafen, probably. The fourth too, but intact. Let's wait 'n see if it'll explode on impact. Silly trees! And if it keeps on pouring—what's happening on the highway, by the way? If it keeps on pouring like this, I won't be able to see a thing. Have the burning pieces gone down there? Nay: that's the middle car burning. Yeahyeah, keep on running. Leave your fucking cars behind and try to get outa there! That's good. Beautiful. God, what heavenly peace.

Oh, I see? Waitasec. Hangon. Was *that* what she was talking about, new school and stuff? Nay nay nay nay nay. Couldn't have known about it. Besides, *I* would never instruct anybody to carry around fifteen kilos. For me, those eleven pounds were just enough. More than two sacks of potatoes. That's typical male. And typical blunder. With me, that kind wouldn't have reached training phase two. There was a lot more than one minute between those two shots. Plus, he even sets one rocket off. At least. The 72mm Strela being the most accurate thing you can get! And four helicopters like neatly pinned to the clothesline of any silly soap commercial being the easiest picking you can dream of! Bet he's always practiced cozily lying in his glorious nook. Over there, in his better Germany. Make sure you don't really have to work, huh? But now he's had to stand up for the first time. On the balcony of his privileged three-room flat. For peace-loving combat forces and other honorable hopes of mankind. In one of those prefab prestige boxes looking like housing projects. On Leipziger Strasse. Holzmarkt. That neighborhood. Or even behind his rayon curtains. Terrific camouflage!

His thunderstorm camouflage though—that's some idea. Not all silly.

They're all outa their minds. What do they want anyway. Didn't I provide for the fattest increase of the Berlin Heart Center? It was big in the paper. AIRLIFT FOR EUROPE'S HEART PATIENTS—DONOR FLOOD IN BERLIN. Four-inch letters. And that was even before I got those bloody bullets at last. Twelve three-round magazines of duplex 7.62×51. Those were original NATO indeed. Don't want to know what kind of gap they'd come pouring through. Hadn't those Baader-Meinhof creeps emptied munitions depots too? Claro. That stuff was kind of burial offerings for some of their buddies, before they dumped them in Stasiland. Behind the Iron Curtain. Sooner or later. Because that sweaty little pug who sold them to me—bet he hasn't set foot in the West up till today. All crying nostalgia for the good old East. Bet he can't even imagine that the words "black market" do *not* sound alien to people who lived under the Warsaw Treaty either. The time it took him to only accept listening to me! Bet if someone in the West offers him a real rare Black Angus, with the correct little blood rivulet, that is, he'll just scream: Miss, the chop isn't done! No doubt he never held a Mauser SP66 in his arms before that deal. Claro. According to him I should have chosen one of his Makarovs or Stetshkins.

"I need a rifle, not a pistol. I've already got one."

"So take a Simonov. Or Kalashnikov. They load 7.62 ammo too. And what's more, you can use our cartridge stock for them. No waiting for supplies. We're overstocked with those."

"They don't have 51mm length. Doesn't make sense for me!"

"But the M43 is top of the line. And given how short it is, it's really fast 'n precise."

"But not fast and precise enough!"

"Your decision. Anyway, the Mauser's currently in short supply. I'm not sure if I can get near NATO midsize bullets these days—the price would be according, of course."

Claro, Comrade Dealer. You're a quick study. Free market economy is when customers are supposed to be so silly that you can tell them a Mauser SP66 7.62 is incredibly difficult to find, right? Too bad if one of them just happens to know that it goes all over the world and may as well come back from there. Really fast 'n precisely. Even to the Jueterbog dump south of Berlin. To former Redarmyland.

Well well well. That's gonna be red alert. Major disaster alarm. All precincts. Must be coming from the industrial harbor, that smoke. It's Westhafen down there. One more real bolt of lightning somewhere, and that'll be it. Bingo. No more planes coming in? Claro: They must have seen it in the tower. Wonder if they reroute them. To Tempelhof? Or Schönefeld southeast of the city—poor passengers. They'll have to squeeze into S-Bahn trains on top. Change trains three times. 'Cause taxicabs—forget about them. One half-filled Fokker 50, and they're all gone. 'Cause the drivers still don't know West Berlin and need twice as long. Plus, after forty years of being better human beings amid the warm-hearted solidarity of socialism they don't feel like calling colleagues when there's business for everybody! I know them. Tried often enough to hail a cab for my crazy hell-raisers who were scheduled for a gig in the West, but stuck in some cheap hotel in the East! Ah, that's the silliest joke of all, the one about how you only need to tell Eastern cabbies your name and they know the address automatically. 'Cause they're all former Stasi agents. But how to *get* to that address —ah, forget it. Anyway, down there the sky is finally clearing. The rain's finally easing too. Actually the kind of weather like the day of my first Mauser mission. Changing real fast, with a thunderstorm brewing. Quite precisely. Breadknife weather. For days. If that pug down in Jueterbog hadn't been so slow with the magazines—given *that* handicap, it's been an absolutely fantastic job! I'd had no time at all to get used to that rifle. And a Mauser's a bloody different feel from the HK G3 I used to work with. For six years. Of my own bloody life! Six damn years of illusion about myself finally getting outa my jail and spreading my wings.

But I simply couldn't miss out on that wedding parade. There were twenty of them, maybe thirty, all at once! Okay, the Mauser is four inches longer and more than a pound heavier—so what! Is it *my* fault that precision guns for po-lice snipers are so difficult to find that I couldn't afford one? Am I Eveline Hartbold? Do I pay lousy wages to the employ-ees of my husband's company for taking care of a bunch of decked-out, coked-out rock stars? No. I'm not. I wouldn't have named the company German Security Technicians Inc., to begin with, and I wouldn't have stuffed it with the kind of lamebrains who just watching them makes you think of German Sleeping Tablets Inc. instead! Claro. Security technicians—*fffhhh*. They can't even *spell* the word "manstopper"! All they can do is play Dick Tracy when they catch another one of those guys playing hooky. 'Cause that's how the boss makes his money nowadays. Li'l bit of personal protection, li'l bit of violation of privacy. Big deal. He doesn't even get near the real Big Deal. Industrial espionage, that stuff. Not for him. Not since Treuhand's gotten the world's largest corporation. Public tycoon privatizing *en gros*. The whole ex-GDR. He wouldn't interfere with state security! He's far too —let alone *her*! Personally checking the gun cases, each time I was done with my shift. To make sure I wouldn't do anything stupid, at least not with toys registered to Strapsky & Harsh! Wonder who came up with *that* name. Big joke, for sure. Bet they had a big laugh all together. When the Holy Couple was *not* around, of course. Claro. Otherwise. Otherwise they all tuck in their tails at five hundred yards distance from the GSTI door. Except for Lincoln, claro. But he feels no need either. He too knows his quality. A-one shot. Ex-GI, what else. And a specialist in surviving. Wonder how *he* copes with his anger. Another one whom they wouldn't promote. All those white pork bellies. Claro. That's something they can't stand, a black man who tops them. The new ones even less, those ex-Stasis. No sense of honor. Never lift their visor. No wonder their jokes all fall flat. Claro. Eveline Hartbold as Strapsky—harharhar! If one of those two has to do with straps it's him, I bet, Hans-Ruediger. *She's* the harsh one. On the ball too. Gets pissed each time somebody calls in sick. Means he costs money. Claro. Cuts in her cash for buying another rotten tenement house in East Berlin to speculate with. Means she'll have to find another company willing to pay GSTI a bundle, to check if one of its workers happens to not lie sick in bed but makes some bucks on the side. Sooner or later. Those folks, they catch them all sooner. Claro. Because it's unjust. Absolutely unfair. German Social Terror Inc.!

Just like that guy with his bloody Strela! Outa his mind too. Who does he think he is—exterminating little people in their little gardens! That's something completely different from—but it *was* precisely like today, two weeks ago! Bright again, really fast. The rain slipped away at once. The ambulances visible from far away. Took quite a bit to come though. Well well well. For those three it was too late anyway. Tough job for someone used to *twenty*-round magazines. Not that I'm keen on continuous fire. But having twenty rounds reserve you can afford a few misses. And I did *not*, just the same. Not a single one. Even though that Mauser's got quite a recoil that I'm not used to. It was precision work, absolutely. Especially since it got dark all of a sudden. Just before the first bolt. Then the downpour. I was nearly sure they wouldn't come anymore, they'd given up the idea of celebrating a wedding by roaring along Schlachtenseestrasse to their bikers' joint at Avus-Treff. And I'd have to pack up and take the next S-Bahn back. But they did come. And how! Didn't look like the usual Rambos from the Harley-Davidson Club this time. No riding a high horse anymore. Eased off on the gas instead, scared shitless. At the first bolt! No more *rrroang-grrroang-grrroang*. Nestled up all together side by side, like chickens! Too late, you assholes! And thanks a lot for driving slow! For being so quiet! Makes my hand even quieter. Steadier than ever. My first one's got the driver with the white ribbon at the handlebar and the chick behind. Precisely between his helmet and his bullet-proof vest. Yeahyeah. They were all wearing one. Good boys. Quite a few bucks invested, haven't you? Hit the left artery. Bloody porridge, that throat. Gone for good, that guy. The second duplex into some neck somewhere in the middle of the gang. The third at the last man's helmet. Where the ear is. And right into it. Precisely one second before he could crash into the whole jumble. Three hits and a dozen dead, at least. Of the rest, some are still not sure to survive. No one's got away clean. *That*'s how things are done, you Strela bungler. None of them will ever jerk off again revving up his engine, panicking everybody on the sidewalk! None of them

will ever roar again across a sidewalk nearly wiping out anyone who happens not to be fast enough for jumping! None
of them will ever shred my eardrums again! Never. That's it.
Over. Bingo.

The downpour, too, was real precision work. The few
passengers standing around at Schlachtensee station on a
Saturday afternoon had taken cover fast, and I had the
chance to take the Mauser apart and put it back into the golf
bag. And slip out of my briarpatch behind the bushes on the
lake side of Schlachtenseestrasse with my parasol and my
folding chair. And move over to the other side of the battle-
field to enjoy the effects of 7.62 duplex bullets from close
up. Claro: All those ambulance horns blaring, that sure was
some more torture. But after them there was peace. Heavenly peace. Absolutely quiet. I even had a chat with two
guys from my old squat. Claro! Yeah, too bad one can't see
anything from down there at the lake, really too bad, otherwise you'd sure get a damn good eyewitness report for once.
Then, even Harry Gross showed up, that rat. Fucking
friendly, for the first time. That should have warned me.
Claro claro claro!

But I *had* been ready to put on the internal blue helmet,
bloody shit! I *had* made my peace with having been fired.
You don't *have* to earn your living with the Berlin police.
Someone with a decent sharpshooter training and a lot of
practice does not depend on the parading politician pack.
There's plenty of clients, more than plenty—*fffhhh*. Claro:
Given all that going crazy about Berlin being the capital
now. They're all outa their minds. Stress, that's the only
thing they're producing! If it were for the motorbikes only.
No. You've never ever seen so many customized BMWs and
Porsches here. You had to go to Hamburg for it. Or Munich.
But now the Wall's come down, and now we finally *are*
somebody: we have to come rattling in now with our own
planes. And anyone who even faintly looks like being able to
fart up some investment in the capital might be a capital
target for an assault, right? Claro! He'd best be supplied with

a complete police snipers special unit of his own right away, huh? Not to mention the stars from glitterland! Shit-scared by their fans all of a sudden, right? Definitely in need of bodyguards now. Claro. Fine with me. No problem in the beginning. Basically, these pop kids are easy to handle. Can't tell a revolver from a pistol, let alone a tear gas gun from a rifle. To them it's all gun. Or cannon. Seen too many cheap mystery movies. Should be faced with a real cannon for once, in front of their coke-noses! Ah, forget it. At least you can put on your earphones as soon as the concert starts.

The GSTI was no problem either at first. Easy to milk, those ex-Stasis running about in companies like that! So proud that not *every*thing they'd had in hand behind their Wall was crap—well well well! Anyway, that ČZ52 was *no* question of short supply. It was a question of two days. Go to the guy and order. Return and pick it up. Nag a bit that this is none of the Ceskas for export and the trigger pulls too softly and the whole thing looks somewhat silly, doesn't it, and did Czechoslovakian soldiers really work with it? How's the guy supposed to know I master a NATO gun? I can handle even the softest trigger. Of every pistol too. Besides, Motzstrasse is not half as far away as Jueterbog.

Of course I didn't rub it in at GSTI! Just kept on dutifully taking that silly tear gas toy from Eveline Hartbold and returning it to her just as dutifully. Lincoln was the only soul to figure out I had a pistol. But that's okay. By then we were buddies. *He* hasn't blown the whistle on me! Like he'd tried to jump on me only once. What was it, actually? Something super cool. Stupid talk. Anyway, I'd just asked him back how old he is and does he remember Aretha Franklin. God, what a dumb glance he had! Really like—whaaa? Well, I said, on account of *R-E-S-P-E-C-T,* you know. Grinning. Leaving him standing there, in the middle of all them white pork bellies. He showed up at the Metropol concert hall half an hour late. Left me doing the band's transport from the Hotel Stadt Berlin all by myself. Bangs a book in front of me, some thriller, by a Melody such and such, USAmerican. Plus a page number. It said something like: A woman who wants

to be real free has to lay the guys flat. Well, either draw them
to bed or blow them away, that is, according to that Melody.
And all the time Lincoln's checking *my* face. Must've had
precisely that dumb whaa-glance, I guess. Claro. But then he
grins and shakes my hand the way he does with his brothers. It wasn't him. No way.

It was this whole bloody shit here. Nothing but stink and
noise lately! Getting more and more. Makes you freak out.
Stop it. Bequietbloodyshit! There's even those first-aid helicopters coming now! Military. The little yellow civil one too.
Claro: Must be hell down there in Westhafen. Too bad I can't
see the gardens. Judging by the noise—now that's insane!
Stop it! I want my Walkman! I can't stand it! The whole time
lately. Getting worse and worse. And warm very early too.
In March already. Must've multiplied like rabbits, those
biker assholes. You can't possibly enjoy any spring or summer anymore in this city! They've all freaked out! Such a
lovely evening. All I did was go roller-skating. Just peacefully. On one of the first warm evenings in March. Didn't do
nobody no harm. Just Lincoln's Tracy Chapman tape in my
earphones, and down along Ku-Damm, quiet and peacefully
between the walkers. All slowly. Lots of people dwelling.
And there's this goddamn piece of shit on his giant bike
coming along, blasting my ears with his insane *rrrummm-
rrrummm-brrrummm*! Right through Tracy Chapman. *Brr-
rummm-brrrummm*! Louder and louder. Closer and closer.
Must be completely insane that creep! Stopityouasshole!
Blowsmyhead! *Brrrummm-grrrunnng*.

I could've kissed myself for being on skates. The shot was
inaudible, too, absolutely. Timed precisely with his last *brr-
runnng*. Claro!

It's true. The first cut is the sweetest. No big plan. Just
straight from the—maybe that, too, was it: I started planning
more and more afterward! That's shit! The shot kind of fades
too far from focus. Claro. It's not spontaneous anymore, like
someone shreds your ear and bang! Away with him! Instead,
it's wait. Check out a good spot. A new one each time.

Preferably after dark. All day long, a dozen Fat Boys or Fer-
raris may saw your nerves apart—you *wait*. Until someone
happens to appear in front of your barrel down in the
bushes where you're crouching. At night. And maybe nobody does! Bloody possible. Appearing instead are three
horny bulls chatting you up! The best spot was Olivaer
Platz. The hottest racetrack indeed. And someone's always
crossing the park there. Zoom—three in a row. None of
them wearing a helmet. Even better! Just let them drive past
and—zoom. Neck's height. The people in the park squeak
and spread away. *That* was okay. There was something
spontaneous about it. And afterward, a curry sausage at Oli-
Food stand on the corner, inhaling the feedback. Claro. Very
supportive. People seemed to like it.

". . . pretty soon ain't nobody gonna dare sit on those
rackety bikes anymore!"

"Well, I think they deserve it!"

"Hey, listen, where's it gonna get us—no way, some guy
can just go an'—"

"Lemme tell ya one thin': If I knew how ta use one a them
guns I—I mean, I can understan' it!"

"They shouldn't be surprised, huh! Makin' a racket like
that while regular folks's tryin' ta sleep . . ."

"Yeah, yeah. Right. Say wha'cha want—'s bin a lot quieter
ever since."

Claro! Same mood among the media people! It wasn't
concealed approval. It was standing ovations in headlines! A
real hot story at last. Big sales. But the bullshit they were
fantasizing—funny experts! Hahah. *Of course* I doctored the
bullets! *Not* with all those flashy frills they were making up,
though! Well well well. A pair of pincers, boys, and snip, off
goes the tip! Rips the flesh apart a bit more. Spreads the
spinal cord a bit more! All right, some bullet may go astray
and get stuck so close to the heart there won't be no trans-
plant supply this time. So what? Am I responsible for the
Heart Center's turnover? No! I'm not. And the bloody
bikeshop owners might well pass on some of their extra
profits to me too. Sitting on a gold mine now, with all this

bulletproof equipment. Claro! Big boom everywhere. Really wonder if the company that produces this thing, this— Papamobile! Bet they've already landed a billion-dollar contract with the federal government!

No dime for me! They're all insane. What are they doing there now? Possible, this idiot doesn't even know how to land on a highway properly? Ohmygodmagn'm! Stop that rotor! Stop! That's it! Can't get my wings folded! Whaaa? Waitasec. Hangon. Yeah, this article. Claro. That was the cutest of all! I was supposed to be the angel of history. Coming straight from the East. They really wrote that! From Marzahn or so. Hellersdorf. Helladwarfs, those journalists! Dream up some Stasi guy from some ex-special unit, some extra-specialist from some supersecret combat commando. Hahah. And the Identikit attempts—well well well! Once blond with mustache, once red-haired without mustache, once black curls with sideburns! Once five feet ten, once six feet three. But no doubt the angel of history that can't get his wings shut, 'cause it's storming! Newspaper poets. Shouldn't feel that important. Tomorrow's fish wrap's what they produce. Angel of history! Ahead of him, the waste dump growing bigger and bigger, behind him, the future looming larger and larger, and what we call progress is nothing but this storm, or so. Well well well. Guess an angel like that has to look like that, five feet ten plus blackred curls plus mustache, right? Claro! 'specially after forty years of planned economy, right? Clarisimo! Hahah. If they only knew. Planning means replacing chance with error. *That* was it. That must have been it. Although—I never hit by chance. Not one single time!

That's what it all started with goddamnitbloodyshit! It was *their* error. Why didn't they plan me in! They're all outa their minds. And that doesn't come just by chance. Any dickhead is allowed to command a unit, but you're not. Not you. Me. *Fffhhh*. Claro: We sure are a precision shooters squad. But that doesn't mean we get a boss who knows his stuff! Sharpshooting, that is. The one important thing is, it's a man, like all the others. The one important thing is, it's *not* a—ah, forget it. At that point you look damn old, girl. From the beginning. But aside from that they were pleased to hire you, right? Claro, you go wherever it gets ticklish. Up on any roof. Where the wind blows strongest, angel! Where a real steady hand is required. Real good endurance. Overview. Covering the whole area. And any fucking little detail. And all of a sudden there's this one wagging his bottle around! And he's dressed all black and wearing a balaclava too and the space around him is clearing out and he's wagging and floundering and still wagging and none of those special unit assholes gets it! They're keeping their dumb glance focused on the line of cars. Like rabbits on the snake! Dutifully on the spot where something could *go* that mustn't go there. By no means on the point where something could *come* from! Bunglers. Fucking bunglers. All outa their— Harry Gross that rat that rooster that goddamn crowing banty rooster. Crowing around like a peacock, just because they told him he'd be next to command the unit. Of all people! Him—not me! Claro. But me, I *see* that guy there wag his bottle. Twisting around. Like a hammer thrower. It *was*n't written on his front, goddamnit! None of them has the faintest idea of what was going on there! While they were peeping at those three super-limos with that politician pack. It could've *been* a Molotov! And in that case they would've all thanked their God. Every single one of them. Kissed my ass in admiration and wasn't that a terrific shot. Claro. That's my kind and you know it, bunglers. That's what pissed you off more than anything else. That I can top you all. Precision hit into his right shoulder. I did *not* shoot him dead. I just correctly put him out of commission. I did *not* freak out! That's a lie! I passed each and every stress test. Always. With bravado. I have the steadiest hand. I've got my nerves under control. Stop bullshitting about me being stressed out. I'm not! You are! About me! Or is it my fault when you don't see anything? No, it's not. Is it my fault when Harry Gross the Failure, of all people, is chosen to lead the commando, but not me? No, it's not! I'd have cho-

sen me. I am top of the line. Am I to blame when this bottle-
wagging creep down there turns out to be just another wino!
How'm I supposed to know! It wasn't written on his front
goddamnitbloodyshit!

Six years! Six fucking years. I should've known. At the latest
during the second round of promotions, when every other
colleague was sent over to the East. The last lamebrain tumbled to some top, but you— This is bound to go on all night
down there. At least those sirens have finished screaming.
Make sure it's in silence when you drive your fucking fire
extinguishers home! Or over to the harbor. Still smoky
above it. Right of it as well. Must be *coming* from there, that
smoke, so where's it going? Claro, I see—it's coming from
the little gardens instead. Moving straight down to the produce market next to Westhafen. Wonder if they're dealing
arms there too. Must tell Lincoln—ah, no. Shit goddamnit!

He even warned me. I should've known. Since the moment Gross the Rat showed up there. I should've known.
That there would be no other dozen.

"Him again, our sniper, huh?" Grinning at me. And gawking. The whole time. Never did it before. "Performing his
masterpiece, our people's hero, right? Seen anything?"

"Besides lightning, nay." Masterpiece. A-one, huh? Claro!
What else? "By the time I got up from the lake it was all
meatloaf up here."

"Heard any shots?"

"Three. Could've been more. There were two or three
thunderbolts." People's hero, huh? If you only knew, you
rat.

He was actually raving! Said they still didn't have the
faintest idea how to catch this master shooter. Of course I
didn't fall for that!

"Yeah, must be a genius, the guy!" That was all I said. It
could've been the golf bag too. Nay nay nay nay nay. First
thing I should've done was ask him what *he* was actually
doing here. Since when do sniper cops investigate a crime

scene? And since when is the Rat able to look me in the eye in the first place?

And Lincoln had even warned me. While I was still convinced that my colleagues were really being friendly. Okay, they fire me, but at least they cover for me in court. Confirming preventive self-defense and the shot not being fatal on intention and that it isn't my fault when this creep crashes headfirst into his bloody liquor bottle and it's curtains! I was still thinking how nice it was that none of them would drop the issue of stress during the trial! What a stupid chick! Claro: You had to wait for Lincoln to come and tell you *why* none of them did! 'Cause it was *all* planned. From A to Z. 'Cause if anyone had even whispered that word —you'd have shot off your mouth, on account of stress according to *you*. Claro: *That* was the point, all those years long. That *they* can't fucking handle the fact that a woman is on top of them. Clarissimo! Wonder how *he* can cope with his anger. I really do. He's saddled with it for even longer than me: You're tops, baby, but we won't let you make it. First it's us. For not just six years. Not just in the police force. Not just at GSTI. Not just. Not just. Just everywhere. Everywhere they're in command. Crashing into your brains with their—with their—their fucking engines. And their fucking self-conceit. And their fucking terror. All day long. Everywhere. They're completely insane, all of them. The whole city, completely insane. Claro. That's what it is. Sooner or later. I even asked them what was *in* their minibrains! Why did they *have* to make all that noise. And all that stink. 'Cause it's a pain in the ass. But that dickhead doesn't say one thing! Just stares at me like *I* am outa my mind. Me! *Fffhhh.* What are they in for? Mustn't be surprised really! Twenty-three, that's what I hit. Twenty-three masterpieces. Claro! What else? No amateur bungling anyway, like those idiots coming up out of the blue slashing bike tires. Or kidding 'round with maze-tins. Just because it makes for big headlines. Pilot fish! Get a life. Bunch of rip-off kids. Nobody's *born* a master! Claro. Claro. Claro. Goddamnitshit. He was shadowing me, that Rat. He already knew it, at

Schlachtensee. He followed me. I could've known it. I should've known there wouldn't be another Mauser mission. He had never been able to look you in the eye. In fact he didn't when he snatched the Mauser out of your hand. Precisely the moment they came roaring 'round the corner on their bikes. Just that one other time. That one single time.

Harry Gross the Failure! Well well well. And it isn't even *his* fault. Shit like him just *gets* promoted. Automatically. That's why he can grin like that. Piss off. Get lost you rat. Get outa my mind! Enough terror in here. Now *she's* coming back with those keys too! Stop it! Quiet! I didn't I just I— outa jail—for—thirty years—my own thirty years of—life that's what they call it! Goddamn! And now I'm even supposed to be grateful, huh? That this isn't the U.S. here, Kentucky or so, huh? Claro: Just another Fried Chick, that's what I'd end up over there. I know. I know. They—I know.

SUSAN DUNLAP was a founding member and a president of Sisters in Crime. Her three mystery series feature a former forensic pathologist turned private detective, Kiernan O'Shaughnessy, in *High Fall*. A second character, Vejay Haskell, a public utility meter reader in the Russian River area north of San Francisco, had her most recent outing in *The Last Annual Slugfest*. And Berkeley police detective Jill Smith last encountered quirky crimes and unusual suspects in *Sudden Exposure*. In "I'll Get Back to You," Dunlap presents a new detective, with a unique problem.

I'll Get Back to You

Susan Dunlap

I'd always thought Purgatory—

Well, no.

The truth is I'd almost never thought of Purgatory. I mean, who does? You hear people discussing Heaven or Hell, but how often do they speculate on the number of eons they may inhabit the lowliest room in Purgatory? *If* Purgatory has single rooms, which wouldn't have been my guess.

If asked, I would have said accommodations in Purgatory were like those of the cheapest traveler's hotel—those coffin-sized chambers in the walls of Japanese airports where businessmen lie abed watching pay TV—roomettes in which suffering could be done in dignified if uncomfortable semi-seclusion. Purgatory would be a shabby place of tedious suffering in which sole souls atone for minor banal sins. If, as in those Japanese airport chambers, the occasional moan could be heard and wriggle felt in the adjoining chambers, so much the more suitable for Purgatory.

But I was wrong.

If I am in Purgatory it's not shabby, not small, not solitary. Maybe this is not Purgatory. It's not like there's a sign in the lobby: *Hotel Expiation, extended stays encouraged.* I can't even find a lobby. What they've got here is just long, off-white halls with spongy walls and carpets that are never the solid ground of knowing. I arrived here without warning, without explanation of what offenses I had committed in life, how I'd departed life, or even who I'd been in it. Much less just what this place is or how long I'll be here.

There are, of course, rules—unspoken rules—here, created by the Boss—the *Authority*—enforced by the Sub-Authority with unseemly zeal. (I'd love to know who *he* was in life.)

I don't know who I was in life, but it's clear to me *what* I was: a rule breaker. *Don't shout!* the unspoken rule here shrieks. Why not? With no one on the hall but me, who's to hear? *Don't spread your wings in the halls! Don't glide!* Well, I mean, what are halls for? I can't prove it but I'll swear the Sub-Authority, a penguin-shaped spirit, hardens those spongy walls; I scrape my wings on them every time.

Don't open the doors! Don't peer into the rooms! Don't look at the sufferers inside!

Fat chance!

If I hadn't opened a door I wouldn't have overheard the Sub-Authority telling the Boss to get rid of me. I wouldn't know that the only reason I'm still in a place as decent as this is because I'm their "designated detective." Their d.i. p.i. (dead eye private eye).

The Sub-Authority is not going to put up with me forever. If I don't figure out who I was, how I died, and why I can't remember a thing about my life, or death, I can never accept the Sub-Authority's offer of forgiveness for all involved, and go on to the Glorious Whatever. It's just a matter of time till the Sub-Authority finds a reason to move me out of here. Out and down.

I can't do that up here. The only chance I've got is to sneak some time down on earth while I'm on my official cases.

So, I hang around outside the Court of Final Appeals—sort of a postmortem ambulance chaser—eager for the next soul who, like me, can't bring himself to forget and forgive.

Usually those souls—Cools, we call them—are huddled in a corner of the court lobby, baffled by their tragic deaths.

(They don't have to have been plucked in the flower of youth or skewered while on a mission of mercy. Passing in their sleep at the age of ninety is cataclysmic if the passer was *them*.) They've just come from the Courtroom where the Sub-Authority read out the list of their transgressions; they're shaken and exhausted. The artists and writers have the worst time; they don't mind being branded as sinners, they'd be insulted with anything less. It's the utter banality of their individual transgressions they just can't accept. A few have actually sprained their necks looking around, terrified someone they know is in the room taking notes, eager to recount the damning discovery to their critics. ("As if they haven't known for years," I always want to shout. But I control myself. That's the kind of behavior that earns you another eon or two here.)

Sometimes Cools are too stunned by their humiliation even to hear the Sub-Authority pause at the end of the sin list, stare them in the eye and pronounce: "All is forgiven. Accept and move on." They don't stop their cervical swiveling long enough to spot his stare, much less agree to his offer of forgiveness for them and everyone involved with them.

Most aren't that dim. They comprehend the offer; they grab it. But there are those who get it but can't bring themselves to accept. Some can't forgive themselves. Without their great and hidden sin what would be left of them? But mostly with the indecisive, it's someone else they can't excuse. Sometimes they don't even know who that person is. My job is not necessarily to uncover their murderer or their victims—whichever they had—but to get them enough information so they can make The Decision. Ideally, the Cool moves on to a blissful realm I can only dream of. But some Cools never can accept forgiveness for themselves, much less for their enemies. Even when the facts of their demise are laid out before them, when they are reminded that their enemies will not ruin their lives, because they, the Cools, are *dead*! They're not about to stop pointing the finger even when it means . . . Those Cools settle into their own personal hells in rooms along the hallway here.

It's rather embarrassing to admit I've had *two* hearings in the Court of Final Appeals. The Sub-Authority insists he read my list of transgressions, my extensive—to use the term he all too lovingly employs—list, at both of my hearings, but if so, it's too painful for me to remember. I don't remember why I died, how I died, or even who I was. All I know about my life is it ended with *The Perfect Crime*. By Leigh Wright. Leigh Wright could be me. Or maybe the book was *about* me. Or maybe the title is just a hint, a tease, a special torture the Sub-Authority has created for me. I saw the book only for a minute, and that by snatching a moment on a case when the Sub-Authority wasn't looking.

If I'm going to get out of this place, off the hall, I'm going to have to do better. I'll get one more hearing—the *final* Final Hearing—and I'd better be able to make my decision then.

So I need a Cool who will provide me an easy case I can dispatch quickly enough to leave me spare time. I eye the Cools as they stumble out of the courtroom, heads down, eyes glazed, bodies tense with fear and helplessness. Their lawyers trot alongside reminding them they have only one last chance.

I spot a man across the room, brow wrinkled painfully, fingers moving back and forth as if about to grab an answer just out of reach. Bingo. I moved toward him, careful not to lift a wing, not to indulge in the forbidden glide. I—

"Let me out of here! I have a meeting!" A brisk, brown-haired woman in her early forties strides out of the courtroom, brushing the worried man aside without breaking stride. Even under her white robe I can tell she's got one of those tight, muscular bodies, the type men covet and women envy. She races forward, legs nearly windmilling, oblivious to the fact she's merely treading space. She is holding a white towel.

Often Cools come to trial still clutching some vital item as if it were a talisman. Not infrequently that item is the picture of a spouse, child, cat. Wizened patriarchs arrive holding the baseball bat with which they hit the winning run fifty *years* earlier! Matrons come clinging to the wedding dress, the pair of jeans, the silk skirt they're still planning to get into again. (When *they* hear about the body falling away, their first reaction is glee.) Executives hold the brass name signs from their office doors.

But the brisk brunette, Tasha Pierce, was holding nothing but her anger. And her towel.

It is a bad sign that I suddenly knew her name. Knowledge comes like that up here. Suddenly you know it, as if you've always known. But you don't know for no reason. I stepped into her path. "You have a meeting, Ms. Pierce? With whom?"

"Selwyn!" Her full dark brows drew low over equally dark eyes. An instant later, when she realized I hadn't reacted to the vaunted name, she insisted, "Selwyn Reed, the CEO. You don't blow off a meeting with the CEO." She was racing her feet, still clad in white running shoes. If I'd had any questions about her haste to get to Selwyn, I needed only note her shoelaces—untied. I could picture her yanking off the pumps that went with her dress-for-success suit, poking her feet into the running shoes as she leapt from her chair, and racing out the door. She had the look of a woman who assumed the purpose of red lights was self-enhancement: the driver's opportunity to apply makeup, the pedestrian's chance at shoelaces.

As if I had perused her file, I suddenly knew that Tasha Pierce had been personnel director. In the home office fifty people had reported to her: the satellite offices under her authority tripled that number. Staffed with her selections, Selwyn Industries "ran like a well-oiled machine," she had announced more than once. Other quotes were: "A company is only as good as the people it employs," and "Dead wood means dead sales."

Ah, *dead wood*. Wood that had seen itself as headed toward being a mighty oak, is not prepared for the ax—in trees or personnel. Perhaps Tasha Pierce had conducted one too many termination interviews. I smiled to myself. Her case could be the easy investigation I needed. I just hoped she hadn't thinned an entire forest of potential suspects. Couching my question in the kind of impersonal terms personnel departments love—words like their title, so close to "personal" as to float the illusion they are concerned about people—I said, "You downsized?"

"Me? No way. I don't do that shit. We've got an outplacement department."

An entire department! Selwyn Industries didn't just thin, they clear-cut! How many people had Selwyn laid off? But that carnage wouldn't have been aimed at my client alone. So much for the easy case.

Still, it looked like someone had done her in. And to say she was unready to forgive her killer was the understatement of the eon. If that person had been lying on the floor, she'd have pounded him to dust with her racing feet. "Look, fellow . . . lady"—she glared at my sexually ambiguous form —"whatever the hell you are. I don't have time to stand around while you get your act together. Either get the asshole who did this or—"

"Which asshole is that?" I asked with renewed hope.

"How the hell should I know? One minute I'm running—"

"Running where?" I struggled to keep my voice calm. The rule is Cools don't remember the days of their deaths. Too traumatic, the Sub-Authority says. (Too much bother for him, I say. If they could run that final day's tape, Cools would spend eternity watching, rewinding, and caterwauling. Each time they'd see some new affront—hospital roommates who screamed, snored, or blared the TV, sisters who looked more longingly at their jewelry than them, brothers who stepped out for a smoke at the moment of death. . . . The Cools would languish in recrimination long after they should have taken the Sub-Authority's offer and moved on. Gladly would they take up the cudgel in memory of their dying selves and stalk out after that offending sibling or roommate—who might well be right here!)

Much as it's a nuisance to my job, I see the Sub-Authority's point. The rule had never been broken—until Tasha Pierce. If I could just squeeze enough from her memory to pinpoint the "asshole" who had caused her death. "Running to where?" I repeated, glancing down at those white running shoes with their undone laces.

"Nowhere," she said, shoving my question out of the way with a flourish of hands.

On earth she might have been lying, but here Cools don't have that option. I grabbed her hands, held them down, and tried to elicit what she did know. "Tell me what you saw as you were running."

Her small face tightened; her hands squeezed into fists; she jerked forward.

"Tell me!"

She let out a frustrated snort. "Trees, buses, people, cars."

"And your meeting with Selwyn, where was that to be?"

"His office, of course."

"In the building you worked in?"

"Where else?" Her eyes added: *you idiot.*

"You were running there. So then, Ms. Pierce, what building were you coming from?"

That stopped her.

"The leaves, the trees, the people: what buildings were behind them? Which buses did you see?"

Her forehead wrinkled, and her eyes almost closed. She was peering inward for all she was worth.

And apparently she wasn't worth much. With a shake of the head she announced, "That tack's not working. Look, honey, I'm not a detail person. Was when I started. Had to be. But now, I'm dealing with the big picture. I've got lackeys to sweat the details. You're going to have to come up with something else."

I could have said . . . Instead I pressed my wings tight to my sides and descended halfway through the floor she had assumed to be solid. A figure-eight flight would have been more effective, but alas, up here we can do little more than they do in the NBA.

"Hey, Angel, don't think you can blow me off with that collapsing routine. I've seen magicians better'n you."

I shrugged and turned toward the corridor. "I'll get back to you."

"I should live so long. We'll do lunch, right?"

I started to reply, but clearly Tasha Pierce was not one to allow extraneous words, at least ones that weren't hers. "Look, I know all the ways of blowing people off. 'I'll get back to you' means: fat chance. I'll call you *right* back, means 'I'll get back to you.' The great thing about being personnel director is never having to bother with that shit. I don't deal with that call-'em-back garbage like I had to coming up through the ranks. Then you've got pests bugging you all the time. 'Did you get my resumé?' 'How come you haven't called me back about the interview?' 'Do you have any other jobs?' as if I had nothing on my mind but them. Now, thank God, I've got a secretary for that. She holds my calls; I deal with them at *my* convenience. I don't have time for calls and messages; they wait."

And so shall you. For all I cared about her convenience she could spend eternity bitching right here. As long as I didn't have to keep running into her. Only the reminder that I had my own reasons for taking this case kept me from speaking out loud. I tried again. Normally I start with suspects' possible motives, but with Tasha Pierce to know her was to be motivated. Whoever killed her should be wearing a big smile. "Let's talk suspects. Your secretary?"

"On my team. I go, she goes. She's probably back in the typing pool already."

"Assistants, sub-directors, people in line for your job?"

"I'm not a fool. In business you don't have colleagues, you've got subordinates. They rise above subordinate status, you move 'em out the door. Otherwise you turn around and they're sitting in your chair."

I asked about family: distant. Friends: none to speak of. Expectant heirs—no will, because it clearly had not occurred to her either that she would die, or that it's more blessed to give. "Selwyn," I last-gasped. "What about Selwyn? Blackmail, exposure, love, revenge? Any motive at all?"

"Selwyn? Puh-lease! Selwyn is sixty-three years old, biscuit-shaped, and too damned self-absorbed to entertain love or revenge. If the man had done anything worth blackmail I'd have died from shock instead of . . . whatever."

It was with some small amount of pleasure that I said, "I'll get back to you."

But by the time I got back to my corridor that little light of glee had faded. This case was my only chance to check out my own death. There was a reason I'd suddenly known so much about Tasha Pierce. Maybe it was the Boss's plan to help me, or it could have been the Sub-Authority tantalizing me for his own amusement. Whichever, I couldn't dismiss Tasha Pierce.

And besides, I wondered as I glided and thumped back and forth, forth and back through the empty corridor (smacking my head more than once on the Sub-Authority's unnecessarily low ceiling), how had the woman died? New York is a big city and she'd probably alienated half of it. But murder? If guns were shot and knives thrown at all the rude and self-absorbed, survivors would have their choice of cabs at rush hour.

But Tasha Pierce had died—in a way she couldn't accept.

I slowed to a flutter. A door beckoned. All the doors on the corridor beckon. The Sub-Authority views unauthorized entry as kindly as does a hotel dick. If he catches me again— But I'm careful. It's an addiction, peeking into these rooms, I know that. On earth I'd be grist for twelve-step, but here what's an addiction going to do, kill me?

One little peek. It'd take only a minute.

I checked to my left. Hall empty. To my right. Clear. I stood dead-still (no great feat for me now). Silence. Then I grabbed for the handle, and pushed open the door.

Inside is a well-appointed dining room. Dinner is over, coffee cups are nearly empty, brandy snifters still half full, the brandy line is still at the neck of the bottle despite the eight glasses poured from it. (That kind of thing—candle oil that burns overlong, multiplying loaves and fishes is commonplace here. The celestial answer to recycling.) I focus on the man at the end of the table. You'd think the man would be smiling—well, you'd think that if you'd been here a lot less time than I have. These are the rooms of those who couldn't accept the offer at the Court of Final Appeals. In these rooms nobody smiles.

He is shouting and slamming his fist on the table as he makes his point. His muddled words echo off the walls. And the echo infuriates him. His face reddens. He shouts louder. He glares down the table, grabs his brandy snifter and swallows too much of the honey-colored liquid, coughs loudly—so loud no one could interrupt him.

But no one will interrupt him—because he is alone. If he lifted his eyes from his snifter, if he took the slightest break from planning his verbal assault or delivering it, he would realize that. The silence of the empty room would reverberate if, just for an instant, he would listen.

That he is forever unwilling to do.

I shut the door; turned.

And gasped.

The Sub-Authority was rounding the corner. Had he spotted me peering into one of the forbidden chambers? I didn't wait to find out.

I flew down the corridor with feet racing about six inches off the floor as if that would speed me out of danger, and ended up back in the courtroom lobby. Not the best spot to hide out. In fact, there was only one place I could be sure of escaping the Sub-Authority. Earth.

Here's the deal: Cools are not the most reliable witnesses. At best, they remember selectively; at worst, they conceal. And as for objectively judging other people, for Mother Teresa: *How much did she help the suffering in Calcutta?* would come after *What did she do for me?* The Sub-Authority understands innate duplicity (in fact it was his committee that first proposed Original Sin). So he realizes I can't count on my clients to be honest about their former lives. I have to do legwork in the field. The field below. I can choose to visit any time in the client's life or the week thereafter.

But like I said, the Sub-Authority understands conniving, he sees evil intent in all actions, particularly mine, so I'm limited to one visit. Usually I interview the client at length, weigh the possibilities, and choose the most potentially most valuable scene.

Usually.

Now I just skidded to a halt in front of the elevator and hit Down.

It wasn't a skyscraper. (There aren't really skyscrapers. If there were, my trips down wouldn't end with such rude bounces.) The first bank of elevators only went down to the seventy-second floor and there I had to change to get to Selwyn Industries offices on the thirtieth, thirty-first, and thirty-second. I pushed 31, the car shot down, and when the doors opened I was facing a glass partition that announced:

SELWYN INDUSTRIES
Personnel Department
Accounting

Inside on the reception desk were two almost tastelessly huge bouquets with big black ribbons draped around their white wicker baskets. There were pale pink roses, white carnations, blue and violet irises, shoots of orchids in varying pastels, and exotic blooms I couldn't name. Conspicuously absent were lilies. Between the two displays I recognized a photo of Tasha Pierce draped in black. Had the flowers been brought from her memorial service? Or were they office memorials, from her subordinates, or the esteemed Selwyn himself?

I stepped back to contemplate that. Invisibility is great, but it does have a downside. People can't see me, but I do have form. I have to be careful they don't run over my toes with their supply carts, smack me with their tossed packages, or, worse yet, back into me, panic, and end up calling everyone in sight to feel around for the soft, cold body they can't see.

As if I had suddenly turned the *volume* to On, I could hear the laughter. Twitterings, giggles, great rolling guffaws from voices too sweet and delicate-sounding to be associated with those great rumblings of glee. Behind the desk the receptionist had to pause to control her laughter before she answered the phone. "No. I'm sorry," she said, her poorly muted chuckle belying her words, "Ms. Pierce is no longer with us." She barely got the phone disconnected before she announced, "Tasha pushed her way out," and burst into giggles.

I expected her to look around the seemingly empty reception area with a mixture of guilt and relief, but the woman showed no remorse at all. She spotted a middle-aged man coming down the hallway and called out, "Pushed her way out!" and both of them dissolved in laughter.

"Gotta say," he said, leaning an arm over her desk, "couldn't happen to a more deserving woman."

"Danger of the fast lane, huh?"

"And the slippery world of periodical publishing."

At this they doubled over. Three more people joined them. A brown-suited man was smacking his fist on the desk as he guffawed.

"You know what they always tell you," a woman in green forced out. They all doubled over again. Fists pounded, sides shook.

I had assumed Tasha Pierce would not be widely mourned, but this! Marley's Ghost drew more tears.

The same thought must have crossed the mind of a woman in gray. She put a hand on the speaker's arm. "Maybe we should cool it. Who knows who's around. I mean, even Selwyn could walk up, and the way we're going, we'd never hear him."

"Selwyn?" the guy in brown said, "you think Selwyn would care that she's dead. He's probably out celebrating over a piece of chocolate pie."

"Two pieces!"

The burst of chuckles was muffled and the laughers glanced uncomfortably behind them. Clearly in Selwyn Industries derision was best aimed at the dead.

"He's probably just relieved never to see her again race into his office, plop that liter bottle of springwater next to the desk and bark out her choice for his secretary, his driver, or his—"

"—wife?"

Any attempt they made at control failed. Hands were slapping, arms swaying so much, I had to jump out of their midst, not for fear they'd notice me, but that in their hilarity they wouldn't and I'd be battered black and blue (or the Hereafter equivalent: gray and gray).

"I heard he tried to put her off an hour earlier," a woman in yellow said. "But, of course, her secretary told him she was on her way."

"Was she?" a blue-suited guy asked.

"Who knows? Even if she weren't she wouldn't have taken the call. She hadn't answered any others this week. I wonder if she's busy telling Saint Peter she'll get back to him."

"Enough!" the woman in gray warned.

"No," I screamed. "Don't stop." But no sound came out.

"We really ought to watch what we say," she insisted.

I wrinkled my forehead and concentrated on transmitting the thought: Gossip is a *good* thing.

They hesitated. The women in yellow and gray were starting to leave when the blue-suited man asked, "But what is the official word? I mean the cause of death."

"Smothered in her towel." And that sent them off again.

The towel. That white towel she'd been clutching. I'd thought it was a strange talisman. Now it made sense. So she'd been smothered with her towel.

No wait, smothered *in* her towel. Not *with* the towel, or *by* the towel, or even *under* it. But *in* it. How does one smother in the towel? She'd have to have been facedown to be *in* it. Was she attacked, and slammed down? But that wouldn't smother her; she'd still be able to breathe through the towel.

Unless her assailant wadded it up around her nose. But that would be being smothered *with*. Not *in*.

Go on, I urged. Alas, discretion, the scourge of detection, had taken hold and one by one Tasha Pierce's co-workers wandered off.

I had come in looking for a notice of a memorial service. I guess I'd heard the real thing.

I did have one more stop, just to confirm my suspicions, but that would take an instant.

Which left me a few minutes leeway for my own work.

But the Sub-Authority was watching me. Maybe not every moment but . . . Would he realize I had solved this case? I couldn't take the chance.

I followed the man in brown through the lobby door into the Down elevator. I got out in one of those faux-marble lobbies, followed the man out to the sidewalk, and found myself, as I'd suspected, in midtown New York.

Sleet was pelting down, so thick I could barely see in front of me. It bounced off the sidewalk and the inadequate women's pumps, men's leather shoes, ubiquitous running shoes. People turned up collars, reached in pockets in hopeless search for gloves. Clearly this day had started out many degrees warmer. These days were the worst, the ones that made you understand why people moved to the suburbs where their cars stood waiting for them. To a one, these people were shivering.

But not me. Death does have its advantages.

Pedestrians raced past me, sliding on the slick sidewalk. A man scraped my side with his briefcase. A woman grazed my nose with her elbow as she raised a manila file over her head in vain effort to save her hair.

I had to get out of there. But where to? Movie theater—across the street!

I ran in front of a double-parked truck and was nearly picked off by a car squeezing around it. Invisibility has its drawbacks. And what's the point of being dead if you can't even fly high enough to clear traffic! The only comfort I could take, I thought as I plopped gratefully in a theater seat, was that cars might hit me but they weren't going to kill me. In any case, I was safe now.

It was a moment before I realized I couldn't just sit here. I might be out of the way of the pedestrians, but *safe* I was not. Not from the Sub-Authority. He'd know the difference between investigating and watching—what was on the screen? *The Return of Raffles* the black letters on the gray-white background announced, as the opening credits rolled —watching an old black-and-white movie about a cricket-loving thief. Not much could be farther from Tasha Pierce. Or me, for that matter.

Was I sure about that? I wasn't. In fact . . . But I couldn't stay here a sitting duck for the Sub-Authority.

I edged out of the theater, pinballing my way between the rushing workers, smacking into the wall, rebounding into a nun, bouncing back into a fat man with an umbrella. Enough! I lowered my head, hunched my wings forward, and steered through the stampede, oblivious to whom I tossed where.

And when I spotted glass doors, I didn't worry about what reaction viewers would have to their opening "by themselves." I yanked one open and flung myself in.

Into, it turned out, the lobby of the Hotel Melbourne. I tossed myself into an empty stuffed chair amid the decorative wrought-iron railings that separated each clutch of chairs. Wrought iron was at the top of walls, too. And while the chair had the heavy look of a British men's club and the carpet was oriental, there were enough palm trees around to suggest the South Seas.

Ah, the Hotel *Melbourne*.

This would do fine as a place to gather my thoughts, make my plan. And a gin and tonic would hit the spot. I raised my hand for the waiter.

It was only after three waiters passed without a glance that it occurred to me how distracted I was. I lowered my invisible hand.

A waiter put down his tray of drinks by the four men and women in the next chair cluster. I reached over and grabbed the nearest glass, and then with a scintilla of good sense, moved behind one of those potted palms to drink it. Who knows what liquor traveling down the esophagus of an invisible dead person would look like? Maybe it would be invisible too. Maybe.

"Where's my drink?" a woman who could have been Tasha Pierce's emotional double demanded of the waiter. "It was a Singapore Sling."

Suddenly I was aware of my feet. They felt light. Ominously light. As if they were merely grazing the top of the oriental rug. The soft brush of it tickled them. I tensed. I knew that light-footed sensation. The pull from the Other Side. Desperately, I grabbed a red book off the table next to me and ran for the door, zigzagging as if I was avoiding gunfire.

The street was still packed, but this time my momentum, coupled with fear, hoisted me over the pedestrians and across the street in two leaps. I raced back inside Tasha Pierce's building, checked the information listing, and pushed onto the Up elevator, smacking two startled executives against the back wall. The red book dropped to the floor, landing partially behind one of the men's feet. *Raffles* was all I could see of the title. Before I could make a grab for it, I was out the door at 3, and into Tasha Pierce's health club.

Women in bright blue and green sports bras and tights with sports briefs over them, or shimmery red leotards with matching headbands, sat poised on Nautilus machines, pushing the black-padded machine arms toward each other. Others straddled pads with their thighs, grunting softly as they forced the pads together on one machine, apart on another. The carpet was a red plaid, the walls yellow. Everything in the place screamed, Faster! All around me women panted, grunted; weights lifted and banged down, shaking the floor like a 6.0 on the Richter scale.

But for the first time since I'd left Selwyn Industries I was relaxed. Here I had legitimate reason to be—getting the final piece of Tasha Pierce's puzzle. I started across the floor.

But my feet were lighter!

"No," I yelled. "Not yet!"

Headbanded heads swiveled toward me.

Could I be heard down here? I looked around, unnerved, but the heads had turned not toward me, but toward the treadmill. Just where I was heading myself. I moved faster, but the tug was stronger. I grabbed the railing on the side of the treadmill. Behind me someone was calling, "Jennifer, treadmill! Jennifer, you're next on the list for the treadmill."

A woman jumped on the treadmill and started the belt, ignoring the call from the sign-up sheet. She had the mill; possession is nine tenths of the law; Jennifer be damned. In a bright green Lycra unitard, she ran on the moving belt, glancing down at the machine's changing display: time elapsed, mileage covered, speed, on the rib-high digital display shelf. A towel hung over the bar on the front of the display shelf, and she almost pulled it loose as she bent, still in stride, to grab her water bottle from the shelf below.

The Sub-Authority's pull was fierce. My feet were off the ground. I grabbed the machine's side bar-railing and held on for dear life.

"Jennifer! Treadmill!"

"I'm Jennifer," a gray-haired, remarkably un-Jennifer-looking woman said bewilderedly as she eyed the occupied treadmill.

My hands slipped. Life, dear or otherwise, was no longer mine.

"So?" Tasha Pierce demanded. We were in front of the courtroom door. "Who's the bastard who killed me?"

"I could tell you," I said, still catching my breath. That pneumatic suction's a killer. "But I think this is one case where they'll let us roll the tape. Right?" I said, aiming my demand at the Sub-Authority.

In an instant I was standing beside Tasha Pierce watching a tape of two women panting on treadmills and one gathering her belongings and stepping off the third machine; it was so real, I could have been in the health club.

I thought of the epitaphs Tasha Pierce's co-workers had given her, ending with: "Smothered in her towel."

The tape grabbed my attention. Tasha Pierce let the health club door bang after her. She ran in, pulling her blouse over her head, slowing to unbutton her skirt and let it drop to the floor, around her untied running shoes. Now in standard health club attire, she put her clothes in her tote bag and made a beeline for the untenanted treadmill, ignoring the sign-up list and the sign posted at the end of the treadmill. With awe-inspiring speed, she plopped the tote bag at the end of the treadmill behind her, the water bottle on the lower shelf, set her Walkman and magazine on the display deck, draped the towel over the bar, and turned on the machine.

The woman on the next treadmill muttered, "Sign-up sheet!" but by that time Tasha had her earphones in place and her tape blaring traveling music. Without a glance, she pushed Faster and the belt picked up speed. She was past the power-walking stage and into the jog.

The woman next to her stepped off her machine, adjusted her turquoise unitard, and tapped Tasha's shoulder.

Tasha hit Faster.

The woman shrugged, checked the list, and called out: "Annie, treadmill!"

To Tasha, the deceased Tasha next to me, I said, "You knew you'd cut in line, didn't you?"

"Yeah, sure. Look, I've got half an hour to be in and out of the gym. I don't have time to wait while every housewife and secretary climbs on the treadmill before me."

I shook my head. If they're not remorseful up here, where?

On the screen the turquoise-clad woman wandered off camera but we could still hear her call, "Annie, treadmill! Annie!"

On her own treadmill, the not yet dead Tasha ran at sprint rate. The water bottle shimmied on the lower shelf; the magazine quivered on the display deck; with each step Tasha's knees hit the hanging towel. Sweat ran down her forehead, glistened on her shoulders, coated her back. Her legs moved faster. And faster.

She stopped pushing the Faster button.

But the machine continued to pick up speed.

For a minute she seemed not to notice. She was running full-out.

"Couldn't bring yourself to admit it was going too fast for you, huh?" I asked, unkindly.

She didn't interrupt her rapt watching to answer.

On screen she hit slower. The machine speeded up. Her face was red, sweat soaked her headband, poured down her back. She was panting in split-second breaths. The treadmill belt was snapping with speed. Sparks came off the sides. She couldn't keep up. Her feet fell farther and farther back away from the read-out deck. She grabbed for the bar.

Missed.

Her shoelace caught under the treadmill; it knocked her forward. Her arms flailed; her head hit the bar. The Walkman and magazine flew off the display deck, onto the belt, and smacked up against her tote bag at the far end. The caught shoelace pulled her leg crooked; she grabbed again for the bar, caught the towel by mistake, dropped it, as she fell, twisting to the racing belt.

Here the tape slowed almost to slow motion and we watched the towel clump at the end of the belt, catching the Walkman. We watched Tasha fall, her head hit the radio, the belt thrust her face tighter and tighter into the wadded towel. She flung her arm out, trying to get purchase, but her hand fell on the slippery magazine, caught at the outer edge of the towel. The big, heavy water bottle flew off the shelf, delivering the final blow.

The women around her were standing around wide-eyed. But if they had any impetus to help her, the sparks flying off the machine kept them at bay.

The videotape speeded up. I had assumed it would end there. It had covered all I'd gleaned of the case, but it continued while they pulled her dead body off the machine, while an employee tried CPR as another called 911, while the medics carried Tasha out. Then the employee who had given the CPR turned to the stunned exercisers and shook her head. "We posted a sign that the machine was out of order," she said in plaintive annoyance. "It was right at the end of the treadmill. She couldn't have missed it."

"She *chose* to ignore it," a woman muttered.

"We called every treadmill 'regular,'" the employee insisted. "I phoned her office myself, early this morning. I left a message to call us." She shook her head. "She just never called back."

Tasha Pierce was given her final chance to accept forgiveness for all concerned. In her case "all concerned" was, of course, only her.

I found myself back in the beige hallway. I stomped down it. I was only an employee, a cog in the greater set of wheels, but, dammit, I had done the work on this case and it was a petty bureaucratic move on the Sub-Authority's part to shift me out of the courtroom before Tasha made her decision. Maybe my whole detecting shtick *was* just for his perverse amusement. I stomped harder, not that it had any effect on the spongy carpet.

Raffles, I thought, trying to distract myself. The Melbourne Hotel, a Singapore Sling, and *The Return of Raffles.* No, just *Raffles.* What could all that have to do with me and my demise? Had I been a thief who traveled to Melbourne and Singapore? A witty, debonair Raffles-like cricketer? If so, death had really changed me.

I paced more slowly down the hall. And back again.

The Perfect Crime. *Raffles,* Melbourne, and Singapore.

I paced.

Perfect crime. Singapore, Melbourne Hotel, *Raffles.*

And back.

After the fifteenth circuit I gave up in disgust, and as much to spite the Sub-Authority as to appease myself I flung open the first forbidden door I came to.

There stands Tasha Pierce, hand on phone receiver, foot tapping.

That didn't surprise me. What startled me were the words coming from the phone: "Yes, this is the Authority's office."

The Authority's office! No one gets through to the Authority. You don't just pick up the phone and call the Boss! If He took calls from everyone who felt they had a problem, the poor Entity would be swamped. No one calls Him direct—not popes, not bodhisattvas, not heads of the altar guild.

But there is Tasha Pierce, brash as life, shouting into the receiver: "I'm being detained here. I need to speak to Him right now."

"Certainly, Ms. Pierce. He's away from the altar right now, but I'll give Him your message and He'll call you right back."

"Yeah, right!" she snarls, and bangs down the receiver. "I should live so long!"

It doesn't occur to Tasha Pierce that the Boss doesn't blow off supplicants. The Authority does not lie. But we all judge by our own standards.

She will, of course, fume, holler, rage, until she grabs the phone and again demands to speak to Him, slams down the receiver again, stalks off again, fumes . . . Eternally.

Hell hath no fury like a woman scorned, as they so sexistly say.

I shut the door on Tasha Pierce and glided slowly down the corridor. The walls seemed not so much off-white as gray, the carpet not spongy but swampy. I had failed. It wasn't my fault my investigation hadn't helped Tasha Pierce, but it hadn't helped me either. I was no closer to getting myself out of here than before. I had failed. I could picture the Sub-Authority's flabby form bent over in laughter, his pear-shaped posterior, spread across his chair as he penned a report on my transgression. How soon would he convince the Boss to shove me in the elevator and hit Down?

Up here there's no place to hide. I trudged on down the corridor. I was almost to the end when I realized: the Perfect Crime, in the Raffles Hotel! In Singapore!

I had died in Singapore! The perfect crime, *my* crime, had been committed in Singapore!

I half ran, half flew to the courtroom lobby to find a newly dead traveler in need of a detective.

HELGA ANDERLE is the editor of the first international women crime writers anthology and has been vice president of the AIEP (the international association of crime writers) since 1993. She worked for international organizations, as well as in journalism, before becoming a writer. Anderle has been published in literary magazines and anthologies from Australia to Mexico. She lives in Vienna, Austria, with her family.

Saturday Night Fever

Helga Anderle

Translated from the German by Tobe Levin

Snot dangled from the chestnut vendor's nose. In suspense, I waited for the man to sniffle or wipe it away with his sleeve. Too late! The drop had grown, lost its grip, and sailed through the air, landing on the crisp slices of potato sizzling on the grill. The cook shoveled them into a paper horn, sprinkled salt over them, and, before I could open my mouth, the innocent customer ahead of me had already imbibed a hearty portion. I let the change I'd already counted out tinkle back into my pocket and turned away, disgusted. My craving for french fries had vanished. Normally I would have smiled about the little scene, but at the moment I had no sense of humor, thinking only about viruses and flu.

It was ten-twenty, Saturday evening, typical November weather: everything so gray-on-gray that you couldn't even groove on your own depression. A night that seemed made for the long overdue physical tune-up: sauna, massage, new polish on fingers and toes, cucumber slices on forehead and cheeks, maybe even the crossword puzzle from *Zeit* magazine—and then straight into the sack for beauty sleep before midnight, done without for God knows how long. Instead, I found myself hanging out on a drafty street corner for twenty minutes, my feet killing me, waiting for some shit photographer. Supposedly, intelligent reporters exist, but

I've never met one. At our paper we have such duds that I even let a machine make my passport photos. I hoped they weren't dumping someone like Fiwonka on me, the worst of the bunch. Just looking at him gave me the creeps! Battle fatigues, military boots, headband, three-day beard, and the collected gold of Montezuma on his hairy macho chest. Matching his outfit he drove around in an open Land Rover even with the mercury hitting minus, like he thought Vienna was somewhere in the jungles of 'Nam. You could just barf. Not that I'd rather have Molny a.k.a. the vacuum cleaner. What magic he performs at press buffets! Before you know it the canapés, cake, sandwiches, anything edible vanishes into his cellophane-lined suit pockets. It doesn't matter that he's already as fat as a sumo wrestler and earns three times as much as I do in my third year as an editor with a union contract.

It really burns my ass the way those bozos pocket the cash for click-clicking a little, while we writers eat our brains out on the brink of starvation. Not to mention the fact that a female doesn't have an easy time of it, up against the chauvinist pigs in the press room. Far and wide not a shimmer of light. Okay, the old farts are full of little stories from the good ole days of typesetting, can be as charming as Maurice Chevalier. In reality they are as misogynistic as Nietzsche and Schopenhauer put together and on the whole thoroughly convinced that the progress of women means the end of the newspaper business.

Still, they're twenty-four karats compared to the younger stars in their cashmere pullovers and designer jeans. A real nest of vipers. Inflated egomaniacs for whom women don't even exist, or only as annoying competitors. They stop at nothing to cut you off from a story or steal it from under your nose. Like right now. At the editorial meeting, no sooner did they let my theme, "For Women, Fear Stalks the Subway," melt on their tongues than they were already storming the boss: Wouldn't it be too bad to let such a good story get fucked up by a woman? Wouldn't it be better if a man did it, dressed of course in dame's clothes and a wig . . . ? But even though the boss usually goes along with the boys' craziest ideas, this time it was too much even for him. Their heads snapped into their shells as he thundered at them, and I left the meeting a good head taller. The story was mine. Mine alone.

Ten-thirty p.m. Where the hell was this idiot photographer? To be absolutely sure we wouldn't miss each other, I had printed the information with a red marker and handed the message to the photo chief myself: PLACE: SCHWEDENPLATZ SUBWAY STATION—EXIT ROTENTURM STREET. TIME: 10 P.M. As I was marching back and forth impatiently, a man suddenly ambled in my direction. A monotone little guy in a camel's hair coat, a velvet propeller under his chin. His bangs made him look like a prematurely aged Viennese choirboy. "Excuse me, madam, but I've been observing you for quite some time. I guess you've been waiting for your escort? Would you care to spend the rest of the evening together?" he said with a stupid grin. Where had he dug up that line from? A Harlequin romance? Grouchy as I was, this was all I needed.

"You shave, I suppose? Then it wouldn't hurt if you looked in the mirror occasionally," I hissed at him. Choirboy came back more quickly than I expected. "Oh yeah? Well, you're not exactly Miss Universe yourself," he snapped, insulted, before beating his retreat. The Egyptian selling newspapers, who'd been watching the incident, tossed me a smile of encouragement and gave the choirboy the finger. A good feeling, that at least the Third World was on my side. Ten forty-five p.m. I'd better just take a look at the other subway exits instead of maybe getting a bladder infection from all this stupid waiting around in the cold.

Spotting myself in a showcase window, I paused. Milk-mustache was right. For Miss Universe I wouldn't have a prayer, but still, I liked what I saw: short, mussed-up, curly brown hair, an intelligent face, with only the region around the mouth a little stormy. Slim figure, bombshell of an outfit, black leather jacket, black jeans, gray turtleneck and low boots with half-high heels. An attractive appearance, all things considered. I only wished I'd put on my long johns.

Subway #1 had just spit out a wave of young people. The Grossfeld high rises with Saturday night fever. Floridsdorf John Travoltas in the finest clothes on their way to the bunny shoot in city discos or the Bermuda Triangle. I went around them and took the escalator in the direction of Laurenzerberg. In summer I liked the area. Wherever you looked, street musicians were performing, and a colorful mix of natives and tourists idled past filled-up benches. The Copa Cagrana rolled out entire clans in all shades of fresh sunburn who stood in line for ice cream at Molin. In the distance, the silhouette of Wienerwald, blue-black, framed by a washed-out yellow shimmer. Colorful neon on the roofs of office buildings edged the Danube Canal, in between the Gothic filigrained peak of the Maria am Gestade tower. The canal exuded an odor as if Vienna were on the sea.

My photographer was leaning, perfectly calmly, on the counter of the hot dog stand and was just washing down the rest of a Langos with a Schnapps. Catching sight of me, he straightened up on the double. His breath made my stomach turn. "Allow me," Nemeth Lajos said, and pressed his dripping-with-garlic-fat lips against the back of my hand. I should have anticipated this. It was typical Lajos or, better yet, typically Hungarian. Not even two world wars and forty years of goulash communism could extirpate their royal equestrian manners from the Magyars. Lajos, the *Schnaps Faucet*—this could even get good! Once a top-notch photographer whose shots of the 1956 Hungarian revolution even appeared in *Life* magazine, he was now a case for Alcoholics Anonymous, only good enough to earn his pittance in the darkroom.

Lajos's motivation for shooting my report was just about zero. Only one thing worried him: "Can't be late or my wife mean!" I was tempted to release the Xanthippe in me and show him how mean I could get. But instead of taking it out on him for making me wait, I stifled it. I still needed him.

Riding down the escalator I tried to get him into the mood of my story. The subway, spooky corridors, confusing long walks. Dark, sinister corners. Soul-lonely women in these horror story labyrinths, accompanied only by fear panting at their backs and the echo of their rushing steps. To be honest, even I was always a little uncomfortable taking the subway home at night. In this situation it did not help much knowing the statistics according to which subways produced more suicides than murders, and far more women were attacked, mugged, and raped on the open streets. I had already collected so much material on the topic, my story would get a lot of attention. The only thing I needed now were a couple of authentic quotes and some smashing photographs.

I'd talked myself up to a high pitch, but Lajos just shrugged his shoulders. "Lady, just say me what photos you want and I make."

"Shoot the escalator from a frog's point of view, that'll turn 'em on!" I suggested. Getting him down on his knees beaded his brow with sweat, and getting him back on his feet again was even harder. I had to relieve him of all his equipment. "Okay, now let's shoot the exit from the number-one with all the kids landing," I panted, propelling him forward. I stopped a young woman, stylish as Madame Pompadour, all gold and glitter, with ten-centimeter stiletto heels. "Do you feel secure at night in the subway?" I asked her, holding the microphone up to her mouth. She chewed absently on a strand of hair and you could easily see how hard things were ticking between her temples.

"I dunno. I don't usually go out by myself. My boyfriend's always with me." As though ordered he shot out of nowhere, placing himself at a protective angle to the blonde. "Ain't you got no sense, what you telling them bitches all your business, them filthy reporters," he said, pulling his goldpiece away. In the meantime it was already 11:15 p.m. and as we got out at Karlsplatz, the opera had just ended. Women in floor-length minks and patent leather shoes, with hairdos that reminded me of the roof construction of post-modern Hollein houses, streamed through the passage. Almost all were hanging on the arm of a Hofrat.* Finally I found a woman traveling by herself. Mid-forties, lawyer's wife type, cultivated Schönbrunn German. "Am I afraid? And how! Vienna has already become pure Chicago!" she babbled old FPO** campaign slogans. "With all this foreign rabble around, a woman can hardly step out of the house! If I hadn't inherited the opera subscription from my aunt, you can be certain I wouldn't be going out alone!" I nodded, full of understanding, thanked her for the words, and pulled Lajos back before he made a grab for the lawyer's wife's hand.

Despite the late hour, there was a lot going on in the opera station. Beside the usual night owls and junkies, a group of Italian tourists was singing "Avanti popolo" at the tops of their voices and behaving as though at a Unità festival. The clochards were hunkering in their usual places and let the booze circle around. Two of them were already leaning against each other, fast asleep, in a puddle of red wine. The drunks didn't look exactly trustworthy, but a woman would really have nothing to fear from them. At most they'd bug you for a smoke or a couple of schillings.

Lajos stopped for a minute to put in a new film. Just as he was at it, all hell broke loose in the station below, as if the Sioux were on the warpath. How could I have forgotten the Rapid vs. Austria soccer game! Riots were as sure to break out afterward as the amen to follow a prayer, and I congratulated myself on already being on the spot. As the enthusiastic kids started heaving at each other, the frightened passengers tried to evade the legs, fists with iron rings, and cherry bombs. I managed just in time to duck behind a pillar; the beer can hurtling like a rocket missed me by a hair. In Lajos the spirit of revolution was apparently awakened. The automatic button on his camera clicked nonstop. Finally! This was something for the front page. The young

* Court Councillor, a title of respect cherished by Austrians even in the absence of a royal court.
** The Freiheitliche Partei Osterreich, a right-wing political party.

stars probably boring themselves to death at the Motto just then would turn green from envy.

Above the shouting and tumult you could suddenly hear whistles and then the heavy tramp of hobnailed boots. A special police unit equipped with nightsticks, helmets, and Plexiglas shields stormed down the stairs. While the first comers began indiscriminately beating anything they got their hands on, the crowd dispersed, fleeing in panicky haste. "Let's get out of here!" I cried, dragging Lajos away from the war zone. Once we were at street level again he marched straight toward the hot dog stand across from the Secession. "Madam, pulease, I could do with a barack!" "Okay, a little high wouldn't hurt me either," I said and let Lajos order. The stuff burned like hell but had a calming effect. I suppose it dulled the nerves. And before I could intervene, Lajos had ordered another round.

I let him drink a third schnapps before driving him back to the subway station to take stock of the damage. The boys had done a thorough job of it. The quai looked like after a bomb attack. The ground was strewn with glass splinters, shreds of clothing and paper, beer bottles, football caps. There was even one nearly new Reebok under the rubble. On the only announcement board still standing, someone had sprayed a swastika. Idiots, I thought, your honored Führer would have sent you delinquents straight into a labor camp.

I let Lajos finish shooting his film. "So now we've had enough, that's it for today. Thanks, you did a good job," I told him, hiding hands in my pockets. Thoughtfully I watched the sad figure disappear in the direction of the opera. If the pictures came out well, I'd pull *Schnaps Faucet* out of the darkroom again. Sure, you had to tell him every little thing, but I clearly preferred to give orders myself than to be commandeered by the other Leica princes.

The pressure on my bladder that I'd carried around for quite a while already had now entirely run out of patience. Despite my dislike of public toilets, I had no choice. I poked around in my pocketbook for change, threw in the coin, and pressed the handle with my elbow. Most of the graffiti I already knew. Only two made it worth my effort to copy them down for my collection. I had just clicked my ballpoint when I heard a noise. It sounded like a groan and came from the next stall. In a flash I remembered the hook stalker, the one who picked his victims from the toilet stalls. Sure, I was scared, but my curiosity got the better of me. Slowly I pushed against the door, which had only been pulled to. Luckily no ax met my effort. On the floor, a girl sat throwing up in the basin. Manuela! I almost didn't recognize her, she looked so awful. Sticky hair, torn clothes, her face corpse white and peppered with fresh scratches, the eyes deeply sunken and without expression. Manuela. It must have been a full five years ago that I'd seen her last. An average pretty girl from the country with the glow of a Valium tablet and the usual kid's hope of a movie career under her perm. Exactly the type which, when left to itself, would be sure to slide downhill. For a little while I took an interest in her. It was pretty stressful since she didn't care about anything other than movies and race car drivers. Then I was doing this volunteer's job, but hot with ambition, I soon had enough of baby-sitting the country's innocents. Manuela had stopped heaving by now. It smelled beastly in the toilet.

"Manuela, it's me, Anna, do you remember me? Are you sick? Do you need help?"

"Anna?" she echoed, and then in slow motion raised her head to look at me with a gaze so mournful, it cut me through and through. I asked myself what I should do with her. To start with, nothing better occurred to me than to pull her out of the stall. But as I tried to lift her, my hand grasped something sticky, moist: her T-shirt was full of blood. Horrified, I let her go. "What happened? Are you wounded? Wait! I'll get the police!"

Manuela's arms zoomed out like tentacles and choked my legs. "No, no! Not the cops . . . I just killed one!"

"You did what?"

"I stabbed the fucking pig." The words came out so muffled that I thought maybe I hadn't heard them right.

I leaned down, took hold of her collar and shook. Manuela's head rocked rhythmically, as though hanging by a
thread. "If you don't believe me, then look for yourself. Outside . . . in front of the dairy . . . in the bushes."

I was suddenly dizzy, slowly sliding down the wall to the
floor. Damn it! Now, of all times, my blood pressure had to
act up on me! Blindly I scrounged around in my shoulder
bag, looking for my medicine. Following directions exactly I
let twenty drops splash on my tongue and waited for them
to take effect. Still a little unsteady, I tottered up and went
out.

The park, now empty, smelled of moist shrubbery. The
fog made pale lanterns of the lights. The tranquillity was
spooky. Apart from occasional traffic noises, I heard only my
own panicky heartbeat. To the left of the path, under the
nearly bald bushes, something was lying. The lawn whispered under my feet and dry twigs whipped my face as I
moved forward, slowly, bent over. Toward the figure lying
inert on the ground. Manuela hadn't lied. She had killed an
officer. His hat hung askew over his face, the uniform had
been pierced by the dead shrubs, a knife plunged up to its
handle in the middle of his chest. Don't play Mother Teresa,
don't touch it, get out of here, my internal voice was warning me. But instead of listening and running, my legs did
their own thing and waltzed the dumbest person in all of
Vienna and its suburbs back into the subway hall.

Manuela was still sitting exactly as I had left her. I tore a
few sheets of toilet paper from the roll, wet them under the
faucet, and wiped the worst dirt from her face. Passively, she
let me do it. Then I buttoned up her coat and helped her to
her feet. A half an hour later a taxi had delivered us to my
apartment.

I put water on for tea, spiked it with a little rum, and
while we were drinking, Manuela started to talk. In a monotone, incoherently, as though delirious with fever. As I was
able to piece it together, she had known the cop for quite

some time. They had a kind of exchange business going: sex for dope. It worked well for a while until he started passing her diluted stuff or placebos. But for tonight he'd promised her something special, and she'd fallen for it. "I couldn't wait for him to get off me and give me the stuff. But he didn't have nothin'. The bastard came up with empty hands. I was mad as hell and started to holler . . . and then he hit me. Left, right, one punch after the other. Then my mind just blew and next thing I know, he's lying there full of blood." I got a blanket and wrapped it around her. Manuela had fallen asleep sitting up. What would happen to her now? If she gave herself up and confessed, maybe they'd be lenient because of the circumstances. But who would believe a junkie like her? And me, what about me? I was dog-tired. Maybe in bed I'd think of something. But I couldn't fall asleep and stared the whole night, eyes wide, into the darkness. Only when I heard the garbage trucks clatter the next morning did a solution occur to me. Manuela would have to leave Vienna immediately, the best thing would be back to her mother. If I remember correctly she was a nurse. Maybe she'd manage to get her daughter into therapy.

Manuela was still sleeping as I got up and put water on for coffee. In my clothes, and with her hair washed, she looked pretty respectable again. She nodded to everything I suggested and padded after me like a zombie. At the station I bought her ticket and put her on the train. "Promise me, no, swear to me, that you'll call me the minute you get home. I'll talk everything over with your mother." She sat there not saying a word, her arms around her raised knees, rocking her body back and forth. "You'll see, it'll all work out," I told her, saying good-bye and wishing I could believe it myself.

If Manuela's telling the truth, that the others don't know anything about their colleague's shit, then she'd be free of suspicion, since any one of an infinite number of junkies or whoever could have done it. I'd wiped the knife; hopefully there weren't any other clues. As the train pulled out, I ran a few steps with it. Depressed, I went straight to the office.

There I was, entirely by accident having stumbled upon an exclusive story, almost witnessing it myself, and what do I do? Destroy evidence, cover up for the murderer, and help her make her getaway. No journalist in even half her right mind would have done such a thing.

With my head on my arms, I stared at the flickering screen. The cursor blinked hypnotically and demanded the subway report. At some point the night chief stuck his head in at the door. "I guess you know your ninety lines have got to be at the copy editor's by eight at the latest." Damn it. With everything going on in my head, how was I supposed to concentrate!

I went to the ladies' room and threw cold water on my face, but it didn't do much good against the chaos in my head. If they caught Manuela and pressured her, I'd be in a real pickle. In my mind's eye the headlines formed: JOURNALIST, ACCOMPLICE IN A COP MURDER! Then I could just pack my bags, I'd be out of job and maybe even land in prison. But what else could I have done? Gotten the hell out of there and let the girl take care of herself? In despair I kept looking at the clock. Manuela must have reached home a long time ago. Why hadn't she called? I tried myself, but nobody answered. It was already nine when I reached Manuela's mother, who had night duty in a hospital. "How Manuela is? I have no idea. Why are you asking? Coming to me? No thank you. I'm happy if she doesn't show her face around here. She's a hopeless case . . . I don't give a damn!" It wouldn't do any good to explain anything to the woman. No misunderstanding that her daughter's fate was a matter of absolute indifference to her. So I merely asked her to promise to phone me as soon as she heard anything from Manuela. It was already midnight when I got home and could listen to the answering machine. A message had come from Manuela's mother. I called back immediately. They had found her daughter. With a needle in her arm. Overdose. "Maybe that's the best solution," she said, sounding relieved. I felt my mouth flood with gall. Damned coldhearted, the loving mommy . . . But who gave me the right to judge her? Maybe it really was all for the best. Manuela had been freed from her troubles and no one could hurt her anymore, not the cops, not fucking life.

I gave her a minute of silence. The minute was not yet up when a new story came to me. The boys could just eat their hearts out.

MARY JACKSON SCROGGINS is the president of the board of directors of Washington Independent Writers, the largest regional writers' organization in the country. She lives in Washington, D.C., where she owns a small publications firm, Nekima, Inc. As Dicey Scroggins Jackson, she is completing **Who the Cap Fit,** an adult mystery, and a slave tale for children, told from the perspective of a ten-year-old slave.

Dreams of Home

Dicey Scroggins Jackson

*For women and children temporarily in shelter,
but away from home.
For Jocelyn, Rose, and Ernestine,
working dreams into realities.
You are not alone.*

"Your name." It was a question without a question's inflection. The little woman-child at the front of the line didn't move or speak. Apparently she expected common courtesy. Obviously, this was her first time in the in-take line. Her first time at A Woman's Place. It would probably be her first night in shelter, not at home. She didn't look the runaway or the castaway. It was warm for late October in Washington, but she was dressed for the season as well as for the weather.

I'd noticed her sad little-girl face—incompatible with its surroundings—before the line started forming at about six-thirty.

She looks a little like Amani, like Amani used to look. Light eyes set in a thin dark face. Only the hair—and her bruises—were really different. Amani's short sandy hair had never been braided with extensions, and this woman-child's dark hair was—professionally.

Somebody cared about this child. Fifteen or sixteen, maybe, and a long, long way from home.

"*I said,* what's your name?" Miss Thing tapped a dull-

pointed pencil on a wooden desk covered with enough graffiti to tag a small building—generational graffiti.

I nudged the child with my elbow, and she lifted her head
toward Miss Thing. "My name is . . . Ra-achel . . . Jackson. I lost my purse . . . my identification was in it, but
I'm—"

She probably knows somebody named Rachel, and everybody black knows somebodies named Jackson.

"Didn't ask you for no ID," Miss Thing said, displaying an
enormous gap in her teeth and one in her manners to
match.

My guess was, Miss Thing had been *in* this line more
often than behind that desk. But memory is short, especially
when you're having fun. And although her tone was flat and
uninterested, she was having fun. No one heaps shit on the
already shat-upon unless they enjoy it, unless they're having
fun.

When the girl didn't move away from the desk and into
the building, I nudged her again.

"Just go on over to the steps. I'll help you out, I've been
here before," I whispered in her right ear, which was bloody
and swollen.

She jerked away. At five-seven and one hundred and forty
pounds, I'm not really a big woman, but I have a big
woman's presence and voice. And, why on earth should she
trust me, a woman without a home and for all she knew
without good sense? But still she reminded me of Amani,
and I sure hoped someone had helped, was helping her.

More than two hours after getting into the in-take line, we
had both gained admission to the in-take room. Here, where
maximum occupancy was posted as fifty, at least a hundred
women waited to be assigned rooms. I sat, and Rachel
leaned on the wall next to my rusty, gray folding chair.

I saw five or six familiar faces. None would be familiar to
Rachel if she could help it. She was not strong on eye contact. I was, even here. I needed to be for Amani. Besides, it
was a habit pounded into me, literally when necessary, by

Gram, who wasn't having any of her children or grandchildren looking down or away "like as if they had something to be shamed of."

Suddenly, I felt Rachel move a nanospace closer to my chair and then grab the side of it.

"Hey, what *you* doing here, girl? Got any smokes?" a tall, too-thin woman said, walking toward Rachel and more than invading her space.

Rachel responded to her nearness or maybe to the unpleasant odor that arrived with her by lowering her head farther into her chest.

Oblivious to the snub, this twentysomething woman, with a sixtysomething face and gait, continued, "That's a baaad jacket you wearing. My name's Grace, Amazin' Grace." She laughed and casually placed her bony hand on Rachel's shoulder. Rachel moaned. "This your first time here?" Rachel's shoulders slumped and her small brown hand moved up my chair, brushing my back.

Whatever was blunting Grace's senses wasn't sufficient to miss that snub. "Look, I'm just trying to be friendly, to conversate." And she probably was, just trying to *conversate,* but Rachel was too far from home to care or to know how to respond. Grace backed up a little and punched out each word separately and distinctly: "Can-you-hear? . . . Huh?"

"Uh huh" was all Rachel could manage.

"Uh huh, you can hear? Or uh huh, this your first time?" Grace said nastily, reverting to her singsong slur and putting both hands where her waist should have been.

I took Rachel's hand and stood, briefly locking eyes with Grace, who was a couple of inches taller than me and a couple of dozen pounds thinner.

"Heeey, sister. Ain't no problem. It's all good!" She backed away.

Backing off was smart. My experience these last few months is that most women in shelter here are smart—unlucky and sometimes self-destructive, but smart.

"Let's go over by the window," I said, and Rachel let me lead her to the opposite side of the tiny, musty room, stepping on newspapers the way you step on peanut shells at The Ground Round. No one moved to let us through.

A woman I'd seen before was sitting on the paint-chipped windowsill.

"Hi. Your name's Janice, right?" I said and matched her I've-seen-you-before-but-don't-think-we're-friends smile.

"Yeah. And you're . . . Gloria?" she said, and I nodded. "Haven't been around for a while. I figured your life was back in order or something. Or you'd decided to go to another place—cleaner, friendlier—you know. You could get into one of those, I couldn't." She patted her pretty hair— thick, unpressed, unpermed—held back with a royal-blue headband encrusted with rhinestones, and shoved her hands into the pockets of a brownish tweed coat two sizes too large. She looked tired, always, and sounded sad. I liked her. I couldn't remember why she had landed here but I wanted to.

"Janice, would you mind letting this kid sit down in the window? She's not feeling well." I moved Rachel toward the windowsill. She did look sick.

"Sure. I'm going back out to smoke anyway." As she walked away, she looked at Rachel and then back at me.

Had I told her about Amani? I didn't think so.

Rachel stood to the left of the window, looking out, but didn't sit down. She scanned the small crowd of smokers, dealers, users, legitimate vendors, pros, and passersby.

"Rachel, why don't you sit down?" Although I wasn't surprised that she didn't answer to Rachel, I didn't know what else to call her. She glanced outside again and then sat down, with her back to the window and her head still bowed.

I sat on the floor beside the low windowsill. "Look, honey, nobody's going to bother you. Really. I know you have no reason to trust me, but do, please. You'll be okay. I'll make sure we're in the same room."

"Thank you, miss," she said in such a soft, vulnerable voice that I wanted to draw her to me, to protect her, to do better by her than I had done by my own daughter.

"I've got a couple of pieces of Kentucky Fried." I tapped my blue canvas satchel. "We can share them. They don't like us bringing food in, but . . ." I said, hunching my shoulders and inhaling deeply. Now, I know cabbage when I smell it. And somebody's got pizza. You wouldn't think anyone could hide a whole pizza on her person and still want to eat it.

"You know, almost anyplace is better for you to be than here, honey. . . . My daughter came here—without my knowledge or my permission—to add real-life experience to a term paper on homelessness. . . . She never, she never came home again," I said. She put her hand on my shoulder, wanting to comfort me now. "Can't you go somewhere else? To a friend's house? Home?" I said. She dropped her hand from my shoulder, detached herself. "How about your grandparents' then?" No response, no reconnection. "You don't want to come back here after tonight. I'll take you to a nicer place up on Georgia Avenue, but I'm not sure they'll let you stay, you're so young. . . . How old are you?"

"I'm . . . eighteen." She lifted her taut little face to convince me, I guess. She was not used to lying. And she probably wasn't even fifteen.

Ms. Bennett, the director of A Woman's Place, appeared outside the doorway. "Okay, ladies, we can go into your rooms now. Remember to keep them neat, and remember only ten to a room and *one* to a bed. Put your belongings close to or under your beds. There is plenty of hot water tonight, ladies, and we can provide soap." She really had a way with the word "ladies." She made it sound like something you definitely didn't want to be and hoped your momma wasn't. A bottom-heavy, nondescript woman, with a sallow complexion and a drippy Jheri-Kurl, Ms. Bennett took pleasure in putting us ladies in our place without being overtly disrespectful or unkind. She would probably genuinely be hurt to know that the women here hated her—not because she was in charge or even because she liked being in charge so much, but because she never let them forget that they were in shelter, not at home.

When we got to Room 7, I shoved Rachel in and steered her toward the last cot on the left, the one next to the wall. I had planned to take the second one, to serve as a buffer for her, but she put her bag down on that one and stared at the wall.

"Please, ma'am, you take the last one," she said, her tiny voice shaking, so I did. She still wasn't sure she could trust me.

It wasn't hard to imagine why she was scared and distrustful, especially since someone had just recently tattooed her little body with bruises.

After devouring a chicken leg but insisting that she was not hungry enough to eat the second piece, Rachel sat at the foot of her cot, holding an expensive overnight bag on her lap, and rested her head on it. It was after ten-thirty and she was exhausted.

"You can lie down. The sheets are always clean on in-take day. Just push your bag under the cot and don't bother unpacking anything. We're getting you out of here tomorrow, and you're not coming back," I said.

Rachel looked at me more directly than she had in the three or four hours since in-take. My eyes—easy to water anyway—hurt to look at her bloodshot, runny right eye. But I held the gaze, not wanting to break contact in any form. Suddenly, she put her hand over her eye, as if to protect me from its sight, and slid around the foot of her cot, closer to me.

"Can I put my bag between our beds instead of on the other side, miss?" she said tentatively.

"Sure. Hand it to me. And, please call me Gloria." Her navy bag was genuine leather, nice soft leather, and the initials on the name tag were not R.J.

"Why are *you* here, Miss Gloria? You don't seem like you should be," she said, again averting her eyes. The eye contact thing is not easily learned after a lifetime, no matter how brief, of looking away.

"Baby, nobody *should* be here. Nobody. But shh . . .

things happen sometimes." I had almost cussed. And to a child. Six months ago, I'd confined my cussin' to a very occasional "asshole." It is hard to wander around in the real world and not to utter "asshole" occasionally. I continued, "This is supposed to be a . . . a . . . safety net."

"But you *really* don't seem like you'd be here. You don't even talk like most of the people."

"First of all, young lady," I said, smiling and playfully, "you haven't really talked to anyone here but me—and me just barely."

She smiled, a shy little-girl smile.

"And, if you listen hard enough, you'll hear lots of different kinds of people, here for lots of different reasons. Some people have gotten used to being here, but nobody really wants to be here. This isn't anyone's dream of home. It is a temporary shelter, Rachel, that's all. And speaking of people who do not belong here . . ."

She turned away from me, rudely and without apology.

Well, a little attitude here. Just enough attitude was good.

She took off her shoes and climbed onto the cot. Just before she pulled the covers up around her ears, I leaned over to whisper, "If you need to get up to go to the bathroom, let me know. I'll go with you, the halls aren't safe for you. Okay?"

Silence was my answer.

The lights—one bulb at each end of the room—went out. The darkness was followed by Ms. Bennett's announcement: "Lights out, ladies. It is eleven o'clock." I guess she thought we wouldn't realize the dim rooms had grown darker without being told so. We were homeless, not stupid. "Good night . . . ladies." *Bitch.*

Five minutes after lights-out, I was always ready to leave A Woman's Place, but I still had business here.

A big macho-stepping roach hopped from the wall onto my cot. I felt it hit the thin bowel-brown cover, then take off pimping toward my face. I snatched the cover over my head and tucked in for the night. I'd keep an ear out for Rachel, but I'd have to provide undercover surveillance.

*   *   *

Dreams are strange when your life becomes dreamlike, nightmarishly so, hard to believe it's yours. Eighteen months ago, I had a husband who loved me and whom I loved back. Robert was my best friend, my best everything. Six months ago, I had a daughter I adored, funny and full of attitude.

Glass shattered, maybe in my dream. I was a heavy sleeper, but the sound yanked me back into the real world.

I listened for more glass to break, trying to tell where the sound was coming from. Room 7 was quiet, except for the requisite snorer.

I tapped the inside of my cover, hoping to frighten combat-ready creatures off before sticking my head out, and threw the cover back. According to my watch, it was four-thirty. Thank God for glow-in-the-dark stuff.

I glanced over at Rachel's cot. It was empty.

"What-do-you-mean, *evidently* she's not here!" I screamed. "Evidently, you don't—"

"Look, we don't usually have to tie you down to keep you in. People want to get in, not sneak out. Did you check the bathroom?" a white man-child trying to grow dreadlocks said. He sat behind the guard's desk guarding his tape player and off-beat grooving to Bob Marley.

"I-am-not-stupid," I said. I sounded calm, reasonable, bracing myself against rising anger and fear. "Of course I checked the bathroom. I have checked the entire second floor, I'd check the whole building if I had access. So, what the hell are you going to do? Right now, what are you going to do? A young girl's missing."

He threw his hands up and patted, pulsed the air. *Well, he wasn't quite the idiot I first thought he was; he didn't pat me.* "Calm down, lady. Just calm down. Do you know it's only five o'clock?"

"I am calm, as calm as I'm going to get until the staff get their lazy butts up and start looking for Rachel." I reached across the desk to feel for a phone, and he jumped from his chair into the wall. I guess he thought I was about to *pat* him. "Where-is-the-phone? I'm calling the police. . . . Please do-not tell me that this is a guard's desk without a goddamn phone. Sweet Jesus," I said. I had never used a phone in A Woman's Place. Amani had, according to our phone records.

My guess is, the guard wasn't thinking this such an easy job anymore. Now, I was not the only one in the hallway who was scared.

"Tell you what, lady, I'll get somebody in charge, I'm just holding the desk," he said, with no disrespect on "lady" intended—even this dreadlock, wanna-be Rasta wasn't going to mess with a crazy homeless lady. "Ms. Bennett was on duty last night, so she's still here. I'll call her, say, in about an hour, okay?"

"No, dear, that-will-not-do." I'm not going to lose another child here. No! Hell-no! "Where's Ms. Bennett's room? Third floor, right? You don't have to call her, I'll go get her."

He came from behind the desk. If he was smart, he was leaving. All six feet of him.

"Don't get in my way, honey. You're somebody's baby, I-don't-want-to-hurt-you." He headed for the front door. They'd probably have to hire another guard.

I spun around at the sound of a raspy, mirth-filled voice. "Yeah, wake her fat ass up. Now!" Five or six women, all unfamiliar, stood near the stairwell from the second floor. I wasn't sure who had spoken.

A short, stout woman with a beautiful gray-blue kente cloth scarf wrapped around her head walked over to me. Like most of the other women, she was fully dressed except for shoes. "Now, what you 'bout to wake Ms. Bennett from her beauty sleep for?" She asked, but they clearly didn't really care, as long as I kicked ass when I found her.

"A young girl who came in with me today is missing. She's just a child, fourteen or fifteen, maybe not that old."

"They don't have no business letting them young ones in here anyway. Ain't even legal. And it ain't good for them, in here with all kinds of folks. You know what I mean. They got other places for them to go," she said. "I didn't know what was wrong, but I sure done called the police. They'll come when they get ready to, though, I shoulda said somebody was dead, somebody white." The Amen Choir of five formed an assenting semicircle around her.

Truth is, the Metropolitan Police Department doesn't care much more about white people in shelter than it does about us. "Homeless" becomes the operative word. It has an homogenizing effect on people's sensibilities. Still, they all laughed at her little funny, even the lone white woman in the group. She probably didn't want to; I couldn't.

The little stout woman moved away from the others and stuck her hand into the pocket of the terry cloth robe she wore over her sweater and jeans. She looked into my eyes, into her pocket, and then back at me again, in a slow, deliberate movement, so I leaned over to peek in. A cellular phone. My God, a cellular phone.

She whispered, "My son gave it to me for protection, you know. This is only the second time I used it here. First time was 'bout a young girl too. Poor thing. A cute little thing with real light eyes."

Real light eyes!

"What do you do around here, just swallow them up whole?" I said, all up in Ms. Bennett's face, as Amani would have said.

Ms. Bennett dropped her hands from her hips and backed up out of her own space to get away from me.

By the time I'd questioned the woman with the phone sufficiently to know that the girl with the light eyes could not have been Amani, Ms. Bennett had appeared waddling down the hall in a thin nightgown, open silk robe, and Barney slippers.

"Miss . . . ? What is your name? I have no idea what you are talking about, but we have rules in this shelter and unless you have somewhere else to stay on a regular basis, I would strongly suggest that you just go back to your room, and I'll forget this little disturbance," she said with perfect diction and learned authoritative pitch. "I'll look into this tomorrow . . . later today." She looked at her watch, disgusted.

"Since you asked but clearly do not care, my name is Gloria Bell. And the problem is, a little girl, a teenager, is missing. She came in beaten up—"

"Beaten up?" She looked away.

"Yes, beaten and scared and now she's gone. I just don't think she left on her own. She had no place to go. So, Ms. Ben—. What's your name, your first name?" I paused to get her name and when she didn't give it, well, let's just say I knew it was about to get ugly up in that hall.

"Okay, B—I can call you that can't I?—like I said, a girl is missing. She gave a phony name, Rachel Jackson. What are you going to do?"

"First," the B said, "any ladies who don't need to be here, that is, everybody but you should go back to her room. You only have a couple of hours left before you will be on your own for the day. I would suggest—"

"So, what are you going to do except suggest that the group disperse? What about the girl?" I said as my supporters walked away even more quietly than they had assembled.

"Who is this girl to you?"

"She is a human being, a scared little person who needs somebody to look after her. She wouldn't have left on her own, she knew I was going to help her," I said. The B appeared to want to laugh. "Now, what are your procedures for searching this *facility*?" Now I could work with "facility" as well as the B could work with "ladies."

"I am not going to entertain this discussion with you. At a decent hour, say, eight o'clock, I will have in-take records checked and—"

"That's almost three hours from now. This can't wait. Where are the records? I'll check them. . . . But, how's that going to help? All the in-take person asked for was her name, which she lied about." I waited for a response.

"I will look into this in a few hours—"

"No, somebody's going to look into it right now. Too much for you? Then just get the hell out of my way, B."

"You're out of here, now," the B said. "I'll call the police if I have to."

"The police were called thirty minutes ago, so you don't have to leave. We can talk a little longer," I said and smiled, a real smile, both dimples deepening.

The little color in her face had completely drained away. The effect was not pleasant. "*Who* called the police?"

"I did," I said. "Maybe if you call too, they'll come quicker."

The police didn't arrive until six-fifteen, more than an hour after the first, and perhaps only, call to them. The B hadn't seemed too pleased at the real prospect of police coming into A Woman's Place to search for another missing child. When they arrived, I was in Room 7 looking around Rachel's cot with my flashlight. I'd looked earlier, when I first noticed that she was gone. When I saw that her leather bag was missing, too, I knew she hadn't just gone to the bathroom or for water. Or left on her own. Where would she go if she'd had to come here?

I should have watched her. I know how dangerous this place can be. First Amani, and now Rachel.

I pushed her cot a few inches to the left, and it bumped the next cot. The elderly woman on it lifted her head and said, in a gentle, sleepy voice, "What're you doing, honey? What time is it anyway?"

I apologized for waking her and told her that it was after six and that the child who had been in the cot next to hers was missing. She looked around, at the other cots, and put her head back down.

"Did you hear or see anything?" I said.

She turned her back to me and pulled the cover over her head. "No, I don't know nothing about nothing, honey. I just come here 'cause I don't have anyplace else to go."

I walked over to her cot, leaned down, and whispered as

gently and calmly as I could, "If you remember anything, please let me know."

I went back to the space between my cot and Rachel's and knelt to look under hers. When my left knee, the bad one, touched the floor, a sharp pain went up my thigh. I raised my knee to find a bright yellow stone. Light from the hallway flooded the room.

"Miss, come with me, please," a young policewoman said, standing small but Rambo-like in the doorway. A male officer—another baby with a gun and a little training—stood to her left, and in the background between the two I could see the B smiling—*not for long*—and talking to someone out of my view.

"Of course, officer," I said. Rachel might still be in this place. Amani surely wasn't, but Rachel, maybe.

I dropped the yellow stone in the pocket of my sweats and walked toward the door, hesitating near the cot where the little lady with the gentle voice pretended to be asleep. "Officer, my name is Gloria Bell, and I want to re—"

"Glo?" I knew that voice. A tall, dark officer pushed past the two younger ones and filled the door. "What's going on? What are you doing here?"

"Lew, thank God," I said. He took two six-feet-three strides in my direction. He smiled down at me, but he wasn't amused.

"I'm waiting for an answer, Glo. This better be good or I'm going to arrest you."

And he would.

It took exactly five minutes to recount what I had repeated at least five times already, the only important facts being, a young girl, beaten up and frightened, had disappeared from this place and no one seemed to care. He stood in front of me. I sat on the windowsill in the in-take room.

"And she didn't tell you her real name?"

"No, but her initials might be C.P.N. They were on her bag."

"The bag could have been stolen or it might belong to a friend."

"If she has a friend who would lend her an expensive leather bag, she probably has one she could have gone to instead of coming here," I said unpleasantly.

He ignored the comment but moved closer to me. He knelt in front of me and took my hands.

"Glo, I'll look into this, but we both know what this is really about."

"Yes, it's really about a young girl missing and nobody caring." I looked out the window. Now I wanted him to disappear.

He stood up, without releasing my hands. "Obviously somebody cares, baby," Lew said.

"Not enough." If I'd cared enough, she might be here now. No, she'd be where I knew she'd have been safe. My house. I could have taken her there.

"Ms. Bennett will look into this and so will I. But you, private citizen, will stay out of it. Got that? I ain't playing with you, baby, I'll throw you in jail if I have to."

"For what? Trying to save a child?" I said, trying to retrieve my hands.

"No. For obstructing justice, public nuisance, vagrancy. I'll think of something," he said, smiling. "Maybe, I'll get you on indecent exposure 'cause you sure ain't too decent now."

"Okay, Lew, you're funny, but can you *find* this one?"

I hadn't meant to say that. And he was right. This wasn't just about Rachel.

He leaned out of my face, stretched his six-three skyward, and lost the smile. My hands were definitely mine again. "Okay, the child is no longer here and Ms. Bennett wants you to be removed from the premises for causing a disturbance. I will personally escort you out. Now, you can either go home or move on to another shelter, but you're getting out of here."

"Thank you, officer. And by the way, why is such a high-ranking officer looking into this little inconsequential homeless-child-missing, homeless-lady-causing-disturbance kind of call?"

"That's it." He opened the door, stuck his head out. "Officer Morrison, please escort Mrs. Bell back up to her room to get her belongings. Bring her back down. She'll be leaving here immediately afterward. See that she does not disturb other residents." He looked back at me. "You have exactly ten minutes."

Officer Morrison, a pretty little thing who appeared too small to make weight and height requirements for the department, stepped into the room. "Yes sir. Let's go, ma'am."

We went up the stairwell in silence. On the second floor, when we got to the second door on the right, I stepped in and she followed. It was still dark. I walked over to the cot against the wall, but someone was already in it and the next one.

"Mrs. Bell, these beds are already occupied. Are you sure we're in the right room, ma'am?" Officer Morrison whispered.

"Oh, it must be the next room," I said, with no pretense at whispering. When I turned to leave the room, I stumbled forward a few steps and fell. My bad knee hit the floor, hard. "Oh God. Ooooh . . ."

My misstep and pain were acknowledged by a chorus of "What the hell?", "Goddamn, can't even sleep in this MFing hole in the MFing wall," and other warm indications of concern.

"You okay, ma'am?" Officer Morrison said, racing forward. I held my knee with both hands and moaned, real moans.

She tried to help me up. Finally, a couple of women came to her assistance. One was Janice. I thought that she'd gone into Room 6, and I hadn't misjudged her character at all.

"I must have tripped over something," I said, all out of breath and weakly.

"Maybe I better get Lt. Davis and my partner. It'll be easier for the men to help you up. Don't want these ladies to injure themselves, too," she said with genuine concern. Somebody had taught her respect for people, just because.

She left the room at a clip. I turned to Janice and grabbed her hand. When she realized I wasn't holding on for support, she pulled away, surprised. I wasn't coming on to her, was not looking for a date.

Officer Morrison was fast and Lew, a natural sprinter, would be worried.

In two minutes flat, Lew was in the room. He shoved the little crowd aside and knelt by me on the floor. He immediately began to massage my shoulder and to rub my thigh, neither of which was hurting. But that was okay. "What happened?"

"I tripped over something and twisted my ankle." He scanned the immediate area without moving his head and only briefly looking away from me. He could really be annoying. "When I fell, I hit my knee," I said.

"The bad one?"

"Yes, but I didn't hit it that hard. I think—"

Before "I can stand" could get out, standing wasn't an issue. He'd lifted me from the floor and was on his way out of the room, down the steps, and out of the front of A Woman's Place. He didn't look as if he felt like a hassle, so I didn't protest. Anyway, my knee really did hurt.

He dumped me in the passenger seat of his black Sable, slammed the door, and got in on the other side. "Okay, Glo, wave at the building. Say good-bye. You're not coming back. I hope you accomplished whatever you planned to in the wrong room."

It would be nice to be home, especially after this absence. It felt good to have a home to come back to, even an empty one. Eighteen months half empty, six months completely empty.

Lew said fewer than ten words after pulling away from A Woman's Place. "Are you crazy, Glo? Do *you* want to disappear?"

"No, but I want my child back," I said and stared out the window. I hated to cry, perhaps because tears came so easily. Every emotion and everything related to emotion came easily. "I . . . I-want-Amani-back! And I needed to protect Rachel. Now they are both gone, gone . . ." I'd yelled at him, accusingly, even though he had tried harder than anyone except me to find Amani, to find out what happened to her.

When we reached my house, a large rambler on 16th Street, Lew pulled into the driveway, came around to open my door, and lifted me out of the car.

"I think I can stand," I said, all cried out now and apologetic.

"I should drop you, right here in the driveway, maybe tripping over air like you did back there," he said and almost smiled.

Inside the house, he put me on the overstuffed sofa in the living room and went into the kitchen. I could hear him talking on the phone, but made out only two words: "another kid." He was a more accomplished whisperer than I.

The teakettle whistled, and Lew returned to the room carrying the rattan tray that he'd given Robert and me just weeks before Robert's stroke. The tea smelled wonderful. The man who made the tea was wonderful. And Robert was almost an impossible act to follow.

"You don't need to stay with me. Thanks for fixing the tea. I'll be fine now," I said. "Besides, I need to get decent."

"Can you get around?" he said with real concern. "Try to stand."

I motioned him away and pushed up from the soft arm of the sofa. My knee didn't feel too bad, but I knew it would get worse. I limped to the opposite wall. Satisfied, he agreed to leave but not before mentioning his need for a home-cooked meal and even supplying a menu—stuffed pork chops and any kind of greens. I started to tell him that I hadn't eaten pork or much of anything fried since Robert's stroke but didn't think he wanted to hear about my dead husband while he was trying to get a date, his first one with me since college.

"Hinting for a free meal, uh? I'd love to oblige but it might be hard while I'm incapacitated," I said, glad to have the playful banter completely back in both our voices. After Robert died, Lew had helped me hold things together without ever overstepping. He was always there to give me what I wanted, what I needed, and nothing more. Only recently, over the last couple of months, had our relationship begun to change, slowly.

"I'll bring the food, spaghetti from that place you like downtown or some real food from Levi's. Sometime between seven-thirty and eight," he said, then walked over to the wall where I leaned, scooped me up—one hundred and forty pounds is never easy for anybody to scoop—and put me back on the sofa. A light kiss that he had aimed for my cheek landed on my lips—my doing—and sealed the date.

On his way out, he stopped at the compact disc player. By the time he reached the front door, "If This World Were Mine," the Luther Vandross–Cheryl Lynn duet, was playing. Without looking back, he left.

He's really a wonderful man. But I was glad to see him leave.

I picked up the phone on the end table, put it on my lap, and waited.

Answer that phone! That must be the tenth ring.

I jerked forward, almost dropping the phone from my lap. My knee was throbbing, and the phone ringing was mine. I must have dozed off—taken a long nap. The last time I'd checked it was only twelve-thirty, and now it was just beginning to get dark. Please don't hang up before I can answer, please don't. I snatched the receiver from the hook.

"Hello. Hello?" I said. No answer. "Janice?"

"Yeah," she said. I could barely hear her.

"So you got the number?"

"From you, this morning," she said. Right answer, wrong voice.

"I wasn't sure you'd even see what I scribbled on the corner of that old Barry flyer," I said, trying to fix on the voice. "You sound a little funny. Are you all right?"

"Catching a cold or something. You wanted me to call you."

"Can you talk now? Where are you?"

"In the phone booth around the corner from the shelter. But I can't talk long. There's a line for the phone. And you know how these people get."

At the moment, those people were being unusually quiet outside a doorless phone booth on a busy noise-free street corner, during rush hour.

"Are you going to help me?" I said, getting right to the point.

"I called you, didn't I?"

"Thanks. I'll treat you to dinner at Southern Grill while we talk. It's only a couple of blocks from you."

She didn't answer quickly. Homeless people rarely hesitated to accept invitations to dinner. I looked at my watch. It was five-thirty.

"No. You hurt your leg. I suggest you . . . let me come to you," she said.

Now, I hesitated. "I'm at 6193 Sixteenth Street, N.W. It's a gray house, third from the corner." I had to talk to her. Whatever she knew, I needed to know now. It had already been more than twelve hours since I'd noticed Rachel was gone. "How soon can you get here?"

"Twenty minutes," she said, and hung up.

Well, she certainly wasn't traveling by Metrobus or the subway. Moving up in the world, aren't you, Janice?

She rang the doorbell at five-fifty. Punctual to a fault, everything to a fault but compassionate.

"Come in, B," I yelled. The door was unlocked.

She came in, slowly surveying the room, and lingered in the foyer.

"How did you know?" she said.

"Why did you lie?"

"You assumed I was Janice so I just let you think that."

"Answering 'yeah' is more than just letting me think you were Janice." Petty point of clarification.

"Well, I thought you might not want to speak with me considering our earlier conversation and your suspicions."

"I'll talk to anyone who can help me find Rachel. Can you?" I said.

"Perhaps. But . . . how did you know?"

I started to ask why she cared, but I didn't have time to play question tag. Rachel might be the loser.

"I know Janice's voice, not well, but I know it. And you have very distinct ways of inflecting certain words, 'suggest' being one of your favorites," I said and beckoned her in, without grace. "Please come in. Into the living room and have a seat."

Even after she finally decided that it was safe, that this was not some kind of trap, she waddle-walked into the living room sweeping for land mines. She stood by the rust-colored armchair in the corner. *Interesting.* She is running a shelter poorly, possibly criminally; withholding information about at least one missing girl, probably two; gaining entrance to my home under false pretenses and demanding a critique of her performance; and she's afraid.

This conversation would be short.

I would have told her to make herself comfortable, to take off her jacket, and to have some cocoa, but I really didn't care about her comfort, I hoped she wouldn't stay long, and she could see the cocoa and the two cups on the coffee table.

"Why did you call instead of Janice?" I said in a neutral tone. Whatever information she had, I needed. I had to remember that. But patience and concealing my feelings were not my strong suits.

She smiled, a lopsided smile, and plopped her abundance in my poor little armchair.

"You gave a note to Janice, so she came to me," she said, as if "naturally" should have followed "so."

"Why?"

"She had given me a little information earlier that might be related to the . . . disappearance."

I wanted to slap her, to beat her with the cane leaning against the sofa. I knew I could take her, was faster than she even in my weakened condition, but I did still need that *little information.*

"Might be related? Could you be a little more specific, B?"

"My name is Bernetta." She threw me a nasty little fat-cheeked smile. "Actually, my friends do call me Bea, a word you have a special way with."

"Okay, Ms. Bennett"—we were not, would never be, friends—"one girl has been missing for months, the other has been missing for almost twenty-four hours." At least it felt that long. "Both were last seen at your place."

"I don't know anything about two girls. That's one thing I wanted to clear up." She clutched her black kid-leather purse a little closer. "I decided to come to your home so that I could explain the situation, without being interrupted or disconnected, so that you would understand my position." She made friendly eye contact. I didn't return it. "You do understand that I didn't have to come here."

"Here, or you could have gone down to the First District to share information with a professional information gatherer." Though Bernetta Bennett might be arrogant and uncaring, I doubted that she was overtly criminal.

This conversation was taking too long, and she was gaining the unacceptable impression of being in control.

"You apparently have connections in the Police Department, but I suggest . . . advise you not to threaten me."

"I suggest that you get on with it. I never threaten anyone, though I've been told that one of my most consistent attributes is 'follow-through,' " I said, with no play in my voice. "Can we get back to business? You've been here for ten minutes and the only information that you've supplied is your first name."

She clutched her purse again, then dropped it in her lap and rubbed her hands together in a greedy little manner. She looked up at me and scanned the room again, with much neck movement.

"Are we alone?"

"Unless you brought somebody with you."

She swallowed hard. "Janice recognized your daughter—"

"My daughter?" I jerked forward, forgetting about my sore knee momentarily. I wondered if she was playing with me, but she couldn't possibly be that stupid or that cruel.

"I—I mean your friend. The girl who came in with you. Janice saw her and thought she looked familiar. Well, she remembered where she had seen her. In church, at the Congregation of the Faithful, Reverend Nelson's church. The girl is the Reverend's foster child," she said, suddenly speed-speaking. "He is a fine man and on our board, so I called him. His wife came for the girl. That's all I know. I hadn't even seen the girl, so I had no way of knowing that she had been beaten or anything like that."

And you didn't care enough to find out why she'd left the Reverend's good home to stay in a shelter. I was jumping to conclusions, this time about the Reverend.

She continued on the fast track. "Mrs. Nelson called to say that she had forgotten the girl's overnight bag, so I asked Janice to get it for me. It's locked in my office now. After your little scene, I wasn't sure what to do with it." She began to regain her composure. I was likely to get more information if she stayed a little uncomposed.

Under the best of circumstances, I would hate this woman. *My little scene.* I may have been premature in judging her not to be overtly criminal.

I reached under a big peach pillow on the sofa. She noticed the movement and stiffened. I pulled out the bright yellow rhinestone from Janice's headband and put it on the coffee table, leaving something—fully loaded—under the pillow for her to get stiff over.

"Please give this to Janice. She's really a very decent woman, and I know she thought she was doing the right thing telling you about Rachel's connection to Reverend Nelson."

"She was. Of course she was. After all, how do we know that the girl wasn't involved with drugs or prostitution or a rough boyfriend or something? Wandered into A Woman's Place . . . uh . . ." she said, losing that composure again.

Enough.

"What is the Reverend's address and what is Rachel's real name?"

"What are you going to do?

"What-is-the-Reverend's-address?"—my hand was involuntarily moving toward that pillow—"And-what—"

"Here, here, I don't know her name, but I've written the address down. I knew that you would want it. But the Reverend is a good Christian man. His church donates money and food to A Woman's Place. The congregation donates clothing and time with residents and occasionally the Reverend and Mrs. Nelson take a woman into their home to help her make the transition—"

"So you sent that baby back to that man and his wife because they donate things and they take other women in. Have you ever talked to any of the women after they've been taken in?" I said, unable to look at her. She had to get out. Now.

"No, but . . . Running a shelter is difficult work, dealing with those people every day who no one else wants to be bothered . . ."

"And you love it, don't you? Just how superior does it make you feel? You are a woman with too much attitude and no conscience. You only called because you knew Janice wouldn't keep this *little information* to herself, she does have a conscience, and you're afraid something really awful like death might happen to Rachel. That might get associated back to your little concrete jungle."

"I always have done what is best for the shelter. I do what is best for the women who make it their home."

"No woman makes it her home, not even temporarily. You see to that."

She stared at me and forced a tiny gasp of indignation. Her eyes shifted to the pillow and remained there as she hoisted herself from my poor little chair. She let herself out.

Every man in my life has hated the extremes of my independence. Lew was no exception. He'd be furious when he found out I'd gone to see the good Reverend and his wife without backup—one of his favorite police words. Actually, I did have backup, but I'd never fired it.

By the time Bernetta Bennett got back to her car, probably parked around the corner, I had called a cab. Cabs came when called to this neighborhood.

Then I called Betty at DHS, hoping she still had foster care connections. She wasn't happy with my request—foster care records are confidential and she could lose her job and her license—but she came through anyway.

In the ten minutes that it took to get to the Reverend's house, I hadn't come up with a plan. So, I just said a prayer, well, not a prayer, but the only Scripture I could think of at the moment. "Jesus wept."

"That'll be four-fifty, miss," the driver, a stocky man with a ready smile but no cabside conversation, said. His dashboard was dominated by the pictures of two dark-haired beauties he said were his daughters, Maria and Ana.

The cab stopped in front of a three-story rowhouse with an immaculate lawn and a small garden dominated by pink azaleas.

"Could you wait here for me? I won't be more than five or ten minutes. I'll pay you twenty-five dollars for a ten-minute wait. If I'm longer than that, please, call the First District police station and ask for Lt. Lew Davis," I said without emotion.

"Miss, please, just pay me the four-fifty and call another cab when you get ready to leave. Hey, how about I call the dispatcher and someone will be here within fifteen, twenty minutes. This is a nice part of town."

I explained the situation briefly: I was removing my child from an abusive environment. I expected no violence or resistance. In fact, I had been told to come and get her. But you just never knew how people would act.

"Okay, miss. Ten minutes, that's all. Ten minutes, and I don't know nothing about this police thing," he said.

Cane in hand, I deftly made my way up the long walk and rang the doorbell. The door opened in the middle of the second ring.

"Hello, can I help you?" Mrs. Nelson, I presumed, said. She was about my height and general build and had an open, friendly face. I hoped she was not a part of this.

"Hello, are you Mrs. Nelson—the Reverend Clarence P. Nelson's wife?" I said officiously.

"Why, yes, I am. How can I help you?" she said in a ministerial tone.

"My name is Rose Cleary, Mrs. Nelson. I'm here to conduct an unscheduled home visit with the child in your foster care," I said and hoped that they had only one. "May I come in, please?"

"Why, of course you can, but I don't understand. We have had other foster children before Akua"—*Akua*—"but never one of these unscheduled visits. And it is so late," she said. When her mild protest was answered by a cold officious smile, she graciously waved me in. She was young, younger than I'd first thought. Probably in her late twenties.

"We schedule these checks at unusual times to be able to observe the normal home and family environment," I said. I stepped into a lovely, airy living room, decorated in warm earth tones. Just my style. "Is your husband in? Akua?"

She pulled her earlobe and hesitated before lying. Thank God for bad liars.

"No, I'm here alone. Why isn't . . . Mrs. Browne, Akua's caseworker, conducting the visit? Perhaps I better call her. Why, I don't know if I should even have let you in without seeing some form of identification."

"Her caseworker's name is Lisa Gordon. She's a short, thin woman with Senegalese twists and a trace of a Jamaican accent. Has someone else indicated to you that she was handling Akua's case?"

I'll have to do something really nice for Betty.

"Oh yes, why, of course, you're right, Miss Gordon. Please," she said, waving me to a pretty paisley chair.

"Let me get right to the point. We received a report of trouble with Akua, and I need to speak to her, privately. I'm sure she is at home now, considering the incident last night.

I just need to reassure myself, for the division, that she's all right."

Mrs. Nelson aged ten years before my eyes. Everything just suddenly drooped, literally, and her open face closed.

"Mrs. Nelson, you don't want this to be any more unpleasant than it has to be for you, your husband, or Akua. If I'm not given access to her, I will have to call the police to have her removed from your home. I can do that, you know."

I hoped she knew less about these matters than I did.

She sat down and put her face into her hands. I wanted to comfort her, but I didn't have time to stop for every hurting person that I encountered. An awful thought, but we all have to pick our spots. I hoped someone had picked Amani.

I had already gone over ten minutes, and I had no idea when the good Reverend would be home, although I'd checked and knew he had prayer meeting until seven. It was seven now. I had a feeling that he wouldn't be as easy to deal with as his wife was proving to be.

"Mrs. Nelson, Mrs. Nelson," I said, walking over to her and putting my hand on her shoulder. *Was this head-hanging, no-eye-contact thing required in this home?* "Please let me speak with Akua." I had to go for it. "In fact, I think you know that you should let me take her away. Where is she?"

She lifted her head and uncovered her tear-streaked cheeks. I thought I should probably take her away, too. I waited for her response.

"She is upstairs in her room, the first room on the right. Here is the key." She handed me a key. I tried to take it without touching her.

No, she wasn't going with me. This sister was on her own.

"You lock her in?" I said, flat but caring.

"Clarence was afraid that she might run away so . . ."

"Did Clarence happen to mention why she might want to run away? But, of course, you would already know," I said, first trying to make it up the steps, but my leg was really throbbing. On the second step, I turned back to Mrs. Nelson. "Go upstairs and get her, now." I put the key on the step.

"I . . . you just don't understand. Clarence is a good man, but he expects a certain standard of behavior both from himself and from all of us. . . . You are probably not a religious woman—"

"Nor are you, or you wouldn't be defending that piss-poor excuse for a man. You are even worse than he is. You are his willing accomplice. He's just a degenerate with a following and an unimaginative cover. . . . Mrs. Nelson, you are a coward, it is one thing to allow yourself to be beaten. I understand the psychology of that, or at least I try. But to allow a child, any child to be beaten . . ." Enough. "Come get this key and let her out, now."

She did. The combination of a big woman's presence and unwavering eye contact made people take you seriously.

Almost immediately, Akua appeared at the top of the stairs and stopped, looking at me and shaking her head almost imperceptibly. Shaking off a dream.

Before she could speak, I said, "Akua, Mrs. Nelson has agreed to let you come and stay with me for a while, if you'd like." She looked confused, so I added, "My house is just a few blocks away over on Sixteenth Street. Would you like to come?" I reached for her hand.

She said, "Yes, ma'am," and looked down the hall before coming down the steps and taking my hand. She noticed the cane.

"I had a little accident," I said. "Let's jet." One of Amani's expressions.

Akua smiled. "I hoped you'd come, Miss Gloria."

I didn't try to hide my tears.

We jetted, me at a quick hobble. And our cab awaited. I'd hoped Maria and Ana's father would wait, would help us.

He took us straight home. I gave him every dime I had in my purse. By nine-thirty Akua was in the guest room asleep. Amani's room was still Amani's.

Lew had left a message on my machine, begging off from dinner but saying he'd call later. When he did call and I told him what had happened, he came over despite my protest that he shouldn't, that everything was all right. He said that he had something that I'd want to see.

He arrived at about ten-fifteen, with a friend, another police officer. Amazin' Grace. She'd been undercover at the shelter since Amani's disappearance.

After a long conversation with Lew and his wife's threat to testify before the congregation, the Reverend volunteered to have Akua officially removed from his home. Betty helped me get temporary custody.

I am not finished with the Reverend Nelson.

I called A Woman's Place about a month after Akua officially came to live with me. The phone rang five times before anyone answered. I prayed that the B was on duty and threw in "Jesus wept" for good measure.

"Hello, this is A Woman's Place. How can I help you?" a woman said. *Very professional.*

"Hello. May I speak to *Bernetta* Bennett?" I said.

"Bernetta? . . . I'm sorry. She'll be with you in just a moment."

Five minutes later she picked up. I am learning patience. Some things are worth waiting for.

"Hello, this is Ms. Bennett," she said, still full of herself.

"Hi, this is Gloria Bell. I called to let you know that I've been appointed to your board to complete the Reverend Nelson's term. He expects to be tied up with the legal system for a while. The board is about to begin upgrading services and staff," I said. "And, oh yeah, I am going to find out what happened to my daughter. If you, either directly or indirectly, had anything to do with her disappearance—"

"I know, you're going to see to it that A Woman's Place is closed down. You're going to destroy it."

"No, Bernetta, if you are involved at any level, I'm going to destroy you. I hope the shelter won't come down with you. I'll be seeing you. Often."

LINDA GRANT is the author of the Catherine Sayler series. Sayler, a San Francisco private investigator, specializes in high-tech crime, taking cases that range from sabotage in a genetics lab in *Lethal Genes* to sexual harassment in a software company in *A Woman's Place*. The first and third books in the series were both nominated for Anthony awards. Grant, a former president of Sisters in Crime, lives in Berkeley, California, with her family.

Hamlet's Dilemma

Linda Grant

I dreamed again last night. It's getting clearer, I think. I can see my father's face down to the small dark mole just above the jawline a bit to the right of his left ear. My sister's face is less clear, but I know now that is not just a memory from an old photo. I've been through the albums. The image from my dreams is not in any of them.

The action never changes, even if the images become sharper. I see more, notice details better. It's like a home movie—the visual quality improved by a stronger projection bulb, but the progression of shadowy images unchanged. They struggle. She is above him, standing on something that gives her height. Her body is slight; his is massive. Her mouth is open, screaming words I cannot hear. Then suddenly she flies backward, up and away, her eyes wide with fright.

My dilemma is this—is it just a dream my warped psyche has manufactured and is now rerunning for its own satisfaction, or is it a memory of a real event? I believe my father is perfectly capable of the acts I see each night. But that does not mean he committed them.

You're thinking I'm talking about repressed memory, the current psychofad. That I'm just another hysterical woman seeking restitution for perceived misdeeds from the past. Or that I'm a victim. Well, I'm neither. I simply want to know what happened and I want justice. Not the warm, fuzzy comfort of public confession à la Oprah or Donahue. Nor the nasty confrontational catharsis of Ricki Lake or Jenny Jones. Justice. The assessment of guilt and where it is found, punishment.

Some family background is in order here. My name is Andrea Wilkes. My father is James Wilkes, chairman of the comparative literature department at a prestigious liberal arts college in the eastern United States (names have been changed or omitted to protect the innocent—and the guilty). My mother, Sara Wilkes, is a faculty wife, which is to say that she has no role in the community other than as my father's spouse. I had an older sister. Her name was Alyson, Aly for short. She died in an accident when I was four years old.

No one talks about the accident, so it's been hard to find out what happened. For many years I was told that she'd fallen from the balcony of our house and that the fall had killed her. Then when I was in junior high, Brian Rigby, a nasty kid with red hair, too many teeth, and a compulsion to sneak into the girls' bathroom, suggested that she had died "of drugs." Confronted with this accusation, my mother admitted that Aly had indeed experimented with drugs and that her fall had occurred while she was high. "She thought she could fly," Mother said, "so she jumped off the balcony on the third floor."

I heard the story many times as I grew older, along with the injunction to stay away from drugs, alcohol, "the wrong kind of people," and everything else that promised to be fun or exciting. I had a very dull adolescence.

My books were my escape. And the means of capturing the thing I craved the most—my father's attention. Never particularly interested in me, he could always be seduced into a discussion of the book I was reading. I became cunning in framing questions to catch his fancy, in proposing arguments he couldn't resist. As a child I presented them to him shyly, as one might offer a handpicked bouquet; in adolescence, I hurled them at him in a theatrical show of defiance. Today, I present them coolly, over lunch at the faculty club or Sunday dinner at home.

I often ask myself why I am still here, living only a few miles from my parents, teaching English in the high school I attended. I could go elsewhere, live in a big city where I could be someone other than James Wilkes's daughter. But I stay. I understand why the idea of flight might have tempted my sister to her death. But my wings were clipped before I learned to use them.

My father is not a violent man. He has never struck me, and I never saw him strike my mother. But I sensed her fear when he withdrew into his study with a bottle and his books and refused to come out or even to speak to us. I have seen flashes of the deep anger he keeps hidden from others. He could kill; I believe that.

But I also know that I have thirty years of resentment to feed my dream. Thirty years of rejection, of offering him my best and seeing it judged not quite good enough. Thirty years of staring at the closed door to his study and longing to be allowed inside. Just as he is capable of killing, I am capable of creating this dream in which he kills.

Having always been a bookworm, I am poorly suited for the job of ferreting out secrets. I find the people in novels much more interesting than those I meet on the street. Real life has always seemed rather pedestrian. I'd rather read about the evil machinations of a Professor Moriarty than the senseless slaughter of drive-by shootings. And I would far rather follow the investigations of V.I. Warshawski or Sharon McCone than explore my sister's death.

But my sister cannot claim justice for herself and the law long ago accepted the explanation of a drug-induced accident, so it is left to me to test the accusations of my dream.

I begin where I think a detective would begin, with the newspaper articles about my sister's death. In a larger city, the back issues would be on microfiche, but here the papers themselves are bound and stored in a small back room where they share space with office supplies and an ancient snow shovel.

Margaret Perkins, the business manager and office staff of the paper, guards the front desk with Cerberus-like ferocity. She is an ageless woman whose wrinkles deepen each year while her hair becomes blacker. I try not to stammer as I make my request.

She does not approve, that much is clear, but she finally allows me entrance to the back room. I realize too late that in coming here I have announced my investigation to the entire town.

The air in the room is stale. The cloying peppermint of disinfectant mingles with the smell of dust and old paper. There is no chair, so I sit on a box of copy paper while I begin my search.

The story is on page one but below the fold, in the right-hand corner. GIRL DIES IN FALL FROM BALCONY, the headline reads. Above it, a one-column picture of Alyson. Her school picture, the one that sits on the end table beside the couch in my parents' living room.

Her hair is long and straight, dark like mine. Her face is an oval, again like mine. As I was growing up, people frequently commented on my resemblance to her. But her smile is broader, her lips fuller and more sensuous. There is a mocking self-assuredness to it that I could never manage.

The story is testimony to the now-dead convention of journalistic restraint, and to my father's power in the community. There is no mention of drugs, of a troubled adolescence, no question of how or why a sixteen-year-old would climb onto the rail of a third-story balcony. Several teachers comment on how bright she was, the drama teacher extols her acting ability. The part about her love of acting is new to me. Everything else is old news. I write down the names of the teachers, though I know none are still at the school.

If anyone knows what happened to Aly, it would be my aunt Hannah. She is my father's older sister and my mother's confidante. She lives in a nearby township, about twenty miles away. The problem is that Hannah adores my father. She would never speak ill of him, even to me.

I go to her immediately, before news of my visit to the paper can reach her. She answers her door wearing a deep rose pants suit and floral print blouse. She is several inches taller than my five feet four, a substantial woman with breasts that jut out aggressively. Like my father, she has a face that is handsome but stern.

She invites me into a meticulously tidy living room furnished with antiques she has collected for many years. I confront my father's picture on the mantel, in a double frame he shares with me.

I must be devious, which is not my way. She will never tell me what I need to know if I am too direct. So I begin not with Aly but with my grandmother. "Why did they move from Boston?" I ask, knowing that just as my father can always be seduced into discussions of books, Hannah cannot resist retelling stories of the family.

She slips easily into storytelling mode, a bit of the sternness of her face relaxing as she talks. She brings out the albums as I knew she would. Then it is an easy matter to flip through them, asking occasional questions, until I reach Aly's baby pictures.

"What was she like?" I ask. "What did she do as a child?"

"Oh, she was smart, just like you," she says. "A very clever child. Learned to read early, played the piano like an angel. A bit of a tomboy though. Always had scabs on her knees and elbows. Used to sneak into the Barneses' pasture and ride their gray gelding. I don't know how many times they chased her off. She just loved that horse; couldn't stay away from him."

She smiles with pleasure. The young Aly is still a happy memory.

"When did she change?" I ask, and in the back of my mind an awful thought forms. Last month at the faculty meeting a social worker lectured on sexual abuse. I remember her saying that you should pay attention to changes in a child's temperament. Aly had changed. Everyone attributed it to drugs. Now I wonder if the drugs might have been a result instead of a cause.

Hannah's smile is gone; her face is sadder than I remember seeing it. "She had a hard time with adolescence," she says. "Some children do. And things were so crazy then. Drugs were everywhere. The students looked like hoboes and they took over buildings, threw rocks at the police. The young were so angry. It was a bad time."

"Was Aly angry?"

"Oh my, yes. She was angry about the war, about the rules at school, about her family. She was a very angry young woman." She pauses. "But not at you. At everyone but you. She really loved you."

I know that. I have been told many times how much Aly loved me. That she was my protector and champion. I've heard the story of how she chased off the Bryants' big shepherd when it frightened me and badgered Derek Bryant until he kept it on a chain. In lonely moments, and there have been many of them, I fantasize about how it might have been different if she'd lived.

"Why did she climb up on that railing?" I ask.

Hannah shakes her head. "Who knows what was in the child's head," she says. "She may have thought she could fly. She may have just lost her balance. But let's talk of happier things. Would you like some lemonade?"

I accept her offer and let her think she's distracted me, but later, after lemonade and more stories of more dead relatives, I come back to Aly.

"Did they test to see if she had drugs in her system?" I ask.

Hannah's expression sharpens, her shoulders straighten as tension creeps into her posture. "Why all the questions about Aly?" she asks. "You know all this."

A clever detective would have a story ready, an excuse to ward off suspicion. I have nothing. "I've just been thinking of her lately, that's all. Trying to understand her death."

"Let it go," she orders. "No point in poking at old

wounds. We'll never know what went on in her head. You'll just upset yourself thinking about it."

I leave twenty minutes later, knowing nothing more than when I arrived. No, that is not quite true. I know that Hannah is uncomfortable discussing Aly's death. She does not hesitate to speculate on the parentage of cousin Clara's bastard child, enjoys repeating the tale of how her uncle shot the grocer in an argument over a gambling debt. Aly's death seems the only subject she will not discuss.

I fill my evening grading papers, mostly quizzes on the first half of *Hamlet*. The play has new resonance for me this year. I have always been fascinated by the ghost. Now, with my dream, I have a ghost of my own. And like Hamlet, I am tormented by its accusations.

Each time I teach the play I explain that Hamlet cannot *know* whether his father's ghost is real or a fabrication of the devil. If real, he must obey it for both his father's sake and his own, but if the ghost is from the devil, killing his uncle will damn him to hell for eternity.

I place them on the scale—duty to father and Hamlet's immortal soul. But the students are unable to weigh them, because for them the concept of an immortal soul is fuzzy at best. They understand the thirst for vengeance, the need to redeem the family honor, to fulfill a dead father's last request. But the concept of the soul and Hamlet's responsibility for it, that eludes them.

Even Joel, the son of a fundamentalist father who's involved the boy in his own fanatical crusade against abortion, cannot understand Hamlet's dilemma. Joel accepts the existence of an immortal soul, the battle of good and evil, but for him truth is "revealed." That Hamlet cannot know whether the ghost comes from heaven or hell is incomprehensible to this child of a true believer.

I am jealous of Hamlet. Of his fixed moral universe. His belief in an immortal soul and ultimate justice. I was born on the empty plain of twentieth-century agnosticism, where faith is unsheltered from the harsh glare of reason. With no hope of justice beyond the grave, I would give anything to have an immortal soul to risk.

The next day I visit Elise Winters, the woman who was secretary of the English department for thirty-five years until her retirement eighteen months ago. I have never liked Elise. She is a woman with no boundaries, no sense of the spaces between people. She will ask anything and expect an answer. Usually, she gets it. Which is what makes her so useful now.

I come at four, after school is out. By now she will know of my visit to *The Sentinel*. She and Margaret Perkins are friends, two crows on the same phone wire. I have created the excuse of asking her to help judge a poetry contest for my class, but she begins her interrogation before I offer a reason for my visit.

"Margaret said you were at the paper yesterday," she says. "What was it you were looking for?"

"I wanted to know more about my sister's death."

Her eyes are bright with curiosity. "An awful thing," she says, but her avid expression does not match her words. "I always wondered myself."

"What did you wonder?" I ask.

"Oh, how it happened. Why. There were rumors she was taking drugs. So many of the youngsters were then."

"And you think that's what happened, that she was taking drugs?"

She gives an elaborate shrug. "Well, we'll never know," she says. "Your father wouldn't let them do an autopsy. I was a bit surprised they didn't insist, but I suppose Sheriff Curtis didn't want any trouble with the college. There was enough town–gown tension in those days what with the demonstrations and all, and nobody wanted to make it worse."

"Surely you had some idea about it," I said. "You've always known everything that was going on."

I'm afraid she'll be insulted, but she smiles proudly. In my mind, I see the crow again with its quick, hungry eyes and sharp beak.

"Well, there were some who suggested it might be suicide," she says. She lowers her voice as she says it, though we are alone in the room. "Marge saw her coming out of the clinic, the one that does pregnancy tests. She said Aly looked upset."

"She was pregnant?" I say.

Elise shrugs. "I didn't say that," she says, "I'm just telling you what the talk was at the time. And since they didn't do the autopsy, there's no way to know. Come to think of it, Aly and the Curtis boy were part of the same group. That might be another reason the sheriff didn't push about the autopsy."

I look around me to escape her sharp eyes. The room is filled with things—armies of porcelain figurines, an entire shelf of owls who stare at me with jeweled eyes, fading photos dwarfed by their ornate frames. I feel surrounded. The air is heavy with Elise's poisonous suggestions, and suddenly I find it hard to get enough oxygen. I know she can hear the fear in my voice as I leave. She smiles at me from the doorway as I flee down her sidewalk.

Tonight I am grateful for the stack of papers that permits me a kind of escape. My fifth-period class is ahead of the others. They have just finished the graveyard scene with Hamlet's "To be, or not to be" soliloquy. That speech has always been a favorite of mine, but today as we read the words in class, they cut like knives.

The boys are impatient with Prince Hamlet. Raised on action-adventure flicks where justice is meted out with an Uzi at a moment's notice, they want resolution. "What's this fool's problem?" Richard asks. Tony announces he'd have taken out the uncle in Act I. He believes in swift action. His brother killed a seventeen-year-old who "dissed" him in front of his girlfriend. "He had to do it," Tony says. "Can't be lettin' no one get away with that kinda shit."

I don't understand Tony's brother; he doesn't understand Hamlet. I wonder what Tony would do about my dreams.

At seven-thirty, the doorbell rings. It's my mother. She's brought me tomatoes and zucchini from her garden, but the real purpose of her visit is to learn why I'm asking questions about Aly's death.

She is gentle and consoling, and she is hurt that I didn't come to her first. I can feel her pain and confusion. Have always been able to feel it. She kept me so close during my growing up that I often felt separated from her by only the thinnest membrane.

I ask my questions, listening not to the words of her answers, but rather for the subtext, for the subtle tones beneath. For years I have hidden behind the protective boundary I erected between us, now I tear away at it. Will myself to feel what she is feeling. I become a human polygraph.

But boundaries built over years do not tumble so easily. I've lost the ability to merge with her. Still, I know one thing. She is frightened by my questions.

Over the next month I assemble bits of information. Nothing conclusive. Much that piques my suspicious mind. I learn that the father I always knew as cold and distant was warm and playful with Aly. The albums confirm it: pictures of him pushing her in swings, her riding on his back. She sits on his lap in the early ones. Later they wrap long arms around each other.

He was younger then, of course. They all say the accident changed him. I can see that in the photos, too. In the early ones he cuddles me, carries me on his shoulders. After her death, there are fewer pictures, and they take on a formal stiffness.

The memories of others awaken memories in me, but where they seem to carry albums of pictures in their heads, I can only manage brief glimpses that fade before they are fully focused. I remember most clearly his voice. And the stories. He was always better at lecture and debate than casual conversation, but he was a master storyteller. With me practically running along beside him to keep up with his longer stride or lying in bed in the dark, he made the tales of Homer, Sophocles, and Shakespeare more exciting and immediate than any movie or television show.

It's hard to connect these memories with the dream. He never touched me as I lay in bed, so why do I suspect he molested Aly? Maybe it is the fact that he seemed to avoid touching me that makes me suspicious. I feel sure that there are holes in our relationship that can only be explained by what happened with Aly.

I construct scenarios. He loved her too much, was enraged when he learned she was pregnant, and killed her. He loved her and he was the reason she was pregnant, so he killed her. Or he loved her and was so wounded by her suicide that he never recovered. Any one could be true.

I have not asked him directly about Aly, but I'm sure he knows of my questions to others. He is worried and preoccupied when we talk. I can no longer seduce him into lively discourse with an inflammatory comment on an article in the latest *New York Review of Books*.

I watch him closely over lunch. He is unusually solicitous, asks several times how I am feeling. The lines in his face seem deeper. His skin is looser; he appears to have lost weight.

The lack of an answer doesn't diminish my need for one. The dream continues to visit me almost nightly, taunting me and demanding action.

Like Hamlet, I still cannot know the origins of my ghost. Maybe if I hadn't spent my youth buried in books I'd know how to proceed, be more capable of action. I should have read Hemingway instead of Shakespeare.

But we use what we have, and I am left with Hamlet, so, of course, my mind turns to the play. Not the tragedy itself, but the play-within-the-play, Hamlet's device to "catch the conscience of the king."

I have almost a hundred and fifty high school students at

my disposal. They're always hungry for extra credit, for anything that doesn't require them to think or write. I could easily assemble my troop of players.

But here I hit a snag. Hamlet's play confronted the king with his actions, accused him directly of the crime. But times have changed. Today, public accusation is as good as conviction, especially when a child accuses a parent. What if I am wrong? There are plenty of people like Margaret Perkins or Elise Winters who would convict my father without a trial, and make of me a false witness.

No, the showing must be private, and subtle. My players must have a text strong enough to carry double meaning.

But where to find that text?

Ophelia, of course. I've never liked her much. Can't see Aly in that role, playing the fool to Hamlet's ravings or killing herself when he rejects her. She'd have been more like Laertes, exacting justice with a sword.

But as I am Hamlet and not Laertes, I will use Ophelia. This good daughter will die again for others' sins. If Stoppard could build a play around Rosencrantz and Guildenstern, I can build one around Ophelia and her father, Polonius.

The stage is set. My parents, my aunt, and a couple of close friends are invited to a reading by students from my junior English class. I have baited the hook well for my father. Talked for weeks of a feminist treatment of the play.

My father hates feminism. He will not pass up a chance to provide the patriarchy's rebuttal to my assault on Western letters. He will be looking forward to wielding the sharp scalpel of his reason.

The students are nervous. They have trouble with this play that seems so thinly connected to the original. But then they also have trouble with the original. "But did Shakespeare mean that Ophelia was murdered?" stern-faced Jennifer asks. She's the brightest of the lot, reminds me of myself at her age, so serious, so anxious to get the right answer.

We are gathered in my living room. It's a bit small, but that means I'll be close enough to my father to watch him closely.

There are so few women in the play, I have been forced to create new characters—friends and confidants for Ophelia, serving women who watch and comment. My action is precisely the activity taking place offstage. I begin not with the soldiers on the ramparts, but with a cozy gathering in Ophelia's chambers where she shares with two friends her excitement at Hamlet's attention.

My *Hamlet* focuses not on the prince's obsession with his father's murder, but with Ophelia's struggle between her duty to her father and her love of Hamlet. Obeying her father's admonition to avoid Hamlet, she finds the prince behaving as if he has gone mad and believes herself the cause. He is bitterly cruel to her, and her father, interested only in the prince, ignores her pain and uses her to try to ensnare Hamlet.

In the scenes with her, the old man is seductive. He is too interested in his daughter's relationship with Hamlet, asks for details and makes inappropriate suggestions. I paint him as a lecherous voyeur and plant suggestions that he could be worse.

We do not see Polonius's death at Hamlet's hands, only Ophelia's reaction when she learns of it. Nor do we see her slip from the willow into the stream and drown. Instead, we witness the serving women preparing her body for burial, and we hear their commentary.

"If the priest had his way, the poor child would lie in unhallowed ground," the first remarks.

"Priests are no lovers of women, save when their horns are up," the second says.

The third objects, " 'Tis church law, a suicide cannot lie in hallowed ground."

First woman: "And was it you saw her jump?"

Third woman: "Not I, but the queen did report it."

First woman: "And she had report from someone else, no

doubt. 'Tis a great convenience for them all to be so easily rid of the maid."

Second woman: "Say you it was no suicide?"

First woman: " 'Twould not be the first time a maid was pushed to her death when her life became an inconvenience to powerful men. The magician tricks the eye away from what he would not have you see. So, too, may clever men lead others to debate 'twixt accident and suicide, so their eyes look not for murder. Once a maid is in the ground, she's soon forgot."

I watch my father closely. His face is the color of old ashes. He stands and stumbles from the room. My mother looks from me to him. I have never seen her so lost.

Aunt Hannah rises from her chair and follows him out.

The girls have lost their lines. They stand confused and embarrassed. There is no need to finish the play. It has served its purpose, but I prompt them and they pick up where they left off.

My father is gone. I heard his car pull out shortly before the end of the reading. My friends are charmed by the play. They discuss the feminist issues with Jennifer, who is pleased by their attention.

After cookies and punch, I herd the students out. My friends follow them. It is only then that Hannah returns to my house. Her mouth is as hard and tight as a bowstring. She has grown in size as my mother shrank.

"Why?" she demands of me. "What led you to this madness?"

"I had to know," I say. "I have a dream in which he pushes her from the balcony. I had to know if it was true."

"Tell her," Hannah commands my mother.

Mother just shakes her head. "No," she says, her voice soft as flannel.

"Tell her."

Mother's head comes up. "No," she says. "And you won't either."

Hannah hesitates. "No, I will tell her. Someone has to."

She turns to face me, and suddenly I am afraid. Her face is cold fury. If she were carved from stone, she would be softer. "You had to know," she says, "so now you will."

"Your dream is true, to a point. James did struggle with Aly just before she fell. But not because he wanted to hurt her. Not for any of the crazy reasons you've imagined. He did it to save you.

"Aly hated you almost from the moment you were born. She was awkward and rebellious; you were cute and lovable. She hated the attention you got."

"It was my fault," Mother says softly. "I failed her. I was so excited about having a baby, so in love with you, I shut her out."

"She shut herself out," Hannah says sharply. "There was room enough for her if she hadn't been so jealous."

"The drugs and the wildness, the boys—they were a cry for help," Mother says. "I tried to reach out to her, but she was so angry, so tough. I didn't have the strength to save her." I hear seas of tears in her voice.

Hannah ignores the seas. Her voice is ice. "The day she died your father found her on the balcony with you. She'd pushed a table to the rail and was lifting you onto it, urging you to play circus with her. He grabbed you from her, set you behind him then reached back for her. She struggled, fought him. We'll never know why, whether she was trying to get at you, or simply to hurt him, but as they struggled she stepped back and fell."

The room is silent as she finishes. My mother stares at the floor, rocking slightly.

"I hope you're satisfied," Hannah says. "I hope the truth is worth the cost. Your father's drinking again. He's locked himself in his study. He almost drank himself to death after Aly. You were the only reason he stopped last time; he wanted to be a decent father to you. You've taken that from him tonight."

I look to my mother, but she won't meet my eyes. She looks unbearably frail. If I reached to touch her, she would shatter into a million pieces.

Hannah voice fills the room with her anger. "I tried to tell you, but you wouldn't listen. You had to know."

I stare at my mother and think of my father in his study and realize my error. I have pictured myself as Hamlet, but I have been playing Oedipus.

MYRIAM LAURINI was born in Argentina, but was exiled from 1976–1980 during a military dictatorship. She lived in Spain for a time before settling down in Mexico. She has had one novel published, with another undergoing final editing. Laurini has appeared in several magazines in Mexico, as well as publishing a report on sexual violence in Mexico.

Lost Dreams

Myriam Laurini

Translated from the Spanish by William I. Neuman

Dead Body

Commander Videla lay faceup. Somebody'd really laid into him, everything was red with blood, his shirt, his bare arms, his pants. I counted at least six knife wounds, wide and raggedy, as if they'd been made with a butcher's knife. His eyes were wide-open, marbles of dark glass, sticking halfway out of their sockets, as if he didn't realize what was going on.

Flashes, one after another, illuminated the scene, turning the stiff corpse into a famous actor: Pedro Infante for a day. Nuevo Laredo's own. All the local papers would run it on the front page, everybody would be talking about it.

The *judiciales* busied themselves outlining the body in chalk, checking for fingerprints, clues. Passersby started to crowd around and the cops yelled at them: Clear out, *bola de cabrones,* and you, *morena,* get a move on. And me: Press, I'm a reporter, I've got a right to be here. And them: The hell with the press, scoot, *morena.*

Videla the corpse was thirty-five years old. He'd trained in martial arts every single day, went without salt to stay trim, cut out eggs for the cholesterol. The *huevos* he already had were enough, the way he figured it. Ten years on the force. The people of Nuevo Laredo loved him. He was fair with the poor and took bribes from the rich, the drug runners, and the coyotes.

He left a wife and two children.

There was a sergeant who threw up when they carried him away. Videla stunk of dried blood and fresh shit. *El miedo puede más que un par de huevos,* my grandpa used to say. Another sergeant, his veins popping with hatred, muttered in a hoarse voice: We'll get even, Videlita.

María Crucita

Seeing Videla's corpse kind of gave me the willies, all that blood and all that stink. That was one part of it. The other part was that I was tired as hell all of a sudden and still had to go write my story. So I decided to grab a bite to eat. I went into the Chinaman's place and sat waiting for my chop suey, rolling little balls of bread between my fingers. That's when I saw her come in. She'd just gotten out of the shower, her hair was wet and she smelled of lavender. Some women are fanatics for cleanliness. Getting up at dawn and taking a shower after spending all night fucking some john wasn't exactly my idea of the good life.

I liked her, though. Maybe it was her aura of sadness. She asked me for a light and I invited her to sit at my table. We're both alone after all, I told her. She was the kind of person who wore her emotions on her sleeve, something that always makes me feel uncomfortable, but in between the empty words she started to tell me her story. I dug into the best chop suey in the state and tried not to let her sob story get to me.

She'd come to Nuevo Laredo like so many others, pretty colored ribbons in her long black braids, huaraches on her feet. Hiding the wild hope in her eyes, her hunger for life. She was fifteen then, with a baby girl she'd left behind in the village with her mother, knowing that if she didn't come back soon . . . Women aren't worth too much up in the sierra, she told me. First the men get what little there is to eat and then, if there's anything left, the boys, and then the women, and then the girls.

She'd survived eating dirt, roots, leaves, chewing on old bones.

I survived because I liked the sun, she said in a quiet voice. And because I could dream, I'm telling you the truth. I used to dream about little things.

When she was twelve she went to work in Mexico City. She ate a lot and the señora would scold her, but María Crucita didn't care, hers was an ancestral hunger.

The family she worked for went on vacation to the Caribbean and sent her back to the village. It's not good to neglect your parents, they told her, you stay there until we send for you.

One afternoon while she was watching some maguey flowers and dreaming one of her little dreams, a boy, barely sixteen himself, came over and started to say silly things María thought were wonderful and beautiful. They did what they had to do and she liked it. She liked it so much that they did it again every day until the sun-tanned family came to bring her back to the city. About seven months later they finally understood why all the diets the señora prescribed for María, so young and so fat, hadn't done any good. She had a fruit in her belly that kept growing and growing whether its mother ate or not. Full of the righteous indignation decent people feel in the face of dishonor, they put María out in the street with only the clothes on her back. The ungrateful little whore didn't deserve to take along the old rags they'd been kind enough to give her.

The baby girl was born in the village. María caught a fever but the sun and her dreams cured her. The boy said the baby wasn't his, there was no way of telling whose it could be, that Crucita girl's a horny little thing, that's for sure.

So, squeezed by hunger once again, pushed on by her dreams, she decided she'd try and make it to the other side.

The maid she'd worked with in Mexico City used to tell her about the other side. Incredible strange things happened on the other side. The very poorest families, poorer than they were, had their own cars, a house with a real floor and windows with glass in them, the women didn't wear braids and they ate every day. The children always had enough to eat too, and they went to school in a special bus that came by just for them. Just like here in this house, said the maid, but there it's the same for the poor folks too.

María arrived one morning in Nuevo Laredo dizzy with hunger and fear. She waited for the other passengers to leave the bus and tried to disappear into her seat. She wanted to go back. Get down now, you, this is as far as we're going, the bus driver yelled at her. María couldn't. Her legs wouldn't work, she was paralyzed, but the man kept shouting at her and finally somehow she got down from the bus to go stand on the dirty pavement, her small bundle of clothes gripped in her hand, not knowing what to do, not daring to look at anything that wasn't that piece of stepped-on gum smeared across the ground. She stayed like that for a while until a handsome tall young man came over and asked her if she was alone. Excuse me, sir? she said. Poor thing, he said, where did she come from, where was she going to, did she have family there, friends? And María answered back like she would have to her sun-tanned ex-boss in the city, and she felt like she could trust the young man who said, yes he was going to help her, yes he could get her across, that on the other side all your dreams become true, stopped being dreams and turned into pure hundred percent reality. But she was going to need money. You had to bribe the guards and the *migra,* and María showed him the fifty dollars she'd changed with the maid and the young man laughed and it seemed like he would never stop laughing, and his fresh spontaneous laughter was contagious and María smiled because she didn't know how to laugh like that, but she promised herself she'd learn. Once, when she'd dreamed about a man who laughed so crazy uncontrollably like that, they'd told her it was the devil but she didn't believe them.

"You've got to get more money," he told her in between bursts of laughter. "What you've got there's barely enough for a Coke and a hot dog. I'll get you a job with a woman who's got a big house, sort of like a barn really, full of little wooden rooms with a bed and a curtain, where you can make the money you need. It's easy work, all you have to do is spread your legs a little." María remembered the first and only boy she'd spread her legs for but she pushed him out of her mind, he didn't know how to laugh like this young man.

She went with the woman, who treated her kindly, cut off her braids and took away her skirt and her petticoat and her huaraches and gave her a dress and a pair of shoes she couldn't walk in. Don't worry, you'll get used to it, the woman said, you can learn to get used to anything, we all do, and María Crucita looked at herself in the mirror and cried a few small tears. She'd have liked to have cried an ocean, but she didn't know how to do that either. After a year of giving the young man all the money she made every day, lying under drunks who puked on her when they tried to put themselves inside, and other men who beat her, and every now and then someone she liked all right but who wasn't any different in the end, she only wanted to go to bed with the young man and she'd forgotten all about the other side. "What do you think?" she asked me all of a sudden, angry, nervous. He finally showed up one day and said, get ready, I'm going to take you over, it's about time now, isn't it? Now all your dreams are going to come true, María. He gave her a necklace and some shiny earrings, and they crossed the bridge without any trouble. She hanging on to his arm, feeling a little sad, like the sun in winter. He left her with another woman, in a nicer room than the last one, with a bed, a dresser, a big mirror, a closet. He promised he'd visit her every month, she was his little María after all, wasn't she?

When the woman told her about the work, María tried to explain that no, no, there must be some mistake, that was all over now, there must be something else she could do. The woman shut her up with her bad Spanish—*si no guster larguer*—but María understood well enough. She went to her room and looked at herself in the big mirror and cried.

She learned to cry an ocean, she spent the next ten years crying and then decided it was time to go back.

"The things I could tell you . . . it was hell. Hell. Look."

She opened her blouse and I saw her burned breasts, wrinkled like prunes with deep black scars. Some asshole threw acid on me, she said. But that was just part of it. That boy lied to me, no one's dreams ever came true, he lied, there aren't even fake dreams there. He lied to me and he broke my spirit.

The Investigation

I went to the commander who'd taken Videla's place and asked him for an interview for the paper. He was more than happy to give it to me. He's the kind who likes to talk, he needs to build up his image if he's ever going to be able to even half fill Videla's shoes.

"Do you have any clues, Commander?"

"Too many. We arrested two drug runners, four coyotes, three black marketers, a couple of drunks. All on suspicion, and they all talked. They talked too much. We let them all go. None of them had any reason to kill Videla, they all respected him. No, it was more than that. In every case the respect was mutual."

"Do you have a make-up on the murderer?"

"Videla's killer was a young man, very strong."

"How do you know?"

"Only someone young and strong could have stabbed him that hard nine times."

"What was the murder weapon?"

"A kitchen knife. We haven't found it yet. How about that? And Videla with his thirty-eight still in its holster. Sounds like a joke."

"From the expression on Videla's face I'd almost say that he knew who his killer was."

"You can go ahead and think that if you want to. I'd heard you'd been pushing that angle, the look on Videla's face, his eyes were all bugged out that way. Every corpse looks the same, young lady, don't let yourself be fooled."

"Some people say that before Commander Videla joined the police force he worked as a coyote, running people across the border."

"Rumors. It's an easy thing to destroy a man's reputation once he's dead. Videla was a good man. Now and then he'd help someone get across, sure. He was a good friend of the gringos, he was everybody's friend, but he'd only do it to help someone out, just like that, for free."

"Yes, of course. How did he decide to become a policeman?"

"We came in together. We were tired of scraping around for work all the time, no steady job, always on the run. So we decided to join the other side."

"What do you mean by 'on the run'? Who were you running from?"

"Excuse me, I didn't mean to say it that way. We were young, you know how it is, women, bars . . ."

"And the ones you helped cross over for free . . ."

"Watch your step, young lady. Just because I let you have an interview doesn't give you the right to come in here and talk to me like that. You can take your little games somewhere else."

"Commander, I didn't mean . . ."

"That's enough. I've got my hands full trying to catch this murderer and you come in here and waste my time for nothing."

"Please, Commander, I didn't mean any offense."

"Offense? What kind of faggot do you think I am? You go ahead and write in your newspaper that we're on the murderer's trail, we know it's a young man, strong, in good physical condition, and that there are witnesses."

"You have witnesses?"

"Yes. A woman. But that's entirely off the record. It could be dangerous for her."

"Give me a break, Commander. Tell me something about her. Who is she?"

"All right, *morena*, but I don't want to hear you've been yakking. I'll have that pretty little tongue of yours cut right out. One of Videla's friends saw the two of them leave the Coconut Club together on the night he died. We found her later on in the Cairo Hotel. She's one of these wetback sluts who's decided she wants to come back home. She was with him when they were attacked. She says she thought it was a holdup, but that the murderer kept saying 'you lied to me, you lied to me,' every time he stabbed him."

"Is she telling the truth?"

"Yes, absolutely. You know how it is, we put a little pressure on her just to be sure."

"Right. Everyone knows the police force never fails in its undying search for the truth."

Lost Dreams

Lost dreams kill hope, they kill the will to live, hide the sun, squeeze a person's guts until they explode in a thousand painful colored pieces.

That's how I found María, sitting on her bed with her head between her hands, small, shrunk into a disintegrating ball, twenty-six years old and with the scars of forty years on her skin, forty years on her shoulders.

They'd moved her into a boardinghouse. A cop at the door said he was protecting her, the only witness. He let me go in to see her. All the cops know me now since I've been working the crime beat.

I went back on my promise to myself again. This destroyed old woman–child got to me somehow. This life I'd never lived started to ache inside me. This life I only knew secondhand, from the outside, from the edge of the edge of nothing.

"What really happened, María? It was you, wasn't it?"

She looked at me and smiled shyly.

"What do you care? What's it to you?"

"They're going to find out sooner or later. Why'd you tell

them you were with him? You could have denied it, said you'd already gone back to your hotel or something. I don't know . . ."

"I told them what I told them because they kept sticking my head in a bucket of water until I thought I was going to die. And I didn't want to die."

"Why'd you kill him, María? Did you hate him that much?"

I'm a piece of shit, I thought, I want to help her but maybe I care more about finding out what really happened, about the story I'm going to write.

"No, I didn't hate him, or, yes. I don't know. There's not a lot to tell. I waited for him for ten years."

In a quiet voice with a chilling clarity, her eyes lost somewhere, her body unmoving, she told me the second part of her story.

When the time had passed even for little dreams. When all she could feel anymore was the desire for death and to kill the young man who'd lied to her, she decided to come back. She went looking for him, the knife hidden in her purse. Finally, that night, she found him. He didn't recognize her. I'm Crucita, remember me? María Crucita, the one with the braids. You gave me this necklace and these earrings. And he was even happy to see her, with her war paint on, her tight cheap silk dress, her high-heeled shoes she could walk in just fine now. A little worse for the wear, but you look real good, María, he lied to her again.

They went to the Coconut Club for a drink and she made a scene. Why didn't you ever come back like you said you would? With his most patronizing smile he told her how his girlfriend had gotten pregnant, how he'd become a cop, how the girl was from a good family and he'd had to marry her for their sake, he told her about his children, his new life, you understand, don't you, Crucita?

But María, who'd always had to understand the señora's bad moods when she'd worked as a servant, the baker's contempt for her dark Indian skin, the denial of the boy who was her baby's father, the hang-ups of the johns when she was a prostitute, María who'd always, automatically, understood and accepted everything, said, No! No, I don't understand, the hell with it! They walked through the park toward the hotel, her mind was made up. You, you had your dreams come true, you told yourself the truth, but you lied to me. He kept quiet. If he'd said something I would have believed him all over again. I swear it to you, *morena*. But nothing, not a word, just the night and the silence, until I couldn't stand it anymore and I took out the knife and stabbed him in the stomach. The blood came out in a big rush and he fell down backward with his eyes wide-open, like when you see something that scares you. His head hit the pavement hard and he didn't move after that, she stabbed him again and again until it felt like his blood burned her skin. She was scared and ran away.

She stuck to the shadows and went back to her hotel. The night clerk was sleeping it off behind the counter. She went to her room, took a shower, and soaked herself with lavender. Carefully she washed her dress, her shoes, her purse, hid the knife under a loose floorboard. She was drowning inside herself. She had to tell someone that the young man had lied to her. That she'd waited for him for ten years. That she'd never learned to laugh that spontaneous uncontrollable laugh. She went back out into the night. She'd lived in the night so long it didn't scare her anymore.

Not Filed

When you write the crime beat, you learn to always start out with the headline. CRIME OF PASSION. No. SHE KILLED HIM BECAUSE HER DREAMS DIDN'T COME TRUE. No, too long. SHE STABBED HIM BECAUSE HE LIED TO HER. No. SHE KILLED THE MAN WHO DRAGGED HER INTO THE GUTTER. No. HE WAS HER PIMP, HER COYOTE, AND TEN YEARS LATER SHE CAME BACK AND KILLED HIM. No. No. No.

I'm Miss Marple. Or Jessica Fletcher. I found the murderer, not them. This story's my ticket to the big time, the female cannonball.

But I need a headline that really drives home, something that says it all. A great story deserves a great headline. WET- BACK MURDERESS. No. POOR INDIAN GIRL LURED INTO SIN KILLS HER PIMP. No. COMMANDER VIDELA WAS SCARED SHITLESS. No, that one could cost me my scalp.

I rack my brain for the right headline while María sits once again through another lineup of suspects. Yesterday the Commander got really pissed off. Not him, no, not him either, not that one either. Wake up, you goddamn wetback Indian bitch! We've got to find the killer, time's running out. Not him, no, not him either, not that one either.

What's the matter with you? You don't recognize any of them? Are you sure it wasn't you? Son of a bitch.

Yes, it was her, Commander, I wanted to shout out loud. But what the hell did I care anyway? I had my scoop, my all-time big story.

To hell with this shit. I threw some clothes into my suit-case and left it at the baggage check at the bus station. I went to her boardinghouse, had a word with the cop at the door, and went in to see María.

They'd beat her up pretty bad but I pretended not to notice. There wasn't any time to waste.

Here's the claim check for my suitcase. Get past the cop, you know how, you learned something in these last ten years, at least. The bus leaves at one-thirty. Change buses in Matamoros for Tampico, and then go on to Veracruz. Don't put on any makeup. Don't talk to anyone. You're María Crucita, the one who never made it as far as Nuevo Laredo. You're María Crucita who never learned to laugh like crazy or cry an ocean. You like the sun and you're afraid of the night. You're an old woman–girl who's just been born.

What a pain in the ass, I've got a thousand headlines buzzing around inside my head and I just thought up the best one yet. I took all my notes for the big story, lit a match. I watched them burn and drank a glass of tequila in memoriam.

Epilogue

The Commander got a well-deserved promotion when he identified a local wino as the strong young man who had murdered Videla.

The reporter quit her job and took off for Mérida. Just to be on the safe side.

No one ever heard from María Crucita again.

ANTONIA FRASER is best known for her historical biographies of such notables as Mary, Queen of Scots and the wives of Henry VIII. However, she has also written a series of novels featuring Jemima Shore, a British investigative reporter. Fraser has been a chairperson of the British Crime Writers Association and lives in London with her husband, dramatist Harold Pinter.

A Witch and Her Cats

Antonia Fraser

At first Jemima Shore thought that the elderly woman was shaking due to the frailty of age. It was bakingly hot outside. For a moment Jemima wondered if the woman, a stranger, was ill, faint, needing water. Then Jemima realized that she was trembling with anger. The woman—seventysomething? Eighty?—was standing on the doorstep, very close to the door itself, when Jemima answered the bell.

"Mine, mine," she was saying, or rather gasping, as if the strength of her anger was robbing her of breath. "How dare you . . . evil, wicked . . . How dare you? Mine, mine." The torrent of words, some of which Jemima could hardly make out, continued for a while. Then, while she was apparently exhausted, the woman shook her fist in Jemima's face.

Amid her general astonishment, Jemima had time to reflect that this was something that had never happened to her before. Fist-shaking belonged to the world of melodrama: outside the opera, Jemima did not think she had ever seen the gesture performed seriously before. She certainly did not expect to open the door of a London house and encounter such a histrionic denunciation.

Part of Jemima's shock was due to the fact that the woman, quite apart from her imprecations, did have a distinctly witchlike appearance. And she was certainly behaving in a traditional witch's fashion: that is to say, cursing. In principle Jemima was dead against labeling older women as witches, simply because they had become skinny and wrinkled with age, had started maybe to mutter aloud aggressively, due to loneliness or disappointment. That was misogynist stereotyping at its worst and quite intolerable. On the other hand, when you were confronted with a shaken fist and a stream of invective issuing from an elderly female, bowed and scraggy in her black dress, with sparse gray hair in a bun and two long prominent front teeth, it was difficult to suppress the instant reaction buried in childhood memories of fairy stories: This was a witch.

At this point Jemima suddenly realized who her caller must be. This was Miss Pollard. Jemima had had that very conversation about the cruelty of describing elderly ladies as witches only a week ago. She had ticked off her goddaughter Claudia for referring to their neighbor as "that old witch" only to have Claudia mutter rebelliously: "old bat, then." But still, Jemima was confident that her point had been made. And now the old witch/bat was gibbering in front of her (as Claudia would have put it). For the invective had started again and what was more, the voice was growing stronger. . . .

It was the emergence of the words "cats . . . my cats! Mine, mine . . . my cats" which gave Jemima at last her clue to what this was all about. Rosy and Rusty, the adorable young marmalade cats—not much more than kittens, really —to whom Claudia had taken such a fancy.

Jemima did not actually own the house in Edwardes Terrace, West London, in which she was currently living, a tall narrow house, with a long thin garden at the back. Recently there had been an insidious unchecked flood in her own mansion flat while Jemima was away. The result had been not only the ruin of carpets and furniture but also the destruction of floors. The only thing to do was to move out entirely while builders wrestled with the damage. And the Edwardes Terrace house—although larger than Jemima wanted—had been available for instant rental.

It was at this point that Claudia Farrow had come to join Jemima. The Farrow parents' ever-troubled marriage was finally coming to an end and the fallout was considerable. Alexa Farrow did not wish her daughter to witness it. So Jemima, as a gesture of godmotherly solidarity, offered to have Claudia to stay until times were calmer. With Claudia came her nanny/au pair, Maureen. And with Maureen, a good deal of the time, came her boyfriend Johnnie. After that, Jemima reflected dryly, the house did not seem in any way too large.

Maureen herself was quite a withdrawn character. She had the kind of ample—not exactly fat—figure which Jemima presumed must give a sense of security to a child; but she certainly could not be described as a jolly, comfortable person. Her hair, brownish and not very thick, was scraped back into a severe ponytail; her face was pale and rather square.

Johnnie the boyfriend was undoubtedly far better looking for a man than Maureen for a woman. He also sported a ponytail but his was a macho masculine ponytail, which set off his neat if slightly wolfish features. Johnnie's only flaw in terms of appearance was in fact that very neatness: he was a little shorter than the lavish Maureen. At the same time, Johnnie was extremely muscular as Jemima could not help noticing from the skimpy clothes, vest and shorts, he generally wore in the hot weather. Either Johnnie's building job had done that for him or else he worked out. Any six-foot man would have been proud of Johnnie's biceps.

If Maureen was inclined to be silent, Johnnie was immensely voluble. The roar of Johnnie's exuberant chatter, pitched to be heard above the television which was also blaring away in the kitchen, caused Jemima much secret annoyance. So this was the way the world had gone: how was she to know that children nowadays had a double escort of nanny and boyfriend? She was herself childless and Claudia was the nearest she had to a surrogate child. But having made her generous offer to Alexa Farrow, she could hardly start upsetting her domestic arrangements.

"Maureen is a bit glum" was how Alexa had put it. "And not wildly intelligent. But you won't have any trouble with her. Claudia is used to her," Alexa had summed up. "And that's important in this situation, isn't it?" The topic of Maureen was dismissed. Alexa had not mentioned Johnnie at all. "Oh Jem," she rattled on, "I'm so grateful to you. You see, I can just about cope with all my future ex-husband's vindictiveness by myself, but having to cope with Claudia—" Alexa was right back into the impossibility of life with Claudia's lying, cheating father.

Claudia was thin, overthin perhaps for an eight-year-old, although once again Jemima was not certain exactly what an eight-year-old should look like. She had an anxious face and dark hair inclined to droop over her forehead. There was something touching about her: indeed, her very anxiety moved Jemima.

The saving grace of the situation in Edwardes Terrace was Claudia's great love of the little golden cats. Jemima, a cat lover, guessed them to be about four months old (she realized that at thirtysomething she knew rather more about cats and their ways than she did about children). Rosy and Rusty still retained all the grace and playfulness of kittenhood, yet were large and lithe enough to go adventuring over the walls of the terrace gardens. From the top floor of the house where Claudia and Maureen slept (and perhaps Johnnie, too, though Jemima hoped not) she could sometimes trace the cats' progress over this wall and that. There would be a flash of golden fur, a gleam of white (one cat had a white face, front and paws) and then another yellow streak as the second cat followed the first. They were always together.

The first time the two cats appeared on the narrow lawn of Jemima's house and began to gambol with each other, Claudia gave such a piercing scream that Jemima thought she had hurt herself, and came running down from her study. But it was a scream of pleasure. Even Maureen allowed herself one of her rare smiles at the enchanting sight of the cat-kittens rolling over and over, biting, cuffing, licking, hugging, pawing each other.

Perhaps Claudia's first words to Jemima should have

warned her of possible troubles ahead: "Oh Jemima, can I keep them? I've always wanted to have a kitten, Mum said that one day I would have a kitten, and now there are two kittens. . . ." Claudia was hugging now one cat, now the other. Her pinched little face was flushed with happiness.

"Darling," said Jemima gently, "I think we'd better find out where they come from. Look, they've got collars." She took the cat with the white face from Claudia and checked the inscription on the medallion which hung, together with a small bell, from the red collar. Rosy, together with her all-gold brother, Rusty. Names but no telephone numbers or address.

"Some milk," Claudia was saying importantly. She cradled both cats together in her arms and headed for the kitchen, which had a glass extension built out into the garden. Jemima hesitated, and decided it would do no harm. Claudia played happily with the cats for the rest of the afternoon and refused to go for a walk in Holland Park. Once again Jemima decided that would do no harm.

She did however ban Claudia from having the cats to sleep in her bedroom. When Claudia went to bed, just about the time that Johnnie came round for his evening session of chat 'n' television, Rosy and Rusty were put firmly back into the garden.

"Jolly little fellows," said Johnnie approvingly. "Although I'm a dog man myself. Something big. Man-sized. You know, it's an odd thing but big dogs are much more affectionate than small ones. When I get another job"—he was currently unemployed—"I'll get a dog." Jemima wondered nervously if Johnnie might be referring to a pit bull.

The next morning, quite early, Jemima looked out of her second-floor bedroom window and saw the small figure of Claudia, still in her pink pajamas, skipping about in the garden.

"Rosy, Rusty," she was calling. Jemima rather thought that Claudia had something in her hand, food perhaps. There was no sign of Maureen. Jemima turned away, wondering what to do—she had to go to the studio early to do some dubbings for her new television series and would not be back until late. She decided to call Maureen, who was both sleepy and surprised—but finally quite sensible.

"She's that excited about the little cats. And you said she would see them again in the morning. So I suppose that when she woke up . . . but don't worry, it won't happen again."

It didn't happen again. At least not exactly like that. But Claudia's obsession with the cats grew and grew. Jemima really believed the little girl thought about nothing else. The drawings she did, at Maureen's suggestion, for Jemima's return from work, were entirely of cats, bright yellow cats since the delicate gold of their fur was impossible to reproduce by crayon. Claudia's letters to her parents, also at Maureen's suggestion, were also concentrated on the same topic. And that was how the argument about the term "the old witch" came about.

One of Claudia's unfinished letters was lying on the kitchen table when Jemima got home. The weather was still so stifling and humid that Jemima's first instinct on her return was to fling open the glass doors of the kitchen-conservatory and breathe deeply in the night air. She had planted some tobacco plants in the decaying tubs by the glass doors —rented houses never had very thrilling gardens—and Jemima stood enjoying their subtle nocturnal scent.

There were various night sounds to be heard in the semidarkness: in the heat, most of the back windows of the houses along the terrace were open. There was at least one television set on, but the noise was low enough not to be a real annoyance. That was fortunate since the terraced houses were all so narrow as to be really close together: from an upper window the various gardens looked like one big green area, punctuated by moderate-sized brick walls. There were about twenty-five houses all told. A few of the houses right at the end of the row backed into some kind of mews. But most of them, including Jemima's own centrally placed house, faced a large high brick building with a flat roof. It looked as if it had been erected in the sixties. There were no windows facing into the gardens, no doubt due to some planning rule or other. Although some of the residents over the years had grown creepers up the blank wall, the effect was still rather prisonlike. Jemima's end wall, for example, simply had a flight of stone steps leading nowhere, and another decrepit tub into which she had injected some white geraniums, at the top of them.

If the effect was slightly daunting, you could also say that Edwardes Terrace was extremely private—secure even, so far as a house in London could ever be really secure. An interloper seeking to enter Jemima's house from the back would have to cross a great many walls to do so. Like the golden cats, in fact . . . Jemima looked speculatively into the darkness. But no cat slithered down to join her. Where were the cats now? How many walls did they cross to get to her garden? For that matter, whom did they belong to?

The answer to Jemima's questions was contained, in a manner of speaking, in Claudia's unfinished letter on the kitchen table.

The old wich got cross with me again today about the cats, she read. *She's so scarry. She lives at No. 18.*

At that moment, as if on cue, Jemima heard a thin, reedy voice calling somewhere outside. "Rosy, Rusty, where are you? Ros-ee, Rust-ee." A witch calling for her cats. (She would, of course, have to speak to Claudia about her letter in the morning.) At least the inhabitants of No. 16 were not guilty this time. The conservatory doors had been firmly closed, according to instructions, when Jemima returned. She could listen to the old witch—*woman*—calling without feeling embarrassed. She could also feel without shame that there was something distinctly querulous about the persistent, nagging calling.

Jemima's complacency was shattered about five minutes later when the all-gold cat streaked out from beneath the kitchen counter and headed for the open doors: the white-faced cat followed.

Oh my God! thought Jemima. Wicked Claudia. Or should it be wicked Maureen? Tones of ecstasy, mixed with wails of reproach, echoed across the garden as the cats and their owner were reunited.

"Naughty cats! Where have you been? Did the horrid little girl get you?" At least, reflected Jemima, the cats had no language in which to answer that question: they could not give away the guilty inhabitants of No. 16. The next morning Jemima happened to be working at home. She took the opportunity to give Claudia that mild little lecture about the word "witch." Furthermore, the cats from No. 18 were never, ever to be locked into No. 16.

Maureen stood impassively by while this scene was being enacted in the kitchen. And as it happened Johnnie was there too. At the time, Jemima felt some annoyance at his presence. But then she thought that Johnnie, too, might benefit from listening. Perhaps it had been Johnnie who, out of unthinking good nature, had helped Claudia, as he saw it, to "adopt" the cats.

Jemima forgot about Rosy and Rusty. Work at the office became all of a sudden extremely demanding. At the same time, her builders wanted a series of decisions. Claudia and Maureen appeared to enjoy an innocuous school-holidays routine of shopping, walks, trips for ice cream, other expeditions, hiring suitable videos mainly made by Walt Disney, all cozily based on Edwardes Terrace. So far as Jemima could establish, Johnnie was slightly less in evidence. Maybe he had a job? Or maybe something of Jemima's inner irritation had conveyed itself to Maureen.

And now there she was, all of a sudden, facing Claudia's scary witch on her own doorstep. In pursuit of her cats. The ghastly thing was that Jemima could not honestly promise that the cats were not in the house. Her visible irresolution had the effect of encouraging Miss Pollard. She stepped into the hall of the house and gave a series of eldritch shrieks up the stairs.

"Rosy, Rusty, where are you? Come to your mother." Jemima found herself praying that no answer would follow from upstairs. It was quite late: something after nine o'clock, and Maureen (and Johnnie) were watching television in the kitchen. She devoutly hoped that Claudia was asleep upstairs—alone and catless. Her prayer was not answered. Almost immediately, to her horror, Claudia's bedroom door opened. There was a light skittering sound, followed by the characteristic small tinkle which always indicated the arrival of the cats. Rosy and Rusty streaked down the stairs, there was a series of sharp mews, and Miss Pollard gathered both cats up into her arms.

A wail came from above her head. Claudia, once more in those pink pajamas, was standing on the landing, rubbing her eyes.

"I'm sorry, I'm sorry . . ." she began. The sight did not move Miss Pollard.

"You wicked little girl! You will indeed be sorry for this, I can assure you of that. Just wait and see. I'm going to curse you. Bad things are going to happen to you because of what you've done. You'll see."

It was an extraordinary scene; for some reason, despite her good sense, Jemima found it quite menacing. She stood frozen, listening to the child crying and looking as if mesmerized at the woman clutching her cats. Then as Claudia's cries became hysterical, Jemima realized she must leap into action.

"Miss Pollard, she's only a child." Jemima spoke as politely as possible, although Jemima did not feel particularly polite. "I apologize on her behalf now, and she will write you a note tomorrow, and so will I, and so, I expect, will her mother. Claudia will not touch the cats again, I promise you that. But as for now, I can't help feeling you must be longing to get home with your cats."

Miss Pollard ignored Jemima. She continued to stare in that disconcerting and rather horrible fashion up at the little girl. After a moment she transferred her gaze to Jemima. Jemima had an impression of a deep malevolence.

"I curse you too," said Miss Pollard in a quieter voice. "I know who you are from television. I curse you too."

Miss Pollard left and Jemima rushed upstairs. When she got to Claudia's room, she could see nothing but a dark head huddled under the duvet. And Claudia beneath her duvet was shuddering with sobs.

"Claudie, dear, don't cry. I'll talk to Mum. You'll get a kitten—two kittens if you like—for Christmas when everything at home is sorted out."

"I'm frightened," Claudia whispered. She finally fell asleep holding Jemima's hand. Later Jemima went rather thoughtfully down into the kitchen and found Maureen and Johnnie still watching the television, the sound having masked all outside noises. Jemima related what had happened—leaving out the curse—and emphasized that on no account were the cats to be allowed into the house or garden of No. 16.

"You must shoo them away."

Maureen said nothing. It was Johnnie who promised ardently: "Oh we will, we will." Jemima walked past them into the hot, dark garden, closing the glass doors behind her. She walked to the end, mounted the steps, and leaned against the blank wall. There were no lights, none at all, to be seen in No. 18. Had Miss Pollard simply gone to bed with her cats? The garden windows—big French windows—were firmly shut. A flicker of light caught Jemima's eye. Jemima realized that whatever Miss Pollard was up to in No. 18, she was up to it by candlelight. Jemima could just make her out sitting at a table. For some reason, she found that whole scene even more disquieting.

It was shortly after that evening, that everything in Jemima's life started to go wrong. It was as though—but that was perfectly ridiculous—some curse really had been put upon her. For example there was a problem with the sound on one of the programs in her new series and no one could fix it, which left everyone blaming everyone else an in edgy way for what looked like being an expensive mistake. No sooner was that crisis surmounted, at some cost, than Cherry, Jemima's longtime assistant and now partner in her production company, broke her wrist playing tennis and was forbidden even to raise her right hand. Given Cherry's mastery of their new computer, this was another disaster. Jemima herself completely forgot to turn up for an important lunch date of a professional nature, something which had never happened to her before. To cap it all, on the very same day, Jemima's builders mixed up their instructions and painted the bathroom the rich somber color intended for the hall. It was not a day to remember. Jemima finally reached Edwardes Terrace having visited Cherry, sent flowers and apologies to her lunch date, and sorted out the builders.

She found herself confronted by both Maureen and Johnnie—not exactly the relaxing welcome Jemima actually wanted. She then understood Maureen to say: "Oh, it's been murder here today." Had Claudia been mischievous? Had there been yet another incident with the cats?

It took a moment for Jemima to understand, yet alone take in, what Maureen was actually saying: "*We've* had a murder here today" were Maureen's words. This horrifying message finally sank in.

"The old witch, Miss Pollard." Was it Jemima's imagination, or was Johnnie giving one of his wolfish grins? If so, what extraordinary taste he was displaying. "Found dead, she was. In her own kitchen. Like ours. You can see into it from the garden. I saw her in the morning, pitched forward onto the table. There was a candle burning. Thought she was asleep, drunk, some of these old ladies take to the bottle, you know. The unmarried sort. Watch out, Jemima—" Johnnie gestured cheekily in the direction of the empty wine bottles (not a few, it had to be said) which were lined up by the sink, awaiting delivery to the bottle bank.

Jemima was not to be diverted, although she did give Johnnie—who was incidentally clutching a can of lager—a frosty glance.

"Go on."

"Like this. It's me that called the police. Me and Maureen. In the evening. You were still out. Didn't know when you'd be back. Because she hadn't moved. The candle was right down. Had gone out. And I could see the cats running, jumping everywhere in that kitchen. They were going mad. And that didn't seem right. So . . ." He hesitated and looked at Maureen. "So we talked about it, didn't we Maureen, and I called the police."

Johnnie's neighborly solicitude for Miss Pollard did him credit; so did his concern for the cats. The trouble was that Jemima did not believe him. That is to say, she believed parts of his story, including the candle burning on the table, something she had seen for herself. But the overall story had an odd ring to it. Jemima's instinct—that famous instinct, feminine or gender free, on which she prided herself—told her that Johnnie was lying.

Her suspicions increased half an hour later when the police in the person of Detective Inspector Gary Harwood from the local station called round. Detective Inspector Harwood was young, pink-cheeked, very clean-looking, and had a professionally easy manner on which he evidently prided himself. It did not take Jemima long—after all, she also had a professionally easy manner on which she prided herself—to discover the main facts of the case. These were roughly as Johnnie had reported, with one significant exception. Miss Pollard was indeed dead. But the house at No. 18 had also been burgled.

"Robbery with violence!" exclaimed Jemima.

"We haven't established the cause of death yet. But yes, robbery. We want to have another word with your Mr. Johnnie Johnson as a result. An old friend of ours, by the way."

"My Mr. Johnnie Johnson? You mean—"

"Recognized him at once. Makes a habit of it. Stupidly he tends to concentrate on this area. Makes life easier for us poor overworked policemen." The detective inspector flashed Jemima a smile: his teeth were amazingly regular and very white in contrast to the ruddy cheeks.

Jemima's mind reeled. Johnnie a burglar? A burglar who, as Detective Inspector Harwood now jauntily told her, made a specialty of getting to know young nannies or au pairs, and then robbing the house next door or thereabouts.

"It gets him access, you see," the policeman added. "It's amazing what latitude you career women will allow your nannies. You take up the references about the nannies, and never ask about the boyfriends."

The moment to disabuse the detective inspector as to Claudia's parentage—and Maureen's real employer—was fast approaching. Nevertheless Jemima took the point. She had simply taken the egregious Johnnie for granted, only too happy that the sullen Maureen had company. Jemima hardly looked forward to breaking this news to Alexa Farrow: it was going to be difficult not to speak in tones of reproach, just as Harwood was speaking to her now. How feckless Alexa had been! Or had she simply succumbed to modern customs? Being too busy, fraught, and unhappy herself to pay close attention to the most vital aspect of her private life. Jemima, being childless, simply didn't know.

She decided to concentrate on the immediate present.

"Murder!" cried Jemima. "He's a killer. What's he doing free? You say he's done this before. . . ." With all her liberal principles, Jemima found herself seized with total indignation at the idea of such a situation.

"No, no, wait a minute. Don't misunderstand me. Johnnie Johnson is not a killer, he's a thief, if you like, a minor thief. But no killings involved, no muggings. Not even a very bright burglar. The kitchen was covered in his prints. But nothing even near the body. He's a chancer, sees the opportunity, can't resist taking it. But then he goes and telephones us! Thinking that makes him innocent. Johnnie Johnson!" The detective inspector shook his well-brushed head with something approaching tenderness.

So part of Johnnie's story was true. Jemima had a mental image of Johnnie, lithe and athletic, scaling the wall as the cats had done so often.

"The cats!" she exclaimed. "What's to happen to them?" Detective Inspector Harwood—it became clear that he was not a cat lover—did not seem to think that the cats were all that important. He murmured something about the RSPCA.

"We'll take them." Jemima took the decision without thinking. That is, she did not think about the reaction of Alexa: she did think of Claudia. At this, Detective Inspector

Harwood began to look quite definitely irritated at having to concentrate on the issue of cats.

"What have cats got to do with a death?" he asked plaintively. "They're not important."

It was only when the cause of Miss Pollard's death was established that he was obliged to change his mind. The cats were important, very important.

Miss Pollard had not been murdered by anyone, let alone done to death by Johnnie Johnson. (His stash of stolen goods was discovered without difficulty, neatly stowed under the bed of Claudia.) Miss Pollard had taken a large cocktail of pills and brandy. She had done so deliberately. She had stated that in a note found in her escritoire—forced by Johnnie in search of plunder.

Coolly, Miss Pollard gave her reasons for taking her own life. It was not worth living, she wrote, without the company of her beloved cats, Rosy and Rusty. Yet her cats wanted to desert her for the company of younger people, like the little girl at No. 16. She had tried to make a home for them but they spent the day trying to escape. . . . Miss Pollard could see no way out but to take her own life. She put her cats' happiness above her own.

Whoever cares for my cats after my death, Miss Pollard ended, *gets my blessing not my curse.*

Jemima did not tell any of this to Claudia. She merely put her arms round her.

"You see now that Miss Pollard wasn't a witch," Jemima said gently. "She wanted you to care for her cats. She specially said so." Jemima edited the will to her own satisfaction.

"She was a witch, Jemima." Claudia spoke firmly, with new assurance. "I know she was. But there are good witches as well as bad, aren't there? And in the end she was a good witch."

To Jemima, it seemed as good a verdict as any on the sad, lonely death of Miss Pollard. She watched Claudia playing with the two golden cats, all her childish tension apparently gone. It was, in a way—wasn't it?—a happy ending.

BARBARA WILSON is the author of five mysteries, most recently *Trouble in Transylvania*, which features translator sleuth Cassandra Reilly. A previous mystery, *Gaudi Afternoon*, won the Lambda Literary Award for Best Lesbian Mystery, and a British Crime Writers' Award for best mystery set in Europe. A collection of Cassandra Reilly mysteries, *The Widow's Curse*, is forthcoming.

Belladonna

Barbara Wilson

I

It is over a year since I spent the day with you on your lovely island—I remember it all very vividly. . . .
—Georgia O'Keeffe,
letter to her hosts on Maui

For a long time I turned up my nose at Hawaii. We who call ourselves travelers are snobs of the worst kind. We would much prefer to be wildly uncomfortable on the cushionless seats of a bus in Bangladesh or a train traversing the Gobi Desert, moving slowly through some strange desolate landscape and feeling either boiling hot or freezing cold, with nothing to eat, no toilet paper and nothing to read, surrounded by hostile people who don't speak our language and perhaps want to convert us to their religion or to steal all our money, than to do anything so gauche as to enjoy ourselves in any sort of tropical paradise, particularly if it means that another Westerner, a mere tourist, might be anywhere in sight.

Luisa Montiflores, the gloomy and recondite Uruguayan novelist, was not of the same opinion. She had just spent three "cold like hell" winter months as a writer-in-residence at the University of Toronto, and wanted to recuperate on the Hawaiian Islands. And she wanted me, as her translator, "my *friend*," to join her.

Luisa had once been my protégé, but over the years the

situation reversed itself. I had been a lone voice championing her difficult, deconstructionist novels, sending sample translations of her work to publishers and writing articles that proclaimed her originality. Now I had lost interest in her work, just as academics and the literary elite were discovering her peculiar blend of poetry and self-pity. Although I suspected that hardly a thousand people in the English-speaking world could have read her work, Luisa attracted honors, grants, stipends, symposia, and residencies all over the world.

"All, all I owe to you," she often said. "I am loyal, you see," and to prove it she frequently stipulated that a translator's salary be part of her agreements. From Stockholm to Adelaide we had traveled the globe together, and if it had truly been my goal in life to be Luisa's literary factotum, I'd have been ecstatic.

We had just been to the University of Hawaii in Honolulu, where Luisa gave a seminar talk on the new Latin American fiction, which was, strangely enough, only about her fiction. Now we were in Maui, where Luisa planned to stay a month and to put the final touches on her latest novel, and talk to me about translating it. We were staying with Claudie, a friend of Luisa's who was an art dealer in Lahaina.

"When Gloria de los Angeles goes to give a talk, they do not ask her about *my* work. Why do they ask me about *her?*" Luisa glared at me. "I still do not understand, Cassandra, how you can also translate her. That idiot and her magic realism. I spit on her magic realism."

"You're writing for different audiences," I soothed her. "Believe me, your work and hers cannot even be discussed in the same breath. Scholars laugh at her. But when they say Luisa Montiflores, they bow their heads in respect."

We were sitting on a terrace overlooking Claudie's magnificent garden of ginger, hibiscus and trailing orchids in the warm, sweet-scented evening. I had managed to keep up my anti-tropical-paradise attitude through this morning's arrival at the Honolulu airport, with its refrigerated leis and prêt-àporter pineapples. But by the time the day was over, I was half converted, and by the time our plane had taken us through an indigo and passion fruit sunset to Maui an hour ago, I was babbling like an idiot. "Just look at that surf! And look, palm trees swaying in the wind!"

"Everyone is reading her," Luisa said. "Every airport I am in, I see her books. Pah! She is a fool. She is *overaccessible,* a tramp."

Claudie laughed. "Oh, Luisa, always the same worries!" Claudie was wearing a silk print shirt in tangerine and lemon over a pair of crisp white shorts and sandals. Her skin was a warm desert-sand tone—Filipina, I guessed—and her straight black hair swung all in one piece like a curtain. I had just been in St. Petersburg, and coming from a bitter winter, my black jeans, cowboy boots, and worn bomber jacket felt completely inappropriate for the lush warm breeze. Underneath my beret my crazed graying hair frizzed out humidly; like Claudie's, it was all of a piece, but more a piece of untended topiary than a swaying curtain of black light.

Luisa took a long drink of iced tea and shrugged off poor, pathetic, overread Gloria. "Claudie," she said abruptly, remembering something. "Where is your Nell? The last time I was here, you had your Nell."

Claudie's smile was almost easy. "Oh, Nell and I have broken up. She goes her way, I go mine."

"But the gallery?"

"She kept it. I got the house. Some of the artists went with Nell, some with me. I'm hoping to get another storefront."

"But Claudie, this is not good. What happened? No, I know what happened! Another woman, no? I'm killing her."

Claudie laughed. "Oh, Luisa, you're always the same. It's too late. It's happened six months ago. One of those things. Believe me, it wasn't easy for any of the three of us. No one's to blame. I could have been the one to leave too."

"That's different, if you leave," said Luisa firmly. "That's passion. Otherwise, it's just betrayal."

"I'm getting used to being single," Claudie began, on a

positive note, and then the telephone rang and she excused herself.

When she was gone, Luisa announced, "That Nell was no good anyway. You know the type: restless, a toughie, a big mouth, always feeling sorry for herself. You know I can't stand that. Claudie is my friend from Paris, we went to cinematography school together. She deserves a good woman. Perhaps you're interested, Cassandra?" Luisa eyed me speculatively. "When are you settling down?"

"When are you?"

"Me? Every day I don't commit suicide is a miracle." But Luisa was laughing now. "My writing is my only mistress. When you see what I have written, you will be amazed and astounded. It is the best work I have ever done, no kidding."

"The most extraordinary thing," Claudie said, returning with more iced tea and sitting down. "That was a woman on the phone named Donna Hazlitt, calling from the Hana coast, on the other side of the island. I don't know what to make of it, whether she's lucid or completely confused. She was talking about a small painting that she said she discovered among her dead husband's things. He apparently inherited it from his parents. It's unsigned and seems not to have been quite finished, but Mrs. Hazlitt seems to think it might be an O'Keeffe. Mrs. Hazlitt is interested in having it appraised and in selling it. She wants me to handle the sale for her."

"O'Keeffe? You mean *Georgia* O'Keeffe?"

"The very same. She came here, you know, in the thirties, courtesy of Dole Pineapple. They hired her to do two paintings for advertising purposes. They set her up on the Big Island, but when she asked if she could live among the workers on the plantation, the Dole people said absolutely not. She never did end up painting any pineapples for them while she was here. Eventually, in desperation, they airfreighted her a pineapple in New York and she managed to paint it, very unenthusiastically."

Claudie put down her iced tea without drinking it and stood up again. "The critics were never very excited about

O'Keeffe's Hawaiian paintings, but I think some of them are lovely. There was an exhibit two years ago at the Honolulu Academy of Arts—it caused quite a stir. Gorgeous flowers, of course—crab's claw ginger, hibiscus, plumeria, lotus, and jimsonweed—which she called belladonna—those lovely angel's trumpet weeds. There were also some landscapes from Maui. She stayed here for a few weeks, escaping the Dole people. Waterfalls and mountains in the Iao Valley, and black lava on the Hana coastline." Claudie paced up and down the terrace. "I can't tell if Mrs. Hazlitt is on the up and up. She just started talking in the middle, as if we'd been discussing this for years. She said it's a flower, an angel's trumpet. Oh, what a coup if this is for real. It would make all the difference to me. Mrs. Hazlitt wants me to drive out there tomorrow to look at it. Why don't the two of you come?"

In a shop in Lahaina, where we stopped the next morning to buy a few provisions, I saw a T-shirt proclaiming I SUR-VIVED THE HANA HIGHWAY.

All too soon I knew what that meant. The Hana Highway was a two-lane road that twisted around the north coast of the island like dental floss around teeth. The landscape was spectacular all right: a dark cobalt sea and only slightly lighter sky, waterfalls at every other turn and black lava rock formations and black sand beaches. Claudie's Toyota, how-ever, was a compact, and although Claudie and Luisa, being small and fined-boned, fit quite well, I had some trouble with my long legs.

And with my stomach, which insisted on lurching in rhythm with the car.

Luisa wanted to know more about O'Keeffe, and Claudie had obliged by giving her a life history, ending with "She was essentially a solitary woman. Even though she was mar-ried to Stieglitz, she still managed to live her own life and spent half the year in New Mexico. I never really think of her as having been married at all."

"Have you ever noticed," I asked, "how much we admire heterosexual women who remained single or *as if* single?

Simone de Beauvoir, Gloria Steinem, Maya Angelou. With lesbians, though, it's a different story. We don't want to discount their relationships, we *want* them to be coupled."

"I am never coupled," said Luisa. "I couldn't ask anyone to share my suffering." As always when she talked about her depressions, she began to laugh hugely.

"I think you're right, Cassandra," said Claudie. "Is it perhaps because lesbians are not supposed to have the problem of being misunderstood and held back by their mates?"

"Or because being a lesbian rests so much on proof. You need to actually have a lover by your side before you're believed."

"I know that part is true," sighed Claudie. "Since Nell left me, a few people—relatives mostly—have asked if I'm seeing any nice men."

"I am opposed to marriage for creative people," said Luisa. "An artist's life is always solitary. You two, on the other hand, are not artists, only the handmaidens to creativity. There is nothing to prevent you getting together with each other. Why don't you?"

In the embarrassed silence that followed, Luisa murmured, "Claudie, pay attention to your curves, please."

Around the small town of Hana was a luxurious resort and clusters of houses on the hillsides. We pulled up a driveway half hidden by ferns and hibiscus bushes to a simple but beautifully constructed wooden house, low and long.

Claudie knocked on the door, but there was no answer. "That's odd," she said, looking again at her scrap of paper. "We're right on time and this is the right address."

We waited for half an hour on the steps, drove away to the resort for a cool drink, and then came back. There was still no sign of Donna Hazlitt.

"I hate to have come all the way out here for nothing," Claudie said, and sounded close to tears. "I guess she changed her mind. Maybe she decided to take the painting to a gallery in Honolulu."

I'd had the feeling there was something odd about this

adventure from the beginning. As the afternoon shadows lengthened, the impression grew stronger. I began to walk around the house, looking for a window I could at least peer into. Most of them were tight with blinds. Finally, in the back, I was able to peer through an opening in the blinds into what appeared to be a bedroom.

The closet was open and clothes were strewn about; the drawers had been treated the same way. And on the floor near the bed lay the still body of an elderly woman in a dressing gown, a still body that did not move when I called out, and would not move again.

The next day back in Lahaina, the news was all over the local paper. Donna Hazlitt, longtime resident of Hana, had apparently been the victim of a robbery-murder. But subsequent editions of the paper backed down: there were no signs of breaking and entering, and nothing of value had been taken, though Hazlitt, the widow of a coin and stamp collector, had many obvious things to steal.

It also appeared that what seemed to be murder may have really been a case of accidental poisoning. Apparently Mrs. Hazlitt had recently been treated at the local clinic for uveitis, an inflammation of the iris, for which she'd been prescribed atropine. The atropine came in a small dark brown bottle with a glass dropper, and was similar to a second brown bottle found next to it on the kitchen counter. This second bottle held Echinacea in a tincture of alcohol, and was a herbal remedy for strengthening the immune system. It was usually taken orally, in a glass of water. Authorities speculated—and then, and after tests, concluded—that Mrs. Hazlitt had mistaken the two bottles. Instead of putting in drops of Echinacea before she went to bed that night, she'd poured atropine in instead. Taken internally, atropine is a poison which attacks the nervous system and causes flushed skin and a terrible thirstiness. If untreated, the symptoms increase to a state of delirium, in which the victim makes spasmodic movements and then falls into unconsciousness and death. The amount of atropine in the glass shouldn't have been enough to kill her, but Mrs. Hazilitt was almost eighty and had a heart condition. She'd certainly shown all the signs of poisoning, including evidence of the spasmodic movements in the disorder in her room.

Donna Hazlitt was known to be a solitary, rather mousy, and inoffensive woman who had inherited her house and money from her husband. They had no children and she had no enemies. The coroner gave a verdict of accidental death by alkaloid poisoning.

Of course, there was no mention in the papers, or anywhere else, of a Georgia O'Keeffe painting.

II

> Everyone has many associations with a flower—the idea of flowers. You put out your hand to touch the flower—lean forward to smell it—maybe touch it with your lips almost without thinking—or give it to someone to please them.
>
> —Georgia O'Keeffe

About a week after our trip to Hana I took a stroll through downtown Lahaina one morning. It had been an old whaling village and a few structures remained from that period. There were a few lovely wooden arcades and a big old house where the Christian missionaries had lived, recording their astonishment at the ways of the Hawaiians, who seemed to enjoy singing and dancing, especially unclothed, as often as possible.

I stopped now outside a gallery window to look at some flower paintings. Many of the galleries in Lahaina catered to tourists of the lowest common denominator and featured canvases of unbelievable awfulness, which depicted mystical underwater scenes—dolphins frolicking amid schools of parrot fish and Moorish idols, and in the background the submerged towers of Atlantis.

But the watercolors displayed in this window were differ-

ent: small, modest, exquisite. There was hibiscus the color
of coral and rose, lying on a yellow tablecloth; a ginger plant
with the cobalt sea in the background; and finally, the single
petal of a plumeria flower, unfurling off the page, softly
shirred at the edges, dark at the center, leading you into its
heart. I thought, if these aren't too expensive, perhaps I'll
buy one for Claudie. She had been so shaken by the whole
experience with Donna Hazlitt that she had hardly come out
of her room for days. She had told the police several times
about the phone call, but it was clear they were not planning
to take her information into much account.

I stepped inside the door and immediately a woman came
forward from between two of the small paintings. She was in
her thirties, with a smooth bronze tan and soft, lingering
brown eyes. Her hair was sun-bleached past blond to something closer to a light lemon cream. Her teeth were startlingly white when she spoke, in a deeper voice than I'd
been expecting, but a voice that fit with how she looked,
attractively roughened by the elements.

"Can I help you?"

I told her I might be interested in buying one of the
paintings.

"Great!" she said, and couldn't help beaming like a child.
"I painted them!"

Her name was Susan Waterman and she was just watching the gallery for the morning while the owner did some
errands. They hadn't sold any yet, so it was thrilling that it
would happen while she was here. This was her first show.
She was actually a botanist at an experimental growing station run by the University of Hawaii.

In the end, overwhelmed by her bubbling gratitude, I
bought two paintings, one for Claudie and one for Luisa.
They weren't cheap. Susan also persuaded me to have lunch
with her tomorrow at her studio, where I could look at her
latest work and see her garden.

*   *   *

Claudie was strangely quiet when I first gave her the package, wrapped up with the label of the gallery stickered on the outside. But she admired the painting.

"I hope you didn't spend too much, Cassandra."

I was afraid to tell her, and said only, "Got it for a song. It's her first show. Susan Waterman. She's a botanist. She invited me over for lunch tomorrow."

"Leave it to Cassandra," Luisa teased. "If there is a woman to be found, Cassandra will be having lunch with her." She had embraced me violently when I gave her her package.

Claudie looked as if she was going to say something, but then excused herself, telling us she had a headache.

"I'm sorry," said Luisa. "I think she is, how do you say, *crushed out* on you. It hurts her feelings that you are going to lunch with someone else."

"Don't be ridiculous. Claudie is definitely not *crushed out*. You know she's been upset since the Hana incident. And anyway, it's only lunch."

Susan Waterman lived in a small house outside Lahaina that seemed surrounded by flowering plants, protea, birds-of-paradise, crab's claw ginger. Inside, the walls were covered with sketches and paintings, and on a table was a copy of Georgia O'Keeffe's *One Hundred Flowers*.

"I'm a great fan of hers," said Susan. "But it's hard to paint a flower without being influenced by her. Women painted flowers for centuries and it was considered terribly feminine and safe, and then O'Keeffe comes along and makes you see everything differently by putting flowers in the foreground and enlarging them so that they push the boundaries of the painting."

On the cover of the book was a great white flower, one of the jimsonweeds from the Southwest. "Don't you have these too?" I asked.

"Yes," she said. "The name in Hawaiian is *Kikania-Haole*."

"Doesn't *haole* mean white person?"

Susan laughed. "Yes. Though *haole* used to mean any

troublesome foreigner. Maybe that's how it got attached to jimsonweed."

"You'd hardly think of it as a weed," I said.

"That's the marvel of O'Keeffe," said Susan. "She makes you see. The critics said her flowers were sexual. O'Keeffe said, don't be silly. But they do give you that feeling, a really powerful, self-revelatory eroticism. The petals both explore and close off entry to the inner core."

Underneath her tan, Susan blushed. "I admire O'Keeffe so much. She didn't seem to need anybody else. Not like me. I'm always getting mixed up in love affairs, in relationships that are bad for me. Right now, I'm in the midst of deciding to break up and go back to being on my own. To really try to be independent." She fixed me with soft brown eyes that implored me to rescue her from this fate.

"Independence is my middle name," I said. "I've always been independent myself."

She looked disappointed, but tried again. "For me, being independent would mean being financially stable, so I could paint full-time. But unless I strike it rich—or find a sugar girlfriend—I'm afraid that's out of the question."

"Your current girlfriend . . . ?"

". . . misrepresented herself badly." Susan smiled. "But enough about me. Tell me what it's like to be a world traveler and translator."

"Well, I couldn't really support myself without my trust fund," I began, just for the pleasure of seeing the infinitely sweet expression that came into Susan's eyes.

That evening when Claudie had gone out to see her therapist and Luisa and I were back to quarreling bitterly over the translations of tiny three-letter words, the doorbell rang. When I answered it I found a woman on the doorstep. Before she could speak, Luisa called, "Hallo, Nell. Claudie isn't here."

"I'm not looking for Claudie."

She wasn't tall, but she was athletic-looking. Her tanned face had a drooping sort of sneer that some might find attractive. Her eyes were blue, a little bloodshot around the iris. She looked about forty, and she looked angry.

"What the hell were you doing with my girlfriend at her place this afternoon?"

"Susan? Your girlfriend?" I stammered. "I bought two of her paintings yesterday. She invited me to lunch, that's all." I was certainly not going to mention those melting brown eyes or the lingering kiss Susan had given me on my departure. I stepped back from the doorway, recalling some karate moves. Luisa was, unfortunately, a total physical coward, so it was no good expecting help from her.

But Nell didn't raise her fists, only her voice. "This is Claudie's way of getting back at me," she said. "I know it. She wanted Susan for herself, and when she couldn't get her, she recruited you."

"Listen, sit down," I said. "Have a glass of water. There's been some terrible misunderstanding. Luisa and I are translating a book, and I thought a flower painting would be a nice present for her. I bought one for Claudie too because she's been so hospitable. Do you think Claudie would have sent me to your gallery on purpose? If you're not on good terms why would she want to give you business?"

For a couple of seconds Nell, considering this, didn't say anything. Then she looked into the room and saw Susan's two framed watercolors propped up against the mantel. Before we could stop her, she'd lifted them up, one after the other, and smashed them, glass and all, on the sharp back of a metal lamp. The delicate pinks and yellows of the hibiscus and plumeria were ripped to shreds.

"You'll get a refund check in the morning," Nell said, and slammed the door as she left.

I was speechless, but Luisa seemed almost admiring. "That kind of passion is common in Uruguay," she said. "You don't see it much in the United States. All those anger management classes."

"She's crazy," I said.

"No," said Luisa. "She's jealous."

III

*The sorceresses of Greek mythology—Hec-
ate, Circe—knew well the narcotic, stimu-
lant and deadly effects of this plant, and
Linneaus gave it the Latin name Atropa
after the Greek Goddess of the Underworld
Atropos, who cut the thread of life.*
　　　　　　　　　　—Dietrich Frohne

I slept on my suspicions overnight and the next morning
took Claudie off for a walk along the beach. "Is there any
possibility," I said point-blank, "that Nell murdered Donna
Hazlitt?"

Claudie's hair blew in a straight line back from her forehead. She didn't say of course not; she said, "Not the Nell I
know. But then, she didn't turn out to be the Nell I knew in
the end."

"What made you think of her?"

"That phone call with Mrs. Hazlitt. You remember I said
she started in the middle talking about this painting. I'm
embarrassed to say I just assumed that she was probably
senile, and that she somehow thought we'd already met. But
afterward it occurred to me, maybe she did really talk to
someone about the painting."

"And that someone might have been Nell?"

"Our old business cards have both the gallery number
and my home number. I kept the house, Nell took the gallery. If Mrs. Hazlitt used the old business card, she might
have called Nell the first time, and then tried the home
number the second and gotten me."

"But why would Nell kill her to get the painting? Did she
want the painting that badly? She must realize she can't sell
the painting now; you'd know."

"I'm afraid," said Claudie, staring at the flat blue sea, "that
she might have done it for Susan."

So the tangled story came out. How Susan had appeared
in their lives, first claiming to be in love with Claudie, and

then when Claudie told her she would leave Nell, saying that she was happy to share. How that sharing turned into Nell's falling in love with Susan, violently in love, and leaving Claudie.

"Susan doesn't really seem like such a femme fatale," I said conservatively, though I remembered the eager touch of her lips on mine.

"She's not at all," said Claudie. "She's more like a puppy dog that you think you're playing with, and all of sudden you realize it has wrapped the leash around your legs so you can't move."

She shook her black hair. "And I wasn't even in love with her the way Nell is. Nell is absolutely obsessed with her."

I thought of Susan's telling me how her girlfriend, soon to be ex-girlfriend, had misrepresented herself.

"So you think Nell wanted to give her the painting to show her how much she cares? Or to ensure their financial future?"

"Oh, I don't know, Cassandra. I lay awake at night, wishing the whole thing had never happened. That poor old woman; she was so excited about her discovery."

"Have you told the police?"

"They don't even believe in the painting; why should they believe that Mrs. Hazlitt was murdered because of it?"

I decided to take Susan up on her invitation to drop by "anytime," but I made sure her car wasn't in the drive first. The little house was locked, but that was no problem for a credit card carrier like myself. I slipped the card in the door and was in in a second. It was the middle of the afternoon and I assumed she was at work. Hopefully it wouldn't take long.

But of course, looking for a flower painting in a studio full of flower paintings was harder than it looked. Over and over I thought, Yes! Then, No . . . There were copies of O'Keeffe paintings, sketches, and watercolors in great piles. Over and over the same creamy white flowers, close-up angel's trumpets, or jimsonweed, or belladonna or *Kikania-Haole,* whatever you wanted to call it.

After two hours I had to give up on finding the painting. But I had found something more important perhaps: a scrap of paper in a book called *Poisonous Plants* by Dietrich Frohne, marking an entry on *Datura.* This was the botanical name of the jimsonweed in the United States, the thorn apple in Britain, the *Kikania-Haole* in Hawaii. It was a member of the nightshade family, which also included red peppers, potatoes, and belladonna, to which the jimsonweed was closely related. Datura seeds had long been used in India for suicide and murder. Criminals used extracts of the seeds to knock out railway passengers and rob them. The term "jimson" came from Jamestown, where the weed had led to a mass poisoning in 1676 that effectively wiped out the colony. Taken orally, the datura seeds caused great thirst and a terrible flushing of the skin. They caused the victim to thrash around and pick randomly at imaginary objects in the air. Further hallucinations followed, then coma and death.

Of course datura was not all bad. Atropine came from the belladonna plant, and was useful in dilating the pupil of the eye.

Susan could easily have answered the phone at the gallery and gone to Mrs. Hazlitt's house. She, not Nell, knew the poisonous effects of plants. She, not Nell, would have known how to recognize an O'Keeffe painting. She, not Nell, had a financial motive. She wanted to paint full-time.

I left Susan's house with the book under my arm and went straight to the police station.

A year later, months after the trial was finally over and Susan Waterman acquitted for lack of more than circumstantial evidence, I got a letter from Claudie.

By that time I was in Indonesia, staying with my old friend Jacqueline Opal, who had suddenly and enthusiastically taken up a spot in an all-women's gamelan orchestra and was spending all her time bonging away on melodious drums. I had more or less forgotten about my Hawaiian trip (and was avoiding letters from Luisa that quibbled about adverb placement in the proofs of her novel), but Claudie's opening brought it all back:

"They apprehended her at the Honolulu Airport, trying to smuggle out the O'Keeffe painting. She confessed everything. How she'd answered the phone at the gallery and talked with Mrs. Hazlitt that first time. The next day when she called Mrs. Hazlitt, she realized the woman had already gotten in touch with me. She raced over to her house that night, frantic that I'd get the painting and she wouldn't. That's when she found out about her eye condition and saw the bottle of atropine in the medicine cabinet. She knew something about atropine because she'd just gotten over an eye infection herself, and her doctor had told her that atropine was poisonous. She made up some story about having heard about Echinacea and got Mrs. Hazlitt to offer her some and to take her dose at the same time, from the wrong bottle. She didn't realize it would be such a horrible death, but then, she wasn't there to see it. She had managed to persuade Mrs. Hazlitt to let her take the painting that night. That's why there was no sign of breaking and entering.

"Susan doesn't really blame you, Cassandra, for making her go through the trial and everything. The important thing, she says, is that Nell was caught. Nell says she needed the money because her gallery was failing without me. As usual, she blames everyone else but herself, me for making her business fail, Susan for wanting to break up with her. Nell wanted Susan to be accused of murder so that she would turn back to Nell for support!

"We don't care now. Susan came to live with me last month and this time, I think it's going to work. She's quit her job and I'm supporting her. It's so important for her to paint full-time. As for the O'Keeffe painting—oh, it's lovely, an earlier version of 'Belladonna—Hana (Two Jimson Weeds).' One of the flowers has a visible green center. The other has its core hidden, so that your eye is drawn deeper and deeper inside.

"The next time you come to Hawaii you'll have to be sure and see it."

SARA PARETSKY's private eye V.I. Warshawski helped to define the "new" female sleuth in modern American crime fiction. Since her first appearance, in **Indemnity Only** in 1982, V.I. has starred in seven other novels and in a collection of short stories. Sara Paretsky and her creation both live in Chicago.

Publicity Stunts

Sara Paretsky

I

"I need a bodyguard. I was told you were good." Lisa Macauley crossed her legs and leaned back in my client chair as if expecting me to slobber in gratitude.

"If you were told I was a good bodyguard someone didn't know my operation: I never do protection."

"I'm prepared to pay you well."

"You can offer me a million dollars a day and I still won't take the job. Protection is a special skill. You need lots of people to do it right. I have a one-person operation. I'm not going to abandon my other clients to look after you."

"I'm not asking you to give up your precious clients forever, just for a few days next week while I'm doing publicity here in Chicago."

Judging by her expression, Macauley thought she was a household word, but I'd been on the run the two days since she'd made the appointment and hadn't had time to do any research on her. Whatever she publicized made her rich: wealth oozed all the way from her dark cloud of carefully cut curls through the sable protecting her from February's chill winds and on down to her Stephane Kelian three-inch platforms.

When I didn't say anything she added, "For my new book, of course."

"That sounds like a job for your publisher. Or your handlers."

I had vague memories of going to see Andre Dawson when he was doing some kind of baseball promotion at

Marshall Field. He'd been on a dais, under lights, with several heavies keeping the adoring fans away from him. No matter what Macauley wrote she surely wasn't any more at risk than a sports hero.

She made an impatient gesture. "They always send some useless person from their publicity department. They refuse to believe my life is in danger. Of course, this is the last book I'll do with Gaudy: my new contract with Della Destra Press calls for a personal bodyguard whenever I'm on the road. But right now, while I'm promoting the new one, I need protection."

I ignored her contract woes. "Your life is in danger? What have you written that's so controversial? An attack on Mother Teresa?"

"I write crime novels. Don't you read?"

"Not crime fiction: I get enough of the real stuff walking out my door in the morning."

Macauley gave a self-conscious little laugh. "I thought mine might appeal to a woman detective like yourself. That's why I chose you to begin with. My heroine is a woman talk-show host who gets involved in cases through members of her listening audience. The issues she takes on are extremely controversial: abortion, rape, the Greens. In one of them she protects a man whose university appointment is attacked by the feminists on campus. She's nearly murdered when she uncovers the brainwashing operation the feminists are running on campus."

"I can't believe that would put you in danger—feminist-bashing is about as controversial as apple pie these days. Sounds like your hero is a female Claud Barnett."

Barnett broadcast his attacks on the atheistic, family-destroying feminists and liberals five days a week from Chicago's WKLN radio tower. The term he'd coined for progressive women—femmunists—had become a much-loved buzzword on the radical right. Claud had become so popular that his show was syndicated in almost every state, and rerun at night and on weekends in his hometown.

Macauley didn't like being thought derivative, even of reality. She bristled as she explained that her detective, Nan Carruthers, had a totally unique personality and slant on public affairs.

"But because she goes against all the popular positions that feminists have persuaded the media to support I get an unbelievable amount of hate mail."

"And now someone's threatening your life?" I tried to sound more interested than hopeful.

Her blue eyes flashing in triumph, Macauley pulled a letter from her handbag and handed it to me. It was the product of a computer, printed on some kind of cheap white stock. In all caps it proclaimed, YOU'LL BE SORRY, BITCH, BUT BY THEN IT WILL BE TOO LATE.

"If this is a serious threat you're already too late," I snapped. "You should have taken it to the forensics lab before you fondled it. Unless you sent it yourself as a publicity stunt?"

Genuine crimson stained her cheeks. "How dare you? My last three books have been national best sellers—I don't need this kind of cheap publicity."

I handed the letter back. "You show it to the police?"

"They wouldn't take it seriously. They told me they could get the state's attorney to open a file, but what good would that do me?"

"Scotland Yard can identify individual laser printers based on samples of output but most U.S. police departments don't have those resources. Did you keep the envelope?"

She took out a grimy specimen. With a magnifying glass I could make out the zip code in the postmark: Chicago, the Gold Coast. That meant only one of about a hundred thousand residents, or the half-million tourists who pass through the neighborhood every day, could have mailed it. I tossed it back.

"You realize this isn't a death threat—it's just a threat, and pretty vague at that. What is it you'll be sorry for?"

"If I knew that I wouldn't be hiring a detective," she snapped.

"Have you had other threats?" It was an effort to keep my voice patient.

"I had two other letters like this one, but I didn't bring them—I didn't think they'd help you any. I've started having phone calls where they just wait, or laugh in a weird way or something. Sometimes I get the feeling someone's following me."

"Any hunches who might be doing it?" I was just going through the motions—I didn't think she was at any real risk, but she seemed the kind who couldn't believe she wasn't at the forefront of everyone else's mind.

"I *told* you." She leaned forward in her intensity. "Ever since *Take Back the Night,* my fourth book, which gives a whole different look at rape crisis centers, I've been on the top of every femmunist hitlist in the country."

I laughed, trying to picture some of my friends out taking potshots at every person in America who hated feminists. "It sounds like a nuisance, but I don't believe your life is in as much danger as, say, the average abortion provider. But if you want a bodyguard while you're on Claud Barnett's show I can recommend a couple of places. Just remember, though, that even the Secret Service couldn't protect JFK from a determined sniper."

"I suppose if I'd been some whiny feminist you'd take this more seriously. It's because of my politics you won't take the job."

"If you were a whiny feminist I'd probably tell you not to cry over this because there's a lot worse on its way. But since you're a whiny authoritarian there's not much I can do for you. I'll give you some advice for free, though: If you cry about it on the air you'll only invite a whole lot more of this kind of attention."

I didn't think contemporary clothes lent themselves to flouncing out of rooms, but Ms. Macauley certainly flounced out of mine. I wrote a brief summary of our meeting in my appointments log, then put her out of mind until the next night. I was having dinner with a friend who devours crime fiction. Sal Barthele was astounded that I hadn't heard of Lisa Macauley.

"You ever read anything besides the sports pages and the financial section, Warshawski? That girl is hot. They say her contract with Della Destra is worth twelve million, and all the guys with shiny armbands and goosesteps buy her books by the cord. I hear she's dedicating the next one to the brave folks at Operation Rescue."

After that I didn't think of Macauley at all: a case for a small suburban school district whose pension money had been turned into derivatives was taking all my energy. But a week later the writer returned forcibly to mind.

"You're in trouble now, Warshawski," Murray Ryerson said when I picked up the phone late Thursday night.

"Hi, Murray: good to hear from you, too." Murray is an investigative reporter for the *Herald-Star,* a one-time lover, sometime rival, occasional pain-in-the-butt, and even, now and then, a good friend.

"Why'd you tangle with Lisa Macauley? She's Chicago's most important artiste, behind Oprah."

"She come yammering to you with some tale of injustice? She wanted a bodyguard and I told her I didn't do that kind of work."

"Oh, Warshawski, you must have sounded ornery when you turned her down. She is not a happy camper: she got Claud Barnett all excited about how you won't work for anyone who doesn't agree with your politics. He dug up your involvement with the old abortion underground and has been blasting away at you the last two days as the worst kind of murdering femmunist. A wonderful woman came to you, trembling and scared for her life, and you turned her away just because she's against abortion. He says you investigate the politics of all your potential clients and won't take anyone who's given money to a Christian or a Republican cause and he's urging people to boycott you."

"Kind of people who listen to Claud need an investigator to find their brains. He isn't likely to hurt me."

Murray dropped his bantering tone. "He carries more

weight than you, or maybe even I, want to think. You may have to do some damage control."

I felt my stomach muscles tighten: I live close to the edge of financial ruin much of the time. If I lost three or four key accounts I'd be dead.

"You think I should apply for a broadcast license and blast back? Or just have my picture taken coming out of the headquarters of the Republican National Committee?"

"You need a nineties kind of operation, Warshawski—a staff, including a publicist. You need to have someone going around town with stories about all the tough cases you've cracked in the last few years, showing how wonderful you are. On account of I like hot-tempered Italian gals I might run a piece myself if you'd buy me dinner."

"What's a nineties operation—where your self-promotion matters a whole lot more than what kind of job you do? Come to think of it, do you have an agent, Murray?"

The long pause at the other end told its own tale: Murray had definitely joined the nineties. I looked in the mirror after he hung up, searching for scales or some other visible sign of turning into a dinosaur. In the absence of that I'd hang on to my little one-woman shop as long as possible.

I turned to the *Herald-Star*'s entertainment guide, looking to see when WKLN ("The voice of the Klan," we'd dubbed them in my days with the public defender) was rebroadcasting Barnett. I was in luck: he came on again at eleven-thirty, so that night workers would have something to froth about on their commute home.

After a few minutes from his high-end sponsors, his rich, folksy baritone rolled through my speakers like molasses from a giant barrel. "Yeah, folks, the femmunists are at it again. The Iron Curtain's gone down in Russia so they want to put it up here in America. You think like they think or—*phht!*—off you go to the Gulag.

"We've got one of those femmunists right here in Chicago. Private investigator. You know, in the old stories they used to call them private dicks. Kind of makes you wonder what this gal is missing in her life that she turned to that kind of work. Started out as a baby-killer back in the days when she was at the Red University on the South Side of Chicago and grew up to be a dick. Well, it takes all kinds, they say, but do we need this kind?

"We got an important writer here in Chicago. I know a lot of you read the books this courageous woman writes. And because she's willing to take a stand she gets death threats. So she goes to this femmunist dick, this hermaphrodite dick, who won't help her out. 'Cause Lisa Macauley has the guts to tell women the truth about rape and abortion, and this dick, this V.I. Warshawski, can't take it.

"By the way, you ought to check out Lisa's new book. *Slaybells Ring*. A great story which takes her fast-talking radio host Nan Carruthers into the world of the ACLU and the bashing of Christmas. We carry it right here in our bookstore. If you call in now Sheri will ship it right out to you. Or just go out to your nearest warehouse: they're bound to stock it. Maybe if this Warshawski read it she'd have a change of heart, but a gal like her, you gotta wonder if she has a heart to begin with."

He went on for thirty minutes by the clock, making an easy segue from me to the First Lady. If I was a devil, she was the Princess of Darkness. When he finished I stared out the window for a time. I felt ill from the bile Barnett had poured out in his molassied voice, but I was furious with Lisa Macauley. She had set me up, pure and simple. Come to see me with a spurious problem, just so she and Barnett could start trashing me on the air. But why?

II

Murray was right: Barnett carried more weight than I wanted to believe. He kept on at me for days, not always as the centerpiece, but often sending a few snide barbs my way. The gossip columns of all three daily papers mentioned it and the story got picked up by the wires. Between Barnett and the papers, Macauley got a load of free publicity; her sales skyrocketed. Which made me wonder again if she'd typed up that threatening note herself.

At the same time, my name getting sprinkled with mud did start having an effect on my own business: two new clients backed out midstream, and one of my old regulars phoned to say his company didn't have any work for me right now. No, they weren't going to cancel my contract, but they thought, in his picturesque corpo-speak, "we'd go into a holding pattern for the time being."

I called my lawyer to see what my options were; he advised me to let snarling dogs bite until they got it out of their system. "You don't have the money to take on Claud Barnett, Vic, and even if you won a slander suit against him you'd lose while the case dragged on."

On Sunday I meekly called Murray and asked if he'd be willing to repeat the deal he'd offered me earlier. After a two-hundred-dollar dinner at the Filigree he ran a nice story on me in the *Star*'s "Chicago Beat" section, recounting some of my great past successes. This succeeded in diverting some of Barnett's attention from me to Murray—my so-called stooge. Of course he wasn't going to slander Murray on the air—he could tell lies about a mere mortal like me, but not about someone with a big media operation to pay his legal fees.

I found myself trying to plan the total humiliation of both Barnett and Macauley. Let it go, I would tell myself, as I turned in the bed in the middle of the night: this is what he wants, to control my head. Turn it off. But I couldn't follow this most excellent advice.

I even did a little investigation into Macauley's life. I called a friend of mine at Channel 13 where Macauley had once worked to get the station's take on her. A native of Wisconsin, she'd moved to Chicago hoping to break into broadcast news. After skulking on the sidelines of the industry for five or six years she'd written her first Nan Carruthers book. Ironically enough, the women's movement, creating new roles for women in fiction as well as life, had fueled Macauley's literary success. When her second novel became a best seller, she divorced the man she married when they were both University of Wisconsin journalism students and started positioning herself as a celebrity. She was famous in book circles for her insistence on her personal security: opinion was divided as to whether it had started as a publicity stunt, or if she really did garner a lot of hate mail.

I found a lot of people who didn't like her—some because of her relentless self-promotion, some because of her politics, and some because they resented her success. As Sal had told me, Macauley was minting money now. Not only Claud, but the *Wall Street Journal*, the *National Review*, and all the other conservative rags hailed her as a welcome antidote to writers like Marcia Muller or Amanda Cross.

But despite my digging I couldn't find any real dirt on Macauley. Nothing I could use to embarrass her into silence. To make matters worse, someone at Channel 13 told her I'd been poking around asking questions about her. Whether by chance or design, she swept into Corona's one night when I was there with Sal. Sal and I were both enthusiastic fans of Belle Fontaine, the jazz singer who was Corona's Wednesday night regular headliner.

Lisa arrived near the end of the first set. She'd apparently found an agency willing to guard her body—she was the center of a boisterous crowd that included a couple of big men with bulges near their armpits. She flung her sable across a chair at a table near ours.

At first I assumed her arrival was just an unhappy coincidence. She didn't seem to notice me, but called loudly for champagne, asking for the most expensive brand on the menu. A couple at a neighboring table angrily shushed her. This prompted Lisa to start yelling out toasts to some of the people at her table: her *fabulous* publicist, her *awesome* attorney, and her *extraordinary* bodyguards, "Rover" and "Prince." The sullen-faced men didn't join in the raucous cheers at their nicknames, but they didn't erupt, either.

We couldn't hear the end of "Tell Me Lies" above Lisa's clamor, but Belle took a break at that point. Sal ordered another drink and started to fill me in on family news: Her lover had just landed a role in a sitcom that would take her out to the West Coast for the winter and Sal was debating hiring a manager for her own bar, the Golden Glow, so she could join Becca. She was just describing—in humorous detail—Becca's first meeting with the producer, when Lisa spoke loudly enough for everyone in the room to hear.

"I'm so glad you boys were willing to help me out. I can't believe how chicken some of the detectives in this town are. Easy to be big and bold in an abortion clinic, but they run and hide from someone their own size." She turned deliberately in her chair, faked an elaborate surprise at the sight of me, and continued at the same bellowing pitch, "Oh, V.I. Warshawski! I hope you don't take it personally."

"I don't expect eau de cologne from the sewer," I called back heartily.

The couple who'd tried to quiet Lisa down during the singing laughed at this. The star twitched, then got to her feet, champagne glass in hand, and came over to me.

"I hear you've been stalking me, Warshawski. I could sue you for harassment."

I smiled. "Sugar, I've been trying to find out why a big successful gal like you had to invent some hate mail just to have an excuse to slander me. You want to take me to court I'll be real, *real* happy to sort out your lies in public."

"In court or anywhere else I'll make you look as stupid as you do right now." Lisa tossed her champagne into my face; a camera strobe flashed just as the drink hit me.

Fury blinded me more than the champagne. I knocked over a chair as I leapt up to throttle her, but Sal got an arm around my waist and pulled me down. Behind Macauley, Prince and Rover got to their feet, ready to move: Lisa had clearly staged the whole event to give them an excuse for beating me up.

Queenie, who owns the Corona, was at my side with some towels. "Jake! I want these people out of here now. And I think some cute person's been taking pictures. Make sure she leaves the film with you, hear? Ms. Macauley, you owe me three hundred dollars for that Dom Pérignon you threw around."

Prince and Rover thought they were going to take on Queenie's bouncer, but Jake had broken up bigger fights than they could muster. He managed to lift them both and slam their heads together, then to snatch the *fabulous* publicist's bag as she was trying to sprint out the door. Jake took out her camera, pulled the film, and handed the bag back to her with smile and an insulting bow. The attorney, prompted by Jake, handed over three bills, and the whole party left to loud applause from the audience.

Queenie and Sal grew up together, which may be why I got Gold Coast treatment that night, but not even her private reserve Veuve Clicquot could take the bad taste from my mouth. If I'd beaten up Macauley I'd have looked like the brute she and Barnett were labeling me; but taking a faceful of champagne sitting down left me looking—and feeling—helpless.

"You're not going to do anything stupid, are you, Vic?" Sal said as she dropped me off around two in the morning. "'Cause if you are I'm baby-sitting you, girlfriend."

"No. I'm not going to do anything rash, if that's what you mean. But I'm going to nail that prize bitch, one way or another."

Twenty-four hours later Lisa Macauley was dead. One day after that I was in jail.

III

All I knew about Lisa's murder was what I'd read in the papers before the cops came for me: Her personal trainer had discovered her body when he arrived Friday morning for their usual workout. She had been beaten to death in what looked like a bloody battle, which is why the state's attorney finally let me go—they couldn't find the marks on me they were looking for. And they couldn't find any evidence in my home or office.

They kept insisting, though, that I had gone to her apartment late Thursday night. They asked me about it all night long on Friday without telling me why they were so sure. When Freeman Carter, my lawyer, finally sprang me Saturday afternoon he forced them to tell him: the doorman was claiming he admitted me to Lisa's apartment just before midnight on Thursday.

Freeman taxed me with it on the ride home. "The way she was carrying on it would have been like you to demand a face-to-face with her, Vic. Don't hold out on me—I can't defend you if you were there and won't tell me about it."

"I wasn't there," I said flatly. "I am not prone to blackouts or hallucinations: there is no way I could have gone there and forgotten it. I was blamelessly watching the University of Kansas men pound Duke on national television. I even have a witness: My golden retriever shared a pizza with me. Her testimony: She threw up cheese sauce in front of my bed Friday morning."

Freeman ignored that. "Sal told me about the dust-up at Corona's. Anyway, Stacey Cleveland, Macauley's publicist, had already bared all to the police. You're the only person they can locate who had reason to be killing mad with her."

"Then they're not looking, are they? Someone either pretended to be me, or else bribed the doorman to tell the cops I was there. Get me the doorman's name and I'll sort out which it was."

"I can't do that, Vic: you're in enough trouble without suborning the state's key witness."

"You're supposed to be on my side," I snapped. "You want to go into court with evidence or not?"

"I'll talk to the doorman, Vic: you go take a bath—jail doesn't smell very good on you."

I followed Freeman's advice only because I was too tired to do anything else. After that I slept the clock around, waking just before noon on Sunday. The phone had been ringing when I walked in on Saturday. It was Murray, wanting my exclusive story. I put him off and switched the phone to my answering service. In the morning I had forty-seven messages from various reporters. When I started outside to get the Sunday papers I found a camera crew parked in front of the building. I retreated, fetched my coat and an overnight bag, and went out the back way. My car was parked right in front of the camera van, so I walked the three miles to my new office.

When the Pulteney Building went under the wrecking ball last April I'd moved my business to a warehouse on the edge of Wicker Park, at the corner of Milwaukee Avenue and North. Fringe galleries and nightspots compete with liquor stores and palm readers for air here, and there are a lot of vacant lots, but it was ten minutes—by car, bus, or L—from the heart of the financial district where most of my business lies. A sculpting friend had moved her studio into a re-vamped warehouse; the day after visiting her I signed a five-year lease across the hall. I had twice my old space at two-thirds the rent. Since I'd had to refurnish—from Dumpsters and auctions—I'd put in a daybed behind a partition: I could camp out here for a few days until media interest in me cooled.

I bought the Sunday papers from one of the liquor stores on my walk. The *Sun-Times* concentrated on Macauley's career, including a touching history of her childhood in Rhinelander, Wisconsin. She'd been the only child of older parents. Her father, Joseph, had died last year at the age of eighty, but her mother, Louise, still lived in the house where Lisa had grown up. The paper showed a frame bungalow with a porch swing and a minute garden, as well as a tearful Louise Macauley in front of Lisa's doll collection ("I've kept the room the way it looked when she left for college," the caption read).

Her mother never wanted her going off to the University of Wisconsin. "Even though we raised her with the right values, and sent her to church schools, the university is a terrible place. She wouldn't agree, though, and now look what's happened."

The *Tribune* had a discreet sidebar on Lisa's recent contretemps with me. In the *Herald-Star* Murray published the name of the doorman who had admitted "someone claiming to be V.I. Warshawski" to Macauley's building. It was Reggie

Whitman. He'd been the doorman since the building went up in 1978, was a grandfather, a church deacon, coached a basketball team at the Henry Horner Homes, and was generally so virtuous that truth radiated from him like a beacon.

Murray also had talked with Lisa's ex-husband, Brian Gerstein, an assistant producer for one of the local network news stations. He was appropriately grief-stricken at his ex-wife's murder. The picture supplied by Gerstein's publicist showed a man in his mid-thirties with a TV smile but anxious eyes.

I called Beth Blacksin, the reporter at Channel 13 who'd filled me in on what little I'd learned about Lisa Macauley before her death.

"Vic! Where are you? We've got a camera crew lurking outside your front door hoping to talk to you!"

"I know, babycakes. And talk to me you shall, as soon as I find out who set me up to take the fall for Lisa Macauley's death. So give me some information now and it shall return to you like those famous loaves of bread."

Beth wanted to dicker but the last two weeks had case-hardened my temper. She finally agreed to talk with the promise of a reward in the indefinite future.

Brian Gerstein had once worked at Channel 13, just as he had for every other news station in town. "He's a loser, Vic: I'm not surprised Lisa dumped him when she started to get successful. He's the kind of guy who would sit around dripping into his coffee because you were out-earning him, moaning, trying to get you to feel sorry for him. People hire him because he's a good tape editor, but then they give him the shove because he gets the whole newsroom terminally depressed."

"You told me last week they met up at UW when they were students there in the eighties. Where did they go next?"

Beth had to consult her files, but she came back on the line in a few minutes with more details. Gerstein came from Long Island. He met Lisa when they were both Wisconsin juniors, campaigning for Reagan's first election in 1980.

They'd married five years later, just before moving to Chicago. Politics and TV kept them together for seven years after that.

Gary rented an apartment in Rogers Park on the far north side of the city. "And that's typical of him," Beth added as she gave me his address. "He won't own a home since they split up: he can't afford it, his life was ruined and he doesn't feel like housekeeping, I've heard a dozen different whiny reasons from him. Not that everyone has to own, but you don't have to rent a run-down apartment in gangbanger territory when you work for the networks, either."

"So he could have been peevish enough to kill Lisa?"

"You're assuming he swathed himself in skirts and furs and told Reggie Whitman he was V.I. Warshawski? It would take more—more gumption than he's got to engineer something like that. It's not a bad theory, though: maybe we'll float it on the four o'clock news. Give us something different to talk about than all the other guys. Stay in touch, Vic. I'm willing to believe you're innocent, but it'd make a better story if you'd killed her."

"Thanks, Blacksin." I laughed as I hung up: her enthusiasm was without malice.

I took the L up to Rogers Park, the slow Sunday milk run. Despite Beth's harangue, it's an interesting part of town. Some blocks you do see dopers hanging out, some streets have depressing amounts of garbage in the yards, but most of the area harks back to the Chicago of my childhood: tidy brick two-flats, hordes of immigrants in the parks speaking every known language and along with them, delis and coffee shops for every nationality.

Gerstein lived on one of the quiet side streets. He was home, as I'd hoped: staking out an apartment without a car would have been miserable work on a cold February day. He even let me in without too much fuss. I told him I was a detective, and showed him my license, but he didn't seem to recognize my name—he must not have been editing the programs dealing with his ex-wife's murder. Or he'd been so stricken he'd edited them without registering anything.

He certainly exuded misery as he escorted me up the stairs. Whether it was grief or guilt for Lisa, or just the chronic depression Beth attributed to him, he moved as though on the verge of falling over. He was a little taller than I, but slim. Swathed in a coat and shawls he might have looked like a woman to the nightman.

Gerstein's building was clean and well maintained, but his own apartment was sparely furnished, as though he expected to move on at any second. The only pictures on the walls were a couple of framed photographs—one of himself and Lisa with Ronald Reagan, and the other with a man I didn't recognize. He had no drapes or plants or anything else to bring a bit of color to the room, and when he invited me to sit he pulled a metal folding chair from a closet for me.

"I always relied on Lisa to fix things up," he said. "She has so much vivacity and such good taste. Without her I can't seem to figure out how to do it."

"I thought you'd been divorced for years." I tossed my coat onto the card table in the middle of the room.

"Yes, but I've only been living here nine months. She let me keep our old condo, but last summer I couldn't make the payments. She said she'd come around to help me fix this up, only she's so busy . . ." His voice trailed off.

I wondered how he ever sold himself to his various employers—I found myself wanting to shake him out like a pillow and plump him up. "So you and Lisa stayed in touch?"

"Oh, sort of. She was too busy to call much, but she'd talk to me sometimes when I phoned."

"So you didn't have any hard feelings about your divorce?"

"Oh, I did. I never wanted to split up—it was all her idea. I kept hoping, but now, you know, it's too late."

"I suppose a woman as successful as Lisa met a lot of men."

"Yes, yes she certainly did." His voice was filled with admiration, not hate.

I was beginning to agree with Beth, that Gerstein couldn't possibly have killed Lisa. What really puzzled me was what had ever attracted her to him in the first place, but the person who could figure out the hows and whys of attraction would put Ann Landers out of business overnight.

I went through the motions with him—did he get a share in her royalties?—yes, on the first book, because she'd written that while they were still together. When she wanted a divorce his lawyer told him he could probably get a judgment entitling him to fifty percent of all her proceeds, even in the future, but he loved Lisa, he wanted her to come back to him, he wasn't interested in being vindictive. Did he inherit under Lisa's will? He didn't think so, I'd have to ask her attorney. Did he knew who her residuary legatee was? Some conservative foundations they both admired.

I got up to go. "Who do you think killed your wife, ex-wife?"

"I thought they'd arrested someone, that dick Claud Barnett says was harassing her."

"You know Barnett? Personally, I mean?" All I wanted was to divert him from thinking about me—even in his depression he might have remembered hearing my name on the air —but he surprised me.

"Yeah. That is, Lisa does. Did. We went to a conservative media convention together right after we moved here. Barnett was the keynote speaker. She got all excited, said she'd known him growing up but his name was something different then. After that she saw him every now and then. She got him to take his picture with us a couple of years later, at another convention in Sun Valley."

He jerked his head toward the wall where the photographs hung. I went over to look at them. I knew the Gipper's famous smile pretty well by heart so I concentrated on Barnett. I was vaguely aware of his face: he was considered so influential in the nation's swing rightward that his picture kept popping up in news magazines. A man of about fifty, he was lean and well groomed, and usually smiling with affable superiority.

In Sun Valley he must have eaten something that disagreed with him. He had an arm around Lisa and her husband, stiffly, as if someone had propped plyboard limbs against his trunk. Lisa was smiling gaily, happy to be with the media darling. Brian was holding himself upright and looking close to jovial. But Claud gave you the idea that thumbscrews had been hammered under his plywood nails to get him into the photo.

"What name had Lisa known him by as a child?" I asked.

"Oh, she was mistaken about that. Once she got to see him up close she realized it was only a superficial resemblance. But Barnett took a shine to her—most people did, she was so vivacious—and gave her a lot of support in her career. He was the first big booster of her Nan Carruthers novels."

"He doesn't look very happy to be with her here, does he? Can I borrow it? It's a very good one of Lisa, and I'd like to use it in my inquiries."

Brian said in a dreary voice that he thought Lisa's publicist would have much better ones, but he was easy to persuade—or bully, to call my approach by its real name. I left with the photo carefully draped in a dish towel, and a written promise to return it as soon as possible.

I trotted to the Jarvis L stop, using the public phone there to call airlines. I found one that not only sent kiddie planes from O'Hare to Rhinelander, Wisconsin, but had a flight leaving in two hours. The state's attorney had told me not to leave the jurisdiction. Just in case they'd put a stop on me at the airport, I booked a flight under my mother's maiden name and embarked on the tedious L journey back to the Loop and out to the airport.

IV

Lisa's new book, *Slaybells Ring*, was stacked high at the airport bookstores. The black enamel cover with an embossed spray of bells in silver drew the eye. At the third stand I passed I finally gave in and bought a copy.

The flight was a long puddle-jumper, making stops in Milwaukee and Wausau on its way north. By the time we reached Rhinelander I was approaching the denouement, where the head of the American Civil Liberties Union was shown to be opposing the display of a Christmas creche at City Hall because he secretly owned a company that was trying to put the creche's manufacturer out of business. Nan Carruthers, owing to her wide and loyal band of radio fans, got the information from an employee the ACLU baddie had fired after thirty years of loyal service when the employee was found listening to Nan's show on his lunch break. The book had a three-hanky ending at midnight mass, where Nan joined the employee—now triumphantly reinstated (thanks to the enforcement of the Civil Rights Act of 1964 by the EEOC and the ACLU, but Lisa Macauley hadn't thought that worth mentioning)—along with his wife and their nine children in kneeling in front of the public creche.

I finished the book around one in the morning in the Rhinelander Holiday Inn. The best-written part treated a subplot between Nan and the man who gave her career its first important boost—the pastor of the heroine's childhood church who had become a successful televangelist. When Nan was a child he had photographed her and other children in his Sunday school class engaged in forced sex with one another and with him. Since he held an awful fear of eternal damnation over their heads they never told their parents. But when Nan started her broadcast career she persuaded him to plug her program on his Thursday night "Circle of the Saved," using covert blackmail threats to get him to do so. At the end, as she looks at the baby Jesus in the manger, she wonders what Mary would have done—forgiven the pastor, or exposed him? Certainly not collaborated with him to further her own career. The book ended on that troubled note. I went to sleep with more respect for Macauley's craft than I had expected.

* * *

In the morning I found Mrs. Joseph Macauley's address in the local phone book and went off to see her. Although now in her mid-seventies she carried herself well. She didn't greet me warmly, but she accepted without demur my identification of myself as a detective trying to find Lisa's murderer. Chicago apparently was so convinced that I was the guilty party, they hadn't bothered to send anyone up to interview her.

"I am tired of all those Chicago reporters bothering me, but if you're a detective I guess I can answer your questions. What'd you want to know? I can tell you all about Lisa's childhood, but we didn't see so much of her once she moved off to Madison. We weren't too happy about some of the friends she was making. Not that we have anything against Jews personally, but we didn't want our only child marrying one and getting involved in all those dirty financial deals. Of course we were happy he was working for Ronald Reagan, but we weren't sorry they split up, even though our church frowns on divorce."

I let her talk unguided for a time before pulling out the picture of Claud Barnett. "This is someone Lisa knew as a child. Do you recognize him?"

Mrs. Macauley took the photo from me. "Do you think I'm not in possession of my faculties? That's Claud Barnett. He certainly never lived around here."

She snorted and started to hand the picture back, then took it to study more closely. "She knew I never liked to see her in pants, so she generally wore a skirt when she came up here. But she looks real cute in that outfit, real cute. You know, I guess I can see where she might have confused him with Carl Bader. Although Carl was dark-haired and didn't have a mustache, there is a little something around the forehead."

"And who was Carl Bader?"

"Oh, that's ancient history. He left town and we never heard anything more about it."

All I could get her to say about him was that he'd been connected to their church and she never did believe half the gossip some of the members engaged in. "That Mrs. Hoffer always overindulged her children, let them say anything and get away with it. We brought Lisa up to show proper respect for people in authority. Cleaned her mouth out with soap and whipped her so hard she didn't sit for a week the one time she tried taking part in some of that trashy talk."

More she wouldn't say, so I took the picture with me to the library and looked up old copies of the local newspaper. In *Slaybells Ring,* Nan Carruthers was eight when the pastor molested her, so I checked 1965 through 1967 for stories about Bader and anyone named Hoffer. All I found was a little blurb saying Bader had left the United Pentecostal Church of God in Holiness in 1967 to join a television ministry in Atlanta, and that he'd gone so suddenly that the church didn't have time to throw him a going-away party.

I spent a weary afternoon trying to find Mrs. Hoffer. There were twenty-seven Hoffers in the Rhinelander phone book; six were members of the United Pentecostal Church. The church secretary was pleasant and helpful, but it wasn't until late in the day that Mrs. Matthew Hoffer told me the woman I wanted, Mrs. Barnabas Hoffer, had quit the church over the episode about her daughter.

"Caused a lot of hard feeling in the church. Some people believed the children, and they quit. Others figured it was just mischief, children who like to make themselves look interesting. That Lisa Macauley was one. I'm sorry she got herself killed down in Chicago, but in a way I'm not surprised—seemed like she was always sort of *daring* you to smack her, the stories she made up and the way she put herself forward. Not that Louise Macauley spared the rod, mind you, but sometimes I think you can beat a child too much for its own good. Anyway, once people saw little Lisa joining in with Katie Hoffer in accusing the pastor no one took it seriously. No one except Gertrude—Katie's mom, I mean. She still bears a grudge against all of us who stood by Pastor Bader."

And finally, at nine o'clock, I was sitting on an overstuffed horsehair settee in Gertrude Hoffer's living room, looking at a cracked color photo of two unhappy children. I had to take Mrs. Hoffer's word that they were Katie and Lisa—their faces were indistinct, and at this point in the picture's age so were their actions.

"I found it when I was doing his laundry. Pastor Bader wasn't married, so all us church ladies took it in turn to look after his domestic wants. Usually he was right there to put his own clothes away, but this one time he was out and I was arranging his underwear for him and found this whole stack of pictures. I couldn't believe it at first, and then when I came on Katie's face—well—I snatched it up and ran out of there.

"At first I thought it was some evilness the children dreamed up on their own, and that he had photographed them to show us, show the parents what they got up to. That was what he told my husband when Mr. Hoffer went to talk to him about it. It took me a long time to see that a child wouldn't figure out something like that on her own, but I never could get any of the other parents to pay me any mind. And that Louise Macauley, she just started baking pies for Pastor Bader every night of the week, whipped poor little Lisa for telling me what he made her and Katie get up to. It's a judgment on her, it really is, her daughter getting herself killed like that."

V

It was hard for me to find someone in the Chicago Police Department willing to try to connect Claud Barnett with Carl Bader. Once they'd done that, though, the story unraveled pretty fast. Lisa had recognized him in Sun Valley and put the bite on him—not for money, but for career advancement, just as her heroine did her own old pastor in *Slaybells Ring*. No one would ever be able to find out for sure, but the emotional torment she put Nan Carruthers through must have paralleled Lisa's own misery. She was a success, she'd forced her old tormentor to make her a success, but it must have galled her—as it did her heroine—to pretend to admire him, to sit in on his show, and to see a film of torment overlay his face.

When Barnett read *Slaybells*, he probably began to worry that Lisa wouldn't be able to keep his secret to herself much longer. The police did find evidence of the threatening letters in his private study. The state argued that Barnett sent Lisa the threatening letters, then persuaded her to hire me to protect her. At that point Barnett didn't have anything special against me, but I was a woman. He figured if he could start enough public conflict between a woman detective and Lisa, he'd be able to fool the nightman, Reggie Whitman, into believing he was sending a woman up to Lisa's apartment on the fatal night. It was only later that he'd learned about my progressive politics—that was just icing on his cake, to be able to denounce me on his show.

Of course, not all this came out right away—some of it didn't emerge until the trial. That's when I also learned that Whitman, besides being practically a saint, had badly failing vision. On a cold night anyone could have passed himself off as me.

Between Murray and Beth Blacksin I got a lot of public vindication, and Sal and Queenie took me to dinner with Belle Fontaine to celebrate on the day the guilty verdict came in. We were all disappointed that they only slapped him with second-degree murder. But what left me gasping for air was a public opinion poll that came out the next afternoon. Even though other examples of his child-molesting behavior had come to light during the trial, his listeners believed he was innocent of all charges.

"The femmunists made it all up trying to discredit him," one woman explained that afternoon on the air. "And then they got *The New York Times* to print their lies."

Not even Queenie's reserve Veuve Clicquot could wipe that bitter taste out of my mouth.

Best known for her detective Sharon McCone, **MARCIA MULLER**'s sixteenth novel with the San Francisco sleuth, *A Wild and Lonely Place,* was published in August 1995. Besides writing mysteries, Muller is also an accomplished Western storyteller. A winner of the Anthony and American Mystery awards, Muller was also awarded the Life Achievement award by the Private Eye Writers of America. She was born in Detroit and received her undergraduate and graduate degrees from the University of Michigan.

The Cracks in the Sidewalk

Marcia Muller

Gracie

I'm leaning against my mailbox and the sun's shining on my face and my pigeons are coming round. Storage box number 27368. The mail carrier's already been here—new one, because he didn't know my name and kind of shied away from me like I smell bad. Which I probably do. I'll have him trained soon, though, and he'll say "Hi, Gracie" and pass the time of day and maybe bring me something to eat. Just the way the merchants in this block do. It's been four years now, and I've got them all trained. Box 27368—it's gotten to be like home.

Home . . .

Nope, I can't think about that. Not anymore.

Funny how the neighborhood's changed since I started taking up space on this corner with my cart and my pigeons, on my blanket on good days, on plastic in the rain. Used to be the folks who lived in this part of San Francisco was Mexicans and the Irish ran the bars and used-furniture stores. Now you see a lot of Chinese or whatever, and there're all these new restaurants and coffeehouses. Pretty fancy stuff. But that's okay; they draw a nice class of people, and the waiters bring me the leftovers. And my pigeons are still the same—good company. They're sort of like family.

Family . . .

No, I can't think about that anymore.

Cecily

I've been watching the homeless woman they call Gracie for two years now, ever since I left my husband and moved into the studio over the Lucky Shamrock and started to write my novel. She shows up every morning promptly at nine and sits next to the mail-storage box and holds court with the pigeons. People in the neighborhood bring her food, and she always shares it with the birds. You'd expect them to flock all over her, but instead they hang back respectfully, each waiting its turn. It's as if Gracie and they speak the same language, although I've never heard her say a word to them.

How to describe her without relying on the obvious stereotypes of homeless persons? Not that she isn't stereotypical: She's ragged and she smells bad and her gray-brown hair is long and tangled. But in spite of the wrinkles and roughness of her skin, she seems ageless, and on days like this when she smiles and turns her face up to the sun she has a strange kind of beauty. Beauty disrupted by what I take to be flashes of pain. Not physical, but psychic pain—the reason, perhaps, that she took up residence on the cracked sidewalk of the Mission District.

I wish I knew more about her.

All I know are these few things: She's somewhere in her late thirties, a few years older than I. She told the corner grocer that. She has what she calls a "hidey-hole" where she goes to sleep at night—someplace safe, she told the mailman, where she won't be disturbed. She guards her shopping cart full of plastic bags very carefully; she'd kill anyone who touched it, she warned my landlord. She's been coming here nearly four years and hasn't missed a single day; Deirdre, the bartender at the Lucky Shamrock, has kept track. She was born in Oroville, up in the foothills of the Sierras; she mentioned that to my neighbor when she saw him wearing a sweatshirt saying OROVILLE—BEST LITTLE CITY BY A DAM SITE.

And that's it.

Maybe there's a way to find out more about her. Amateur detective work. Call it research, if I feel a need to justify it. Gracie might make a good character for a story. Anyway, it would be something to fool around with while I watch the mailbox and listen for the phone, hoping somebody's going to buy my damn novel. Something to keep my mind off this endless cycle of hope and rejection. Something to keep my mind off my regrets.

Yes, maybe I'll try to find out more about Gracie.

Gracie

Today I'm studying on the cracks in the sidewalk. They're pretty complicated, running this way and that, and on the surface they look dark and empty. But if you got down real close and put your eye to them there's no telling what you might see. In a way the cracks're like people. Or music.

Music . . .

Nope, that's something else I can't think about.

Seems the list of what I can't think on is getting longer and longer. Bits of the past tug at me, and then I've got to push them away. Like soft summer nights when it finally cools and the lawn sprinklers twirl on the grass. Like the sleepy eyes of a little boy when you tuck him into bed. Like the feel of a guitar in your hands.

My hands.

My little boy.

Soft summer nights up in Oroville.

No.

Forget the cracks, Gracie. There's that woman again—the one with the curly red hair and green eyes that're always watching. Watching *you*. Talking about you to the folks in the stores and the restaurants. Wonder what she wants?

Not my cart—it better not be my cart. My gold's in there. *My gold* . . .

No. That's at the top of the list.

Cecily

By now I've spoken with everybody in the neighborhood who's had any contact with Gracie, and only added a few details to what I already know. She hasn't been back to Oroville for over ten years, and she never will go back; somebody there did a "terrible thing" to her. When she told that to my neighbor, she became extremely agitated and made him a little afraid. He thought she might be about to tip over into a violent psychotic episode, but the next time he saw her she was as gentle as ever. Frankly, I think he's making too much of her rage. He ought to see the heap of glass I had to sweep off my kitchenette floor yesterday when yet another publisher returned my manuscript.

Gracie's also quite familiar with the Los Angeles area—she demonstrated that in several random remarks she made to Deirdre. She told at least three people that she came to San Francisco because the climate is mild and she knew she'd have to live on the street. She sings to the pigeons sometimes, very low, and stops right away when she realizes somebody's listening. My landlord's heard her a dozen times or more, and he says she's got a good voice. Oh, yes—she doesn't drink or do drugs. She told one of the waiters at Gino's that she has to keep her mind clear so she can control it—whatever that means.

Not much to go on. I wish I could get a full name for her; I'm not even sure Gracie is her name. God, I'm glad to have this little project to keep me occupied! Disappointments pile on disappointments lately, and sometimes I feel as if I were trapped in one of those cracks in the sidewalk that obviously fascinate Gracie. As if I'm being squeezed tighter and tighter . . .

Enough of that. I think I'll go to the library and see if they have that book on finding people that I heard about. Technically, Gracie isn't lost, but her identity's missing. Maybe the book would give me an idea of how to go about locating it.

Gracie

Not feeling so good today, I don't know why, and that red-haired woman's snooping around again. Who the hell is she? A fan?

Yeah, sure. A fan of old Gracie. Old Gracie, who smells bad and has got the look of a loser written all over her.

House of cards, he used to say. It can all collapse at any minute, and then how'll you feel about your sacrifices? *Sacrifices.* The way he said it, it sounded like a filthy word. But I never gave up anything that mattered. Well, one thing, one person—but I didn't know I was giving him up at the time.

No, no, *no*!

The past's tugging at me more and more, and I don't seem able to push it away so easy. Control, Gracie. But I'm not feeling good, and I think it's gonna rain. Another night in my hidey-hole with the rain beating down, trying not to remember the good times. The high times. The times when—

No.

Cecily

What a joke my life is. Three thanks-but-no-thanks letters from agents I'd hoped would represent me, and I can't even get the Gracie project off the ground. The book I checked out of the library was about as helpful—as my father used to say—as tits on a billygoat. Not that it wasn't informative and thorough. Gracie's just not a good subject for that kind of investigation.

I tried using the data sheet in the appendix. Space at the top for name: Gracie. Also known as: ? Last known address: Oroville, California—but that was more than ten years ago. Last known phone number: ? Automobiles owned, police record, birth date, Social Security number, real estate owned, driver's license number, profession, children, relatives, spouse: all blank. Height: five feet six, give or take. Weight: too damn thin. Present location: divides time between postal storage box 27368 and hidey-hole, location unknown.

Some detective, me.

Give it up, Cecily. Give it up and get on with your life. Take yourself downtown to the temp agency and sign on for a three-month job before your cash all flows out. Better yet, get yourself a real, permanent job and give up your stupid dreams. They aren't going to happen.

But they might. Wasn't I always one of the lucky ones? Besides, they tell you that all it takes is one editor who likes your work. They tell you all it takes is keeping at it. A page a day, and in a year you'll have a novel. One more submission, and soon you'll see your name on a book jacket. And there's always the next manuscript. This Gracie would make one hell of a character, might even make the basis for a good novel. If only I could find out . . .

The cart. Bet there's something in that damned cart that she guards so carefully. Tomorrow I think I'll try to befriend Gracie.

Gracie

Feeling real bad today, even my pigeons sense it and leave me alone. That red-haired woman's been sneaking around. This morning she brought me a bagel slathered in cream cheese just the way I like them. I left the bagel for the pigeons, fed the cream cheese to a stray cat. I know a bribe when I see one.

Bribes. There were plenty: a new car if you're a good girl. A new house, too, if you cooperate. And there was the biggest bribe of all, the one they never came through with. . . .

No.

Funny, things keep misting over today, and I'm not even crying. Haven't cried for years. No, this reminds me more of the smoky neon haze and the flashing lights. The sea of faces that I couldn't pick a single individual out of. Smoky sea of faces, but it didn't matter. The one I wanted to see wasn't there.

Bribes, yeah. Lies, really. *We'll make sure everything's worked out. Trust us. It's taking longer than we thought. He's making it difficult. Be patient. And by the way, we're not too sure about this new material.*

Bribes . . .

The wall between me and the things on my list of what not to remember is crumbling. Where's my control? That wall's my last defense. . . .

Cecily

Deirdre's worried about Gracie. She's looking worse than usual and has been refusing food. She fed the bagel I brought her to the pigeons, even though Del at Gino's said bagels with cream cheese are one of her favorite things. Deirdre thinks we should do something—but what?

Notify her family? Not possible. Take her to a hospital? She's not likely to have health insurance. I suppose there's always a free clinic, but would she agree to go? I doubt it. There's no doubt she's shutting out the world, though. She barely acknowledges anyone.

I think I'll follow her to her hidey-hole tonight. We ought to know where it is, in case she gets seriously ill. Besides, maybe there's a clue to who she is secreted there.

Gracie

The pigeons've deserted me, guess they know I'm not really with them anymore. I'm mostly back there in the smoky neon past and the memories're really pulling hard now. The unsuspecting look on my little boy's face and the regret in my heart when I tucked him in, knowing it was the last time. The rage on his father's face when I said I was leaving. The lean times that weren't really so lean because I sure wasn't living like I am today. The high times that didn't last. The painful times when I realized they weren't going to keep their promises.

It'll be all right. We'll arrange everything.

But it wasn't all right and nothing got arranged. It'll never be all right again.

Cecily

Gracie's hidey-hole is an abandoned trash Dumpster behind a condemned building on 18th Street. I had quite a time finding it. The woman acts like a criminal who's afraid she's being tailed, and it took three nights of ducking into doorways and hiding behind parked cars to follow her there. I watched through a hole in the fence while she unloaded the plastic bags from her cart to the Dumpster, then climbed in after them. The clang when she pulled the lid down was deafening, and I can imagine how noisy it is in there when it rains, like it's starting to right now. Anyway, Gracie's home for the night.

Tomorrow morning after she leaves I'm going to investigate that Dumpster.

Gracie

Rain thundering down hard, loud and echoing like applause. It's the only applause old Gracie's likely to hear anymore.

Old Gracie, that's how I think of myself. And I'm only thirty-nine, barely middle-aged. But I crammed a lot into those last seventeen years, and life catches up with some of us faster than others. I don't know as I'd have the nerve to look in a mirror anymore. What I'd see might scare me.

That red-haired woman was following me for a couple of nights—after my gold, for sure—but today I didn't see her. How she knows about the gold, I don't know. I never told anybody, but that must be it, it's all I've got of value. I'm gonna have to watch out for her, but keeping on guard is one hell of a job when you're feeling like I do.

It must be the rain. If only this rain'd stop, I'd feel better.

Cecily

Checking out that Dumpster was about the most disgusting piece of work I've done in years. It smelled horrible, and the stench is still with me—in my hair and on my clothing. The bottom half is covered with construction debris like two-by-fours and Sheetrock, and on top of it Gracie's made a nest of unbelievably filthy bedding. At first I thought there wasn't anything of hers there and, frankly, I wasn't too enthusiastic about searching thoroughly. But then, in a space between some planking beneath the wad of bedding, I found a cardboard gift box—heart-shaped and printed with roses that had faded almost to white. Inside it were some pictures of a little boy.

He was a chubby little blond, all dressed up to have his photo taken, and on the back of each somebody had written his name—Michael Joseph—and the date. In one he wore a party hat and had his hand stuck in a birthday cake, and on its back was the date—March 8, 1975—and his age—two years.

Gracie's little boy? Probably. Why else would she have saved his pictures and the lock of hair in the blue envelope that was the only other thing in the box?

So now I have a lead. A woman named Gracie (if that's her real name) had a son named Michael Joseph on March 8, 1973, perhaps in Oroville. Is that enough information to justify a trip up to Butte County to check the birth records? A trip in my car, which by all rights shouldn't make it to the San Francisco county line?

Well, why not? I collected yet another rejection letter yesterday. I need to get away from here.

Gracie

I could tell right away when I got back tonight—somebody's been in my hidey-hole. Nothing looked different, but I could smell whoever it was, the way one animal can smell another.

I guess that's what it all boils down to in the end: We're not much different from the animals.

I'll stay here tonight because it's raining again and I'm weary from the walk and unloading my cart. But tomorrow I'm out of here. Can't stay where it isn't safe. Can't sleep in a place somebody's defiled.

Well, they didn't find anything. Everything I own was in my cart. Everything except the box with the pictures of Mikey. They disappeared a few years ago, right about the time I moved in here. Must've fallen out of the cart, or else somebody took them. Doesn't matter, though; I remember him as clear as if I'd tucked him in for the last time only yesterday. Remember his father, too, cursing me as I went out the door, telling me I'd never see my son again.

I never did.

I remember all the promises, too; my lawyer and my manager were going to work it all out so I could have Mikey with me. But his father made it difficult and then things went downhill and then there was the drug bust and all the publicity—

Why am I letting the past suck me in? All those years I had such good control. No more drink, no more drugs, just pure, strong control. A dozen years on the street, first down south, then up here, and I always kept my mind on the present and its tiny details. My pigeons, the people passing by, the cracks in the sidewalk . . .

It's like I've tumbled into one of those cracks. I'm falling and I don't know what'll happen next.

Cecily

Here I am in Oroville, in a cheap motel not far from the Butte County Courthouse. By all rights I shouldn't have made it this far. The car tried to die three times—once while I was trying to navigate the freeway maze at Sacramento—but I arrived before the vital statistics department closed. And now I know who Gracie is!

Michael Joseph Venema was born on March 8, 1973, to Michael William and Grace Ann Venema in Butte Hospital. The father was thirty-five at the time, the mother only sixteen. Venema's not a common name here; the current directory lists only one—initial M—on Lark Lane. I've already located it on the map, and I'm going there tomorrow morning. It's a Saturday, so somebody's bound to be at home. I'll just show up and maybe the element of surprise will help me pry loose the story of my neighborhood bag lady.

God, I'm good at this! Maybe I should scrap my literary ambitions and become an investigative reporter.

Gracie

I miss my Dumpster. Was noisy when it rained, that's true, but at least it was dry. The only shelter I could find tonight was this doorway behind Gino's, and I had to wait for them to close up before I crawled into it, so I got plenty wet. My blankets're soaked, but the plastic has to go over my cart to protect my things. How much longer till morning?

Well, how would I know? Haven't had a watch for years. I pawned it early on, that was when I was still sleeping in hotel rooms, thinking things would turn around for me. Then I was sleeping in my car and had to sell everything else, one by one. And then it was a really cheap hotel, and I turned some tricks to keep the money coming, but when a pimp tried to move in on me, I knew it was time to get my act together and leave town. So I came here and made do. In all the years I've lived on the street in different parts of this city, I've never turned another trick and I've never panhandled. For a while before I started feeling so bad I picked up little jobs, working just for food. But lately I've had to rely on other people's kindnesses.

It hurts to be so dependent.

There's another gust of wind, blowing the rain at me. It's raining like a son of a bitch tonight. It better let up in the morning.

I miss my Dumpster. I miss . . .

No. I've still got *some* control left. Not much, but a shred.

Cecily

Now I know Gracie's story, and I'm so distracted that I got on the wrong freeway coming back through Sacramento. There's a possibility I may be able to reunite her with her son Mike—plus I've got my novel, all of it, and it's going to be terrific! I wouldn't be surprised if it changed my life.

I went to Mike's house this morning—a little prefab on a couple of acres in the country south of town. He was there, as were his wife and baby son. At first he didn't believe his mother was alive, then he didn't want to talk about her. But when I told him Gracie's circumstances he opened up and agreed to tell me what he knew. And he knew practically everything, because his father finally told him the truth when he was dying last year.

Gracie was a singer. One of those bluesy-pop kind like Linda Ronstadt, whom you can't categorize as either country or Top 40. She got her start singing at their church and received some encouragement from a friend's uncle who was a sound engineer at an L.A. recording studio. At sixteen she'd married Mike's father—who was nearly twenty years her senior—and they'd never been very happy. So on the strength of that slim encouragement, she left him and their son and went to L.A. to try to break into the business.

And she did, under the name Grace Ventura. The interesting thing is, I remember her first hit, "Smoky Neon Haze," very clearly. It was romantic and tragic, and I was just at the age when tragedy is an appealing concept rather than a harsh reality.

Anyway, Mike's father was very bitter about Gracie deserting them—the way my husband was when I told him I was leaving to become a writer. After Gracie's first album did well and her second earned her a gold record, she decided she wanted custody of Mike, but there was no way his father would give him up. Her lawyer initiated a custody suit, but while that was going on Gracie's third album flopped. Gracie started drinking and doing drugs and couldn't come up with the material for a fourth album; then she was busted for possession of cocaine, and Mike's father used that against her to gain permanent custody. And then the record company dropped her. She tried to make a comeback for a couple of years, then finally disappeared. She had no money; she'd signed a contract that gave most of her earnings to the record label, and what they didn't take, her manager and lawyer did. No wonder she ended up on the streets.

I'm not sure how Mike feels about being reunited with his mother; he was very noncommittal. He has his own life now, and his printing business is just getting off the ground.

But he did say he'd try to help her, and that's the message I'm to deliver to Gracie when I get back to the city.

I hope it works out. For Gracie's sake, of course, and also because it would make a perfect upbeat ending to my novel.

Gracie

It's dry and warm here in the storage room. Deirdre found me crouched behind the garbage cans in the alley a while ago and brought me inside. Gave me some blankets she borrowed from one of the folks upstairs. They're the first clean things I've had next to my skin in years.

Tomorrow she wants to take me to the free clinic. I won't go, but I'm grateful for the offer.

Warm and dry and dark in here. I keep drifting—out of the present, into the past, back and forth. No control now. In spite of the dark I can see the lights—bright colors, made hazy by the smoke. Just like in that first song . . . what was it called? Don't remember. Doesn't matter.

It was a good one, though. Top of the charts. Didn't even surprise me. I always thought I was one of the lucky ones.

I can see the faces, too. Seems like acres of them, looking up at me while I'm blinded by the lights. Listen to the applause! For me. And that didn't surprise me, either. I always knew it would happen. But where was that? When?

Can't remember. Doesn't matter.

Was only one face that ever mattered. Little boy. Who was he?

Michael Joseph. Mikey.

Funny, for years I've fought the memories. Pushed them away when they tugged, kept my mind on the here and now. Then I fell into the crack in the sidewalk, and it damn near swallowed me up. Now the memories're fading, except for one. Michael Joseph. Mikey.

That's a good one. I'll hold on to it.

Cecily

Gracie died last night in the storeroom at the Lucky Shamrock. Deirdre brought her in there to keep her out of the rain, and when she looked in on her after closing, she was dead. The coroner's people said it was pneumonia; she'd probably been walking around with it for a long time, and the soaking finished her.

I cried when Deirdre told me. I haven't cried in years, and there I was, sobbing over a woman whose full name I didn't even know until two days ago.

I wonder why she wasn't in her hidey-hole. Was it because she realized I violated it and didn't feel safe anymore? God, I hope not! But how could she have known?

I wish I could've told her about her son, that he said he'd help her. But maybe it's for the best, after all. Gracie might have wanted more than Mike was willing to give her—emotionally, I mean. Besides, she must've been quite unbalanced toward the end.

I guess it's for the best, but I still wish I could've told her.

This morning Deirdre and I decided we'd better go through the stuff in her cart, in case there was anything salvageable that Mike might want. Some of the plastic bags were filled with ragged clothing, others with faded and crumbling clippings that chronicled the brief career of Grace Ventura. There was a Bible, some spangled stage costumes, a few paperbacks, a bundle of letters about the custody suit, a set of keys to a Mercedes, and other mementos that were in such bad shape we couldn't tell what they'd been. But at the very bottom of the cart, wrapped in rags and more plastic bags, was the gold record awarded to her for her second album, "Soft Summer Nights."

On one hand, not much to say for a life that once held such promise. On the other hand, it says it all.

It gives me pause. Makes me wonder about my own life. Is all of this worth it? I really don't know. But I'm not giving up—not now, when I've got Gracie's story to tell. I wouldn't be the least bit surprised if it changed my life.

After all, aren't I one of the lucky ones?

Aren't I?

LIA MATERA has written ten mysteries featuring either the left-wing lawyer Willa Jansson or tough defense attorney Laura Di Palma. Her books have been nominated for Edgar, Anthony, and Macavity awards. *The New York Times* described Willa Jansson as "one of the most articulate and surely the wittiest of women sleuths at large in the genre." Matera herself is a recovering lawyer, but in *"Performance Crime"* she abandons the world of lawyers and writes about another kind of performance artist.

Performance Crime

Lia Matera

I was about as stressed out as I could be. In addition to my work year starting at the university, I was trying to help get the Moonjuice Performance Gallery's new show together. After last year's fiasco, Moonjuice needed something accessible. And that would never happen unless someone displayed some sense, however tame that might seem to the artists.

But the artists weren't the main problem, the main problem was Moonjuice's board of directors. The "conservative" members were two wannabe-radical university professors. The middle-of-the-roaders were a desktop publisher and an aspiring blues guitarist. On the avant-garde extreme was self-proclaimed bad girl and dabbling artist Georgia Stepp. I, an untenured associate professor, was so far to the right of other board members it was laughable. I was a fiscally responsible Democrat, which practically opened me to charges of fascism.

I was trying to make my point about being sensible to Georgia.

"We have to be careful after last year," I insisted.

"Last year was fun." Georgia opened her long arms for emphasis. She wore a satin camisole, emphasizing a fashionable bit of muscle. Her nails were long and black. Her blond hair was cut short and dyed black this year. "We freaked out all the prisses."

She meant "prissy" board members who'd resigned in protest, convincing our sponsors to defund us and our program advertisers to boycott us.

These were liberal restaurateurs and bookshop owners, hardly Republicans.

"We have less than a quarter of last year's budget because of that show! We've got artists working for free"—that got her—"and feminist university students volunteering elsewhere."

"Art can't follow money like a dog in heat!"

"It can't treat sponsors like fire hydrants, either. There just aren't that many patrons of the arts around," I pointed out. "Especially art by lesbians. And we lost their support over what? Way-out, nonpolitical—"

"Way-out *is* political." Georgia looked happy. And there's no one more beautiful than Georgia when she's happy. But that doesn't make her any less wrongheaded.

"Clothespins with glued-on feathers don't make a statement, I'm sorry." The "art" that made our advertisers bail included a woman in studded leather pinning feathers on her naked partner.

"It wasn't supposed to be a statement." Georgia leaned closer. "It was a dance. A dance, serious one."

"Clothespins on my nipples always make me want to dance."

"But it was about artists, not you." Georgia certainly hit the nail on the head.

"Yeah, well it wasn't about our advertisers, either. Not to mention Viv and Claire." The two former board members. "We've got to get our sponsors and advertising back, Georgia. It doesn't matter what kind of show we put on this year if no one's willing to pay for the next one. We're not Andy Hardy. We're not putting on shows to pass the summer."

She shot me a look. To her, practicality is somehow demeaning.

Marlys, legal secretary and blues guitarist, strolled in. Georgia considers her a best friend and ally. Which Marlys proved by changing the subject.

"You guys see the paper this morning?" She was short and heavy, with the usual layered haircut. The look she gave Georgia made me wonder if she minded Georgia's going to bed with every dominatrix and poet to cross our stage.

"What, daaaaarling?" Georgia liked to do Kate Hepburn, imitating gays in drag. I was never sure if I thought it was funny or disrespectful.

"Somebody broke into Greg Purl's house and shot all his cereal." Marlys was flushed, eyes sparkling as she watched Georgia.

"A cereal killer!" She practically shrieked. "Was that the point? I love it! A pun crime!"

"Plus, Greg," Marlys pointed out.

Purl was a local boy who'd made good. He'd gone to Hollywood to make big-budget lowest-common-denominator movies. His latest was about—you guessed it—the serial killer of teenage girls.

"Did the papers get it?" Georgia wondered. "Cereal killer, serial killer; his movie?"

"They got the pun." Marlys looked gratified. "They didn't really go into his movies."

Marlys and Georgia were friends with Purl before he "sold out." It always amazed me how superior they could feel, despite their obscurity and their day jobs. It's not that easy to sell out, after all. Someone has to want to buy what you've got to pander.

"Purl wasn't hurt?" Once again, mine was the lone voice of practicality.

"No, it happened at his house here. He's down in Hollywood. Someone broke in and shot his cereal boxes," Marlys explained. "According to the papers."

"How funny!" Georgia struck a pose. Give her a cigarette in a long ivory holder and she surely could be some thirties star. Or RuPaul. "Cereal killer. I'm just surprised the papers got it."

"We would have, even if they didn't." Marlys smiled.

"Was his house damaged? Did they just fire into a cupboard or what?" I loathed his last movie's relentless reliance on "sexy" violence. But that didn't give anyone the right to shoot up his kitchen. "He must feel so . . . violated."

Georgia laughed till tears sprang to her eyes. "It's almost like a Hollywood version of karma, isn't it?"

Marlys answered my question. "I guess the person took all his cereal outside and dumped it on his lawn before shooting it full of holes." She was watching Georgia, still grinning. "I knew you'd like it!"

"Well, I don't think it's funny," I put in.

Georgia cackled. "Ha! 'That's not funny'—the PC lesbian mantra."

"You're just too young to remember what it was like when everyone was politically *in*correct! It was irritating and demeaning—"

"Like political correctness," Georgia countered.

Moonjuice was going to drive me insane some day. Especially if performance artists kept embracing things we used to fight against, like pornography and the word "dyke."

"Fine, Georgia—don't get it. There's certainly plenty I don't get—like the idea of a naked choir." One of the proposed acts for our yearly fund-raiser was a naked twenty-person choir. Georgia and I had been bickering about it all afternoon. "They don't even say what they're going to sing. Like we're prurient twelve-year-olds who'll like them just because they're naked."

"Well, why not?" Georgia asked. "Haven't you ever wondered what choirgirls' breasts look like when they sing loud?"

"No!" I responded. "And I'm sure our sponsors haven't either."

"Nan's partly right," Marlys said generously. "We should judge art by itself. If they can sing, let them sing naked. If they can't, let them go streak through college campuses."

Georgia shot her an *et tu* look. "All right, all right; we'll ask them for details. But not in a philistine way."

Georgia called me at the university the next day. "Nan, come down." Down into town, where Moonjuice Gallery is.

It's a long ride to the dark little storefront full of folding chairs facing a creaky stage.

"I have students coming in forty minutes."

"Then come right away." Georgia hung up.

Georgia wouldn't be able to get away with acting like that if she looked like me. Or maybe if I had Georgia's personality, I'd look more like her; I'd be skinny and daring with strange hair and long nails.

But I didn't need Georgia's big clothing and makeup bills. I had car payments to keep up.

When I got to Moonjuice, I was surprised to see cats fighting in the empty lot across the street. It seemed ominous, somehow. But I teach classics; things tend to look symbolic to me.

When I walked into Moonjuice, I found Georgia onstage tearing through all the costumes. Feather boas were curled around her feet and spangled dresses were tossed over chairs. Some of the comedy costumes—a fast-food clerk, a secretary, a hockey player, a number 32 football jersey, a fireman—were strewn across the floor.

"What are you doing?" I couldn't keep exasperation out of my voice. Who knew when we'd be able to afford new costumes? She was trashing our assets.

"I can't find anything!" She wore a black turtleneck, a tight black mini, and black stockings today. With her black nails, lips, and hair, she looked like a Parisian model for the vampire collection. "Where are the costumes from last year?"

"What costumes? You mean the whips? The clothespins?"

"The overalls, the ginghams. They've been stolen!"

She couldn't say this over the phone?

"Of course they weren't stolen," I reassured her. "Who'd want to steal gingham dresses?" Overalls maybe. "They're probably at someone's house or in the attic where they're supposed to be."

"Will you go up there and look?"

"Now?"

She nodded. "These were already down here, backstage. I can't go up to the attic—it's so dusty. My allergies."

"I'm supposed to be meeting students!"

"They'll wait."

Georgia worked nights as a cocktail waitress—but not that steadily. She always contrived to have a guest room to crash in if she couldn't make rent. To her, jobs were trifles.

She clattered down the stage steps. "Nan, please?" She linked her arm through mine. I loved the way her body felt. I know I'm not supposed to, but I get turned on by skinniness. And there just isn't that much of it in our community.

"Why do you need them?" If I relented and did this for her, I'd beat myself up over it all week. It wasn't right to put myself out for someone gorgeous if I knew I wouldn't do the same for a frumpy friend.

"I was thinking the naked choir could start out wearing them and then strip them off."

"Why?"

"I found out what they sing. They sing gospel." To her that made sense.

Don't ask me how she talked me into it. I'd be embarrassed to analyze it.

I dragged out attic boxes and searched through them. I never did find the overalls and ginghams. But I found the boxes the costumes on stage had come out of. Their paper wrappings were still scattered all around.

By the time I got back downstairs, I was late for my appointment. I tore out of there with hardly a word for Georgia. Just as well. It wouldn't have been a kind word.

On the way out, I noticed cats were still fighting across the street. The funny thing was, they were different cats this time.

When I got home from work, I showered first thing, still feeling grimy from my visit to the Moonjuice attic.

Then I ate dinner in front of the TV. I always feel guilty when I see "Kill Your Television" bumper stickers in Moonjuice's parking lot. But I work long days, deconstructing and analogizing, and dealing with students' problems. Channel surfing is my big vice.

Local news was on. "The pun-loving bandit has seemingly

struck again!" The female anchor was a fluffy bit of a thing. She was my secret lust object.

I shoveled pasta into my face while she explained: "A ransom note was sent to Ygdrasil Herbs today! To ransom its *president,* you ask? No, to ransom its . . . *catnip.* That's right, *catnip*—that fragrantly psychedelic herb . . . psychedelic to *cats,* that is. Last night, someone broke into the Ygdrasil plant on Teenmore Avenue and stole their *entire stock* of catnip. Ygdrasil supplies over seventy percent of the catnip sold in this country, according to its spokesman. So better keep on kitty's *good side* for a while!"

The Ygdrasil spokesman came on the screen, explaining that the ransom note was signed "Catnip Kidnap."

The newscasters could hardly keep a straight face. "Catnip Kidnap," the airhead newswoman giggled in closing.

I thought about the cats fighting across the street from Moonjuice. It was a cat synchronicity, I guessed.

But the next day, I wasn't so sure it was a coincidence.

The media had fallen in love with their Pun-loving Bandit, reporting every conceivable connection between the Cereal Killer and the Catnip Kidnap. But that was nothing. By evening, news people were delirious with soft-news joy: Someone had stolen every meat patty from the town's most popular fast-food joint.

The first words out of the newscaster's mouth were "Burger Burglar!"

I could hardly contain my agitation as the newscaster described the burglary. The meat had been stolen during the busiest part of the lunch rush. No one had noticed anything odd. But when they went to the freezer to replenish, the patties were gone. One manager thought he'd spotted a new employee, but turnover was such that he hadn't been sure, and he'd been too busy to check.

The fast-food place had once donated a costume to Moonjuice. I'd seen it just yesterday strewn with the rest of Georgia's mess.

Georgia. She was all panache, all show. If something had

style, that was enough for her. It didn't have to make sense or be wise or look good to people who mattered.

I was sure Georgia was doing it. Performance art just wasn't enough anymore. Now she'd taken to performance crime, damn her.

I wanted to strangle her. Didn't she realize these childish tricks were felonies? That she could go to prison? That Moonjuice would sink under the scandal?

I wouldn't let it happen. I drove immediately to a mall pet store. They had very little catnip, most of it from Ygdrasil. I left it there, instead buying a small box of the other brand.

I had to go all the way across town to find another pet store open. It too had mostly Ygdrasil catnip. I bought the other brand.

Then I drove to Moonjuice.

I felt like an idiot scattering the catnip in the vacant lot. Then I hurried across to Moonjuice, letting myself in with my key.

I was in the "kitchen" area—a sink, a coffee urn, a paint-splotched table, a garbage can. I dumped the empty catnip boxes into the garbage. If anyone else had noticed the cats across the street, if anyone connected catnip to Moonjuice, I would point to these empties. I would make up some story. I didn't quite know what, but the main thing was to disassociate from Ygdrasil.

As soon as I dumped the boxes, I dashed through rows of folding chairs and ran up the stage steps.

The costumes were wildly tossed about, just as they'd been yesterday. But I couldn't find the fast-food worker uniform. I was afraid I knew why: because Georgia hadn't returned it to Moonjuice.

She must have gotten the Burger Burglar idea from seeing the uniform. Foolish!

"What's up?" Marlys had entered the room. She wore slacks and a mannish shirt and jacket—the uniform of her office day job.

I nearly screamed. "Oh, God, you scared me!"

"I noticed." She tossed her backpack down. "What happened here? Cyclone Georgia?"

"Yes."

She climbed the stage stairs. "It would never occur to her to clean up, that's for sure." Her tone was fond, not frazzled.

She started picking up dresses, putting them on hangers. She shook her head when the rough floor pulled a spangle off one.

"I'm surprised so many costumes are down here," she mused. "Shouldn't some of these be up in the attic? We're not using them this year are we?" She glanced at me. "I get a little sick of the hoo-haw dresses and boas. What next?" She struck a pose. "Joan Crawford and Judy Garland?"

"Right orientation, wrong gender," I commented.

I forced myself to calm down. I helped Marlys fold costumes and hang dresses. We talked about this year's show. She agreed with Georgia about the naked choir, which surprised me. She's usually pretty levelheaded.

I didn't want to bring up the Burger Burglar or Cereal Killer or Catnip Kidnap, but I wished she would. I was looking for an excuse to let off steam, talk about it before the pressure blew my socks off. I even considered voicing my worry about Georgia. Marlys was both her friend and a reasonable person. She could counsel me, help me. She'd see the need to protect Georgia from her own excesses. And, as important, to protect Moonjuice from more scandal.

Marlys, work clothes and all, schlepped most of the costumes to the attic. I went into the tiny office area and switched on our most valuable resource, a laptop computer we'd purchased last year before our sponsors jumped ship.

I didn't have any work to do on it, but Marlys wouldn't know that. I wanted to stay longer than her. I wanted to search for evidence.

Marlys came down. She saw me at the laptop. "Bookkeeping, poor baby?"

"Yes," I lied. I saw with annoyance that the computer battery was low. The adapter kept the juice on, but it wasn't recharging the battery. Either that or another board member had been using it.

"You have to do that now? I was thinking a mixed drink would taste good."

"No thanks." I was tempted, but I had something I wanted to do here. Alone. "Call Georgia?" I suggested.

"I've been trying her all afternoon. She's not home." She walked to the phone and dialed. A moment later, she smiled. Georgia had an outrageously campy telephone tape. "It's Marlys again, calling to see if you want dinner." She hung up, looking disappointed.

To me, she said, "You're sure you won't go play, Nan?"

"Sorry."

She shrugged, patting me on the shoulder before she left. I watched through the window as she tossed her pack into her old Honda, then drove away.

I ran up to the attic. A little guiltily, I reopened boxes Marlys had just neatly packed with costumes. I tried not to unfold any as I looked through.

I finally found the fast-food uniform at the bottom of a box in the corner. It wasn't one of the newly repacked boxes toward the front.

Georgia must have noticed the costume during yesterday's mess-spree, then thought of a clever way to use it. She must have brought it back sometime today and packed it away. It would, of course, never have occurred to her to put away the other costumes. That's what she had me and Marlys and a dozen other women with crushes on her for.

It was irritating. But I couldn't risk what she was willing to risk. I wouldn't feel safe until the uniform was no longer here to incriminate her. I carried it back downstairs with me.

If anyone noticed the cats out back and checked for catnip, they'd find my empty boxes of non-Ygdrasil brand. I'd say I'd noticed cats fighting and sprinkled catnip to pacify them.

And no one would find the fast-food uniform at Moonjuice. I'd see to that right now.

I turned off the laptop, turned out the lights, and carried the uniform away under my jacket. I drove to a beach cliff. I bundled the uniform into a tight ball, tying it with its own sleeves and pant legs. Then I dropped it off the cliff and went home.

I was watching the eleven o'clock news and eating ice cream when I learned disaster had struck anew.

A local computer company, the anchor informed me, a major manufacturer of laptop computers, had reported a break-in. Someone sneaked in and poured salt, pounds of regular table salt, all over the laptop battery assembly area. Thousands of dollars' worth of batteries had been ruined.

I waited for the anchor's inevitable statement. I was shocked when it didn't come. Maybe this one was too subtle for the folks at Channel 6. But someone would get it before tomorrow's paper rolled off the presses.

I would most certainly wake up to the headline SALT ON BATTERIES.

It was close enough to "assault and battery" to be Georgia's kind of pun. Georgia had struck again.

I guess performance art gets boring after a while. I guess it takes a criminal component to give art its edge.

I hardly slept at all that night.

I was a wreck the next day at work, barely following the convoluted ditziness of my students, barely jittering through a staff meeting, barely keeping my temper when the library accused me of damaging a book.

As soon as I could, I rushed to Moonjuice. Most of the other board members were there. Georgia waved at me. She and two others were going through some papers. Georgia was laughing, saying, "Yes yes yes," as a woman named Marie insisted, "We can't put that into an ad!" Another woman, Heidi, was gushing, "Oh, Georgia's right! Let's shake them up."

I didn't even want to know what kind of pornography Georgia was trying to sneak into a Moonjuice ad. She wore a lavender bodysuit with a silver sarong. The outfit had looked better on her when she was a blonde, but it was still eye-popping.

I went into the kitchen to pour myself some coffee before going in to join the wrangle.

Someone knocked at the back door. Usually people come in through the front.

I opened the door, alarmed to see a policeman.

"Hello." He smiled warily. This town has baggage about its treatment of lesbians and gays. The police have been trying to project a kinder, gentler image.

He carried a brown paper bag.

"What—? Who do you—? Hi." I had to calm down. He looked way too interested in my nervousness.

He showed me his ID. Then he waited, as if for me to blurt out some incrimination.

I knew, at that moment, that something had gone wrong. That he was here to question Georgia. That she'd been linked to the crimes. I wanted to box her ears for being so stupid.

"Do you mind if I come in?" the cop asked politely, as if I'd forget the Police Department's recent homophobia.

"No. What do you . . . ? Is there something?"

"Yes. I was hoping to speak to someone here? Anyone in charge?"

I didn't want him speaking to Georgia, that was for sure. But there was something I very much needed to do right now, before he did any more snooping.

"I'll get Marlys," I said. "She's in charge. Kind of."

I dashed out of the kitchen, going straight into the office. I'd fetch Marlys in a minute. First, I was going to hide the laptop. I wanted no association in the cop's mind between Moonjuice and the salt on batteries.

I unplugged the laptop and kicked the power cord out of sight. I folded the screen down, and picked it up, brushing its dust outline off the desk. I turned with the laptop under my arm. I was going to stick it in the cupboard under some towels. Then I was going to hurry and get Marlys.

Instead, I stood there. Just stood there, holding the laptop.

The cop hadn't waited in the kitchen. He'd followed me.

Followed me! I wanted to crab, Don't you need a warrant? Don't you have any manners? But maybe it's police procedure to follow people so they don't go get shotguns or something. I wish I'd thought of that earlier.

Marlys appeared in the doorway behind him.

I said, "I was just coming to get you. He wants to talk to you."

The cop had turned so he could keep an eye on us both. Georgia was coming toward us.

"I thought you two could talk in here," I said lamely. "I was just going to take the computer, and work in the kitchen."

Marlys, picking up on my freak-out, looked alarmed. Georgia strode into the middle of the situation like a bull into a china shop.

"Police?" She fiddled with her sarong as a child might. "We haven't even put our show on yet."

I was absolutely paralyzed. Georgia had the glitter-eyed look she gets before she flies into the ozone. Though I'd just said I was leaving with the laptop, I didn't.

The cop held up his paper bag. "We wondered if you could identify this for us."

I thought for a second he was going to pull out a gun, the one used to shoot Greg Purl's cereal. In retrospect, that might have been preferable.

He pulled out the fast-food uniform I'd tossed over the cliff last night. It looked damp and sandy.

"Our costume?" Georgia asked. "Is it?"

Marlys was frowning at her as if trying to warn her to be a little guarded for once.

The cop turned the collar inside out, showing the words "Moonjuice Gallery" in felt-tip marker.

Damn. Who'd been organized enough to do that?

I put the laptop back on the desk.

"I just labeled it!" Georgia exclaimed. "How funny! I did it because the overalls and ginghams disappeared."

I had to hand it to her, she was cool under fire. She smiled at me.

"I thought I'd get some brownie points from you, Nan. And I forgot to even mention it!" She looked at me expectantly. "I did it two days ago."

"What a good idea," I said meekly.

"Well." She held out her hand for it. "Thanks for bringing it back." When he didn't return it, she looked confused. "I noticed a bunch of costumes were gone from the stage. I didn't realize they'd been stolen. I guess I thought Nan had one of her cleaning fits."

"I did," I told her. "We put them back in the attic."

"We think this may have been used in a burglary," the cop said. "Do you mind if I have a look around here?"

"Do you have a warrant?" Georgia said. She'd pulled herself to her full five feet ten inches. She looked regal. Rather, she looked like she was playing at looking regal.

"You object to me looking around?"

"No, of course not," Marlys interjected.

But Georgia elbowed her, saying, "Yes, we do. Without a warrant, you can't look around!" Her tone was adamant, and the look she shot Marlys clearly said, Shut up.

"Don't be silly, Georgia," Marlys insisted. "Why invite trouble? He just wants to look around. We don't have any secrets."

The cop glanced at the laptop I'd returned to the desk. He glanced at the fast-food uniform in his hand. He didn't look convinced we had nothing to hide.

And who knew what else Georgia had stashed here. Maybe even the gun.

"I agree with Georgia," I said. "As a matter of principle—"

"And history!" Georgia was on her high horse now. "We haven't forgotten Verboten." Verboten was a lesbian bar the cops had raided years ago, cracking heads and leading to the creation of a citizens' review board.

"Oh, you guys!" Marlys looked peeved. "You're making a

mountain out of a molehill! We don't have anything to hide." She looked at me, clearly surprised. "Nan?"

But I repeated, "No. He should get a warrant if he wants to search. On principle."

I've never been so scared in my life. Not even Georgia's warm look of approval helped.

"Go!" Georgia said to the cop. "Go away. No warrant, no search."

Still, the cop lingered. He caught Marlys's eye.

But Marlys looked at Georgia and knew she was licked. She said to the cop, "Where did you find the uniform, anyway?"

"Some tidepoolers brought it in."

Behind us, another board member—I hadn't seen her join us—said, "The Burger Burglar! You think he used our costume?"

Marlys, watching Georgia, looked ashen.

When the cop left, Georgia began prancing, repeating, "No warrant, no search; no warrant, no search." She treated us to a dazzling smile. "I've always wanted to say that."

"It was a damn stupid thing to say!" Marlys pushed past her, leaving the room.

"I wonder when they'll be back with the warrant," Georgia said. "Let's look around and make sure there's nobody else's business lying around for them to get into."

She went straight out of the room and up into the attic.

I could have hit myself with a hammer for doing that dumb thing with the laptop.

In the cop's mind, Moonjuice was connected to the burger burglary. Now my idiocy had reminded him of the salt on batteries, too.

I went into the kitchen. I had to get rid of the catnip boxes. They'd provide an additional associative link with the Catnip Kidnap. The boxes would be more incriminating than unincriminating now.

I pulled them out of the garbage. I went out the back door to put them into my car trunk.

I'd just closed the trunk when I turned to find the cop behind me.

"Do you mind if I ask you a few questions?" he said.

My heart sank.

"You know, I only came here to return the costume. Get some routine information." He stood too close. "But your attitude about this uniform, your behavior with the laptop computer, and now the catnip boxes." He shook his head. "Why don't you make it easy on everyone and talk to me."

But I'm the careful one, the practical one, the meticulous one. It's supposed to be Georgia who screws things up, not me.

"No," I said. "No. I can't."

I was so intimidated, I'd have confessed any of my own sins. But I couldn't deliver Georgia to the cops. This whole thing had been about protecting her.

I walked past him. I went back inside.

I'd ruined everything. I couldn't believe it. I'd put Georgia in peril of arrest. I'd undermined all our work at the gallery, and whatever reputation it still sustained.

I found Marlys sitting at the table.

"I've wrecked everything for Georgia," I confessed in agony. "They're going to investigate now."

"For Georgia?" she repeated. "Georgia's upstairs feeling important and dramatic." Marlys sounded almost bitter. "She'll be fine. She always is."

I tried to say more, but she waved me away. She didn't want to talk, that was apparent. I thought she must, in her heart, understand what I'd done to Georgia.

But I didn't fully understand the sparkle of tears in her eyes for three more days, until the cops came and made their arrest.

I should have known Georgia wasn't organized enough to pull off performance art crimes. I should have realized that Marlys was.

I should have realized Marlys wanted to feel she was more than just Georgia's friend, that she was also a kindred spirit.

I should have recognized her need to distinguish herself from the rest of Georgia's entourage.

Marlys. If I'd known, I'd have trusted her to take care of things. I'd have butted out.

After the arrest, the story didn't get much press; Marlys wasn't pretty enough to be a celebrity. Georgia was extravagant in her admiration, but only at first; her attention span was too short to visit Marlys in jail. I thought Marlys would become a legend in the performance art community, but artists get depressed if they have to admire someone else.

By the time Georgia sang in the naked choir, nobody talked about poor Marlys anymore, that's for sure.

Permissions

Match wits with the best-selling
MYSTERY WRITERS
in the business!